Heart of Glass

OTHER NOVELS BY DIANE NOBLE
At Play in the Promised Land
The Blossom and the Nettle
When the Far Hills Bloom
The Veil
Distant Bells
Tangled Vines

(WRITTEN AS AMANDA MACLEAN)
Westward
Stonehaven
Everlasting
Promise Me the Dawn
Kingdom Come

NOVELLAS
Come, My Little Angel
"Gift of Love" in *A Christmas Joy*
"Legacy of Love" in *A Mother's Love*
"Birds of a Feather" in *Unlikely Angels*

NONFICTION FOR WOMEN
Letters from God for Women
It's Time! Discover Your Gifts and Pursue Your Dreams

Heart of Glass

DIANE NOBLE

To Marlene
This is truly
a book of my heart—
Enjoy!!
Diane Noble
Zeph 3:17

WATERBROOK
PRESS

HEART OF GLASS
PUBLISHED BY WATERBROOK PRESS
2375 Telstar Drive, Suite 160
Colorado Springs, Colorado 80920
A division of Random House, Inc.

All Scripture quotations, unless otherwise indicated, are taken from the *King James Version*. Scripture quotations marked (NKJV) are taken from the *New King James Version*. Copyright © 1982 by Thomas Nelson, Inc. Used by permission. All rights reserved.

The characters and events in this book are fictional, and any resemblance to actual persons or events is coincidental.

ISBN 1-57856-400-X

WATERBROOK and its deer design logo are registered trademarks of WaterBrook Press, a division of Random House, Inc.

Printed in the United States of America
2002—First Edition

10 9 8 7 6 5 4 3 2 1

To Father Tom and Susan Johnson,
and our beloved church family at
Saint Hugh of Lincoln Episcopal Church
in Idyllwild, California.

I thank my God upon every remembrance of you,
Always in every prayer of mine making request for you all with joy,
For your fellowship in the gospel from the first day until now.
—Philippians 1:3-5, NKJV

Acknowledgments

Heartfelt thanks to my editors at WaterBrook Press: Erin Healy, Lisa Bergren, Traci DePree, and Paul Hawley for their remarkable work. To my literary agent, Sara Fortenberry, for her advice, expertise, and support. And special thanks, as always, to Liz Curtis Higgs for her prayers and encouragement as this project took shape. Thank you especially, Lizzie, for providing the CDs of glorious mountain dulcimer music to listen to as I traveled with Fairwyn March on her heart journey!

To my brother Dennis and sister-in-law Kathi for providing a wealth of information on Salisbury, North Carolina, the fictional setting for Oak Hill, and especially for providing the blueprint for the Deforest estate and gardens with their own lovely home.

To Tom, my husband, for his historical expertise, his patience, and his loving support through my long months of work on *Heart of Glass*. I couldn't do it without you!

I also want to mention the following works, all instrumental in my research of the Mission at San Juan Capistrano and the folklore and folk songs of the Great Smoky Mountains, and listed here for those readers who might want to take a peek into the fascinating threads of history covered in *Heart of Glass*:

Smoky Mountain Voices: A Lexicon of Southern Appalachian Speech, Harold F. Farwell Jr. and J. Karl Nicholas, Editors.

Our Southern Highlanders: A Narrative of Adventure in the

Southern Appalachians and a Study of Life Among the Mountaineers, Horace Kephart.

American Folk Tales and Songs, compiled by Richard Chase.

The Mountain Dulcimer: How to Make It and Play It, by Howard W. Mitchell.

Musicmaker's Kits, Inc.: Complete Plans for Making the Hourglass Mountain Dulcimer, P.O. Box 2117, Stillwater, MN 55082-3117.

A Guide to Historical San Juan Capistrano: A Comprehensive Guide for Architecture, Heritage, History, and Preservation, by Mary Ellen Tryon.

Little Chapters About San Juan Capistrano, St. John O'Sullivan, first published in 1912.

One

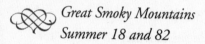
Dearly Forbes arrived at the top of the trace, his red head poking up first, barely showing above the tall meadow grasses at the top of the treeless mountain. The boy's hair stuck to his face, and his eyes seemed bright as a bird's even from the distance between us. His scrawny shoulders were bare and browned by the summer sun, and wide galluses held up trousers big enough to be his pa's.

When he saw me standing on the porch of my chinked-log cabin, he made his way across the meadow, grinning all the way. "Fairwyn March! Thar's a body acomin' through the piny woods to see ye!"

I couldn't help smiling back, so contagious was his pleasure at being the one to bear the news. "Well now, Dearly," I said, "that's not such an unusual event, in my thinking. Might it be Selah with some eggs? Perchance she's bringing a fresh-shot razorback ready for smoking?" Selah Jones was a good aim, known to all in these parts, and such a prize wouldn't surprise me.

He climbed the porch stairs, huffing and puffing. "This one's a furriner," he said between noisy gulps of air, "a furriner like as ye've never seen afore."

With this, I indeed perked up. "I'll bring ye some water, son, if ye care to sit a spell." I nodded to one of the two stick rockers near me.

"Yes ma'am, that'd be right fine."

I returned from the kitchen a few minutes later with a cup of water. He gulped it sprawled in the rocker next to where I sat. I resisted the urge to ruffle his hair. He smelled like a warm puppy that had been playing too long in the sun. This beanpole boy had long ago twisted himself around my heart.

"Now then," I said. "Tell me about this furriner on his way for a visit."

Dearly leaned forward and gave me a nod. "Well ma'am," he said, rolling his eyes with importance. "He calls himself a professor. Says he hails from North Carolina. Rode right up to Caudill's General Store, slid off'n his horse, and announced he'd come to study our folk tales. Says he's awritin' a book on us." Dearly reached down to his ankle and gave it a scratching.

"Then why's he coming to see me?"

"Everbody knows ye're the bestest song scribe round these parts. And the bestest storyteller to boot." He rested his back against the slats of the rocking chair, pushing it to and fro with his bare feet, taking pleasure in the rhythmic creak on the weathered boards of the porch. He shook his head slowly. "I like to never seen anybody dressed like the professor. All done up with a highfalutin hat and fancy trousers. Carrying a walkin' stick with a silvery knob." He grinned again, shaking his head. "And ye should see his poke. Made o' shiny leather with brass letters on hit."

Few outsiders came to Sycamore Creek. I could count on one hand the numbers who'd made their way to where I lived with my granddaddy Poppy. "When you expect this professor to land at my front door then?"

"He's marchin' up the trace right now. Huffin' worse'n me."

"So you passed him on your way?"

"Yes indeedy." He let his gaze drift from my eyes.

"Dearly Forbes," I scolded, causing him to look back, "did this professor ask you to show him the way?"

Dearly stared hard at his feet, then reached down to pick at one grimy toe. "Well now, I reckon."

"But you ran off without him?"

"I jes' moved up the trace faster'n him."

"Dearly, ye need to go back and fetch him. Right this minute. The poor man may already be lost."

The boy stood, scratched his head, and hiked up one of the galluses that had slipped off his shoulder. "Well, if'n ye say so." He slumped off the porch, looking put out. He halted at the bottom step and gazed back with a grin. "Can I stay then, listen to ye tellin' the man yer stories?"

"If that's what he's come for, then yes, lad. Ye can stay."

He skipped off through the meadow, bare feet flying, the afternoon sun gleaming on his orange hair.

I shelled beans from the back garden as I rocked in my rocker and waited for Dearly to pop up again from the trace. I'd just finished the second bushel and was starting on the third when, sure enough, Dearly skipped from the hilltop to the edge of the meadow. His grin was wider than before, and he shouted a big hello.

For just an eye bat I thought he was alone, but before I could let out a disappointed sigh, up from the trace rose another figure.

The professor stood there, shading his eyes and gazing my direction. His head back, shoulders erect and proud, he stayed in that one spot while I stood, ready to walk out to him. He looked

magnificent and golden in the slant of the sun. Then with Dearly
Forbes at his side, he began striding through the grasses toward
me, scaring up a joree-bird into a flutter, whilst all around him
swallowtails flitted and bees worked the mountain daisies and
purple pennyroyals.

Minutes later he was on my porch, tapping his walking stick
against a loose board as if such motion might nail it in place. He
gave me a smile that flushed my cheeks, and I stared dumbfounded into his eyes.

Poppy and Me had a stack of books that I'd read so often I
could scarce make out the gold-stamped words on their worn
leather spines. At the top lay *Great Expectations* by Mr. Dickens,
and on page six of that book there was a man that long ago had
captured my spinster heart: *Joe was a fair man, with curls of flaxen
hair on each side of his smooth face, and with eyes of such an undecided blue that they seemed to have somehow got mixed with their
own whites.*

How I dreamed of such a one coming to my door. This man,
with his flaxen curls and pale blue eyes, so resembled my imagin-
ings that immediately—even before he spoke—I figured him to
be good natured and sweet tempered, the same as Mister Dickens's
man on page six.

The professor's lips tilted upwards again, which truly set my
heart aflutter. "Miss Fairwyn March?"

I nodded slowly, thinking I could not bear to keep my eyes
locked onto his pale eyes a heartbeat longer. So I studied my lace-
up brogans. No one had ever called me "Miss" before. Just plain
Fairwyn. It was a fitting name, Poppy used to say when I was
young, because of my delicate look and my way of moving quiet-
like along the trace. Like unto floating, he said. Though I knew as

well as he did that "delicate" was not a consideration that did me proud in these parts. It didn't help that I was known for my dulcimer playing instead of my sweet-egg pie.

"My name is Zebulon Deforest," he said, drawing my eyes to his once more.

"I'm pleased to make your acquaintance," I said.

"And I, yours." He was still smiling.

Dearly spoke up from behind me. "This here's the furriner who's come to hear yer music, ma'am."

Zebulon Deforest laughed, a sound that warmed my heart. "I've heard you're the best song scribe in these parts." His rushing words reminded me of the swift-moving waters of Sycamore Creek in the spring. "I'm told you sing and play a dulcimer." He frowned, obviously puzzled. "A fairy dulcimer."

I laughed softly, enjoying the admiration I saw in a place deep behind his eyes. "Years ago such a tale was begun," I said. "I suppose on account of the way I play." I gave him a half-smile and shrugged. "I'm prone to hold my face heavenward whilst strumming. And I have a certain way of telling tales and singing at the same time. Story songs, fairy tales, some about my kinfolk from years past. I suppose folks in these parts have mistaken me for the fairies in the stories I tell."

He leaned forward, furrowing his brow. "Your language," he said, "it's not the same as the others I've met. Are you from here? Originally, I mean. Are you from the Great Smokies?"

"From Blackberry Mountain itself," I said. The door was open, and I gestured toward the bookshelf beside the fireplace. "The language in my books isn't like that of my mountain kin. I suppose I speak both ways, depending on who it is I'm speaking to."

"May I have a look?" His eyes met mine with a spark of

curiosity, and I nodded. He strode to the bookshelf, Dearly trailing at his heel. I stood by the doorway, watching as the professor leaned forward, squinting in the dim light, running his fingers over the spines. *"Great Expectations..."*

"Yes." I smiled at the back of his flaxen head.

"Works by Tennyson, Robert Browning, Lewis Carroll, Hans Christian Andersen...Melville...Charlotte Brontë."

He glanced back to me in amazement, then returned to making his way through the stack, reading each title aloud. *"The Old Curiosity Shop, The Deerslayer...* Thoreau's *Life in the Woods."*

"One of my favorites," I said, leaning against the doorframe.

He grinned. "Fitting." His face sobered. "You've read these all?"

"Many times."

"Are ye gwine to tell yer tales?" Dearly said. "When are ye, ma'am?"

The professor chuckled at the boy's impatience, then looked to me once more, raising a well-formed brow. "Would you be so kind?"

" 'Tis no trouble," I said and nodded to the porch.

He passed through the doorway trailed by Dearly, and I reached for my dulcimer that was propped in the corner of the cabin. When again I joined them, Dearly was sitting on the top step, and the professor was in the rocker nearest the end of the porch floor. Laying my dulcimer across my lap, I settled into the rocker nearest my bushel baskets of fresh-shelled beans.

The professor leaned forward, his gaze on my instrument. "Did you make it yourself?"

I strummed a few chords. "Most do in these parts, but I've never learned the art. My granddaddy—Poppy—made this one for me. 'Tis from his own recipe, as he calls it. Won't tell anyone his secrets."

Zebulon Deforest studied me as if taking note of every word I said. "Whom did he learn from?"

"He's never said." I shook my head. "Poppy's one to keep things to himself. 'Tis my prayer that someday he'll pass along his dulcimer-making secrets to me." I stroked the smooth soundboard, relishing its warmth beneath my fingers. "Making something of such beauty would be a wonder."

"But are ye gwine to sing fer the furriner?" Dearly said, scooting closer. "Whyn't ye sing the one about 'Yonder Mountain'?"

With a wink and a nod toward Dearly, I lifted the dulcimer closer and strummed a few chords in the key of G. Tapping my foot, I began a lively rendition, lifting my voice in song.

At the foot of yonder mountain there runs a clear stream,
At the foot of yonder mountain there lives a fair queen.
She's handsome, she's proper, and her ways are complete.
I ask no better pastime than to be with my sweet.

Dearly clapped his hands and joined with me on the next verse.

But why she won't have me I well understand;
She wants a freeholder and I have no land.
I cannot maintain her on silver and gold,
And all the other fine things that my love's house should hold.

I glanced at the professor, who seemed better pleased than a chap chasing butterflies.

"Reminiscent of Cornish lore. Pre-Saxon, I think," he murmured, biting his lip. "Pre-Christian perhaps."

I laughed, shaking my head slowly. "I'm not sure of your meaning, but I've heard tell our kinfolk brought it from Virginia."

"These are the threads I'm searching for, Miss March," he said. "You can call me Fairwyn."

"An unusual name." He gave me another smile and nodded.

"Hain't atall," Dearly piped up from the stairs. "Everbody round these parts knows Fairwyn March."

"It means light," I said to Zebulon Deforest. "Fairlight would be another way of saying it." I could not help sounding proud. It had been a family name as far back as anyone could remember.

He studied me, his eyes crinkling at the outer corners as he puzzled. "There is a place by that name, your name—Fairlight—in England. And *Wyn*…" He paused with a frown. "That's Welsh, is it not?" He leaned forward with interest. "Do you know anything more about your ancestry?"

"My family's been in the Appalachians at least a hundred years," I said. "Tales are told of how they came…"

His elbows resting on his knees, his fingers dangling between, he seemed keen for me to continue.

"Poppy says it was his granddaddy Anwar March who came to our land first. He was a smithy in Wales, a seaside village called Aberystwyth. He took a wife from Fairlight—the same we were just talking about—a lass who was orphaned and who'd come to work as a maid in the big house where my great-great-granddaddy lived. She was the first to be called Fairwyn, from Poppy's recollection.

"Anwar and Fairwyn came to the new world by sailing ship, then moved deep into Virginia, gradually making their way across the mountains to Sycamore Creek. It was here they bore nine babies, all named for places in the old country." I laughed. "That's why we are all related, it seems, here in Sycamore Creek. I have more cousins than you can shake a black birch stick at. Poppy can tell you more about such things when he returns from his hunting trip."

The professor seemed to be puzzling something. "March," he said after a time. "There is a legend of a warrior in ancient times named Meirchyawn." When I frowned, he went on, "It has the same meaning as March. Have you ever heard of such a legend?"

Such a string of related family going back through the generations caught my imagination. "Meirchyawn," I said quietly, pondering the strange word. "I'm sorry, but I haven't heard it before."

The professor nodded. "For my book," he went on, "I'm studying the genealogies connecting the Appalachian people to England, Scotland, and Wales. Legends such as the one about Meirchyawn that have been carried from the old country and how they connect to tales and folk songs here."

I thought of the books on my shelf, the authors I'd long held in high esteem. I'd already decided that this man was fairer than I'd ever seen, and now I knew his mind was sharper than a scythe at harvest. I met his eyes, imagining the storehouse of knowledge behind them. A flush warmed my cheeks at the nearness of such a one.

"You will be famous for your book someday? Perhaps another Mister Dickens?"

He laughed lightly, shaking his head. "I'm hoping for acclaim, of course. But fame such as Dickens…?" He chuckled again. "I hardly think so." His face was glowing, and I could see that my admiration pleased him.

He was studying my face when he again spoke. "About your playing…" he said gently, "excuse me for not saying so earlier, but the others are right. Your songs are surely the best example of mountain music in this region." He paused. "They're lovely."

My music was a part of my very soul and had been so since I was a small girl. There was no separating my heart from my dulcimer, my fingers, or even my voice. My cheeks flushed again. Too often this afternoon they had turned crimson. I felt like a schoolgirl.

"Please," he said, "play something else."

" 'Dabblin' in the Dew'!" Dearly shouted.

Grinning, I let my fingers dance through the beginnings of "Dabbling in the Dew." The rhythm flowed from my heart straight to the tapping of my toes.

Oh, where are you going, my pretty little dear,
With the red, rosy cheeks and the coal black hair?

By the time I got to the last of the four verses, Dearly was singing at the top of his lungs. And surprise of all surprises, this sophisticated furriner had picked up the tune and joined in.

What's a ring on the finger if there's rings around the eye?
For it's dabbling in the dew makes the milkmaid fair.

His gaze was bright when we stopped, and I knew it was his mind working that caused his joy over the song. "It's Elizabethan," he whispered reverently. "*Elizabethan.* Imagine such a find."

"My grandmother taught it to me, and her mother before her…"

He smiled with his eyes of undecided blue. Then he stood abruptly and began to pace the porch, his brow furrowed, each step causing the planks to creak. Dearly looked up at him with a puzzled frown, then back to me and rolled his eyes.

Zebulon Deforest stopped and stroked his smooth face. "Think of it," he finally whispered, his voice quivering with emotion. "This is a thread that may lead to some monumental discoveries."

He strode back to the rocker and sat, again bending toward me. "Have you heard of Chaucer?"

I nodded. "The name, yes."

"Fairwyn, he was born in 1342 in London. A poet like none other—perhaps even greater than Shakespeare who came after him." He leaned even closer, narrowing his eyes in thought. "You must read *The Canterbury Tales*. You must." He seemed to consider me an equal. My heart skipped into a dance. Before I could comment, he hurried on, "It's truly one of the greatest poetic works in English. I will see that you get a copy." He went on to tell how our mountain language matched that of Chaucer and that he wanted more time to explore this new find.

By and by he pulled out a chain-watch, an elegant gold disk with flowery engravings, studied its face, and then placed it again in his trouser pocket.

Queer disappointment washed over me at the thought of his leaving. I wanted to speak more about Shakespeare and Chaucer, letting his words fill my mind with new ideas and wisdom from the past. As we stood, Dearly hopped down the steps behind us, but Zebulon met my gaze as if he had nothing else in the world to think about but me.

"I must see you again." His pale eyes bored into mine, and my heart danced as surely as my feet would the minute he left. "Please tell me I may."

"Yes, please come again," I managed.

"Good then." He smiled, dazzling me again with those strange pale eyes.

"Surely, you can come again tomorrow," I said when I could breathe.

Just as the mountain shadows were inching toward our house, Poppy strode up the path from the woods. Squirrels hung from both ends of a strap slung across his shoulder. His yellow hunting dogs followed along, nosing the ground. Leaning against the door, I watched him prepare the critters for cleaning on the rough oak tabletop at the far end of the porch. He had barked them, I could see. Shot the tree trunk close to their heads to bring them down without a wound.

While he skinned the squirrels, I told him about Zebulon Deforest. But the more I told, the deeper the lines creased around his mouth.

"A furriner, eh?" Poppy frowned as he slit open the second squirrel's belly with his hunting knife.

I dropped the first skinned critter into the iron pot hanging over the fire where the wild onion broth was simmering. I came back to the porch just as Poppy pulled the entrails from the second squirrel, tossing them away from the house for the yellow dogs to finish. Then he skinned the animal clean to the muscle.

"Sometimes I can't help but wonder…" I said mostly to myself as I stared at the lavender hills above the meadow. Just before nightfall they reminded me of a giant, magical flower, its petals fading into the sky. "Sometimes I wonder what life might hold outside Sycamore Creek." I laughed lightly. "Even for an old maid like me."

Poppy looked up. "Lass," he said, "ye canna keer about what canna be. 'Tis a useless chase."

"The professor says our songs and tales come from ancient legends in the old country. He told tales about books and poets like as I'd never heard."

"He's fillin' yer head with folderol same as Welsie True." His face darkened at my friend's name. "Same entirely." He looked down at the bloody mass of squirrel fur.

"He's planning to write a book about the connection of our kinfolk to those in the past." I hesitated, already knowing Poppy's reaction. "He wants to see me again," I said finally.

Poppy looked hard at me. "Ye need to stay away from this furriner, lass. He's already fillin' yer head with nonsense. Next thing I know ye'll be hankerin' to leave."

"My heart aches for more books," I said as I went to the fireplace to stir the pot of stew. While moving the big iron spoon in a slow circle, I looked back to where my grandfather stood leaning against the doorjamb. "Sometimes I think I'd near sell my soul to fill my head with the wonders of this world."

His face softened to a look of sorrow. "I ken yer hankering, girl. I ken." He turned to head to the creek to wash up. At the top step, he looked back. "But ye're mountain borned, and 'tis here ye'll stay."

Blackberry Mountain
August 24, 18 and 82

My dear Welsie True,

Oh, what a joyful thing I have to tell you. A professor came striding across our bald mountain today. My heart danced when I saw him. Truly he was easy on these old-maid eyes, but truer still was the treasure of his mind. Never had I been more grateful for all the books you've sent through the years than I was today. Considering that I never once spent a day in a schoolhouse 'twas a glory to understand the least possible bit of his ponderings. He's coming back tomorrow. I scarce can wait for his visit!

Whenever I sit down to pen a letter to you, I think how far this scrap of paper will travel. I try to picture the route from all you have told me. I see the mail train traveling across wide fields of tall grass called Great Plains, across the jagged Rocky Mountains, on to salt deserts so flat you can see forever, and finally to where you live in California. Sometimes I dream about your little cottage by the sparkling sea with your flower garden and picket fence. I can almost hear the mission bells in the distance. And it makes me long to come see you.

Today again, I thought of leaving. But Poppy says I will never leave, and I know he's likely right. Sometimes I think my heart will twist in two at such a thought. I am resigned that I likely will never wed. But oh, how I want to see the world, to truly live! I want to experience life beyond these hills, glorious as they are. Sometimes I think my heart is like unto a stagnant pond—no pure waters bubbling in to renew my life.

I will tell you more about the professor after he visits next.

Until then I remain
Your devoted friend,
Fairwyn March

The next morning, just as the eastern light caused the dew to dance on the laurel leaves, the professor helloed from the top of the trace.

I stood at the doorway, watching as Zebulon Deforest made his way through the meadow grasses, his leather poke bouncing with each step, the silver knob of his walking stick twinkling in the sun. He smiled as his gaze caught hold of mine, and he bounded up the porch stairs. Off came his hat, and he bowed at the waist as if I might be a queen.

"Miss Fairwyn," he said. My heart caught at the sound of his voice.

"Mister Deforest," I said with a tone of awe.

"Please call me Zeb," he said, which pleased me no end. His smile spread wider across his smooth face. "Mind if I sit with you?" He nodded to the rocking chairs at the end of the porch.

"I have some cross-vine tea brewing. Would you like a cup?"

He nodded his approval, his eyes not leaving mine, and settled into the far rocker. The porch boards creaked beneath his weight. I listened to the rhythm of his rocking while I poured two cups of tea, then returned to join him.

Zeb took a long draw, looking satisfied with the taste. He now fixed his gaze over the slope of land at the top of the trace, pondering something in the distance. He turned to me after a time. "I must return home," he said, "but I would like to come again to Sycamore Creek."

Pleasure settled into my heart. Without comment I sipped my tea and cast a shy glance at him above the rim of the cup.

"I would like to bring you some books in exchange for your help." Setting his cup on the nearby porch handrail, he sat back in the chair and studied my face. "Besides Chaucer, what would you say to a few volumes of Shakespeare?"

I didn't hide my pleasure. "That would be a treat indeed," I said, a smile spreading wide across my face.

"What I would like, if you wouldn't mind…" He pulled a notepad from his leather poke. "If you could write as many family tales as you can remember, I would be much obliged."

Now I couldn't stop smiling. " 'Twould be an honor. Truly."

"This help…with my book, I mean…is invaluable. Your self-taught education…" He seemed to be having trouble finding the words. "Finding someone like you in these mountains. It's like finding a rough-cut jewel."

I blushed at the compliment and tilted my chin downward, peering at him from beneath my lashes, feeling suddenly shy, too stunned to speak.

He laughed, a low pleasant sound. "I'm sorry if I spoke too intimately. What I meant was that you're not like the others I've met here. You're better read than most of the women I know in Oak Hill." His eyes were bright with admiration. "With a little push in the right direction…" He let his words fall away.

Embarrassed, I stared at my brogans while I took another sip of tea.

"I'll be back before long—perhaps before winter," he was now saying. "I'd like it if you could travel with me into the hollows and coves of this area. I'll need your help gaining the trust of the people." I met his gaze again. "After all," he laughed, "I'm a 'furriner.' "

He swallowed the last of his lukewarm tea, and, with the lift of a brow and a smile of promise, he stood. Too soon, he walked toward the trace, his stride strong and sure, like that of a happy razorback heading to steal from the corncrib.

Two

By harvest Zebulon Deforest indeed returned to Sycamore Creek, but he didn't come up Blackberry Mountain to my cabin.

Most of our mountain folks weren't as standoffish as they had been before. But there were still some who met him with expressionless faces, rifle-guns at their sides, and refusing to answer even the simplest of questions.

All this Dearly Forbes reported to me with glee. The boy always seemed to be the bearer of news both good and bad, and he told me every detail over a tall glass of goat's milk and some warm corncakes. I didn't let on to Dearly, but when I discovered how long the professor had been in our mountains, I was fearful he had changed his mind about bringing me the Chaucer and Shakespeare tomes. Each night as I lay upon my corn-tick, I thought how it would be when he came again across our meadow. My spinster's heart beat fast at the thought of seeing him coming toward me. I imagined how his eyes would seek out mine, his keen affection clear as our gazes met. I could almost see the sharp sunlight falling slantwise across the grass, turning his hair to gold, his face to bronze. I dared to dream that someday in that shimmering glint of light, his arms would open to draw me into their embrace.

Stronger than all the images I conjured was that look of admiration for my self-taught book learning, for my gift of dulcimer playing and singing, that I'd seen in his eyes.

I waited. And waited. And more often than not I allowed myself my outlandish daydreams, hoping and praying that Zebulon Deforest would soon return.

The morning was bright and rain-fresh when I saw him rise above the trace at last. Pine smoke hovered low to the ground, lacing among the chestnuts, maples, elms, sycamores, willows, beech, and birch trees that formed a half-circle behind the cabin.

I'd just come around the side yard, propping a bushel of corn against my hip as I carried it toward the weathered narrow sled out front. There was to be a corn-shucking party at Selah Jones's this very night. Poppy and I had been working since dawn picking the late ears and carrying them up the mountain since our field was a ways behind the cabin on a terrace as steep as a cow's face, and the road was too treacherous for a wagon.

Poppy had just left for Selah's when I spotted Zebulon. I stopped dead still, my heart soaring on wings as sure as a hawk's riding the wind into the sky.

At first, he didn't see me, so intent was he on weaving his way through the rain-puddled meadow. Had I not been so caught up in the romantic sight of him, it might have been amusing to watch him dart and hop, his leather poke bouncing against his shoulder with each step.

A few steps from the cabin he seemed to remember his manners and halted to hello the house. He'd barely uttered the word when he spotted me standing there. His eyes studied mine—almost as if looking for something he'd been searching for, and for the briefest moment I thought he might make my daydreams come true, that he might open his arms so I could fly into them. But instead, he stood there without saying a word.

Finally, he swung his hat from his head and strode toward me.

When he was an arm's-length away, he stopped again. And glory of all glories, I saw that same admiration as before in his pale eyes—the same I'd been conjuring for weeks. But it hadn't been my imagination. Truly, it hadn't.

A small grin started—I couldn't help myself—and spread across my face. "Good morning, Zebulon Deforest," I said. "Welcome back to Blackberry Mountain."

He laughed, a low and warm rumble, making my heart thud faster. "I've brought you what I promised." He swung the poke from off his shoulders, letting it drop to the ground.

"If you'd like, you can come in," I said, nodding to the cabin door and thinking that I couldn't wait another minute to feel the new books in my hands. " 'Tis too cold out here to stay unless you're willing to work to keep warm." I glanced at the sled half piled with corn.

"I heard about the corn-shucking and play party tonight."

Queer disappointment filled me for an instant, thinking he'd come just so I'd invite him along. But before I could ponder it further he walked to the bushel I'd set down, and with a heavy grunt, he hefted it and set it onto the sled. He rubbed his hands together and shook his fingers as if they ached from the cold.

"About the play party and husking," I said.

His eyes brightened. "May I go with you?" Then he hesitated, a warm smile spreading across his face. He gave me a slight bow. "Forgive me. I should have said, 'Fairwyn March, may I have the pleasure of your company this evening?' "

As he straightened, I laughed softly and inclined my head. "It would be my pleasure, kind sir." I thought my heart might never stop its dancing.

He followed me into the house then, and sat by the fireplace in one of our two chairs, his poke by his side. After reaching for our best china cups and saucers on the kitchen shelf, I turned back to where the coffee was boiling over the coals. I could feel his gaze on my back as I wrapped a towel around the handle and poured the dark liquid into the two cups.

My cheeks heated from the warmth of the fire or from his nearness, I couldn't tell which. I turned back to him, handed him his coffee, and sat opposite him. After a moment of letting his coffee cool, he took a swallow, his eyes still on mine above the rim.

"I brought you the books I promised," he said, setting his cup and saucer on the wood-planked floor. He reached for the bag and placed it atop his bent knees, without making a move to withdraw the contents.

I couldn't bear to meet his eyes, so fearful was I that my hunger for the leather poke's contents would show. Like the starving cougar cub I'd once found caught in a bear trap over by Troublesome Creek, I hungered for book learning.

"Shakespeare," I murmured. "And Chaucer."

"Ah, you remembered!" he said as if it had been a test. He seemed to take extra care and time opening the parcel. At last, he beamed and held out the first large book.

I reached for it, quickly wrapping my fingers around the leather binding. The tome lay heavy in my lap, and I traced my fingertips over the gold lettering: *A Treasury of Shakespeare's Plays and Sonnets.*

"Open it!" Zebulon said, scooting his chair closer and resting the second book atop his knees.

Slowly, I turned back the front cover.

"No, no, no!" He said, taking the book from my hands. "Like this! Like this!" He closed the cover, then proceeded to demonstrate opening the book in the center, slowly bending back the spine, cutting each side in half, then in quarters, each time bending gently as before. He carefully smoothed the pages, touching them as gently as a mother touching a newborn infant. Or a lover touching his beloved.

"Welsie True never told me about this," I said quietly. I turned my attention to his method of preserving the spine and tried not to be offended.

He looked up, and his expression turned sheepish. "I shouldn't have spoken so," he said. "Forgive me." He handed the heavy book back to me. "Who is Welsie True?"

I smoothed the pages, aware he still watched my hands, judging them. Some of the joy had worn off his gift. "She is my dearest friend in the world."

"Someone nearby then? A neighbor?"

I shook my head. "I've not yet set eyes on her. But someday I will." I said no more for I could see that he had lost interest.

"Read something," he urged. "There, on the first page...*The Tempest*." He reached across the distance between us and pointed to a place halfway down the page. "Ah, my dear, with your lovely voice...I cannot wait to hear you read Shakespeare." He then surprised me by settling back into his chair and closing his eyes. "Read."

I frowned at the unfamiliar words and began. The words came slowly at first, and then—almost unbidden—the fey magic of the language took root in my soul. "Heigh, my hearts! cheerly, cheerly, my hearts! yare, yare! Take in the topsail. Tend to the master's whistle—Blow, till thou burst thy wind, if room enough!"

I continued on, images of ancient mariners filling my mind. Time passed without my awareness. It wasn't until I heard footsteps on the porch that I realized I had read for an hour or more. Poppy was home for our midday meal.

The door burst open, letting in a blast of light. "What's this?" Poppy growled. "Who's here with ye, lass?"

" 'Tis Zebulon Deforest," I said, placing the book on the floor and standing awkwardly, the chair tipping over with a clatter behind me. "He's returned." I wondered why I felt the need to explain Mr. Deforest's presence or protect him from what would surely be Poppy's displeasure.

Zebulon stood and set the other book in his chair. "Good day, sir." He strode across the great room, extending a hand to shake Poppy's. He towered over Poppy's elfin figure.

Scowling up at him, my grandfather ignored the gesture. "So ye've come to take away me Fairwyn."

"No sir," Zebulon said quickly. "I've done no such thing. I've come again to learn about your people, those things your grand-daughter can tell me about your culture. Your stories, your songs. That sort of thing."

"Ye mayn't ken ye're takin' her away, but ye're pullin' her away from me, true."

I stepped forward and laid my hand on my grandfather's rough sleeve. " 'Tis only as he says, Poppy."

Poppy set his gaze on the Shakespeare volume at my feet. "What's this?"

"A book for your granddaughter," Zebulon said. "I saw her hunger for reading when last I was here…I thought—"

My grandfather turned his hard-eyed gaze to Zebulon. "Ye're putting notions in her head. That's what ye're doing. Bad as Welsie True, ye are. Worse'n Welsie True." He moved to the book and picked it up. "Fairwyn don't need yer gifts. You pack 'em in yer poke and git." He snapped his galluses, looking scornful.

"Sir…" Zebulon's voice quaked with either anger or fear, I

couldn't tell which. "Sir, you have no right to keep your granddaughter from reading what she wants. She is a grown woman, able to make her own decisions about such things."

He studied the book still in Poppy's hands, then moved his gaze to my grandfather's face. "These are classics of the finest order. Beautifully bound. Valuable beyond your imagination. There is a bright spark of intelligence and yearning in your granddaughter's soul. You cannot forbid Fairwyn to have them."

I stood rooted to the bare planks beneath my brogans. *Bright spark of intelligence?* My cheeks warmed. The professor saw such a thing in me? The gift of the books paled in comparison to the gift of his compliment.

Poppy turned toward the corner where his rifle stood, and I quickly took three steps to stand in his way. "Poppy," I said gently. "Ye needn't do anything more. Mister Deforest was about to go."

Looking pale, Zebulon met my gaze, and with a slight nod he headed first to retrieve his leather poke, then outside. I followed him onto the porch, leaving the door open behind me for Poppy's sake.

"Will he allow you to keep the books?"

I smiled. "His gruff manner is only that. He loves me and only desires to protect me. He fears that book learning will make me dissatisfied with my lot. With Sycamore Creek. I'll assure him that your gift has nothing to do with my desire to leave. He'll not understand, but he'll agree to let me keep them."

He leaned against the porch rail. "You've considered leaving this place?"

"I think about it every day." I laughed and shrugged. "But where would I go? What would I do?" Then I sobered. "Besides, this is the only home I've ever known. Poppy's raised me, and I'm the only one left to care for him."

He studied my face. "About tonight, will there be a problem if I walk with you to the party? I mean, your grandfather—will he object?"

I glanced back through the doorway to where Poppy sat by the fireplace thumbing through the Shakespeare volume. His thin shoulders were hunched, and he frowned in concentration. His lips moved slowly as his index finger traced over the words. "I'll convince him that he has nothing to fear from you," I said when I turned back to Zebulon.

Zebulon stepped onto the bottom stair, which creaked beneath his weight, then turned and looked up at me. My heart caught at the earnest expression in his eyes. "When I first met you it was your mind—your undaunted thirst for learning—that captured my attention," he said as if to himself. "But I'm finding your spirit captivates me as well." He turned then and headed into the meadow, almost loping as he went.

"Be here by sundown," I called after him.

Without turning he waved a hand over his head, showing me he'd heard, then disappeared down the trace.

"Ye're just like yer momma," Poppy said between spoonfuls of possum stew. "I fear for ye, lass, I do. Fear ye'll be sweet-talked by barren promises jes' like she was. Came to no good, it did. And my sweet girl lost her life jes' because of it."

The scent of onions, beans, and cooking meat mixed with the aroma of burnt hickory filling the room. The stew still bubbled in the kettle hanging by its handle over the fire, and a pan of cornbread warmed on the coals beneath.

"You shouldn't judge me by the choices Momma made." I

thoughtfully stirred my food, looking across the scarred table at Poppy. "She made her choices on her own. Mine are mine alone to make."

Poppy's face grew red, and he set down his spoon so hard it rattled. "Now listen here, lass. Ye canna ken the trouble of those days." His voice rose in anger. "Ye weren't a part of what befell yer ma, but ye were a result of her sin." Then he looked down again as if ashamed to have divulged even that much to my yearning soul.

I leaned forward to take his hands in mind. "Poppy, tell me what happened. You've always kept it to yourself. You tell me over and over that I'm bound to make the same mistake—tell me about the troubles that took my momma's life. How can I avoid them, if I don't know what they were?"

He withdrew his hands from mine, and set his lips in a straight line, refusing to meet my eyes as he continued eating. It was always the same when I asked about my mother and father.

We finished our meal in silence.

During the afternoon we loaded the rest of the corn into the sled and then hung two more razorbacks in the smokehouse, fresh-killed by Poppy that morning. He said nothing about the books Zebulon brought, and when I looked at the slant of the sun and said that Zebulon Deforest would be here soon to fetch me for the play party, he turned away, his narrow shoulders sloped with a kind of resigned sorrow.

Yet when Zebulon arrived, Poppy made it clear that he expected to accompany us.

With the sun low in the western sky, we started up the trace leading to Selah Jones's cabin at the topmost knob of Blackberry Mountain. Poppy led the way with Blinken, our sorry one-eyed mule, pulling the sled. I suspected it was on purpose he wanted

Zebulon at the south end of that foul-smelling creature, though I was there as well.

We met a passel of kinfolk and neighbors along the way. Empty-handed Charlie Beck hollered out that he was fit to be tied over the poor crop of late corn, then he fell into stride beside Poppy to talk of the woes of an early frost.

Rosie and Alpha Green joined us next, two ancient old-maid sisters who skittered like waterbugs up the trace. White-haired and wiry, they cackled as much as they talked. I never saw much of them unless there was a play party. I had always figured I would be like them someday. Known for my tale-telling and singing, considered one of the ancient keepers of our stories and songs by the generations to come. But never loved as a woman by a man.

As darkness fell, I turned to watch the swinging lights coming up the trail, twinkling as the bearers wove through the autumn forest. A sharp breeze blew from higher on the mountain, biting into my cheeks, bringing with it a flurry of falling leaves. I quickened my stride to keep warm. Beside me, Zebulon drew in quick breaths of air, obviously winded at the climb.

Selah Jones was one of the few knob folks with a barn, and as we came up the trace, the glow from a ring of torches around it welcomed us. Already, music spilled into the night air, fiddles and mountain dulcimers sawing prettily, jaw harps twanging, and a washtub drum beating its bumpy rhythm into the starry sky.

Selah spotted me right off and hurried over, hobbling all the way. "Fairy lass," she said, peering through the dim light to Zebulon. "Who's this ye've brung?"

Poppy held no great esteem for Selah and was already leading Blinken to the far side of the barn where a group of men was unloading their sleds of corn.

"Zebulon Deforest," I said to Selah, looking back to her. "He's here from North Carolina to study our ways."

He stepped forward, his hand hanging limp as if he didn't know quite what he was supposed to do.

"Pshaw," Selah said and spat to a place beyond Zebulon's shoe. Then staring at the same fancy shoe, she brightened and peered again into my face. "Ye goin' walkin' together, lass?"

I shook my head, but I couldn't help grinning at the change in her. Seemed everyone in these mountains except Poppy wanted to marry me off—even to a furriner.

"He asked to come along. Wants to see our dances, hear our folk tales and music."

Selah put her hands on her hips, frowning. "Ye shoulda axt if'n I keered." Behind her, the fiddlers started in on a Virginia reel, a foot-tapping rhythm I could scarce resist. I glanced longingly at the open barn door.

But Selah was looking hard at Zebulon, still not letting us pass. She was small but mighty. If she wanted Zebulon to leave, he would have no choice.

"It's just for tonight, Selah," I said.

"Perchance if'n he's acourtin'—"

I held up a hand to interrupt, but before I could speak, a low rumbling laugh made my heart dance as fast as the tapping feet in the barn. At my elbow Zebulon leaned closer to Selah and whispered so I could barely hear him. "Now, how will I ever find out if Fairwyn and I are meant to go walking together, if I can't watch her dance and listen to her tell tales?"

Selah blinked her bright eyes at him, a hint of a smile playing at the corner of her lined mouth. "Well sir," she said. "Ye have a quare way o' puttin' hit, but I reckon ye're right."

"You don't mind if he stays then?" I grinned at her, then looked up at Zebulon, who winked at me. *Winked!* Surely, goodness and mercy!

Around us clusters of kinfolk and neighbors stared curiously, whispering among themselves. I figured they would since I'd been an old maid for a decade or more already. I squared my shoulders and shot another smile at Zebulon, allowing him to take my arm and lead me into the barn. My face tilted upward with pride to be with such a refined and educated man.

Zebulon met my gaze with an expression of wonder as we made our way through the play-party game already in progress. The place was filled with music. On a low platform in the middle, Poppy was strumming his dulcimer while Billy Butler and Ruffy Hill played on their fiddles. Granny London was sitting proud as a peahen by the washtub drum, tapping and clapping, and Jonce Reed twanged away on the jaw harp.

"You keep calling this a play party," he whispered in my ear as soon as we were seated. "It looks like dancing to me."

I gave him a nod, though I kept my eyes on the whirling and dipping couples in front of us. "Long time back a circuit preacher came through telling folks that dancing is a sin. No one stopped dancing, but now they call it a play party, playing games set to music—much like children do." I turned to smile at him.

But he was lost in watching the activity on the hay-covered floor. "They're the same as English country dances," he said slowly with a frown of concentration. "Straight off the courts of Henry VIII and Elizabeth I, I'd wager."

Then he turned to me, still puzzling something in his mind. "There's a book called *The English Dancing Master,* which ran through seventeen editions from 1650 to 1728. I've seen copies of it, drawings of the dance forms." He turned back to the dancers. "What's this called again?"

" 'Molly Brooks.' "

"The squares—or sets, as they're called in the *Dancing Master*—are identical." He turned to me again. "And the one before, the Virginia reel, was originally called 'Sir Roger de Coverly.' It's the same tune and rhythm." In his enthusiasm, he grasped my hand. "These dances go back hundreds of years. I've known it was true, but to see the purest form of Elizabethan dancing is…well, almost overwhelming."

He leaned closer as if taking me into his confidence. Something deep inside me welled with pride, and I bit my bottom lip to keep my happy smile from spreading.

"Think of it"—he squeezed my hand for emphasis—"we might find the key to rituals and games and songs that go back even further. I'm searching for those that are from pre-Christian rites. Pagan, if you will. Perhaps those taken from sword dances, English Morris dances, traditionally done by teams of men. I have a theory that they arrived in America before all the rest. I want to trace their history."

I blinked with surprise, trying to comprehend his meaning. "I've never heard of such thing in our mountains."

"If you ever do, Fairwyn, please note it in the journal I gave you. Perhaps something was mentioned by your kin years back. Something of rites or rituals that struck you as queer."

Again, a flush of gratitude and wonder filled my soul near to overflowing, knowing he valued my mind, my help with his work. I was afraid to show him the longing for more that surely shone in my eyes. So I merely nodded as answer to his request and then turned to watch the double lines of dancers finish their promenade.

"Time to hear Fairwyn," shouted Dearly Forbes from the far side of the barn.

"Hear, hear!" Granny London called from her seat by the washtub. "Fairwyn, sing us a pretty."

I was glad for the break from the professor's intense stare and the whirl of unsettled emotions inside my heart. I stepped onto the squat platform and took my place near Poppy. He glanced at me with pride and handed me his beautifully crafted dulcimer.

Dearly wound through the crowd until he was sitting at my feet. "The one about the groundhog," he whispered loudly.

Grinning, I strummed a C-major chord and began tapping my foot.

> *Groundhog married the baboon's sister;*
> *Smacked his mouth, and how did he kiss her?*
> *Kissed so hard he raised a blister!*
> *First couple out on the floor!*

Dearly hooted and slapped his knee as though he'd never heard the song before. Granny London grabbed white-haired Horace Mitchel, and they hobbled to the center of the floor to start a play-party square. Next came Rosie and Alpha Green and the Braugham brothers, widowers both, to take their places across from the old women. Then came pretty young maids Molly, Honey, Maudie Mae, and Beulah, peering toward the passel of young men who were standing shylike at the far end of the barn. By the time I got to the second verse, four of the boys had shuffled to join the girls to complete their square. Soon another half-dozen couples followed, and the barn floor was filled with laughter and song.

I launched into the third verse, joined by Billy Butler and Ruffy Hill on their fiddles. Poppy sat to one side, grinning and clapping as I strummed. He cocked his head as if to better hear my voice and watch my dancing fingers.

"More, more," Dearly shouted at the end.

Without missing a beat, I began "The Old Gray Goose Is Dead," followed by a rousing "Paddy O'Doyle." Most of the folks stopped their dancing and lifted their voices in song. When it was quiet once more, I sang "At the Foot of Yonder Mountain."

When the play party was done and people had drifted away from their dancing squares, the room fell still in anticipation of the storytelling time.

"Tell us the beggar story," Dearly said before anyone else could get out their requests.

It was indeed a favorite of mine, and I put down the dulcimer and stood to begin.

"An old couple had invited the Lord to supper, and he was late acomin'. They kept the supper hot and waited and waited, but still he didn't come.

"Directly a beggar came to the door and asked for something to eat. The woman thought, 'Well, I'll let him have my part.' But they were so poor they had scarce enough for the three of them. She went ahead and fed the beggar, and he thanked her and left.

"They still waited and waited and kept looking out the door. Then a little ragged boy came along. He looked cold and starved, so they took him in. The man told his wife, says, 'I'm not much hungry. He can have my supper.' So they fed the boy and let him sit and get himself warm. Tried to get him to stay the night but he said he couldn't, and before he left the man got a coat and wrapped him in it so he'd keep warm.

"The old people kept the fire going and kept Jesus' supper ready. And finally they looked out and saw him coming. They went to meet him at the gate, and said, 'We waited so long! We were afraid you'd never come.'

"The Lord took their hands, and said, 'I've already been here twice.' "

At the story's end, Zebulon hurried across the room and stood before me. His eyes were damp, and I thought it was from my story, for it seemed to cause tears each time I told it.

He shook his head in wonder and said, "The story is ancient, from a region of the world I hadn't considered would have an influence here. This is an even greater discovery than anything yet." I felt my heart sink in disappointment.

He caught my hands, smiling as happy as a wee chap chasing swallowtails, and looked deep into my eyes. I was only vaguely aware of the hush that had fallen over my kinfolk and neighbors as they stopped talking and turned to stare.

He leaned closer, and for an instant I thought he might kiss me, the old maid of Sycamore Creek, right there in the crowded barn. But instead he whispered in my ear, "Tolstoy tells a similar folk tale. It's Russian, Fairwyn! And I discovered it right here in the Great Smokies!" He leaned back and hooted like a screech owl, raising his joyous fists toward the rafters.

From the exchanged looks and instant murmurs of young and old around us, I knew everyone thought I had caught myself a beau at last.

I met Zebulon's triumphant gaze, unable to stop smiling.

Three

Zebulon Deforest walked me home in the light of a harvest moon as round as a big brass pot. Poppy stayed behind to help the rest of the men with the shucking.

"Why is the husking done by moonlight?" Zebulon reached for my hand to help me down a steep section of the trace. "I've heard of it, but I don't know the reason."

I laughed. "It does seem simpler to do it in the daytime. But it's always been done this way—at least as far as I know. Always by the light of the first harvest moon. Same with planting. It's always done during a new moon." I decided not to tell him about the other legend about corn growing healthy and strong if sweethearts strolled among the rows, right after the planting, whispering of their love and dreams and the babies to come.

We walked along without speaking. The crunch of our feet on the damp, leaf-covered trace, a soft drip of moisture from the barren tree branches, and the voice of a hoot owl in the distance carried through the chilly air. Wood smoke from nearby cabins lay low to the ground, mixing with the mushroom scent of the loamy soil.

When the cabin I shared with Poppy was visible in the moon-lit distance, Zebulon halted and turned to me. A tuft of his hair, looking almost silver in the light, had fallen across his forehead. I wanted to reach up and comb it with my fingers.

"May I accompany you again?" His eyes locked with mine.

I pondered whether he meant to go walking with me or whether he just needed me to introduce him to others in Sycamore Creek, others who might help him find connections to the legends and songs so important to his work. He didn't seem to notice that I didn't answer, for he rushed on, now looking heavenward as if gloriously happy for what he'd discovered in our mountains. "The keys are here!" He shook his head slowly. "They're here!" Then he looked back to me.

"Fairwyn, I can see by the expression on your face that you understand the importance of what I'm doing." He reached for my hand and held it between both of his. And as we stood there, he began to tell me of the English-American heritage of folk tales, folk songs, and folk dances. He said the lore was not static, it was ever-changing and needed to be recorded now before any more time passed.

We started to walk through the meadow, the moon creating a gemlike sparkle on the heavy dew. With each step, the fragrance of crushed autumn grasses rose. Zebulon kept hold of my hand, squeezing it with emphasis from time to time as he spoke.

I was drawn into a wider world than I'd ever imagined, even in my dreams. He spoke softly out of his passion for study, explaining each detail with great patience. I listened, enchanted.

"Our American usage of the English language—in our literature, ballads, and folklore—comes from the North of Europe," he was saying when we reached the cabin's porch. "Each region has kept its distinct identity in its folk traditions."

He took both my hands again, gazing into my eyes. "Even the scale you used to sing your songs tonight is part of your heritage. There are four such modes, or scales—each reflecting the spirit of the heritage. Most singers have never heard the name of their mode…" He raised a brow, and I shook my head. "But they use these modes in their music." He went on to explain the Mixolydian, Dorian, Phrygian, and Lydian scales. "Tonight you were singing in the major or sol-fa scale. As in *do, re, mi, fa, sol, la, ti*."

I stared up at him, my heart catching. How I ached to learn more. "Hum the Mixolydian scale," I demanded with a smile.

He grinned and gave me a rusty hum. *"Do, do, sol, sol…"*

"Now the rest…"

Still looking immensely pleased, he complied. I joined him tentatively at first, then boomed out the scales. He threw back his head and laughed. "Your quick mind is second only to the glory of your voice." Again, high regard shone in his eyes, and I felt my cheeks warm.

"I'll come back to see you tomorrow," he said.

"I would like that." His gaze met mine, and I wondered with awe about his knowledge of a world I hadn't yet discovered. I felt drawn to the riches of such a mind as his.

"Tomorrow then," he said with a slight nod. And he turned to leave me.

October 4, 18 and 82

My dearest Welsie True,

Oh, how I wish you were here beside me to listen to all I have to tell you. I suppose I must be content with writing to you, knowing you will soon read these words and rejoice with me.

Zebulon Deforest did indeed return! I thought he

would never arrive, so great was my anticipation. But he came striding up the trace and across our meadow to stand before me, tall and handsome and—dare I say it?—seeming almost enchanted with me.

Imagine such a thing! Here I am, twenty-seven years old, and someone like Professor Zebulon Deforest travels all the way from Oak Hill, North Carolina, to see me.

Now that I have said what my heart dreams, I will tell you what my mind tells me is the real truth. I can see you smiling at the mention of the battle between my heart and mind—you have spoken of such a battle within yourself! My mind says that he has returned to find out more about our mountain culture, not to see me. Or that, if he has come to see me, it's merely to further his studies.

O Welsie. My heart is drawn to him. I have never known love, so I feel inadequate to judge what it is or isn't. All I know is that I love listening to him talk about the world I hunger for, about the knowledge he has gained from deep study and years of reading.

I have never known anyone could be so full of information. His brain contains riches such as I long to have as my own.

When I am with him, he treats me as if I have the capacity for such learning, that I'm not a backward mountain girl, but almost...his equal. He makes me think that my dreams of an education can come true.

Is this love, Welsie? 'Tis utterly confusing. How I long for you to sit beside me and tell me what love truly is. Please write soon and tell me what you know of love.

    Until then I remain
    Your friend,
    Fairwyn March

That afternoon, right after I rode Blinken down to Caudill's Store to post my letter, I took my dulcimer deep into the wood near Quicksand Creek. It was cool beneath the bright crown of chestnut trees and stands of pinwheel poplars, the air sweet with ferns and moss and decaying leaves. I fairly skipped along the deer path as my music called me forward.

I settled against the carcass of a hollowed-out log and strummed, eyes closed and fingers dancing along the neck of my instrument, the taps along the fretboard and the soft zing of the strings filling the mountain air.

The song was one I had scribed, from tune to words. For now, I kept my lips silent and entered that room in my heart where music lives. I do not know how long I stayed within it—for when I enter the glory of the place, I forget even my own given name. Poppy will call me from the top of the hollow and I scarce can hear him. No sun rising or sun setting, no seasons, no longings or heartaches. It is only me and the music of my heart.

But today a sense of coming change swept like a whirlwind through my heart, causing me to sing of love and courtship and marriage. My voice dropped as I pictured Zebulon standing before me, and I sang to him, daring to imagine him asking me to go with him to Oak Hill to become his bride.

"Fairwyn?" A voice interrupted my reverie and song as Poppy touched my shoulder. My face flamed.

I laid the dulcimer in my lap as he sat down beside me. "I figured ye'd be here, lass." He jingled something sounding like stones in his left hand, but he didn't open it for me to see. "When a lass fancies a lad," he said, " 'tis thoughts of love that draw her like a ha'nt. I knew ye'd be here strummin' and dreamin' o' the professor.

"Yer own momma did the same," he said, letting his gaze drift away from mine. "Came here after she figgered herself in love with that polecat da of your'n. Came here and sang ever song she knew about love."

It pleased me to hear that my mother loved so much, no matter the outcome. "Tell me about him." I tried to keep the note of pleading from my voice, but it still filled my tone. "I'm a woman grown, and it's time for me to hear the truth."

He met my eyes again, his as hard as flint. "Ye'll make the same mistakes as her if'n ye hain't keerful."

"Poppy, didn't ye hear me? I'm a grown woman. Tell me what Momma did that was so wrong?"

He spread his fingers open, dropping the pieces into my palm. "I fashioned these for ye."

I stared at the tiny carved tuning keys, then looked back into his worn, lined face. Poppy was known for his dulcimer making and repair all through the Great Smokies. I studied the small round keys, wondering how Poppy's big, callused hands could carve something so delicate and sturdy. I looked up into his piercing eyes.

"Aye, they're for ye." He looked away at the leaf-moldy ground. From a poplar branch above him, a phoebe dived for a beetle that skittered toward a toadstool, then lit on the ground and looked at me. "Poor little critter," Poppy muttered. "Picked the wrong froggystool."

I wondered if I would ever know the mystery surrounding my mother's death and my father's identity. I clutched the tuning pegs near my heart and, with my other hand, reached for Poppy's.

"I know ye're hankering to leave this place something fierce."

"I can't deny it." I tried to laugh, but found the music of it would not leave my throat. It came out more like a cry.

"As sartin as summer follers spring, lass, this professor of your'n will try to take ye away from me."

Another beetle crawled across a dead maple leaf propped against the toadstool. The same brown phoebe cocked its head, watching, waiting.

Poppy stood, looking down at me until I finally raised my face to his. "Yer ma turned no good on me. Fergot ever thing I ever larned her about love and loyalty. I loved her—yer Granny Nana and me both did. We never figured she'd be so bereft o' her senses."

Without another word he turned and walked back down the damp leafy path, making no sound, almost seeming to float above the trace. Floating, just like folks always said I did. I had not thought of it until this minute, but I must have learned my way of walking from Poppy.

Professor Zebulon Deforest did not return that afternoon as he promised, and I was sorely disappointed. After my chores were done, I waited at the top of the hill and sat beneath the stand of maples, playing my music, while the leaves fell and the cold mists blotted away the sun.

That night, I read out loud from the Shakespeare volume with the fire crackling behind me, popping and sizzling, almost in rhythm with my heart as my fears and hopes rose and fell.

At length, Poppy waved away my Shakespeare. "Read a shepherd's song," he said. "I expect I'd like to hear the forty-second."

I leaned deep against the slatted chair and, balancing the big book on my knees, turned the wrinkled pages to the place marked The Psalms, my finger tracing along the numbers until I found the one Poppy intended, then began to read. "As the hart panteth after the water brooks, so panteth my soul after thee, O God. My soul thirsteth for God, for the living God: when shall I come and appear before God?"

I paused, looking into Poppy's face, craggy and soft in the firelight. He nodded, telling me without words to continue. I finished reading verse number eight: "Yet the LORD will command his lovingkindness in the daytime, and in the night his song shall be with me, and my prayer unto the God of my life."

Poppy held up his hand to halt my reading. "There now, lass. This'n is the onliest song that should be in yer heart."

"Perhaps God's given my heart room for more than one song," I said, looking into the fire. I folded shut the big *Holy Bible* and walked across the room to place it near *Great Expectations* before returning to my chair. "You've always said he created all of me, even the song in my heart. Wouldn't that song—no matter where I sing it—always belong to him?"

He stared into the firelight for a good long while. Outside, a hoot owl called from someplace deep in the hollow. Another answered from the edge of the meadow.

Poppy turned his face to mine. His voice was low and soft when he spoke. "Ye have the will to do as ye please—jes' like yer ma."

I nodded, swallowing against a bone-dry spot in my throat. Before I could speak, he went on, "Furriners are different than us. Once't I was down in Dover Town to see a man about my fiddle makin', and I saw how folks there look on mountain folk. Like mockingbirds, they were, mimickin' my way of speakin'. And they laughed, they did, right in my face.

"Yer furriner," Poppy said, "if you follow him to that fancy school of his, he'd change ye like a prize piece of sassafras wood. Same as I carve and plane and sand to fashion a dulcimer, Zebulon Deforest would fashion ye into something ye aren't."

Hot tears stung my eyes. "Think of the music your dulcimers make once you finish. A block of sassafras could not make such a sound."

Poppy's sorrowful eyes peered hard into mine. "That's why ye must listen for God's song in the night, lass." His voice quivered, and for a long while only the hoot owls and the sizzle of flame filled the quiet of our old homeplace.

" 'Tis his song rightly belongin' in yer heart. No other."

Four

The sun had just begun its rise above our hollow the next morning when Zebulon Deforest emerged through the mists at the top of the trace, paused a minute, then headed into the brown meadow grasses. I was standing on the porch shaking out my counterpane when he spotted me. He stopped and stared. Then he galloped like a red-gold coyote across the distance between us and bounded up the porch stairs.

For more thuds of my heart than I could count, he stood staring at my face, the blaze of his smile filling me with joy. He leaned closer and took my hand in his. "I'm sorry to have stayed away yesterday, Fairwyn. I got caught up in my writings, trying to decipher the notes I'd made from the night before."

I couldn't speak, so overcome I was with how he studied my face. He laughed as if he knew my heart's ponderings, my desire to draw him closer. "Did you miss me?" he said, his voice soft and gruff at the same time.

The sunlight cut across his forehead, and he combed his flaxen hair back with slender fingers. It seemed his eyes fairly shimmered with book learning, and I longed to sink into their depths to see what they had seen.

"I have something to ask you." He pulled me down from the steps toward the meadow, and we ran into the tall grasses.

Zebulon's laughter rang out as we whirled in the meadow. My

voice joined his, right along with a flutter of startled quail that exploded skyward.

He halted midstep and grinned, cocking his head. "I was awake most of the night," he said, looking as if he couldn't bear to contain his news a minute longer. "I pondered my studies and these mountains"—his smile turned gentle—"and you," he finally finished. "I thought about you, Fairwyn March."

I bit my bottom lip, afraid to breathe.

"Your intelligence, your heart for learning, your knowledge of the region. You've already helped me make connections that might have taken months."

I didn't know whether to be flattered or dismayed. I tried not to think about what I'd rather have heard him say about me.

But before he could say more, Poppy appeared like a ha'nt from around the side of the house. He strode toward us, his face dark as he scowled at Zebulon. I figured he'd seen us twirling.

"Are ye plannin' to keep company with my Fairwyn?" Poppy said.

My face flamed, and I bit my lip.

Zebulon stepped closer to Poppy, his face now serious. "Please forgive me any impropriety, sir. I never intended to—"

"Ye canna dally with Fairwyn." Poppy's voice was a growl. "I willna allow it."

"I wouldn't do that, sir."

I stared at my feet, wondering at the troubled thoughts that filled my head, the voices that condemned me for my spinster state. Would I never be worthy of a man's notice?

"Then tell me yer intentions."

Zebulon studied the ground, working the muscles in his jaw as though he was chewing on a sassafras stick. He looked back to

Poppy and said, "My intentions are to ask your granddaughter to come back to Oak Hill with me."

I caught my breath. But before I could speak, Poppy reached for my hand and held it fast. "I've been expectin' yer question. And I already got an answer fer ye. And that answer is no." He stepped closer to Zebulon, now emphasizing his words by thudding his index finger at the younger man's chest. "Fairwyn's mountain folk, Mister Deforest. Ye're citified. I canna see her heart broken for the likes of ye."

Zebulon held his hands up as if in defeat and took a step backward. "I can assure you, Mr. March, I have nothing but honorable intentions toward Fairwyn." His voice dropped and took on a condescending tone. "My offer was merely one of furthering her education—"

Poppy's face turned dark gray. "Ye're using her for yer fancy book." He let go of my hand, and his white-knuckled fists, hanging at his sides, twitched. "Ye'll take her nowhere."

"I understand your concern, but I can assure you, I would guard her feelings, her well-being, with every ounce of energy in me."

I couldn't keep silent a minute longer. I glared at them both. "Shouldn't I have a say in this?"

Stunned silence followed, and Poppy spun to look me straight in the face. "Ye'd go agin' my wishes, lass?"

"You know my heart for book learning, Poppy," I said, trying to keep my tone soft and reasonable. "You know how I long to know more, to see the world beyond our mountains and read more than just the books Welsie True sends me. What Zebulon offers is a gift. It's a present wrapped in wonder and hope."

I glanced at the professor, my heart so filled with longing I thought I might die if this opportunity passed me by.

"When I return, I'll bring a traveling companion for Fairwyn," Zebulon said, "a proper lady from a good family, a student of English folklore like me. She'll travel with Fairwyn and me so you needn't worry about Fairwyn's reputation. Her name is Miss Eugenia Barton."

He smiled at me then, which lifted my heart. "I think you will like Jeannie. She will help you feel comfortable in Oak Hill society," he said gently.

I studied my brogans, my worn and mended homespun skirt, then lifted my eyes to his again. Poppy frowned, his lips white. "Fairwyn hain't agoin'. No matter what kind of highfalutin offer ye might make."

During the weeks before Zebulon's return, Poppy refused to discuss Oak Hill. I tried reasoning with him, cajoling him, and appealing to his love for me. He said no more about my mother and her transgressions, but I knew he thought of her every time he set eyes on me, every time I mentioned leaving him.

The matter still hadn't been decided when Zebulon returned with Eugenia Barton.

They climbed the trace together, talking and laughing like old friends as they crossed the winter-barren bald. They swung their leather pokes from their shoulders, and the small parcels landed with hushed thuds on the worn planks by the handrail.

"Jeannie, meet Miss March," Zebulon said grandly when they stood at my door.

Eugenia's smile was warm when she reached for my hand. "May I call you Fairwyn?"

It pleased me no end, and I grinned in return. "Aye," I said.

She was younger than me with dark, luminous eyes and a complexion the color of Devonshire cream. My freckles and yellow corkscrew hair seemed ordinary compared to her delicate, exquisite appearance.

"Call me Jeannie." She glanced at Zebulon as if looking for his approval.

Before I could invite them into the house, he said, "Did you notice Fairwyn's use of *aye?*"

"Of course." She raised a pretty brow.

"These hollows are so isolated the people have clung to the idioms of the Old Country. Fairwyn's speech rarely reflects it, as I mentioned, but you'll notice that many of the mountain folk speak some of the purest forms of middle English found today."

Jeannie asked questions about the Celtic influence, and for several minutes I thought they'd forgotten they were still standing on my porch.

Finally, Zebulon turned his attention back to me. "I've told Jeannie about the corn-husking." His eyes seemed to warm with the memory. "I would love to take her to Selah's place, have her meet the old lady. Do you think it's a possibility?"

I glanced up at the wintry sky just beyond his shoulder. "Today?"

He nodded, his face bright with anticipation. Jeannie stooped to pull a small pair of leather gloves from her poke, then turned up the collar on her heavy woolen coat. "We'd best be on our way," she said cheerfully, smiling up at Zebulon, taking his arm as if for an afternoon stroll.

I wondered how much of her brightness was for Zebulon's sake and how much was a naturally sunny nature.

I pulled my woolen shawl from the hook by the door and led

the way to the trail to Selah Jones's cabin. Zebulon, like a horse used to being in the front, passed me on the first switchback. Jeannie hurried along to walk beside him as he told her about the husking party in greater detail. The sounds of the forest were punctuated by her bell-like laughter as they trudged along. I listened to their friendly banter, longing to be a part of it.

Jeannie seemed to sense my ponderings, and when she stopped to catch her breath, she reached for my hand and drew me closer to them both. She was so kind and gracious that I felt my heart lighten.

"Tell me more about the knob people," she said as we started to walk again. This time she marched by my side, letting Zebulon continue in the lead. "Zebulon tells me the people here often refer to each other as that."

"Or piny-woods folk," I said with a grin.

She stepped over the root of a bare-branched maple. "Tell me more unique idioms."

"Dawn is the *peep o' day*," I said, enjoying the awe in her expression. "And there's *blossom bushes, froggystools,* and *mushyrooms.*"

She laughed, obviously taken with the turns of phrase.

"And there's a *piggin* for a small wooden pail, *purty* for pretty, and *quare* for queer. *Mebbe, kitch,* and *keer, keerful,* and *keerless.*" I grinned as the words rolled off my tongue. "And right now we're *wigglin'* and *winglin'* along…"

Jeannie stopped midstep. "This is fascinating. Have you ever thought about developing a lexicon of the language?" Before I could answer, she had turned her piercing gaze to Zebulon. "This could work itself into a publishable paper, Zeb. Truly, it could." She looked back to me. "He's right in what he told me about you. You are a treasure. Right here in the midst of the backwoods." She grinned. "The piny woods!

"Tell me more about your mountain folk," she said once we started up the next hill.

"If it's their songs and ballads you want to hear, mostly you'll be disappointed," I said. "They'll stop singing the minute we draw nigh." We turned onto the last long switchback leading to Selah's cabin. "Clamp their mouths shut."

"Can't say I blame them," Jeannie said, now breathing hard with exertion. "I'm not certain I wouldn't do the same if the circumstances were reversed."

I shot her a smile, impressed by her respect for our private nature.

"They need to realize that by recording their folklore and ballads," Zebulon said from up ahead, "we're doing them a service. This might even be called a preservation effort."

"I doubt that my people would understand why it's necessary," I said. "No need to preserve something that isn't in danger of disappearing. Life is the same now as it's always been. Why would it change?"

"The twentieth century approaches. Already coal mining companies are buying up land north of here. Mining towns are cropping up where farms used to spread across the land." He shrugged. "Likely it won't be long till they arrive in Sycamore Creek. Then change will come, believe me."

I shuddered at the thought.

"Change isn't necessarily bad," Zebulon went on. "The mines are bringing in positive developments—regular paychecks, company stores, schools, and the like." He grabbed a tree limb to help himself around a steep curve.

"It seems to me," I argued, "that a man might sell his farm, sell everything—then heart, soul, and body belong to that mine and the company running it."

"Hear, hear!" Jeannie said. "I've been telling Zeb the same thing. It's wrong to rob the mountain people of their way of life—no matter the benefits."

Zebulon laughed, holding up his hands in surrender. "But back to my original point," he said, "change is coming, and now is the time to record how the heritage of the Appalachians springs from its English roots."

We scrambled single file up the steepest part of the trace, now just a few yards from the mountain bald and Selah's cabin.

"You were saying about the knob people…?" Jeannie said, looking over her shoulder toward where I walked behind her.

"I was telling you about their shyness," I said. "It's only because Selah has met Zebulon once before that I would attempt—" Before I could finish my sentence, Selah was glaring at us from the top of the trace with a rifle in her hands.

Jeannie turned the shade of the pale sky overhead.

"Ma'am," Zebulon said, doffing his hat toward Selah, " 'tis a pleasure to see you again."

I stepped forward, and Selah's face softened. "Fairy lass," she said, "what're ye doin' up here with this furriner agin?"

"Miss Barton and Mr. Deforest are here to learn more about our singing and storytelling," I said gently. "They're writing down our history."

Selah's wrinkled brow furrowed as she puzzled my meaning.

"You remember Zebulon Deforest from the husking."

She nodded.

"This is a friend of his from the city. Jeannie Barton."

Selah squinted into Jeannie's face. The younger woman looked startled, then broke into a smile. She gave Selah a small curtsy.

Selah grinned, her eyes brightening. "Well now, fancy that."

"They want to know if our music comes from blood kin," I continued, "back before they sailed from across the sea."

"Pshaw," Selah said, shaking her head. She spat into a patch of rabbit grass.

Zebulon spoke up again. "You see, I'm writing a book about your people, your ancestors, how they came here—"

Selah cut him off with a wave of her rifle. "Hain't hankerin' to talk 'bout no blood kin."

Jeannie stepped forward. "What about your songs? Would you sing for us?"

Selah's small, round eyes peered into mine. She liked nothing better than to smoke her old clay pipe, settle back in her porch rocker, and lift her warbling voice in song. She shunned dulcimers and even jaw harps and fiddles, calling them newfangled. Just her voice, she always said, was plenty sound enough for her.

"Selah's the best there is," I said. "She's known all over Blackberry Mountain and parts even farther flung."

Selah smiled at me, and I saw affection in her eyes. She was the closest thing to a grandmother I'd known since Granny Nana died. She always put up a gruff front, seldom hugged or kissed me, but I suspected she'd walk across hot coals on my behalf if she had to. She might even sing for furriners.

I wasn't wrong. Selah opened her mouth and started in on "Dabbling in the Dew."

At the first words I felt its rhythm vibrate from my heart clear through to my bones and could not keep from joining in. Jeannie caught my eye as I sang, and I saw in her face a wonder—I supposed, at the music of my voice.

"Sing with me," I said between verses. Jeannie gave me a quick nod and tried to keep up with the words. Her voice was husky and off pitch, but her joy in the attempt made up for the dissonant sounds coming from her throat.

Oh, fine clothes and dainties and carriages so rare
Bring gray to the cheek and silver to the hair.
What's a ring on the finger if there's rings around the eye?
For it's dabbling in the dew makes the milkmaid fair.

The thin wintry sun was high when Selah started singing, and she was still going strong when it began its downward slant. All the while Zebulon and Jeannie scribbled notes and exchanged looks that spoke of their delight in their discoveries.

A full moon rose behind Selah, glowing like a halo around her. There'd never been a prettier sight than her hair shimmering silvery-white in the moonlight, or a more comely sound than her gravel voice floating on the air toward heaven itself.

A few days later, Zebulon came to see me alone. I was surprised that Jeannie had stayed behind at the boardinghouse in town.

We walked into the wood behind the cabin, and I thought to take him to my singing place, the toppled log. A light snow had fallen the night before, and our footsteps crunched along the hard, frosty ground. Poppy had left early that morning to deliver a dulcimer to Ruffy Hill over near Lean Neck Creek and wouldn't be home till nightfall. I breathed easier, being with Zebulon, knowing we wouldn't have to deal with Poppy's obstinate, thin-lipped anger.

"Have you spoken to your granddaddy about leaving?" Zebulon said.

"He won't discuss it."

Zebulon stopped walking and turned to me. "Would you consider coming with me without his approval?"

I'd asked the same question of my heart at least a dozen times each day since Zebulon first suggested it. I swallowed hard and looked through the bare branches with their frosting of thin snow. "I want to with all my heart."

"But you're feeling obligated to him, to this place."

I glanced at Zebulon, surprised that he understood so clearly. "He and Granny Nana raised me after Momma died, then he took on the task alone. Now he depends on me."

"He can't care for himself?"

"Well, no. I don't mean in that way. He's as independent and ornery as they come."

"He would be able to live without you then?"

"Oh yes, quite well. But it's his broken heart that I can't bear thinking about."

"Still, you want to come with me." Zebulon's face was kind.

"More than you know," I whispered.

"And I want you to come more than *you* know." He took my cheeks in his hands and tilted my face upward slightly. After a moment of gazing into my eyes, he brushed my lips with his.

I gasped slightly and blinked, only to see his eyes smiling into mine. Without a moment's hesitation, he covered my lips with his once more, this time with greater feeling. When he released me, I stepped back in awe, bringing my fingertips to my mouth and staring into his face.

He laughed lightly. "Please, dear Fairwyn. Come with me. Please say yes—no matter what your granddaddy says. You mustn't let your mind go to waste." He took my hands and gently squeezed my fingertips. "You will be astonished at the worlds that will open to you at Oak Hill."

He drew me again into his arms. I let him hold me close, finding it easy to slip my arms around his waist and glory in the warmth of his cheek resting on the top of my head.

When he spoke, his voice seemed to rumble from his chest. I sighed and cuddled closer. "I came here with my book in mind," he said, "and I found you—a diamond newly mined and still caught in its rough encasement."

"A diamond?"

He laughed softly. "A prized jewel, Fairwyn March." For a moment he didn't speak. "You have great beauty, a classic kind of loveliness. With an education…the right sort of training…you could become the toast of Oak Hill."

He pulled back slightly and looked into my eyes again. "I dream of helping you become more than you ever thought possible," he said softly. "I see all of what you are now—beautiful and intelligent and charming—and I imagine what you could become if given the chance.

"You hunger for an education. I see it in your eyes every time it's mentioned. But Fairwyn, there's more to life than that. There's love and adventure, travel… I can show you so many things, if you'll let me."

"Why would you want to?"

He reached for my hands and brought my fingers to his lips. He kissed their tips, then my knuckles. Then gently rubbing the calluses on my palms, he kissed each one. "Haven't you guessed by now?"

My heart beat wildly. "Guessed?" I whispered.

He cocked a brow. "I've grown to care deeply for you—dare I say it?—to love you." He drew me closer once more. "And I can see your affection for me reflected in your eyes." He studied my face. "Please tell me you love me, Fairwyn." He lifted my chin with the crook of his index finger. "Tell me you do."

But before I could answer, he had again covered my mouth with his. The tenderness of his kiss made my knees weak, and when he pulled away, I could see a sweet vulnerability in his face, like a little boy.

I ran my hand along his strong jaw and gazed at him, unable to speak words of love. How could I when I didn't know what it was I felt? "My singing place," I finally managed, my voice shaking. "It's been a magical, special—even secret—place all my life. I'd like to show you."

When we arrived at the hollow log, now covered with a thin sifting of snow, he gave it only the merest glance. "So this is where you sing," he said, rubbing his hands against the chill. After a moment of awkward silence, we turned back. He took my hand in his.

"I've been teaching at Providence College in Oak Hill for three years," he said, his tone once again filled with enthusiasm. "The youngest ever to gain an assistant professorship in the department of English Literature. By writing a book"—he laughed—"any book, I will solidify my position at the college." His voice softened. "What you've done for me here will never be forgotten."

"Whether or not I come with you?"

His frown lasted only as long as a glint of sunlight on a leaf in the wind. He squeezed my fingers slightly, and his voice was warm when he spoke. "I hope you'll use good sense even though your grandfather opposes it. This may sound harsh, but it's your mind that you need to follow, not your heart."

A salty sting burned the top of my throat. "I desire an education more than anything, but I can't leave the one who's raised me."

He stopped, turning toward me. "It's your granddaddy who's wrong, Fairwyn." His face turned dark, and he dropped my hand. His voice rose slightly as he continued, "Think like an adult instead of a child. Think of yourself for once. You can stay here in the backwoods, letting your mind languish"—he waved one hand toward the direction of my hollow log—"or you can expand your mind and your world without limit."

I stared at him, knowing there was truth in his words. Also knowing there might be greater truth in my heart.

He walked away from me, standing stiff-shouldered as he looked through the barren trees toward the cabin. A redbird flittered from one branch to another above his head.

"I'm sorry," he said as he turned back. "I'm speaking as if you're one of my students." He shrugged. "It's just that I see a spark of longing in you—" He fell quiet, glancing into the branches, so wet-dark against the pale sky. "I give you my word, Fairwyn, if you don't like what you find in Oak Hill, I'll see to it that you are sent safely back to Sycamore Creek."

But your kiss, I wanted to say. *What about your kiss and your words of caring…of love?*

He returned to me, taking my hands in his. "Your visit wouldn't have to be for long—perhaps a month. I could show you around, introduce you to some of my colleagues. You could get a feel for the place. Couldn't your granddaddy spare you for just that long?"

I drew a breath, feeling a heavy weight on my shoulders. As I looked up into his eyes so bright with knowledge and affection, I knew my answer. I couldn't say no. All he offered had been buried in my mind for as long as I could remember.

"I will come with you," I said at last.

Above me the redbird fluttered to another branch, and a falling leaf drifted through a shaft of pale sunlight on its way to the ground.

I had just been offered my heart's desire. I wondered why I trembled so.

The next day Poppy found me sitting on the hollowed-out log, my dulcimer lying beside me. I'd gone there to consider what lay ahead, to do my grieving without showing him my tears. I didn't want to hurt him any more than I already had.

His tread was so quiet along the deer trail that I didn't hear his approach. I was weeping, and when he saw me, his furrowed face drooped with sadness.

"Oh, Poppy." I wiped my wet cheeks with the hem of my skirt. "Please give me your blessing."

He settled down beside me on the log, and for several minutes he didn't speak. The wood was silent, a dusting of snow muting every sound, even our voices.

"If'n ye go," he said, "I'll be waitin' fer ye to come home agin." He looked off into the wood. "I cain't stop ye from what ye've decided. So go, lass." He let out a deep sigh. "Ye're as stubborn as yer grandpappy."

"I am."

He turned then and smiled. "Ye have a gift from God himself.

Ye've a curious heart, one that is full to overflowing with wonder at the good Lord's world. Not everyone's got that kind of yearnin'. I always feared ye'd leave someday. I drug my feet agin' it, but all along, I knew ye'd go."

"It's not for long," I reminded him. "Only a few weeks, then I'll return to you."

He studied my face a good while before speaking. His lips moved as if he were trying on the words before letting them out of his mouth. "It's yer Mister Deforest," he said, "that vexes me. I want ye to promise ye'll be keerful of yer heart." He paused, staring out in the shadows of the wood. "I tremble for ye, Fairy lass. I do."

I reached for his big, gnarled hand. "Thank you for saying yes, Poppy," I whispered. "Thank you." Even as I spoke, dread fear caused me to tremble.

Three days later, I made my way down the trace with Zebulon Deforest.

Five

It took Zebulon, Jeannie, and me nearly a week of mule-riding through Cumberland Pass, across the razorback ridges through Pigeon Roost and Hardburley, past Defeated Creek and into the eastward leaning hollows and coves of the Smokies before we finally headed along switchbacks leading down the mountain into Dover Town, where we were to stay the night.

I stopped with a sigh of wonder when Dover Town rose into view. The buildings were stacked double high, made of red bricks and mortar and trimmed in fussy designs. Along the streets, flanked by houses with gardens and picket fences, carriages rumbled and horses trotted and people strolled. I couldn't help my staring at the clothes the womenfolk wore. Only in books had I seen pictures of such wonders. Ruffles and lace and bonnets with feathers.

That first night, I took pleasure in the washtub of warm water that was brought to my room. The soap smelled of roses and bubbled high above the rim of the tub.

Then I climbed into the tall bed. It was the first time I rested on a feather-tick, and I planned how I would describe it to Poppy once I got home and to Welsie True in a letter even sooner than that.

The next morning, Jeannie took me to the mercantile. Wide-eyed, I circled the place, fingering the materials and ready-made frocks.

"Choose any you like," she said, then caught my hand and

drew me to a rack of bright dresses. "Oh, you must try this one!" She pulled out one the color of a meadow in spring—a pale leaf-budding green with little blue and purple and gold flowers.

Unable to stop smiling, I put it on in the back storage room. It fit perfectly, with a trim bodice and pretty white lace collar. I'd never seen such a glorious dress, and there it was on me! I stepped out to where Jeannie sat waiting on a flour barrel.

She assessed me carefully, finger to chin, having me turn one way then another. Her brow furrowed. "I think we can do better," she said at last.

I chose one the hue of my Smoky Mountain skies at sunset with puffy sleeves and a full, gathered skirt. Again, I stepped into the back room and then emerged with it on. I waited while the shopkeeper fastened the multitude of buttons up the back.

When I stepped back into the main room, Jeannie gave me a quick nod. "It's beautiful. Suits you perfectly."

There wasn't anything wrong with the dress—it looked fine. But it didn't have the same effect on my heart as the first one. Still, it was a gift, and I was determined not to be ungrateful. Besides, Jeannie knew more about looking fine and proper than I did, so I resolved to trust her good judgment.

"It shows off her hair," the lady said, her voice pleasant. "It fits so well, it's hard to believe it's a ready-made dress. Such a lovely shade. Depending on the light, it's sometimes gray, sometimes blue."

"May I see?" I ventured, feeling shier than ever before in my life. "Do you have a looking glass?"

The shopkeeper smiled. "Of course." She turned to lead me across the room, but Jeannie stopped her.

"How about shoes?" Jeannie looked down at my brogans then winked at me. "Something a bit daintier, perhaps?"

The woman bustled around the storeroom and soon emerged with a pair of leather lace-up shoes with heels shaped like Poppy's hourglass. "You can walk in such things?" I asked with awe.

"These will do you for dress-up or for everyday," she said. "If you can buy but a single pair of shoes, these are the ones to have."

"Try them on," Jeannie said with a grin. Her expression said they would be perfect.

I sat on the flour barrel opposite her and hiked up my considerable skirts above my knees, grabbing my ankle as I did. The shopkeeper pulled out a tool that looked like something Poppy used for scooping out sassafras wood.

"It's called a shoehorn," she explained and forced my foot into the small space. Before I could complain, she laced the shoe up tight and tied the two leather thongs into a bow. Never had I felt such grief in my feet. My toes cramped, and my ankles smarted.

Then the woman squeezed my other foot into the remaining shoe. I was on my feet wincing as I slowly followed her across the store. Each step threatened to topple me, and I grabbed ahold of bags of flour, bolts of cloth, and the pickle barrel to keep myself upright as I made my way.

I glanced at Jeannie, who looked ready to explode in laughter. I frowned, offended at first, then realized how silly I must've looked. I bit my lip to keep from giggling. But Jeannie let out a squeak and a sputter that caused me to release a peal of my own.

She came over to help me, circling her arm around my waist until I could take a step without falling. "They take some getting used to," she said sweetly.

The shopkeeper turned a large looking glass on a stand toward me.

With a gasp, I moved closer. I had seen my face in a small

ivory-handled mirror given to me by Granny Nana years before, but never had I seen the whole of me. Now there I was, from tip to toe, and I could only stand and stare.

I knew not whether I was comely or homely. Only that I had a mess of hair the color of corn silk that frizzed around my face like furled leaves on a spring-sprouting dogwood. I seemed of a smaller size than most, though the skirts on my new frock made me feel awkward and oversize. And my trying to balance in the tiny shoes caused me to look as old and bent over as Selah Jones.

I stepped closer to peer into my face, touching it in amazement. It had likely been years since last I looked in Granny Nana's looking glass. I had forgotten about the freckles that covered my nose and cheeks. I'd even forgotten the color of my eyes—and now I saw that they matched the dress perfectly.

The shopkeeper approached again, this time with a hat such as I'd never seen in my life. Its brim was made of straw with a mound of paper daisies on one side. I tied the ribbons beneath my chin then turned to the mirror to look again.

Jeannie stepped up behind me, and I met her eyes in the reflection. Her gaze was warm with friendship, something I'd never known with a girl my own age on my mountaintop. It struck me, watching her in the mirror, that no matter what transpired in Oak Hill, I'd made a friend, perhaps one to last a lifetime. "Have you never seen yourself before?"

"Some years back," I said.

"I saw how your eyes sparkled with that first dress," she said. "Let's take both. They're beautiful on you and will be perfect for the days ahead." She turned to the shopkeeper. "Zebulon Deforest asked that they be put on his account."

I touched the silk at my cuff and looked at the woman.

"Would you mind bundling my old things for me?" I thought of my homespun skirt, poke bonnet, and shawl once belonging to Granny Nana, their scent of wood smoke from winters sitting with Poppy by the fire. "I'll likely be needing them again once I return home," I said, unable to resist one last glance in the looking glass. I smiled at myself, a twinge of sorrow filling me as I took in the color and fit of the dress, the dainty design of the silly, high-heeled shoes. Where would I wear such finery once I returned to Sycamore Creek?

The bell atop the door jangled, and in strode Zebulon Deforest. His eyes were fixed on me as he approached.

He looked me up and down, a smile beginning in his eyes and spreading to his smooth jaw. "My, my," he said, then made a sound like a soft whistle. "My, my, my."

Jeannie's face shone with a smile at the sight of him. "Isn't she lovely?" She beamed at me.

I took a single step forward, but my ankles wobbled, and I started to fall. Zebulon caught me, and with his arm circling my waist, he pulled me toward him, steadying me. My cheeks grew warm at his nearness.

I glanced at Jeannie, who seemed to be studying Zebulon's face and then mine with curiosity.

"I'll need to teach you the ways of a lady, Fairwyn," she said gently. Zebulon released me, and I stepped back, this time careful to maintain my balance. "A lady should take a man's arm, or allow him to place his hand on her back to steady or guide her. Like this."

She tucked her dainty hand in Zebulon's arm, and the two promenaded across the room. Then she stopped and he placed his hand in the small of her back and turned her gently. They moved in perfect harmony, like a well-rehearsed song.

"All right now," she said when they had finished. "You try it."

Zebulon stepped toward me and smiled into my eyes. "It's easy," he said softly, bending toward my ear. "Just follow my lead." He tucked my hand in the crook of his arm, and we started. I held my breath with each step, feeling faint with worry. My ankles wobbled, my gait mismatched with his.

He patted my hand. "Let's try something else," he said and drew me closer. Now his arm circled my waist, which truly threw me off balance. My heart began to pound. I leaned toward him to keep from falling. "That's it," he said and slowed his stride. "Easy does it. You're catching on nicely." I tried to relax, and finally I took a step without wobbling. Then another and another.

We stopped and my face flushed with my success. "I did it," I whispered.

Jeannie was at Zebulon's elbow. "Yes, you did!"

Dover Town
October 15, 18 and 82

Dearest Welsie True,

You will not believe it!

Here I am in Dover Town with Zebulon Deforest and Jeannie Barton. We arrived this very day, early in the morning, and we will leave tomorrow on the first train to Oak Hill. I haven't stopped smiling since we got here— except when I find myself gawking at the ladies' stylish dresses and hats, the tall brick buildings, and the fancy carriages pulled by high-stepping horses rattling down cobbled streets.

And wonder of all wonders, Jeannie took me to a mercantile today. I have now in my possession my first two ready-made dresses ever! Oh, they are a glory!

But the greatest wonder of all is the new hope in my heart. In the past I've told you how I've cried myself to sleep at night for fear my life would never change. I've worried to death that I would remain the old spinster of Blackberry Mountain.

All this is changing, Welsie True, for when I look into Zebulon Deforest's eyes, I am breathless with expectancy. I cannot tell what the future holds—I scarcely know my own heart and soul well enough to describe it. I only know that change is coming into my life. Joyous change, frightening change, but change nonetheless.

I wish you were here right now, for I surely need a friend to help me sort out the stirrings within me.

Until I write again, I remain

Faithfully yours,

Fairwyn March

The next morning I walked to McKenna's Store early to post my letter to Welsie True, then hurried back to meet Zebulon and Jeannie. After breakfast at the hotel we hired a carriage to take us to the train station. I was laced into a dress I thought might cause me to draw my last breath—especially after my big breakfast of flapjacks, butter, and honey. I was altogether in misery, with my hair balled tight at the back of my head, a straw hat set just right, and shoes too small and unsteady to be trusted.

I wouldn't have missed it for the world.

Zebulon stood between Jeannie and me, and they both turned to watch my face when the fearsome locomotive with its clacking and screeching and belching steam pulled into the station.

"Mercy!" was about all I could whisper as it whooshed and groaned to a halt.

Jeannie caught my hand and drew me to the open doorway as soon as the steam cleared. Zebulon followed behind, lugging parcels, pokes, valises, and—most important of all—my dulcimer case. My heart pounded as we neared the machine, then stopped to gaze up at the gigantic wheels and smokestack. "Mercy!" I whispered again.

We climbed into a middle car and settled onto a bench, Jeannie on one side of me, Zebulon on the other. My stomach rose into my throat when we began to move. None of the other passengers seemed to pay any mind to the motion. Two little chaps jumped up and down in front of us. I was afraid the momentum would send them toppling, but they held on, stout-hearted and steady. Some folks were talking, while others leaned their heads back and closed their eyes.

I swallowed hard as the machine gained speed. My hand flew to my mouth, and I nibbled my bottom lip, surprised at a small dark fear that settled into my stomach.

"This is safe?" I asked. " 'Tis a safe mode of transportation, I mean?"

Zebulon covered my hand with his and squeezed my fingers. "Of course," he said, with a laugh that seemed meant to relieve my fears. "Safer by far than riding a horse."

For a long time I studied the countryside as it raced by. I was unable to shake the fearful darkness that seemed to accompany the rhythm of the wheels on the track and the dizzying speed. To rid my mind of the growing discomfort, I closed my eyes and imagined sitting in our meadow, braiding a crown of buttercups, bluets, and mountain daisies to wear in my hair, just as I did as a child. I strummed an imaginary dulcimer and hummed a song of Selah's.

> *Ducks in the millpond,*
> *Geese in the pasture;*
> *If you want to marry,*
> *You'll have to talk faster.*
> *I love you little, I love you lots.*
> *My love for you would fill all the pots,*
> *Piggins, keelers, kettles, and cans,*
> *A four-foot tub, and ten dishpans.*

I blinked to discover Zebulon grinning down at me. He leaned toward my ear and whispered, "You were singing of love."

My cheeks flamed, and I sat up straight. "I thought I was humming."

Jeannie turned to me, smiling. "Sing it again, Fairwyn. The words are lovely." If she'd heard Zebulon's whispering, she didn't let on. I sang the tune softly, and for a long while Jeannie didn't speak. She just kept her gaze on the passing countryside.

Zebulon leaned his head back against the seat and closed his eyes.

Six

The train wound through rolling green hills and across flat-lands with soil so red it seemed on fire. We passed fields high with weeds and burnt-out bones of buildings ten times higher and wider than the double-highs in Dover Town. In some places, great pillars stood quiet and sorrowful with nothing behind but rubble. The war. I frowned and leaned closer to the window.

"It'll take decades more for the South to recover," Zebulon said. "And the carpetbaggers are still set on making it impossible."

"Oak Hill is a different picture entirely," Jeannie said, looking across at Zebulon on the far side of me. "At least our city was spared the horror of Northern aggression."

When I gave her a confused look, she went on, "A woman was the cause." Her tone seemed proud. "General Nicholas Appleby rode into town, itching to set fire to our stately mansions. He came to the grandest house in town, his horse and his men tramping all over Mrs. Hall's boxwood hedge. She rushed outside, shouting that she didn't care who they were, she'd planted that boxwood herself, and she would thank him kindly to remove his horses from its midst.

"The general was a gentleman and ordered his men to remove their horses from the prized hedge. In talking to her, he found out that this woman was the wife of the doctor in charge of the local prison camp. Immediately, he ordered his men to halt their plans to torch the city. He'd already been to the prison, had seen the

67

humane treatment of the Union soldiers, and had a deep respect for Dr. Hall. So, while he used the Hall mansion as his headquarters, he left it intact—silver, china, fine furniture, and Chinese rugs—when his regiment moved on.

"The city got through the rest of the war untouched, and so Oak Hill retained its glory—and now we're trying to pick up where we left off," Jeannie concluded. "Providence College is one of the few fine institutions of higher learning in the South that's not in shambles."

Zebulon leaned forward, obviously ready to take charge of the conversation. "What Jeannie means is that whereas many Southern cities suffered greatly and have much to rebuild, we are fortunate. Many of our families lost husbands and sons—and their suffering will never be erased. But our city stands undefiled."

Outside the window, the land raced by at a speed that caused my eyes to dizzy and my fears to return. I reached down to touch my dulcimer case for reassurance.

Zebulon settled back and crossed his legs. "I'm thinking literature might be of interest to you, Fairwyn. Ancient as well as modern. I would like to have you attend some lectures while you're with us."

"Literature," I said, my spirit quickening. "You couldn't please me more." I imagined the college campus where he lectured, with old oak groves and lush, stately lawns, the library that surely must be there. I almost couldn't breathe for the wonder of it. "Of course I would love to attend."

"I've more books for you as well." He paused, watching my face. "Mark Twain. A humorist and writer who's making quite a name for himself." He chuckled deep in his throat. "You must get to know his work."

I asked Zebulon question after question about the literature he taught in his class, feeling as if I'd just been led to a clear creek of running water after a long thirst. And he began talking, seeming pleased with the rapt audience he had in me. I memorized everything he said, planning on writing it all to Welsie True come nightfall.

Jeannie turned to join the conversation, delighting me with stories from Socrates to Edgar Allan Poe, from Cicero to Plinius. Zebulon enjoyed her tales as much as I did, roaring with laughter.

Darkness fell on the passing fallow fields and burnt-carcass plantations, and soon the train slowed as we approached the Oak Hill station.

Zebulon pointed out the single carriage waiting just beyond the platform. As he escorted Jeannie and me toward it, I scarce could walk for my aching feet and wide-eyed wonder. One train had been nearly too much to take in during a single day, but now I counted seven of the beasts all lined up on the silver tracks, spewing steam like dragons in fairy tales.

Finally, his "man," as he called the carriage driver with the midnight face, opened the door of the fancy rig, and Jeannie and I climbed in. Zebulon followed, settling in beside me, leaving Jeannie alone on the seat across from us.

"My parents are expecting us. I sent a telegram from Dover," Zebulon said.

"I'll be mighty pleased to meet them," I said.

He leaned back in the plush, upholstered seat, crossing his legs at the ankles. "The guest room is on the top floor with a wonderful view of the gardens. I think you'll be comfortable with us."

The carriage passed by ashen trees and fields, then tall-pillared houses scattered here and there, light glowing from their windows.

We made our way along the winding road, the horses' hooves clacking along the cobbles.

We stopped first at Jeannie's family home just south of Oak Hill. Never had I seen such a mansion. Double pillars stood on either side of a wide porch. Lace curtains hung from windows tall as a hundred-year-old chestnut tree back home. A welcoming glow of lamps shone through the glass.

Jeannie said her good-byes and reached to give me a hug. "I'll see you tomorrow," she said with a smile that again made me think of the promise of friendship.

A few minutes later we rounded the corner to Bank Street. Zebulon gazed at me from across the carriage, his eyes bright with pride. "This is home," he said.

It must have been the sound of the jangling reins and clopping hooves that drew his mother and father to the broad porch, because they appeared just as we drove up the winding road near the front of the house.

"Halt!" Zebulon's father called up to the driver, and the man indeed slowed the prancing horses to a standstill, then climbed off the tall bench where he'd been driving and opened the door for us. He took my hand as I stepped to the ground then stopped dead still. I gawked in wonder, letting my gaze travel upward, taking in the magnificence of this house.

With a prideful grin, Zebulon let go of my hand and raced to his mother and father, hugging his mother first, a pretty woman who looked as prim and proper as Jeannie, only older, and then his father, a tall, stately man. He wore a mustache that curved down to his chin, giving his face the appearance of a perpetual frown.

"Mother," Zebulon said after a moment, "I would like for you to meet Fairwyn March of Sycamore Creek."

He turned to me with an encouraging smile. "My mother, Charlotte Deforest."

I moved to close the distance between us and stuck out my hand. She smiled and reached for it. I shook hard just as Poppy had taught me, but she looked alarmed and withdrew her fingers. "What an unusual name," she said with a honeyed voice.

" 'Tis a family name," I said. "It comes from Wales."

Mrs. Deforest did not once stop smiling, just nodded, and said, "How nice."

Zebulon guided me toward his father. "Meet Zebulon Deforest, the Second," Zebulon said.

"I'm pleased to make your acquaintance, Mr. Deforest," I said.

His answering smile warmed my heart. I wondered if Zebulon knew how blessed he was to have both a mother and a father.

Mr. Deforest bent over my hand and kissed it. I couldn't stop smiling when he straightened.

Zebulon's mother stepped closer as if to scrutinize me in the dim light. "Dear," she said in the same slow, honey-sweet voice. "You must be utterly exhausted. Let me show you to your room. You must surely want to refresh yourself."

I followed her through the tall front door then stopped, dumbfounded, in the entry. A chandelier, grander than any I'd ever read of, hung from the second-story ceiling. I turned in a slow circle, taking in the curved banister, the gold-framed paintings of folks in old-fashioned garb lining the walls.

Mrs. Deforest stood back, seeming pleased with my admiration. "These are Zebulon's forebears," she said with pride. "A portrait of him will join them someday. With that of his wife." She seemed to be studying my expression, and I felt my face grow warm. "You've already met his intended, I believe."

"Intended?"

She nodded and half turned on the bottom stair to begin her ascent. "He's betrothed to Jeannie Barton, the daughter of Providence's president."

A small gasp escaped my lips. "They are engaged to be married?"

"Oh yes, my dear. I thought surely they would have told you."

I trailed her as she climbed the stairs, one delicate hand on the rail, the other daintily gathering her full skirts. Her back erect, she didn't turn when she spoke again. "Their union has been planned since they were children."

We reached the landing, and I stared blindly at a hunting scene, trying to push the stark dismay from my mind. Not only had Zebulon been trifling with my feelings, just as Poppy had suspected, but he had acted as if he were free to court me.

Blinking back my tears, I tried to concentrate on the plush and colorful rugs, the ornate carved furnishings. " 'Tis grander than I could have imagined," I said in a hushed voice. "Books about such décor can't begin to describe finery like this."

Mrs. Deforest smiled, seeming pleased. "Well now, dear. I thank you for your kind words. It really isn't much. Truly." She turned and pushed open the first door on her right.

When she had shown me around the guest room and placed clean towels in my hands, she turned to leave. "Join us again when you're refreshed, dear. We'll have a light supper at nine o'clock."

I nodded, and she turned to leave.

"May I ask you something?" I said.

She turned. "Of course."

"I will be writing to a friend while I am here, and it's important that I post the letter right away. Is it possible?"

She flicked her fingertips. "We have servants for such tasks.

You write your letter, and we'll make sure it is posted. Tomorrow, if you like."

"Thank you kindly."

"Your friend…is this someone you met at school?"

I laughed without meaning to be rude, but she blanched at the sound. "Oh, goodness no. For one thing, I've never been to school." I shrugged. "There's no schoolhouse in Sycamore Creek. No schoolmarm has ever set foot in our valley."

"Really."

"And to answer your question about Welsie True. I've never met her. She's written to me for as long as I can remember. Before Poppy's eyes went bad—when I was just a lap baby—he read her letters to me."

"And you've corresponded all these years. My."

"She won't answer questions about who she is to me or why she writes, but she has been my friend, my mother, my sister, even a kind of teacher to me through all my years."

Mrs. Deforest stepped back across the thick carpet to where I stood and placed a hand on mine. "Zebulon hasn't mentioned much about your family. When he was here last, he did say that you're fatherless and motherless." She looked distressed.

I smiled gently, trying to put her at ease. "My mother died when I was an infant."

"I'm so sorry, dear," she said. "How did she…succumb?"

I wondered how much I was required to answer, and studied her face for a moment while I decided.

"I'm much too nosy," she said, filling in the silence. "You must forgive me."

"Childbirth," I said at last. "My mother died bearing me. And I never knew my father. No one has ever said if he's dead or alive."

A small gasp escaped her lips. "You're not..." Her voice trailed off in hushed horror.

"Illegitimate?" I finished for her. "I truly don't know. No one will say."

Her complexion had turned the pale hue of the lace-trimmed linens on the tall, four-poster bed. She squared her shoulders, and when she spoke again, her voice had a slight edge. "About your letter," she said. "You write to your friend. One of our boys will take it to the post office."

Mrs. Deforest closed the bedroom door without a sound, leaving me standing in the center of the room, trying to sort out the whirl of emotions that the silken voices in this place had stirred in my heart.

Oak Hill
October 16, 18 and 82

Dearest Welsie True,

Today I came by train to Oak Hill, and I am so overwhelmed by all I've seen and done it would take sheet upon sheet of writing paper to begin to tell you every detail.

First I will tell you about this mansion that Zebulon calls home and his mother says "really isn't much." It is filled with the grandest furnishings you might ever imagine. Sofas of brocade with a shine prettier than sunlight dancing on a meadow. Striped drapes and lace hang before windows that are taller than the old chestnut out back of Poppy's cabin. And the bed is so soft and high I get dizzy just looking at it.

I will write more tomorrow, because my eyes are almost

closing of their own accord. I'll tell you then of the devastation I've seen from the War, also the fascinating story of what happened to this town during the occupation.

I'll explore the grounds, gardens, and fountains and report on it all, for I know you are interested more in those things than the house itself.

You've always encouraged me to stretch my wings like a butterfly coming out of a cocoon. You would be proud of me for coming here. Tomorrow I shall begin to fly.

I remain

Your loving friend in Oak Hill,

Fairwyn March

P.S. I haven't been entirely honest in what I wrote so far. Instead of being ecstatic with wonder as it appears above, my heart is troubled. I didn't want you to worry, so I hesitated to say anything. But you always seem to guess what I'm "writing between the lines," so I will tell you that my mind is a bundle of confusion right now. I thought I might have been falling in love with Zebulon only to find he's promised to another.

Back in Sycamore Creek he kissed me, Welsie True! And he spoke words of love. Were they empty words?

I will write more tomorrow. —*FM*

As the sun rose the next morning, I stretched out on the big feather-tick, confused for a time about my surroundings. The room was flooded with warm light. Two round lamps with painted roses sat atop table-stands that flanked the bed. A wardrobe of shining wood such as Poppy might've used for a fiddle or dulcimer stood in the corner, and on the ceiling just above me was a golden chandelier holding more gaslights than I could count.

I stretched again, threw back my counterpane, and stepped to the floor. In the corner was an oval looking glass in a frame as big as me. Surprised, I ran to it, almost not recognizing myself. I was wearing sleep garments belonging to Zeb's mother. They were made of the softest lace and cotton. They flowed to the ground like a queen's train.

I walked to the window, opened the shutters, and leaned out to take in the view. Though the grasses were brown with the season, I saw the outline of what surely would be a glorious garden come spring. My eyes widened. I'd read of fountains but had never seen one before. This fountain rose up through the center of four perfectly round bowls and then spilled over the edge of each in a wondrous waterfall.

With a cry of delight, I raced from my bedroom in my flowing nightclothes, down the wide staircase, through the long hall on the first floor, and searched for a door leading outside. Open-mouthed servants stopped their dusting and stared.

Mrs. Deforest rounded a corner, coming from the room Zebulon had told me was the library, and froze dead still, looking me up and down.

Thinking she'd stopped to greet me, I nodded and continued my quest to reach the back of the house. When I didn't stop, she followed me, her stride nearly matching mine.

"Go find Zeb," she muttered to a servant who was brushing off a chandelier with long feathers. "And hurry. Tell him to get in here now."

Finally, I spotted a glass door that led outdoors. With no one between and Mrs. Deforest on my heels, I hurried toward it, only to have it open before I got there.

Jeannie and Zebulon stood in front of me, blocking my way. My confusion about their relationship flooded again into my mind. I looked at them uncertainly.

"Where do you think you're going?" Zebulon's voice was stern.

I stared at him in surprise.

Mrs. Deforest's gaze flew to her son's, but her voice was in perfect control when she spoke. "What will the neighbors think, Zeb? Please, do something."

"The neighbors?" I said as I looked to Jeannie, whose face held the only kindness in the group, but even her perplexity was evident.

Jeannie circled her arm around my shoulders and led me a few steps away from the others. "It's your dress," she said gently. "It isn't proper to be seen in your, ah, nightclothes." She reddened. "It's considered indecent."

Ashamed, I put my hand to my mouth and, blushing furiously, backed away from the three and fled upstairs.

After I was dressed, I slipped past the dining room without being seen, unable to bear facing Zebulon's family again. I found the garden and fell into a small white bench of iron filigree by the fountain, burying my face in my hands. *Indecent?* Somehow the word made me feel unclean, something I had not felt before coming here.

I heard footsteps on the gravel path.

"Fairwyn?" Zebulon said from behind me. I looked up, my eyes so watery he was but a shimmering blur.

"Fairwyn, I'm sorry."

But instead of saying anything, all I could do was weep. For lost dreams, for not fitting in, for the joy I had thought I would find in the world outside my mountains.

Seven

Each day I met in the family library with Zeb, as he asked me to call him now. Sometimes we spoke of Chaucer and Shakespeare; other times Zeb seemed more interested in my mountain stories, ballads, and dulcimer playing. He would settle back in his chair by the fire, his eyes closed while I sang. It seemed we couldn't get enough of each other, the talk, the laughter, the discovery of thoughts.

There was only one subject I hadn't asked about. I desperately wanted to know about Jeannie, but looking into his eyes, I thought I couldn't bear it if they were indeed betrothed.

"Fairwyn," Zeb said one evening at the end of the first week, "I can't imagine your ever leaving here." The fire lit his handsome face in shades of crimson, and his voice was a hoarse whisper.

"I promised I would be home in a month."

"And I plan to honor that promise to your grandfather," he said solemnly. "But I also made a promise to you—to further your education. Come to some lectures, mine and perhaps some others on English literature or world history."

When he walked me to the library door, he stood very close, then reached out to touch my face. He seemed to be pondering something and drew back without so much as a brush of his fingers.

"I want you to come to the college with me tomorrow," he said. "Walk with me through the campus. Then when you're comfortable, we'll meet with the faculty and my publisher. You can tell them your stories and sing your songs." He smiled. "Perhaps seeing the college will change your mind about going home."

October 17, 18 and 82

Dearest Welsie True,

I was awake in the night, thinking about you and praying for your health. I pray your chest pains of last year have gone away. But still I am filled with anxiety for your well-being.

It seems I will be here for three more weeks. How I wish we were face to face to talk over all that is spilling from my heart and mind. I don't want to go back home again. After only a week here with Zeb, talking about world history and English literature, I know I shall shrivel up and die if I must stay in Sycamore Creek. I'll die an old maid with no one to talk to but Poppy and Selah and Blinken, though I admit I love to talk with Selah more than just about anything in the world.

I hope you will write to me soon, Welsie True. I miss your caring words, your sound advice. You are my truest friend, and I love you.

Your devoted,
Fairwyn March

Late that afternoon, before supper, I slipped to the garden to play my dulcimer and sing. The fountain splashed and harmonized, reminding me of the river back home.

Zeb's mother would be thankful that I was missing their social hour. I'd become so nervous eating with them, I always seemed to be dropping my fork with a clatter or knocking over a glass of sweet tea. Mrs. Deforest gave me tight smiles and never raised her honeyed voice, but the strain in her face was clear.

This afternoon would be mine alone, with my music filling my heart, with the empty garden and no one to frown with doleful eyes. Smiling to myself I started in on "Dabbling in the Dew," and had just reached the second verse...

Oh, suppose I were to carry you, my pretty little dear,
With chariots of gold and fine horses rare?
Oh no, sir, oh no, sir, kind sir, she answered me,
For it's dabbling in the dew makes the milkmaid fair.

...when I heard footsteps coming up the path behind me. I stopped my strumming and turned. It was Zeb.

"Fairwyn," he said, his voice low, "I was hoping to find you here." He settled across from me, a book in his hand.

My fingers moved quietly along the strings while we beheld each other.

I glanced at the volume. "Mark Twain?"

He smiled. "You don't forget anything, do you?" He flipped open the book and began to read:

"Tom!"
No answer.
"Tom!"
No answer.
"What's gone with the boy, I wonder? You TOM!"

No answer.

The old lady pulled her spectacles down and looked over them about the room; then she put them up and looked out under them. She seldom or never looked through them for so small a thing as a boy; they were her state pair, the pride of her heart, and were built for "style," not service—she could have seen through a pair of stove-lids just as well. She looked perplexed for a moment and then said, not fiercely, but still loud enough for the furniture to hear:

"Well, I lay if I get hold of you I'll—"

Zeb's voice was rich and deep, and his words filled me with delight. I chuckled out loud, so full was my joy.

He looked up as I swiped at a tear that had rolled to my chin. He saw through to my soul in that instant—I could see it in that place behind his eyes. Smiling, he handed me the book. "It's yours," he said reverently.

I took it into my hands, feeling the rich leather under my fingertips. "Mine?"

"Open the cover," he said, leaning toward me, his eyes bright.

"It says here, 'Mark Twain,' in cursive." I admired the slant of the penmanship as the import of the name sunk in. "The author signed this?"

"I asked my editor to have it signed to you. It's *Tom Sawyer,* Twain's first published book," he said, laughing. "His publisher—the Century Company—is the same that will be publishing my book."

"It says, 'to Fairwyn March,' " I breathed, running my finger over my name, which seemed to shine on its own. I gave Zeb a wide smile. "Thank you," I said. "It's a wonderful present."

He stood and reached for my hands, pulling me up before him. The winter light was fading. "You are beautiful," he said, his voice hoarse with softness.

Behind us the fountain sang, and above us a sharp breeze blew through the big elm tree, causing its bare twigs to bend and rattle.

Zeb drew me closer until I could feel the warmth of his nearness. I held my breath for the beauty of him, his flaxen hair gleaming in the slant of the sun, his eyes filled with knowledge and desire.

"My feelings…" he began, then swallowed hard. "I didn't mean for this to happen. I swear I didn't. I've tried not to care, since that day in the forest when I kissed you. I swear, I've tried not to love you."

I reached up to touch his smooth face, running my fingers along his jaw. He trembled and caught my hand in his, then turned it and kissed my palm.

"Oh, Fairwyn," he whispered. "You've captured my heart!"

Now his eyes closed, almost as if unable to bear the emotions between us. He sounded ready to cry when again he spoke. "You don't know the complications my love for you will bring. You can't know how impossible this is!" He dropped my hand and turned away from me.

I stood as still as death and puzzled his meaning. "Jeannie," I whispered. "Is she what makes this impossible?"

He buried his face in his hands and nodded, without saying a word.

"Your mother told me you're promised to each other."

"Our parents arranged it, or tried to. I thought I loved her. We've known each other since childhood. I do love her, but it's friendship. Not love." He looked up, his face ragged. "Not the way I love you." His eyes filled with tears. "But I don't want to hurt her."

"She's become my friend," I said. "I understand—"

He frowned, cutting me off. "You can't possibly know how close we are, what this will do to her."

"I didn't mean to compare my friendship with her to yours…"

He turned again to me, and for a long moment, he stared, speaking not a word. "Come here," he said at last in a husky voice. "Come here, Fairwyn, before I lose my mind." He opened his arms.

He looked like a lost child reaching for someone to love him. I walked slowly across the distance between us. Desperately he clutched me, and with a small cry held me tight, so tight I could feel the wild thump of his heart. "It is wrong," he whispered in my ear. "I know it is, but I can't help myself."

Gasping, I pulled away from him, feeling I might faint because I was trembling so. His face looked ragged and worn. "I can't let you go," he cried. "God help me, I can't!"

He stepped closer and lifted my face until I was looking him straight in his pale eyes. "Don't you understand, Fairwyn?"

I shook my head.

"I want to marry you!" Then he bent to kiss me again, first on my lips, then all over my face. "I'll have it no other way," he said when he'd stopped. "No matter what Mother or Father or Jeannie or her parents or anyone else might say." He caught my hands in his and whirled me into a dance. Then throwing back his head, he shouted it again, "I will marry you, Fairwyn March! I will!"

I stepped backward, staring at him, my heart pounding. "It's not entirely up to you, Zeb. Don't I have a say in this?"

He moved closer. Raising my hand to his lips, he kissed my

fingers. "Indeed you do, my dear," he said with a smile. "Indeed you do."

October 17, 18 and 82

Dearest Welsie True,

I'm writing to you for a second time today because tonight Zeb kissed me again. He said he wants to marry me! He will not take no for an answer. I should be blissful that a beau might finally ask Poppy for my hand. But instead, my heart pounds with fear. A small voice inside me says, 'tis wrong, Fairwyn March, 'tis wrong! But I can't help dreaming of my life as Mrs. Zebulon Deforest III.

I asked you once what love is, and you replied that it is everything I've said about appreciating Zeb's mind, his tenderness toward me, his way with words—all of these things and more.

It's that "more" that bothers me, Welsie True. I think you mean that I should love his heart. Sometimes I think I do, other times I'm sure I don't.

How I long to be in love! Can I make love come? That's what I need you to tell me. If I already love his other qualities, can't I work on the rest?

I don't want to be an old maid forever—this might be my only chance. Oh, tell me, Welsie, what I should do!

With love

I remain,

Fairwyn March

Eight

Loud wailing from down the long hallway drew me from my sleep the next morning. It sounded like Zeb's mother in her suite of rooms, along with the lower tones of Zeb and Mr. Deforest. Each time they spoke, she only cried the louder. I hadn't known she had any other voice but the one that spoke in silk and honey.

When I finally realized what they must be speaking of, I sat up in bed, my eyelids flying open. Zeb was surely telling them about his proposal to me.

I swung from the tall feather-tick and ran to the wardrobe, hurrying into my day dress and struggling with the back buttons and sash. Ignoring my shoes, I picked up my dulcimer and ran from my room, through the house to the garden, feeling I might suffocate if I didn't get away from Mrs. Deforest's crying.

Once there, I drew in a deep breath and settled onto the iron filigree bench. I closed my eyes, trying to think. This should have been the happiest time of my life, so why did my heart feel hollow and scared?

Setting aside the dulcimer, I stood and walked nearer the fountain, letting my fingers stir the chill water. The ripples danced and sailed in silvery rows across the small pond.

Upstairs, faint but sure, the argument continued. It seemed they now were closer to the window, for I heard whole snatches of their conversation.

"You'll be ruined by marrying the likes of her, Zeb! Can't you see it?" his mother wailed. "She doesn't even have family."

"She does. There's a grandfather," said Zeb's lower, calmer voice. "You'll grow to cherish having her as part of our family, Mother. Give her a chance."

There was more weeping. "You'll be sorry." His mother's voice dropped. "You marry her, and it's forever, Zeb. Can you imagine being tied to someone like Fairwyn March forever? You'll be the laughingstock of all Oak Hill." Her last words dripped with disdain.

"Now, now, dear," said his father. "Calm down. I'll admit this is a queer notion Zeb's come up with, but no more queer than some of his other exploits. He'll get over his little infatuation before the month is out." He laughed a nervous-sounding chortle before he continued. "Zeb, you need to think long and hard about this notion of yours. Consider carefully the impact of marrying beneath your station. It could mean your career."

There was a moment of silence before Mrs. Deforest spoke. "Your father's right. Think of your career. You'll be ruined. You're supposed to wed Jeannie…what will she say? Jeannie's father…" Fresh wailing began. "Think of the responsibilities a faculty wife carries. She'll be an embarrassment to all of us with her backward ways.

"What if word gets out that she's…" Mrs. Deforest didn't have to finish. I knew the word that followed—*illegitimate.* It was a word I had feared all my life.

I looked down, ashamed of my dress, my bare feet, and my disheveled hair. I lowered myself, creating a rumpled pile of cotton and petticoats around me. Another word, and I might surely die of a broken heart. I rested my forehead on my arm, stretched sideways along the fountain bowl.

Then Zeb spoke. I could hear his disapproving tone.

"Fairwyn has more charm than you credit her with, Mother. She's not an embarrassment to me, and if you'll give her a chance, she won't be to you."

I tilted my face toward the window, holding my breath to see what might come next.

"She's worked hard to better herself all her life. She's taught herself to read. She's eager to learn everything I teach her. She'll learn fast how to adapt to our life—how to make small talk, how to serve tea at faculty affairs, all of it."

There were more murmurings that I couldn't hear as the voices moved away from the window.

I waited until long after I knew the family was breakfasting in the dining room before slipping in the back door and up to my room. I scrubbed my face and feet at the washstand and took special pains with my hair, pinning it back in a small round knot, just the way Jeannie had showed me.

Then with my chin tilted high, my spine picket-straight, I swept down the stairs and into the dining room.

"Good morning, Mrs. Deforest," I said, measuring out my words like sorghum from a scoop.

Then I nodded to Zeb's father. "Mr. Deforest," I said pleasantly.

Zeb stood, smiling his approval as he moved to pull out my chair. I waited until he had pressed it against the backs of my knees, then with all the refinement I could muster, I sat down gracefully, nodded my thanks, and unfolded my napkin, smoothing it into my lap. I tried not to notice how my fingers trembled.

With red-rimmed and swollen eyes, Zeb's mother stared hard at me. "You're late, dear. Too late, I'm afraid, to eat with the family." Her voice was silky as a spider's trail, and her smile spread wide across the bottom of her face. "We'll have to see if there's anything left in the kitchen that might still be warm." She rang a tinkling silver bell for the servant.

"Sukie," she said when the dark-faced woman entered, "take Miss Fairwyn with you out to the kitchen, see what you can find for her to eat. She can take her late breakfast with the help." She gave the word *late* an extra long drawl.

Sukie glanced uncertainly toward me, then back to Mrs. Deforest. "Yes ma'am."

"Mother!" Zeb stood and threw his napkin onto the table. "That's unnecessary. Fairwyn can and will eat in here. I'll wait with her, if you and Father must leave."

I stood, my heart fluttering like a bird in my throat for fear I might say something I would soon regret. I gave them all a hard look, feeling my heart twist inside. "I'm not hungry after all," I said, and rushed to the doorway. I wanted only to be away from this place, this fresh heartache.

Zeb followed and, just as I passed the shiny, dish-laden sideboard, he reached for my arm. I swung away from him, and to my horror, my elbow knocked against a tall glass decanter. It teetered for a heartbeat then crashed into the awful silence of the room, splintered pieces spraying across the polished wood floor.

Zeb's mother let out an agonized moan, brushed past me, and knelt. She tenderly picked up a broad shard, pricking her finger. Her tears fell on her trembling hands.

She looked up at me then, her eyes hard. "This belonged to my mother," she said softly, "and her mother before that. It's crystal. From Austria. But I suppose you wouldn't understand the importance of this sort of an heirloom."

"I am sorry," I said quietly. I stooped to help her gather the glass splinters. "I am so sorry."

I looked at my hands. Pinprick drops of blood mingled with the pieces of glass. "I am so sorry," I cried once more as I stood and fled the room.

I paced the guest room, feeling more confused than ever about my place in this family. I considered leaving but couldn't bear the thought of going home in shame. Just before noon, Zeb sent a housemaid up to fetch me for our daily talk.

I tapped the library door softly, and when Zeb opened it, I entered. "I still aim to marry you," he said as I sat in one of the chairs by the fire. A new and stubborn look of determination shone bright in that place behind his eyes. He stood by the fireplace for a moment, then commenced to pace the room.

"I heard your mother and father this morning, speaking of me. They are set against any union between us."

Zeb turned to take my hands, examined my fingertips and palms, then kissed them tenderly. "I'm sorry you had to hear their sorrow."

Sorrow? I was just beginning to see how in this household harsh truths were buried under flowery words. Pushing aside these thoughts, I shook my head and raised my eyes to him. "You stood up for me. Thank you."

Still gently holding my hands, he helped me rise. "Nothing has changed. I feel more strongly than ever that this is the right course for us."

I was trembling now, relief flooding through my veins, and Zeb gathered me into his arms. "Do you want to marry me, Fairwyn?"

The voices inside me started up again, voices telling me how silly I would be to say no, telling of the grand life I would have as the wife of Zebulon Deforest III. Especially telling of the learning that would be mine, the riches of knowing all that my heart desired.

When I didn't answer, he went on, his voice low and tender. "Oh, my sweet Fairwyn, I care not what anyone else thinks. We are the ones that matter. We've got our whole lives ahead of us, together."

"But your life here, your career...I don't want you to lose it all because of me."

He kissed my fingertips. "We'll show them it doesn't have to be that way." He paused. "But I'll need your help."

I nodded.

"You must learn how to be a faculty wife—one who knows how to entertain, fulfill the responsibilities required of that position."

I nodded again.

"Jeannie's father is the president of Providence; that may add some additional hurdles." He laughed lightly. "We'll be starting over together."

I reached up and brushed a shock of hair away from his forehead. "I'll help you however I can."

He looked proud. "I know you'll learn fast."

"I'll learn to pour tea, to chatter about clothes and recipes...as long as you promise me that I can take advantage of the college lectures. I want to study literature and music, history..."

He threw back his head in a hearty laugh. "Ma'am, you drive a hard bargain."

I smiled, already dreaming of the day I would enter the classroom as a student.

"You still haven't said yes." He leaned back against his desktop, feet outstretched, ankles crossed, and raised a brow playfully. "Before you give me your answer, come to the college with me today." He chuckled again. "Perhaps you'll see why my world is the one you belong in." At his words my heart began to lighten.

For a moment the only sound in the room was the mantel clock. Then, standing, he pulled me close and kissed me again.

It was going to the college that made up my mind, just as Zeb knew it would. He ushered me into the biggest room I had ever seen, seated me in the back row, and disappeared. The floor had a slope like the inside of a mountain cove, curving rows of seats falling away to the platform in front.

A group of young scholars filed down the center stairs and took their places in the rows before me. There were a few curious glances in my direction, but mostly I was ignored.

A door to the side of the platform opened, and a reverent hush fell over the students. There was a rustle of cloth behind the doorway, and Zeb stepped forth, resplendent in black robes, a red and gold sash draped over his broad shoulders and circling his back.

He drew his forehead into a scholarly scowl and stepped onto the platform. When he began to speak, my mouth dropped open, and I nearly forgot to close it. His deep voice was resonant with authority and confidence as he told of an ancient poem called the *Odyssey* by a poet-scribe from the faraway land of Greece and of Odysseus, a warrior and leader of outstanding wisdom whose endurance, resourcefulness, and courage captured my imagination.

Zeb's depth of knowledge was like brilliance itself, shining brighter than the sun on a summer day, his voice like that of the siren's song he spoke of. To me, he *was* Odysseus, just as he'd become Mr. Joe from *Great Expectations* with the flaxen hair and eyes of undecided blue. I watched as he moved about the platform, his fist pounding the lectern, barking questions to the scholars or answering theirs in turn. He seemed taller than before and in such command of his world, this landscape of his creation. I could not take my eyes from him.

Long after the students left, I sat still, my head filled with images and ideas I'd just glimpsed.

His robe swishing with each step, Zeb came up the stairs to me, more handsome than I'd ever seen him. He reached to help me stand. "How did you like it?" he asked.

I stared into his pale eyes. "I adored every moment."

"I knew you would love this as I do." He turned me toward the door, his hand on the small of my back as we walked. "You may attend every class, Fairwyn, if you like."

Outside the students milled and chatted on their way between classes. Here and there the robed figures of the professors and deans were hurrying across the grassy knolls and along stone-lined pathways.

The air seemed electrified—as if before a lightning storm in summer—with the excitement of new discovery and ideas. And when he took me around to meet some of his teaching colleagues, introducing me as the one who had helped him with his book research, my heart fluttered in my chest like a brown phoebe readying to take flight.

Later on, when most folks had left the grounds, Zeb stood by my side, and we surveyed the long shadows falling across the campus. He cocked his head and smiled into my eyes. "Well?"

I knew what it was he waited for. I knew my answer.

"You must ask Poppy for my hand," I said.

Nine

Our visit to Poppy filled me with sorrow. He refused to give our marriage his blessing, which Zeb said was "ignorant" and "stubborn." I tried to make peace between them, telling Poppy about all that Zeb could offer me and explaining to Zeb that Poppy's stubbornness was born out of his deep caring and being responsible for me all these years. But Zeb's anger grew inside him with each word Poppy spoke against our union. Finally Zeb went off by himself, not speaking at all.

Poppy still fussed and stewed at Zeb, paying no mind that my beau wasn't talking back. And all the while, Poppy watched me with sorrowful eyes that nearly broke my heart.

When Zeb had gone across the meadow and down the trace to Lettie Jameson's boardinghouse, Poppy and I sat alone by the fire.

"I'll be leaving tomorrow," I said.

"I reckon."

"Please come to Oak Hill with us," I pleaded. "I can't get married without you."

His eyes bright and damp, he snapped his galluses and shook his head. " 'Tis a mistake ye are makin', lass. Ye mark my words. Ye'll rue the day."

I touched his arm. "Poppy, please. It's a different world there. One you can't know unless you visit. You'll set your heart at ease if you'll come see for yourself."

"I canna," he said, his face turned away from me.

"Can you give me your blessing, Poppy, even if you won't bless us both in marriage? It's a new life I'm starting. I'll need your blessing for that, leastwise." Tears filled my eyes.

"I canna, lass," he said turning to me at last. "Aye, I'll pray for ye every day of yer life. But I canna give ye my blessing. My heart breaks hard, and I want ye to change yer mind."

I fell to my knees beside him. "Pray for me then, Poppy. Pray for me."

"So like her," he said, turning his face away from me. "Jes' like her."

I buried my face in my hands, and silent sobs shook my shoulders. "I'm afraid, Poppy. Sore afraid." I looked up at him, tears streaming from my face and dripping from my chin. "You warn me about my mother, but you don't tell me what she did to hurt you so. And never once have you even mentioned my father's name. Does he still live? Can I find him and know him? Every wee lass needs a da—and you in your bitterness and sorrow have kept him from me."

Never had I spoken to my beloved Poppy with such spirit. I went on. "You've nursed your own heartaches, never once thinking of my own. And now, when it seems I've at last found some happiness, you won't even give me a proper send-off." I bowed my head, afraid to look up.

His rough fingers tilted my chin until I was looking him in the face. I saw the sorrow in his eyes and felt ashamed, because I knew—oh yes, I knew—his deep ponderings about my union with Zeb Deforest. Without words, he told me about his fears, no doubt the same fears he'd had for my mother. He told me about his unfulfilled hopes for me. He told me about the music in my heart, music that belonged to God and no one else. All without words.

I turned my face away from the pain I saw in his eyes. Then I felt Poppy's big hand on my head.

"Father God," he said in a hoarse whisper, "I bring ye yer daughter Fairwyn March. She belongs to ye, naught anyone else. Watch over her, guide her according to yer precepts. Keep her mind fixed on ye."

Holding my breath, I waited for his blessing, hoping he would relent. But he remained still and quiet as if waiting for me to pray. I couldn't bring myself to utter a word, so frozen was my heart.

When he finally went on, his voice was trembling, and so was his hand. I realized then that he had been too overcome with weeping to speak.

"Our father in heaven," he whispered at last, "I ken I am a stubborn old man, and when tryin' to fathom yer ways, allus pick the wrongun. Bless this yer lassie through all her days. Allus be her light in the night. Allus be her sun in the day. Remind Fairwyn March ye're nigh even when her darkness turns into midnight. May she ne'er forget ye're with her unto the ends of the earth. Yea, ye'll ne'er leave her alone."

He laid his hand on my head then, and when I opened my eyes, Poppy was staring hard at me, his own eyes bright. "Do not go, Fairy lass. Do not. As sartin as I'm asittin' here, I know it's a wrong thing ye're aplannin'."

"I love him, Poppy."

"I see the change in ye already," Poppy said. "And I fear the love ye think ye have is only attraction fer what he can give ye." He paused, nodding slowly. "There's a new brittle cover to yer heart like frost on the edge of a pond. Ye know what is right, but ye're stubborn as yer Poppy, and surely ye're going to do what ye will."

"It's only book learning you see in me," I argued. "My eyes are beginning to open to the world outside. I've gained a wealth of knowledge already, and it's only begun. I'm still your Fairwyn March, Poppy. My heart will not change. Ever."

"Dinna go," Poppy repeated as I stood. He caught my hand. "I fear for ye, lass. Dinna go."

That night, long after I lay on my corn-tick, Poppy sat out in the cold, rocking on the porch and smoking on his clay pipe. I could not sleep for the worry of him as I listened to the creak of the chair runners.

A hoot owl cried, and in the far distance, coyotes yipped and sang. Hot tears filled my eyes as I turned on my side and let them run onto my pillow.

On June the third of 18 and 83, I stood before Zebulon, gazing into his eyes, and spoke the words that bound me to him forever.

We stood beneath a rose-covered arbor in the garden behind the Deforest house, the fragrance of fresh-planted gardenias, ever-lastings, and daylilies drifting on the light spring breeze. A small string ensemble played softly a few yards from the arbor, and in the distance the splash of the water fountain blended its music with that of the violin, viola, and cello.

Zebulon squeezed my fingers when the ceremony was done, and my heart quickened at the love and adoration in his eyes. And when we turned to our guests and Dr. Merriam Browne, the college chaplain, pronounced us man and wife, I caught my breath and almost forgot to breathe. Plain, uneducated, mountain-born,

old-maid Fairwyn March was *Mrs. Zebulon Deforest III!* I wanted
to kick up my heels, but instead I remembered my new manners
and gazed up at Zeb adoringly.

As soon as the ceremony was done, I tucked my arm in Zeb's
and strolled with him across the sweeping lawns to greet our
guests. I moved gracefully with my head tilted upward. *Think of
it! Mrs. Zebulon Deforest III.* I was in my glory.

When the wedding supper was served, I daintily picked up the
proper utensils in the right order, and from the corner of my eye
saw Charlotte Deforest's nod of approval. I properly chose the correct sterling implement for everything from honey ham to the sug-
ary white wedding cake, lifting the correct crystal goblets, with my
pinkie finger poised, for sweet teas and mint juleps.

I wore an imported gown, chosen for me by Mother Charlotte.
I had memorized every detail of the description that accompanied
it from Belgium, quizzing myself at night, and with Zeb's help
learning the foreign words so I could share them with Welsie True.

My bride's *toilette* was made of ivory *mousseline de soie* trimmed
with garlands of roses and greenery. My draped bodice, also of
mousseline, was held in place with a spray of orange blossoms, a
trim repeated around the draped layers in the skirt. Attached to a
halo of roses, my veil was fashioned of tulle. Underneath it all I was
dressed in silk lingerie, from my empire matinee to my flounced
petticoat. Even my shoes were made of silk.

Zeb patted my hand as we walked toward a group of deans and
their wives. My heart pounded with nervousness, being presented
as Zeb's wife, their equal. If they had misgivings about our union,
they didn't show it. One by one, they congratulated us both, kissing my cheek and shaking my husband's hand.

Jeannie stood behind them slightly and off to one side. She

looked up and met my gaze with a ready smile, but in her eyes I saw a depth of sadness that nearly took my breath away. I skirted the group of Zeb's colleagues and their wives to reach her, Zeb a few steps behind me. By the time I stood in front of Jeannie and held out my arms, her expression had changed. Though pale, she laughed happily, and gave me a warm hug. She took Zeb's hand and simply said, "Congratulations, Zeb."

Jeannie's heart was kind. From the beginning she had been my friend. She had kept her distance during the wedding preparations, and Zeb and I hadn't pressed her to be part of our celebration. I'd wanted to ask her to stand with me as my maid of honor, but I knew that might hurt her even more, so I kept my silence.

Jeannie wouldn't purposely hurt anyone, yet Zeb and I had hurt her. I sought out her eyes again, wanting her to know how sorry I was, but she kept her gaze turned away. Just as she had done on every social occasion since the announcement of our betrothal.

I didn't encounter her again until after the wedding dance. Zeb and I had whirled and dipped and laughed with our guests. I danced with Zeb, his father, and every colleague from Providence. Even Jeannie's father.

As blisters rose on my heels, I asked Zeb to escort me to one of the linen-covered chairs. Gratefully I sank into it. At the same time the ensemble began to play, Jeannie walked from the garden alone.

"Darling," Zeb smiled at me. "It's Stephen Foster. We must dance this one."

"I can't," I groaned. "My feet…"

But Zeb wasn't listening. His worried gaze was on Jeannie. He turned to me, an eyebrow raised, asking a silent question.

I nodded. "Ask her," I whispered.

By the end of the first stanza, I was sorry I'd given my approval. "I dream of Jeannie with the light brown hair" floated out across the night air as Zeb took my friend's hand in his, and soon she was floating lightly in his arms.

She gazed up at him with adoration, and for a moment their eyes met, Jeannie's filled with tears. Our guests, conversing in small knots across the lawn, hushed their voices and turned to watch.

After Zeb escorted her from the dance floor, he returned to me. As we sat out the next song, we spoke of everything else but his dance with Jeannie.

That night, when we had retired to Zeb's suite of rooms in his parents' house, I sat down on the edge of Zeb's tall-poster bed, and Zeb knelt before me to remove my shoes. I stared at the top of his head as he unlaced my shoe.

Now that the ceremony was over, the confusion and misgivings I'd had for months began to creep back into my mind. The layers of *mousseline de soie* wedding gown, the Stephen Foster music, the laughter and conversation, my day of proving to everyone that I was indeed good enough for Zebulon Deforest III, all of it gone.

My beautiful day was over, and my life with Zeb was about to begin.

I stared at my new husband, thinking of my wedding vows. Everyone had been against our union, from Poppy to Charlotte to Zebulon II. What if they were right? What if I had just made the biggest mistake of my life?

My heart thudded in fear, and the threat of tears stung my eyes. This was forever. I had just given myself to this man…to have and to hold every day for the rest of my life.

Zeb broke into my thoughts as he unfastened my stocking and let it fall in silken folds down my calf. He let out a low whistle as he examined my heel. "Oh, these blisters, darling…" He frowned. "You should have said something."

"I did," I whispered. *But you weren't listening.*

He found the lace garter on my left leg, then unrolled the second stocking, lightly touching my toes, my arch, my heel, as the silken material slid off. So carried away he was with bathing my feet with his kisses he seemed oblivious to my wince at his every touch.

After a moment, he rocked back on his haunches, staring into my eyes with deep yearning. "How I've waited for this night," he whispered, his voice low and hoarse. He lifted my hand and kissed my fingertips, letting his lips linger on my palm. The new ring on my finger glittered in the lamplight. "From the first moment I saw you, I've waited. Oh my beautiful Fairwyn, how I've longed for you." His last words came out in a soft moan.

Then lifting himself to sit beside me on the bed, he turned me gently and began working the long row of pearl buttons on the back of my wedding gown. After a moment he extinguished the lamp.

Long after Zeb had fallen asleep at my side, I lay awake, staring into the dark, wondering where the music in my heart had gone.

Ten

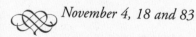
My dearest Welsie True,

Forgive me for causing you worry. You said you were
ready to travel all the way here by train to see about
my health. I know your meaning was in jest, but how I
would rejoice in such a visit! It has been months since
last I wrote, and I beg your forgiveness. I have not been
well, but it is an illness of spirit, not body.

I received your wedding gift, and my countenance
lifted at the sight of it. How well you know my heart,
dear Welsie. How well you knew what I might need to
bring light again into my dark spirits. A sterling candleholder fashioned in the form of flying swallows. You once
told me how they return to the mission in your town, flying with wings of silver and sunlight, singing to each
other as they find their spring nests in the bell towers.

How my heart longs to take wing, to sing with aban-
don as I did long ago. No longer do I feel like singing,
not with the joy that once bubbled from my soul. When
I sing—and I do not want to mislead you, for I still do
often—it is to forget my world, not to add joy to it.

Perhaps that seems like so much folderol, as Poppy always says, but it's true. I disappear into the meadows and hollows of my memories, content to live there instead of my present reality.

I made a mistake, Welsie True, when I married Zeb Deforest. I knew it for certain on our wedding night, though I have not admitted it to anyone but you. My heart has weighed heavy ever since.

No one knows here in Oak Hill how it is with me. I smile and try my best to be a good wife to Zeb, a help-meet in all ways. I hold in my worries about seeming foolish and backward to his equals. But how I long to let my spirit loose just like your swallows flying toward the sun, to speak my mind no matter what words I use—plain mountain talk or the soft, elegant speech of Oak Hill. On the day after our wedding, I asked Zeb if he would love me as much if I returned to my mountain ways, kicked off my shoes, and spoke again with words like agin, ye, and once't. He laughed and said not to be ridiculous.

That night I cried myself to sleep, taking care not to wake Zeb, but all the while longing for something I could not put in words.

So you see, dearest Welsie True, this is how it is with me. Zeb wants babies. A lot of babies, he says. Perhaps when I write next, I will have that news to tell you. Maybe it will help and give us more common ground to walk on.

I am sorry to burden you with my troubles. Even as I write this letter, I move my gaze to your candleholder, thinking of your love and friendship. The candle glows from atop my cherry wood writing table, casting light

across the room. It is a beacon, calling me to a place I do
not know but long for.

> I remain
> Your devoted,
> *Fairwyn March Deforest*

February 18, 18 and 84

Dear Welsie True,

Your latest letter caused such grief in my heart. I am
troubled about your health. You've never told me your age,
even though I've asked many times, especially when I was
a lass and did not know it was ill-mannered. But since you
are complaining of pains in your chest and cannot always
catch your breath, I worry that you are failing. I have
longed to see you in my lifetime, but must be content with
your precious letters and caring for me across the miles.

Once I asked Zeb if he thought I might someday
travel to California to see you and the mission you love.
He spread out the plans for our new house, then asked if
I thought we would have any money for such a "frivolity,"
especially since we are still paying for my schooling at
Providence.

I'm in the third term now, and my subjects are
ancient history and English literature. I passed each of
my earlier courses with honors. Zeb is proud. Oh yes,
crows about it to anyone who will listen. His wife is the
smartest woman on campus, he says. Then laughs and

says it's because there are only two women at Providence—Jeannie Barton and me. My studies are all that keep me going most days. My passion for learning has never ebbed, and I must admit I've discovered more than I'd ever dreamed possible.

Since the wedding, Zeb has had three desires. I have told you about the first—his wish for children—but I will tell you the others now. Zeb wants to be in charge of Providence College before his thirty-fifth birthday, not that long off. First he must become head of his department, he says, then dean of his section, then president of the college. He's driven by this desire like a dog worrying a bone. And he wants his book, *Celtic and Gaelic Traditions Carried from the Old World to the New World through Subsequent Generations,* to meet great acclaim. It will publish next month with the Century Company, and he is as proud as a banty rooster every time it is mentioned in conversation.

With Zeb busy writing his second book and me busy with my studies, there is little time left for the two of us together—though I would gladly set aside my books if he would just want to talk the way we used to, if he would still listen to me as if he cares.

Forgive me for telling you of my troubles when you have plenty of your own. In my present darkness I have nearly forgotten how to pray, but I lift your name to heaven each night and ask for God's mercy in your regard. You are my treasured friend, and I remain

Your devoted,

Fairwyn March Deforest

May 30, 18 and 84

My dearest Friend,

I understand your concern, but no matter what you say, I cannot feel God's love and care for me. I have never even breathed this truth before now, not even to myself, but I know it was not God's best for me to marry Zebulon Deforest III. I have pondered it long and have concluded that the still, small voice warning me was God speaking to my heart. I disobeyed him, so my present darkness has much to do with disobedience.

Since last I wrote we bought land for our two-story brick house. Charlotte Deforest has chosen essentially everything—from the floor plan she deems most "appropriate" for a future college president, to the drapes and wallcoverings. I've given up trying to argue with her; Zeb only takes her side anyway.

It gives me great peace to know your health is better. Yes, please do tell me of your new friend, Micheil. I am filled with curiosity. You say he is troubled greatly because of his exile to the "hinterlands," as he calls San Juan. Where is he from that such a fate could befall him? And whatever crime has he committed to require such a penance? No matter his past, tell him I am ever in his debt for the care he is giving you, my friend.

I remain

Loving you always,

Fairwyn March Deforest

June 8, 18 and 85

My dearest Welsie True,

Just now as I penned today's date, I realized Zeb and
I have been married two years this month.

I finished putting in the garden I told you about
back in March. Since then I made a trip back to Poppy's
old cabin on Blackberry Mountain. Poppy helped me dig
up some mountain daisies, bluets, and buttercups. I
brought them, roots and all, back to North Carolina.
After I dug the soil in my garden and put them in,
I added lilacs, roses, hollyhocks, irises, and black-eyed
Susans. Now they are a glory of color. How I wish you
could see them.

Zeb bought three Arabian mares and pastures them
just beyond the pond. Most of his hours at home—
which are not many—are spent working with his horses,
training them and riding. The cost of such creatures
seems extravagant on a college professor's salary, but each
time he brings in a new filly or colt, I hold my tongue.
'Tis something I still have not learned very well.

To answer your question about children, there is
nothing to tell. I see a low-burning sadness in Zeb's eyes,
and I fear he blames me for our barren state. And to
answer your second question, I still find it hard to fit
into Zeb's world.

I am still studying hard for my exams. This is my last
term before upper division classes. I would tell only you
such prideful news! But I have you to thank for my every

success, Welsie, for it was your love of books that made me love them, your gifts that allowed me to read.

Soon I must hitch up the buggy and head to town to mail this letter, but first I want to ask you for your prayers. My darkness is descending more often now, sometimes so great I think I cannot go on. I have taken to walking deep into the wood on the far side of the pond, often bringing along my dulcimer and losing myself in its music.

Pray for my countenance, O Welsie True, my dear friend, because no matter what you say about God waiting and listening, I cannot pray for myself. The darkness is too great for even his light to break through. You have always listened kindly and loved me through these bouts, and for that I am grateful. But now I am feeling selfish because so little in my letters has to do with you. Please write and assure me of your good health. Tell me more of your love for that crumbling mission and the man who is running your ranch, the gentle-hearted ex-priest.

Until then, I remain
Your devoted,
Fairwyn March Deforest

P.S. Last night as I lay upon my bed unable to sleep, I was so overcome by fear that a terrible image came to me. In it I was cowering in a corner, curled in a ball, my head covered by my hands. My heart pounded, pulsing in my throat, and I thought the ugly image might never flee my mind. Then I remembered your candlestick and rose to light it. Holding it, I traced the flying swallows with my fingers and thought of your bright mission by the sea. My darkness finally left when I imagined what it might be like to visit you there. —*FMD*

One morning the next spring, as we lingered over coffee in the dining room, Zeb announced that I would be sailing to Europe to visit a fertility clinic in Switzerland. He did not ask, he merely presented it as something I would clearly see I must do. Somehow, I was not surprised.

"I've taken great pains to arrange this," he said. "It's the wisest course, given your inability to conceive." He took a loud sip of coffee, sighed, then placed his cup in its saucer. It rattled, and he touched it to quiet the motion. "If you leave now, you'll be back for spring term."

"I won't go alone, Zeb," I said without hesitation. "Think of how long I'll be away." My voice softened as I tried to convince him. "The crossing itself will take weeks. I may be gone from home six months." I imagined him holding me in his arms on the long voyage. "Shouldn't we go together?"

"Perhaps a year," he said, ignoring my question, "including the time you will stay in the sanitarium for the tests."

"When have you arranged for me to leave?" I spoke between tight lips.

He smiled then and squeezed my fingers, a look of triumph on his face. "You'll sail on the tenth of next month."

"You've arranged it without knowing what my decision would be?"

He gave me a narrow look. "I knew what you'd decide, Fairwyn. I knew that when you considered the small life you hold in your hands, our child's life, you would agree."

I bit back all the things I wanted to say, and when I spoke, my voice held no emotion. "I must visit Poppy before I go."

He stood. "Of course, darling. I knew you would. It's been too long since your last visit."

Within the week I was on my way to Sycamore Creek, by train to Dover Town, then by hired horse into my beloved mountains. It was early spring, the time of year when tight-curled buds on the dogwoods were readying to unfurl in the warm sun. All around me, the redbirds sang, and the bees worked the laurel and rhododendrons. The sweet scent of damp soil and the delicate colors of the bursting leaf buds flooded my senses, and I filled my lungs as a thirsty traveler might gulp water from a spring. My heart lifted, and my darkness drifted away like the morning mists as I rode up the hollow and across the meadow to Poppy's place.

I helloed the house before sliding from my saddle, so glad was I to be home. "Poppy!" I cried as I lifted my skirts to my knees and bounded up the porch stairs. "Poppy, I'm here! Your Fairwyn March is home."

Only silence met my ears. "Poppy!" I called again, this time quieter, as I pushed open the front door and peered inside.

The house smelled musty, as if it had been empty for a long time. His worn counterpane was folded on his bed, his pillow in place at the head. The fireplace was long cold, and the shelves where we kept our iron kettles and pans and dishes were shrouded in dust. It was as if Poppy had left on a journey, planning never to return.

A great fear squeezed the breath from my lungs. I ran from the house, around to the smokehouse, the empty barn. No chickens scratched in the yard, no yellow dogs yipped and barked, no Blinken brayed a greeting. "Poppy," I breathed, "where are you?"

But in my soul I already knew.

Leaving my horse pastured near the barn, I removed my shoes and petticoats and took off by foot through the wood, to climb to the top of Blackberry Mountain.

I headed up the switchbacks, feeling slightly winded. And I remembered the time I had climbed this trail with Zebulon and Jeannie. Brambles reached out to tear at my city dress, but I didn't care. My eyes were already damp as I hurried upward, still upward.

At the top of the trace, I helloed to Selah Jones. When she didn't come to her door, I called again. Finally she appeared, holding the door half open and staring out, the lines in her face furrowed in a puzzled frown.

" 'Tis Fairwyn March," I said, drawing closer so she might see me better.

Her face split into a near-toothless grin as she tottered across the porch, letting the door slam behind her. "Fairy lass," she said. "Ye've come home at last."

"Poppy?" I breathed. "Do you know where Poppy is?"

Her rheumy eyes peered hard into mine. She reached for my hand then, Selah did, hers feeling light as parchment in mine. Blue veins on them looked like slender branches on a winter willow. She pulled me close, her wiry arms hugging me tight.

"I sent word," she said, her voice both hoarse and soft. "Your Poppy went last winter."

"You sent a letter?" I whispered.

Selah nodded, looking worried. "I wrote it myself."

"Oh no," I whispered. "I received nothing."

" 'Tis true. He went of a sudden. 'Twas his heart. I told you in the letter." Her face saddened. "Perchance I didn't mark it clear enough."

"Were you with him? Was anyone?" I couldn't bear to think of his passing all alone.

Her face drooped. "Near's we know, he passed sommat between comin' here for Sunday dinner and Monday nearin' high noon when Dearly Forbes climbed the trace to buy some eggs. It was Dearly what found him." She patted my hand. "Near's we know, yer Poppy went quick."

I turned from her then, looking out across the valley beyond Blackberry Mountain.

She walked the few steps between us to stand beside me. Her hand settled on mine, and the warmth of it comforted me.

My eyes filled. The trees and mountains shimmered as if the whole world were about to shed my tears. "I need him," I said, though mostly to myself. "He's always been here, loving me from afar. What will I do?" I turned to Selah.

"Your granddaddy wouldna want ye jes' mopin' and mournin' fer someone gone. Soon enow, ye'll know life goes on." She stared at me hard then. "Ye do not look like yer farin' well, lassie. And I can tell 'tis sommat besides your poppy that troubles you."

"I'd like to see where he was buried," I said quietly.

"I figured ye'd be comin' to see the place. I been waitin', lass." She turned to walk down the trail.

I followed her to the graveyard. For nearly a hundred and fifty years my kinfolk had buried their dead in this place.

Selah held on to my hand as we wound through the flat grassy yard. "Over there," she said, pointing. "Beneath yon chestnut tree. Thar's the place where yer granddaddy rests."

I hurried to the place and fell to my knees before Poppy's grave. A rough stone rested at the head, and chiseled on it were the words, *Angus March, 1795 to 1886, husband of Gorawyn Maxin, father of Fairwyn Enid March. May He Rest in Peace.*

Fairwyn Enid March, the mother I never knew. I touched her name on Poppy's gravestone, wishing I could go to her now for comfort, wondering what it might be like to have a mother's arms around me.

I stood and moved to the two granite stones to the right of Poppy's and knelt again: Gorawyn Maxin and Fairwyn March, my grandmother and my mother. The space beside my mother's was empty.

Poppy took the knowledge of my da with him to his grave. I blinked back fresh tears as I stared at Poppy's headstone.

Choking back the sorrow that filled my heart, I crumpled on the empty place next to my mother's grave, feeling the loss of much more than Poppy. Feeling the loss of my da I never knew, and of a mother's love.

I felt a light touch on my shoulder. "Fairy lass," Selah said. "There's sommat else ye need be knowin'. Come with me."

I stood to follow her.

"It be sommat yer granddaddy left fer ye. Sommat he said to give ye without fail."

"Word of my da?" I said, hoping above all hope. I caught her hand. "Is it?"

She stared at my queerly without speaking. "Naw," she said. "That's sommat ye're better off without."

She shook her head slowly as I followed her back down the trace. "Naw, lassie. 'Tis not word of your da. 'Tis something else entirely."

I took hold of her hand again and gently halted her midstep. "You know then? You know my pa, who he was?"

Again came the queer stare, and in her eyes I saw that she was hiding a secret knowledge. Then she started down the trail again. " 'Tis not for me to say."

"Did you ever know a Welsie True?" I called out as we walked.

She halted dead still, and turned, her bright round eyes curious. "So ye know her then, lassie?"

"Aye."

She stared then, her eyes turning damp. "I should've knowed it," she whispered. "Aye, that I should have." But she would say no more. She turned and motioned me to follow.

Eleven

Selah dusted off a small chest, hobbled across the porch with it, and set it down beside me on her front steps. "This here be what yer granddaddy left ye."

I recognized the box as one that Poppy had made with inlaid scraps of maple and black birch and sassafras, their grains fitting together with perfect artistry. I trailed my fingers gently over the polished top, imagining Poppy's big hands fashioning the piece.

"Open it, lass," Selah said impatiently.

I lifted the hinged lid. Inside were papers, folded and yellowed with age. Fingers trembling, I unfolded the first, a long document with a fancy border. I read through it, and a fresh wave of sorrow filled my heart. It was the deed to Poppy's house and acreage. He had signed at the bottom, giving it all to me. I unfolded the second paper, glanced at his signature, then read it through, trying to understand its meaning. Someone else had written the document, a bank officer, it appeared. Poppy had made the difficult journey to Dover Town, it seemed, within the last few months. Only one deposit was listed, in the amount of $91.36.

I blinked in surprise, knowing it likely had come from his dulcimer sales all these years.

"He done saved it fer ye, lass," Selah said. She walked across the rough boards between us and sat down with a small groan. "All his life savin's, it was. And he wanted ye to have ever penny."

" 'Tis a fortune."

"Nobody knowed he had it, till he gave me this days afore he up and died." She tapped her temple. "Seemed he knowed it was acomin'."

I folded the paper again, tucked it beneath the first, and opened the third.

Selah's voice was reverent and low when she spoke. "This'n's the fairest, Fairwyn March." She leaned close to look over my shoulder. "The fairest of all."

Too moved to speak, I nodded. With delicate, sometimes shaky lines, Poppy had drawn every step to making a dulcimer, along with notes on the secrets of his craft that he'd never told a living soul. Except me. I clutched the wrinkled paper to my heart, feeling a light warmth creep into the dark corners of my soul. " 'Tis indeed the fairest."

I stayed on at Poppy's place. But it was not to be helped. Every day, I felt a new freedom, running bare toed through the meadow, dancing in circles with my arms straight out among the swallowtails and painted ladies, listening to the music of the red-birds and brown phoebes. Sometimes I sang while I danced, letting my voice carry into the deep wood behind our house. Only the does and fawns tilted their heads, their liquid brown eyes looking puzzled. At that, I laughed and twirled to sing some more.

Sometimes I stretched on my back in the midst of the butter-cups and mountain daisies, paying no mind to the bees that busied themselves among the clover and fairy puffs. I just stared straight up at the sky, at the clouds that built themselves into castles and bears and coyotes and owls, then grew weary with their play and marched off to the other side of heaven.

I seldom thought of Zebulon Deforest and our home in Oak Hill. It was as if that life had been a mere imagining, and I was finally free of the demands and restrictions that bound me there.

Selah Jones came at sunup every second day to bring me a bucket of milk, some eggs, fresh-made biscuits, and honey from her own gum. "If'n ye're stayin'," she said one day, "I'll bring ye back yer Poppy's chickens."

"The smokehouse is full," I assured her. "I have plenty. You must keep them." I laughed and marveled at how good it felt. "Besides, the old scrawnies might up and quit laying if we confuse their roosting habits."

She chuckled with me then, a rusty sound, and as if understanding my need for solitude, she left me as quickly as she had come.

Sunsets faded into sunrises; nesting birds flew off, and their younguns, still apuff with baby feathers, followed. Leaf buds unfurled and gloried in their new life.

Then one day, I knew it was time to play my music again, to play not to escape as I did in Oak Hill, but as an expression of my joy. To play the way I had as a child. I picked up my dulcimer and headed to my quiet place atop the hollowed-out log. I began a lively song, tapping my foot almost like dancing.

> *Oh, where are you going, my pretty little dear,*
> *With the red rosy cheeks and the coal black hair?*
> *I'm going a milking, kind sir...*

I halted, dead still. Dread filled my heart, and I clutched my dulcimer to my chest as though it was a baby. The image I dreaded came again—myself huddled in the corner, cloaked in impenetrable blackness. I saw myself weeping, my heart in despair.

That pretty little dear, with so much love for life and promise…where had she gone? I buried my face in my hands. All my heartaches and disappointments, my fear of making mistakes that could not be undone, the certainty that I was somehow the cause of Zeb's unhappiness, his desire to run to everything but me, poured from my heart in sorrowful torrents too deep for words.

I stood and ran deeper into the wood along an old favorite deer trace. I do not know how long I moved along the trail, only that my heart pounded and my lungs stretched to the point of collapse, my breath coming in quick, painful sobs. My toe caught on a root, and I stumbled and fell atop my dulcimer. I heard the twanging break of the strings, the splintering of wood. I rolled to one side and touched the gaping hole in its back, knowing my soul was pierced as deep.

Then I heard a voice. A man's voice. It was off in the distance at first, then drew closer. The man's tone said he was not surprised to encounter another traveler, even one as disheveled and tattered as I, along the trace. I looked up from where I lay stomach down by my shattered instrument, but I saw no one.

Fairwyn March, said the voice from just inside the woods.

"Come out," I demanded, bringing myself to sitting while swiping at the tears now drying on my cheeks. "Bring yourself out from hiding. Tell me how ye know my name."

It's not yet time, Fairwyn March, he said.

I stood and dusted the soil from my palms. "Why not?" I took a few steps closer to the voice, my curiosity overtaking my fears.

The voice laughed, a gentle, loving sound that drew me yet closer. How could this one know me?

I told you, my child, it's not yet time.

"You're my father? My da?" I said, hope burning deep inside. "If so, then why can't you say it?"

The voice had come from near a chestnut tree, the tallest of all in the wood, with its canopy crown stretching thick and wide. When the man didn't answer, I feared he had gone on down the trace from whence he came.

Frogsong rose, and from the canopy of trees a mountain blue-bird called and a titmouse sang, joined by another.

Finally the man spoke again, and his voice was low and rest-ful. *Do not be afraid, Fairwyn March. No matter what comes, no matter the darkness, do not be afraid.*

My heart skittered at that, and I thought I was surely speaking to a haunt. Especially since the words reminded me of something Poppy said long ago. Then it struck me—maybe it was Poppy's ghost. His haunt too unsettled to leave for heaven.

"Who are you?" I whispered, my mouth dry with newborn fear.

Just remember, child, what I have told you.

"I want to see you in the flesh. Then I'll decide." I wasn't about to promise anything to a haunt.

Do not be afraid, beloved. Remember my words. His voice seemed filled with light, though I couldn't see it. It had the sound of rushing waters. And wind. Aye, even the wind.

When I heard it, my fears evaporated like the mists in the sun. I threw back my head and laughed, so lighthearted I felt. Surely, goodness and mercy me, it was a wonder! Who was this man to have struck my heart with such gladness? It was as if he had smote the darkness inside me with a weapon of light.

I ran to the chestnut tree, but the place was deserted. I dropped to the ground, searching for footprints, but the soil was too filled with loam and leaves to tell if one had passed by.

"Where are you?" I called, worried at once that the dark fear might invade my heart again once the light of his voice was gone from me. "Show yourself! Please, oh, please…" I covered my face. "Please, come back."

Behind me, the sounds of voices, familiar this time, carried on the wind to where I now lay curled atop the soil. I rolled to one side, realizing I'd been asleep.

Zeb came through the wood along the trace with Jeannie Barton slightly behind him. They spotted me, and with a small cry Jeannie ran toward me.

"Oh, Zeb, she's hurt. Look at her!"

Zeb stooped gently beside me and gathered me into his arms.

"Did you see him?" I whispered as he held me. "Did you?"

"See who, Fairwyn?" He pulled back a bit and frowned into my face. "Who did this to you?" He looked down at my tattered dress, my soiled feet, then moved his gaze to take in my dulcimer, my wild hair. "Who did this? Oh, my dear one," he said, holding me close again, "tell me what happened."

I pushed him away slightly, puzzling his meaning. "Nothing happened, Zeb." I brushed off my hands and tried to stand, but the emotion of the dream made me weak. I reached to Zeb for support.

"Nothing happened?" he said, frowning. "Look at you. Of course something happened." Zeb exchanged a glance with Jeannie. "You've obviously had a scare, Fairwyn. Something frightened you."

I looked down at my clothes, suddenly struck by my condition. Wild. Dirty and disheveled.

Zeb peered into my eyes as if looking for something hidden there. For the first time I noticed accusation in that place behind his eyes. But of what, I couldn't fathom.

I laughed lightly then, a sound like tinkling bells that I hoped conveyed, *Of course I'm all right. I'm just a silly little woman who's had a slight case of the vapors. That's all. Silly little me.* I touched Zeb's jaw, then stepped back. "I came here to find that Poppy died. It's been a trial." I smiled to ease their discomfort. "As you might think, I've had a difficult time dealing with his death. He was all the family I had."

"Poppy died?" Zeb came to me then and wrapped his arms around me. "Poor Fairwyn," he murmured, his chin resting on my head.

That night, we stayed at Poppy's old homeplace. After I fixed a supper of eggs, bread, and honey from Selah, and ham from the smokehouse, we sat in the great room. Zeb and Jeannie talked about Oak Hill and Providence College as if I were not there.

I said not a word about the wooden box of precious treasures Poppy had left me. The small chest sat, shining like the lodestar on the shelf next to *Great Expectations*. Zeb's gaze rested on it from time to time, which troubled my heart. I didn't want to share its contents with him—it was my secret, my treasure. Had I known Zeb might come for me, I would have hidden it away.

I excused myself early, telling Zeb and Jeannie that I was deathly tired. I turned down the covers on my old iron bedstead for Jeannie, then retired to Poppy's corner, thinking Zeb would surely join me in a little while. I fell into an exhausted, dreamless sleep, then woke when the moon was high. Zeb was not beside me, and I rested on my elbow, looking around the ash-gray darkness.

Whispering murmurs carried to me from the porch, just beyond the window where I lay.

"What do you think?" Zeb's voice was low.

"Fairwyn must have had a nervous breakdown. Not unusual for women. It's often accompanied by hysterics."

"I've been worried for some time."

"I know, I know." I could almost see Jeannie patting my husband's arm.

There was a long pause before Zeb spoke again. "I can't send her to Switzerland in this state."

I heard the crunch of footsteps moving farther down the porch. I sat up, straining to hear. Another long silence followed.

Jeannie murmured something so softly I could barely hear it. But my heart froze at the words I thought I'd heard: *I can't leave you.*

Holding my breath, I climbed down from the bed and tiptoed to the window, pulling aside the homespun curtain. I could see them clearly in the pale light. They stepped from the porch and walked along the edge of the silvery meadow, bathed in moonlight. I choked back the taste of betrayal, praying that what I feared I was about to witness would not happen.

Zeb stopped and turned toward Jeannie. For the longest moment they stared at each other. Zeb leaned in close as if for a kiss. Then Jeannie shook her head almost imperceptibly and held up one hand. She spun and ran back to the cabin. By the time she reached the door, I had returned to bed and lay as still as death. I was still awake when I heard Zeb slip back into the cabin an hour later. He didn't sleep next to me but spent the night in Poppy's chair, which he pulled close to where Jeannie rested in quiet slumber on my old cornhusk-tick.

It would be a long while before Zeb shared my bed again. And instead of Switzerland, he took me to an asylum.

Twelve

Nearly three weeks after our return to Oak Hill, Zeb and I headed to the train station. We were traveling to the State Hospital at Morganton, one of the better known insane asylums in the region, according to Zeb. Without the word being spoken aloud, I knew that he thought me mad. Worse, I suspected it of myself. This was a journey I dreaded.

My stomach clenched tight as the carriage rounded the corner and I beheld the imposing edifice. It rose from the earth like a dark castle, sides and turrets of stone, roof of slate. I counted four stories, imposing pillars accenting each below a center dome, and so many windows on each wing that I deduced the place surely housed hundreds of patients. The carriage wheels clattered into a rut, and the vehicle swayed. I grabbed hold of Zeb's arm and swallowed hard, unable to tear my gaze away from the monstrous building.

Dr. August Crawford met us at the door of his office. A stocky, bearded man with wiry gray hair, he smiled and gestured for us to enter. As I crossed the threshold and passed him, the scent of sweet pipe tobacco wafted from his clothes.

His office was dimly lit, with heavy drapes pulled across the four floor-to-ceiling windows except for a two-inch space between the panels. Bars of light streamed through each opening and puddled on the dark red carpeting. Light from an ornate brass candlestick-shaped lamp on the doctor's desk cast a flickering glow on the walnut-paneled walls.

Shivering, I seated myself in the chair farthest from the doctor, close to a window with its bar of light. He hadn't stopped smiling since we entered, and he fixed his gaze on my eyes. The scent of tobacco seemed stronger, almost sickening in its sweetness.

Dr. Crawford pulled a chair toward me and sat down. "You have nothing to fear, Mrs. Deforest," he said. His tone was quiet, soothing, which only frightened me more.

I didn't trust myself to speak and looked away from him, fearful I was acting mad. Swallowing hard once more, I stared at the intricate pattern in the rug.

"Dear woman," he said, "please don't be frightened."

"I don't want to be here," I said, lifting my gaze at last. But it wasn't the doctor's eyes I met. It was Zeb's, who stood a distance away, observing me dispassionately. I wondered if he planned to admit me without my consent. "Please, Zeb," I whispered, "please don't leave me here."

He started to step forward, but Dr. Crawford held up one hand and shook his head almost imperceptibly. "Leave us alone for a few minutes, Mr. Deforest," he said.

Without a word, Zeb turned and walked silently across the thick rug to the door. A moment later, it closed solidly behind him.

"Now," Dr. Crawford said, "what is it you are afraid of?"

I raised my chin, willing myself to stop trembling. "Of being left here against my will. That's what I fear." I had to convince him I wasn't mad. Even if I was.

For a moment he didn't speak. He made a soft humming sound and nodded slowly. "What if you came of your own volition? Would you be afraid then?" As I pondered the question, he went on. "This is a place of rest. A place to restore your spirit, your soul, if you will. A place to replenish depleted emotions."

His tone was soothing, like a lullaby. I closed my eyes and briefly considered the notion. The darkness in my soul, my sense of despair, was too familiar from long acquaintance. But I had heard about asylums, their practices, their treatments. My eyes flew open, and I stared hard at Dr. Crawford and finally spoke. "Perhaps it's a place to succumb to whatever fears may lurk in one's heart."

One wiry gray eyebrow lifted, but he didn't seem surprised at my comment. "There is fear in your heart." It wasn't a question.

"If there is, I know as surely as I'm sitting here that being admitted to such a place would only serve to convince me of my own madness."

He leaned forward. "You fear that you are mad."

I didn't blink. "Yes. Sometimes…in fact, often, I worry about my sanity."

Again he hummed softly, nodding his head. "Go on."

"Sometimes I think I'll die if I can't find solitude, time to ponder things, to sing and play my music…or read my books until dawn."

He smiled. "If that be madness, then I join you in it."

I tilted my head and smiled. For the first time in days, my burden seemed lighter. "I long to skip barefoot through the woods, hold out my arms, and twirl. Lie down on my back and stare up at the leaves, examine each one as part of God's creation. Each furled bud of spring, each vibrant color of harvest."

He watched me earnestly. "You surely know such notions aren't a sign of madness."

I did know. But there was more.

And he had guessed. "What else causes you to fear for your sanity?"

I considered how to answer. His eyes seemed kind, but it was a practiced look to get me to divulge more about myself. Then again, maybe such unjustified mistrust was part of my madness. I stared hard at him, wondering how much to say.

"It's a darkness that haunts my soul," I said finally. "A dread darkness that I can't shake. It strikes me when I least expect it and drives me to my knees in despair." I didn't tell him how I wanted to curl into a tight ball and stay there, my head covered with my arms. How I sometimes wanted to die with the agony and fear of it.

"When did it begin?"

I thought back to the day I married Zeb. "It's been so long I really can't remember." My cheeks warmed at the lie, and I bit my bottom lip and let my gaze drift to the bar of light streaming through the window, the particles of dust that floated in it.

"Women often complain of such a malady," he said. "Often it begins in midlife. You're how old…?"

"Thirty."

"A bit young," he said thoughtfully. "But you're barren, is that right?"

"My husband told you?"

He nodded. "Does that upset you?"

I frowned. "Zeb sometimes tells others about our personal lives. It's only later I find out about his…betrayals." I swallowed hard to keep my slow anger in check. "I'm certain he gave you my physical and emotional history. All for my own good, of course."

"Of course. The man of the house often takes charge without consulting his wife." Dr. Crawford smiled as if I were a child who'd pleased him with my answer. I thought he might pat me on the head. "Women struggle with symptoms such as you describe. Others may come on as well. The darkness, or depression, as it's sometimes called, is directly related to your reproductive organs. From the times of ancient Greece, they've been known to be the seat of a woman's emotions. Hysterics, the condition is often called. Madness can occur in extreme cases. You need to be aware, be watchful, for any deterioration of emotion."

My eyes dampened with fear. I licked my dry lips and nodded.

He frowned and leaned slightly toward me. "There are treatments. We've come a long way since the ancient Greeks." His smile was gentle.

"What…what kind of treatments?"

"I would prefer to discuss them with your husband present," he said. "It will be his decision to make, of course."

I frowned. *I have no say in this?* I wanted to spout, but I held my tongue.

As if reading my mind, he said, "As I'm sure you understand, it will be up to Mr. Deforest to take care of any, ah, arrangements."

"Arrangements?" I leaned forward, my heart pounding. "So you think I should be admitted?"

He raised a hand. "Please, dear woman, remain calm. It isn't my intention to upset you. Let me bring in your husband, and we'll discuss our options together."

Apprehension swept through me, but I said what was expected of me. "Yes, of course. That would be best."

He stood and headed for the door. Zeb was obviously waiting nearby, for he strode through the doorway only moments later. He didn't meet my eyes but settled into a chair next to me, his gaze fixed on Dr. Crawford's. He looked worried. "What do you think, August?"

I glanced up in surprise. There was understanding, even sympathy in Dr. Crawford's expression as he nodded slowly toward my husband and took a seat opposite us both. The look—the use of the familiar form of address—said they were equals discussing a patient they were both concerned about. I felt betrayed. Strangely, betrayed by them both.

August Crawford stroked his beard in thought. "As I mentioned before, this is a relatively common malady among women of a, well, certain age. Especially barren women."

"Hysterics," Zeb said.

Dr. Crawford leaned back in his chair, gazing thoughtfully from Zeb to me and back to my husband. "I see three options here. One would be for Mrs. Deforest to become pregnant. That would alleviate much of the darkness within her emotions." He smiled brightly in my direction. "And we all know the joy and delight that children bring to a woman. They can also do much to close the distance that can develop between husband and wife during times of these sorts of female troubles."

Zeb glanced at me, his expression both hopeful and kind. For a moment neither of us spoke. Then he turned again to Dr. Crawford. "And the other two choices?"

"There is a new procedure, still experimental at this point, involving surgery."

I gasped and reached for Zeb's hand. He folded his fingers tight about mine.

"This would be to surgically remove Mrs. Deforest's uterus through hysterectomizing. Because it is innovative and not widely practiced, I would recommend it only as a last resort."

"We will not consider such an operation at all," Zeb said, his lips in a thin line. "I absolutely forbid even discussion of it." He squeezed my fingers, and the warmth of his hand helped me take a breath at last.

"I agree," I said, my voice trembling. "It's unthinkable."

"That leaves the last alternative," Dr. Crawford said. He stood and went to his desk where he fished around for his pipe and tobacco. After he'd filled and tamped the bowl, he lit the cherry-scented leaves and drew in a deep breath. Smoke circled his head, and I resisted the urge to cough. Watching him made me miss Poppy and Selah and their clay pipes and pungent smelling smoke.

"The alternative is one I'm sure you've guessed—and the most likely given the circumstances." He settled again into his chair across from us. "That is for Mrs. Deforest to be allowed time to rest here in the hospital. Regain her emotional strength."

"Tell us more," Zeb said.

"Our methods are those perfected by Dr. Kirkbride, superintendent of Pennsylvania Hospital, one of the finest mental institutions in the country." He drew on the pipe, and the smoke circled slowly toward the ceiling. "Dr. Kirkbride advocates the creation of a humane and compassionate environment for patients, a beautiful setting"—he waved his pipe—"such as we have here."

Dr. Crawford set his gaze on me. "You will find, dear, that such a setting will help restore you to a more natural balance of the senses."

He stood and walked to the center curtained window, pulling back one-half of the heavy drape. Sunlight flooded the room, and I winced in pain at the sudden brightness.

"Dr. Kirkbride," he continued, "planned his building in a linear mode, buildings arranged *en échelons*. We have matched his style—from the domed center building you first entered, to the patient wings on each side." He turned to me. "Come, dear. Come here and look."

I stood and moved on leaden legs across the carpet toward the window.

"There. You see? Each ward is enough out of line with the others to afford plenty of fresh air from all sides." To judge from his proud tone, he might have designed the building himself. He pointed toward the ward opposite us. It rose dark and forbidding against the cloudless sky. "Yet each ward cannot be observed from the other wards."

"Why is that?" I ventured.

He raised a brow and considered me for a moment without answering. "Some of our patients are, well, unable to contain their, ah, voices. Actions. Some cannot sleep. They act out their disturbances, their inner turmoil, in ways that can bother others. It's distressing enough to hear them, but to see them as well…"

I waited for him to go on, but he said no more. It didn't matter. I'd read enough about asylums to let my imagination run wild.

Zeb had joined us now and stood slightly behind me, close enough for me to feel the warmth of his arm near mine. I longed for him to put his arm around me or to simply touch my hand, to let me know that he understood my fears, that he was with me in this. I was so cold inside that I had begun to tremble again.

Looking thoughtful, Zeb moved back to the chair and sat down. "How long do you think it might take for my wife to recover from her, ah, nervous breakdown?"

I waited for the doctor to correct Zeb's terminology. I thought I had a common case of female hysterics. But Dr. Crawford said nothing. Instead, he turned and walked from the window, and left me standing alone to study the bleak scene outside. He sighed deeply as he sat across from my husband. The cushions in the plush upholstered chair squeaked softly as he settled back. "That depends on Mrs. Deforest herself," he said.

I turned to face them both, leaning against the windowsill. I folded my hands together to keep my moist cold fingers from shaking.

"If she entrusts herself to our care with the sole purpose of recovering her health, she will improve accordingly. If she is institutionalized against her wishes, we will have her feelings of anger and betrayal to deal with as well. Obviously, these emotions will only compound her recovery."

Institutionalized against my will? My breath caught as I waited for Zeb to answer. His gaze met mine. I was surprised at his cool, calm expression. It was as if he were dealing with an ordinary decision. Not one that could shake my soul to its foundations.

"Tell me," I said, forcing calm into my voice, "tell me, Dr. Crawford. If I were to agree to a 'visit' here at your facility, how long do you think it might take until you released me?" I shuddered, thinking of the brick wards, the cries at night.

He smiled, turning to me again at last. "Ah, my dear. That would be entirely up to your cooperation, your willingness to work with us to lessen your pain, to dispel your dark spirit."

"How long?" I pressed.

He was still smiling benignly. "Truly, I cannot say."

"It would not be up to me to decide when I could go home?"

He glanced at Zeb, then back to me. "No, dear woman. It will be up to the experts to decide about your well-being. You might think you're recovered, when indeed you are not. Truly, it is a matter for the doctors—and we have the best—to determine your treatment and your stability."

"I could be here for years."

He nodded solemnly. "Yes."

"Unable to leave."

"Yes."

My gaze flew frantically to meet Zeb's. "You wouldn't," I began, then my voice faltered. "Please, tell me you will not leave me here against my will." Hot tears filled my eyes, and I swiped at them with the back of one fist. "Tell me you won't."

I saw my life in this brick-walled institution. I saw myself standing at a locked window, looking out at the seasons in the barren fenced yard, unable to gaze upon my beloved hill country, unable to gather bluets or make a daisy crown or touch Selah's parchment hand. I would reach out to touch only the windowpane in my ward.

I held my hands to my ears to stop the dulcimer music that played forlornly in my head. As if a haunt, it played alone without my foot tapping, without my strumming fingers. It played through the seasons that passed without me being a part of them. I saw them all, the seasons, the years, pass by without me. And I was filled with more sorrow than I had ever known.

"I want to go home," I said to Zeb.

He stood, crossed the few steps between us, and took both my hands to help me from my chair. Circling his arm around my waist, he moved me to the window again. I leaned against his shoulder, staring at the brick wing where I might be housed.

"Dearest Fairwyn," he murmured, holding me close, "I just want you to get well."

He pulled a handkerchief from his vest pocket and wiped my tears.

Thirteen

Once we had settled into the carriage, Zeb held me all the way to the train station. Unable to stop my trembling, I rested my head against his chest, grateful for each moment that passed, for each mile that stretched between the hospital and me.

"Thank you," I whispered against the rough tweed of his jacket.

He rested his cheek atop my head and didn't answer.

"I would have died if you'd left me there."

Still he said nothing.

"Of a barren spirit, of the silence in my heart."

He pulled back slightly, and I looked up at him. The carriage swayed as it rolled over a bump. I grasped the upholstered bench seat and held on tight, my gaze on Zeb. His face wasn't as kind as I expected. Instead, he seemed perplexed as he studied me. "What do you suggest might be the answer?"

"You mean as a cure for my...illness?"

He raised a brow and let his gaze drift over my shoulder to the passing landscape. "Yes."

I studied my hands, surprised that I was now clenching them in my lap. "Dr. Crawford suggested pregnancy." I blushed at the word. "He said children..."

Zeb turned his gaze again to me. "You can't take care of yourself. How can you take care of infants? Little children?" His brow furrowed, and for a moment I thought I saw the glitter of tears.

"I know how you've wanted them—"

He held up one hand, palm out, to stop me. I moved away from him to the opposite corner of the carriage. "But what do *you* want, Fairwyn?" Before I could answer, he went on. "I've given you everything. I built you a lovely home. I have seen that you receive an education to rival that of many women in our day. I have given you access to my library. I have seen to it that you're invited out socially, but you constantly decline those same invitations.

"Your only friend is Jeannie, and she's…"

At the mention of her name, I tilted my head to meet his eyes. "She's what?"

"Nothing." His voice was soft. "Nothing at all."

I leaned forward. "You were going to say that she's my friend because of her loyalty to you?" My voice dropped. "Because she's in love with you."

He laughed, but the sound carried no merriment. "She's my friend. My dearest friend. Has been since childhood."

I loved Jeannie like a sister, and my heart caught even as I spoke. "She's in love with you."

His smile faded. "That's your imagination."

"I've seen it from the beginning."

"She knows I'm in love with my wife."

We rode in silence as the carriage rattled and rocked.

"Are you?" I finally said.

He narrowed his eyes, and his words were measured when he spoke. "There you go again, Fairwyn. You can't accept the gifts I've given you. Not even my love."

"Poppy once told me that you wanted to marry me so you could change me. That you saw me just as he saw a block of sassafras, waiting to be fashioned into a dulcimer."

He made another mirthless sound. "Is that what you've thought all this time?"

"You have, you know, wanted to change me. Subtly at times. Other times more blatantly. I wasn't acceptable in your life, in Oak Hill, the way I was when we met. You told your mother I would grow and change to fit in."

"And you have. You've learned your lessons well."

"Perhaps that's what's caused my darkness. Those lessons. Trying to fit in." I let my gaze drift away again. "Maybe my spirit is exhausted from trying too hard and not succeeding. No matter my education, no matter your gifts…none of it makes up for feeling a misfit." I sighed. "I'm just not suited to be your wife."

"Self-pity is unbecoming." He studied my face as my cheeks turned red, then continued. "You're saying that if you went back to your mountain ways you'd be happy again?"

His tone seemed devoid of emotion, as if his spirit was weary. I was afraid to look at his face when I answered. "Perhaps."

Zeb reached across the distance between us and grasped my forearm, forcing me to turn to him. *"Perhaps?"* he echoed. "You would leave me?" He shook his head. "You can't. I'll not allow it."

I stared hard at him. "Ask yourself why, Zeb."

"What do you mean?"

"Is it because you would miss me, or is it because it would embarrass you before your colleagues?" He didn't answer, and I went on, plunging the knife deeper into his heart. "And you kept me from being admitted to the hospital for the same reason." I laughed. "I'm realizing just now that it was not for my sake. It was because of the extreme embarrassment it would bring you."

"Why do you think I brought you here, if not to explore all medical therapies? Your argument makes no sense."

I raised a brow as a new idea occurred to me. "Perhaps you wanted to frighten me into acceptable behavior."

His face flushed, and I wondered if I'd dug into a place in his heart he didn't want me to see. I didn't care if I'd falsely accused him.

"It's all about appearances, isn't it, Zeb?" My voice was soft. "And that's why my spirit is starving. I'm tired of pretending everything is as it should be on the outside, when every day I die a little more on the inside."

The driver turned onto Alexander Street, and the train station came into view a half-mile away. Minutes later, as the vehicle drew to a stop, Zeb turned to me.

"What about you, Fairwyn?"

I frowned. "What do you mean?"

"Where is your love for me?" His voice was low with sorrow. "Have you ever loved me…or has it always been those things I could offer you that you loved?" He held my gaze, his eyes damp. "Or was I a convenient escape from your spinsterhood?" Before I could answer, he opened the door and stepped down, then reached to take my hand and help me to the ground.

We spoke no more about such things during our journey back to Oak Hill. Nor in the weeks and months to come.

May 8, 1887

My dearest Welsie True,

You asked me how it is with Zeb and me, saying you read between the lines in my last letter that all is not well. We will soon have been married four years. I haven't wanted to burden you with my problems, for I am better off than

many women. I have never known a day of hunger; I
have never gone without life's necessities. I have a library
full of books, and I often walk in the woods and sing.
I never did repair my shattered dulcimer; somehow its
heart was broken that day in the woods as surely as mine
has been since.

I can't tell you that my life is not pleasant. Nor can
I tell you that it is full. I have kept my dark fears at bay.
My heart sometimes longs to soar—just as it did in the
old days. But it can't as long as I am so shut inside
myself. I do not know what happened to that spunky
young woman who came to Oak Hill so full of life and
dreams.

It still seems that Zeb and I cannot truly find love in
each other. For months now he has been lost in his own
world; sometimes I think he forgets he has a wife. Maybe
he wants to forget.

Since the day he took me to the hospital we have
been more distant than ever. Those words we spoke in
the carriage, those honest and hurtful words, cannot be
taken back. I suspect he grieves as much as I do.

I've wanted to talk to him, to ask his forgiveness, to
give him opportunity to ask for mine, but it seems the
days and weeks and months pass without true conversation of the heart. We speak of everything else, from the
garden I'm planting to his newest Arabian colt, but not
of our feelings for each other.

Most of all I grieve for my mistake in marrying Zeb.
I've cried before God, asking his forgiveness, but the deed
is done, and there's no going back. I have no sense of his

forgiveness, perhaps because I can't forgive myself. I have caused deep heartache for Zeb, because he suspects I don't love him the way I should. I don't know how to convince him that I might—if he would just love me in return.

O Welsie True, perhaps you shouldn't have asked. I don't want to give you cause to worry, especially now that you are suffering ill health. Please write soon and assure me that you are well again.

You asked if Micheil might write to me. I hope you haven't asked because you fear for your health and want him to have means to contact me if something should happen to you. I will welcome his letters. But I hope it is not worrisome news they bear.

I remain
Your dearest friend,
Fairwyn March Deforest

At night sometimes I lay awake wondering about Welsie True's world. I dreamed of traveling to California to meet her at last. I thought of the sunlight and waves that she said crashed high and lacy against a crystalline sky. I imagined the mission bells that resounded across her valley, but most of all, I pictured meeting my lifelong friend, the woman who had revealed so little about herself but so much of her love for me.

As for Zeb and me, we continued in our separate lives, mine filled with reading, gardening, and singing, his filled with college affairs and work on another book, his third.

I had almost given up my hopes that our lives would change when one evening in June, Zeb arrived home from the college, a flush of wonder on his face. I was working in the garden and could see his smile even as he drove the one-horse buggy up the road to our house. He pulled back on the reins and nearly leapt from the vehicle, so intent was he on reaching me.

My heart caught; I'd not seen such passion in him for a long time. He drew me into his arms.

"Fairwyn!" he said, looking me full in the face. "Finally, my time has come!"

"Your time, Zeb?"

"My deepest desire!" He practically shouted the words. "The head of the department!"

"It's yours?" I caught my hands to my face. He hadn't mentioned it for months. I thought he'd given up on advancement at the college just as he had stopped hoping for a child.

His face fell. "Well, not exactly. It's rumored that my name is with the president and his administrative committee."

"Zeb!" All the feelings I'd harbored—the wonder of watching him lecture, the pleasure of walking with him through the greens at Providence College, seeing him talk to the other professors and the scholars—all of it rushed back into my heart, filling me with pride.

We moved up the walkway toward the house. On either side of the brick path stood the glory of my gardens. Their sweet fragrance filled the air.

Smiling down at me, Zeb put his hand on the small of my back, guiding me gently the way he had done in our days of courtship. I caught my breath at the sudden wonder of his nearness. He reached to open the door for me, but just before I stepped inside, he kissed me. In my surprise and delight, I couldn't help the smile that spread across my face.

"You're blushing," he teased and let his fingers trail along my cheek. "I haven't seen you blush for, well, forever, it seems." He laughed, looking pleased.

I moved through the open doorway, aware of his closeness as he shut the door behind us.

"I have something I want to talk to you about," he said once we were inside. "Plans I need you to help with."

"It sounds serious."

He laughed lightly and crooked his finger. "Follow me, milady."

Curious, I followed him to the library. A stone fireplace dominated the far end of the room, flanked by floor-to-ceiling shelves full of books covering every topic from medieval folklore to European history, science to mathematics, Renaissance art to modern politics. Books Zeb had given me, including all of Mark Twain's works, filled an entire wall. Because I spent hours reading here— at least when Zeb was at his college—I'd arranged a small settee flanked by two striped chairs near the window that faced the back garden and the pasture beyond.

I settled into one of the chairs, across from Zeb, and leaned forward eagerly. Maybe there was hope for us yet. It had been years since Zeb said he needed my help. I half expected I'd misunderstood and that he would laugh at the absurdity.

But he didn't even smile. "We need to campaign hard for my position."

"Campaign?"

"Administrative politics plays a large part in the awarding of these positions."

"Especially because you didn't marry Jeannie."

His eyes met mine with a look of warning. He ignored my

words and continued. "My thoughts are these… You see, Fairwyn, I'm of a mind that we will put on the soiree of all soirees for all of Oak Hill. Not just for the college"—he nodded thoughtfully, almost as if the ideas were coming to him as he spoke—"I wouldn't want to be that obvious. No, we'll put on a charity event."

He raised an eyebrow. "And my idea is this. We'll have a benefit for the people of Appalachia."

The idea appealed to me, and I smiled, catching his enthusiasm. "Go on." He knew I'd been closely following the potential devastation of mines throughout Appalachia.

"Though coal mining has brought some good change, it is also causing men to leave their families, their lands. They're selling their souls to the companies. Some are moving to the mining camps alone, others are uprooting their families. All are suffering." He shook his head slowly. "Many suspect economic devastation is coming; others deny it—especially those who are tied to the business of mining."

I was touched that he cared. "It's a fitting thing to do."

His face softened. "I know how difficult it's been for you to feel you fit into my world. I thought this might be a way to blend your world and mine together." His look was earnest, his voice low. He reached across the distance between us and took my hand. "Let's have a dinner here, perhaps on a Sunday afternoon."

"I've never put on such an affair, but I suppose I can find someone to help…"

"Jeannie has already offered," he said. "She said she'll help you in any way she can." He leaned back and smiled. "It was her idea to make it a picnic. She suggested that we set up tables around the yard. It will be a perfect setting—your gardens have never been more beautiful."

He grinned. "I was also thinking we might try our hand at a Western barbecue."

I put aside my uneasy feelings about Jeannie and smiled at my husband. "Even Mark Twain speaks of the beef roasted over an open hearth outdoors."

"Or smoldering on a spit over coals." His eyes twinkled.

He walked to his desk, pulled out a sheet of paper, and lifted his pen from the center drawer. Still looking pleased, he sat down, dipped the nib in the well, and began writing names. "We'll charge them a nominal fee of course. But that will be for the Appalachian poor." He continued his list. "There's something else," he said, looking up finally.

"What is it?"

"I want you to sing."

I laughed. "Sing? Oh, Zeb. I haven't sung for anyone since I broke my dulcimer."

He rose and circled from behind his desk, then sat beside me on the settee. "Think of it, Fairwyn. This will be a way for your true self, your mountain voice, to shine." His eyes met mine. "It would make me so proud."

I swallowed hard and nodded slowly.

"I want you to play your dulcimer and sing—just as you did when we met."

Years before, I had loved an audience. I smiled finally, thinking of it. Perhaps that part of my heart was still alive after all.

He rose and came to stand beside me. "It will work—for you, for us both."

I turned to look up into his face. He was pleading with me. I could see it behind his eyes.

"Your career rests on it?"

"You might say it's in your hands, Fairwyn."

I thought of my instrument, broken and dead, in the barn. "I need time to fix my dulcimer."

"That old thing?" he scoffed. "I'll buy you another. It's probably no good anyway by now. Wood too moldy to save." He hesitated, looking deep into my eyes. "Why did you quit playing? You could have bought another instrument anytime." He was holding my hand again, rubbing his thumb across mine.

All my longings, my heartaches, my faded dreams, came flooding into my soul. I craned my neck to look up at his face, surprised by the tenderness I saw. Maybe it truly was time to sing and play again. And bring that dulcimer back to life.

He bent to nuzzle my neck, then moved his lips up to my earlobe. Finally he kissed me. "I think it's time we made some music of our own," he murmured, his voice husky. He swept me into his arms and carried me from the library and up the circular stairs.

The next morning I pulled my dulcimer from its shelf in a dark corner of the barn. I'd lovingly wrapped it in Poppy's counterpane for protection. I coughed as I brushed the dust and cobwebs from the faded, worn cloth, turning it in my arms until I could pull out the instrument.

A splintery hole gaped at the back of the sound box, and the strings hung limp and lifeless. But Zeb was wrong; the instrument had not a spot of mildew on it. I turned it around completely to examine Poppy's workmanship. It had no other damage. I rubbed my fingers over the smooth, satiny wood, then took it out into the sunlight, holding it tenderly against my chest. Sitting on a large stone by a stand of hollyhocks, I tightened the strings on the tuning pegs. Gingerly, I worked some of the larger splinters toward the flat top, patting them into place. Small holes remained.

I strummed a few chords and winced at the thin sound. I worked the splinters a few more minutes then tried strumming again. It was no better. Then I smiled. I knew Poppy had repaired many a dulcimer. Perhaps his instructions for dulcimer making would give me a clue. Gently putting aside the instrument, I raced into the house and up the stairs. I fell to my knees before the bureau and pulled out the drawer where I'd hidden the small chest he'd left for me.

The light caught the brass latch. Just the sight of it lifted my heart. I reached for the box and set it on my lap. Opening it, I wondered what Poppy's thoughts must have been when he first placed these treasures inside.

I unfolded the brittle yellow paper with his drawings, smiling as I traced the lines with my fingers. Step by step, his illustrations showed the fine art of dulcimer making, but there wasn't a bit of instruction on repairing injured instruments.

I opened the next document, frowning as I peered into the near empty box. My eyes went back to the paper. It was my savings account, looking the same as the last time I checked.

Then I noticed what was missing: the deed to my land, my inheritance. Frantically, I looked around where I was sitting. Perhaps it had fallen out when I opened the box. But there was nothing, nothing at all.

I stood, puzzled. Could I have taken out the deed some months ago? I thought hard about the times I'd lifted the same box from its hiding place, fingered through the papers, and thought about Poppy. But nothing came to me. I knew I'd left the deed in the chest. I wouldn't have been so careless as to take it out and not replace it.

Trembling, I swallowed hard. Where could it be? Only one answer came to me. Zeb. Had he taken it? And why?

I raced down the stairs to his desk in the library. Frantically, I rummaged through his papers, looking for files, old letters, anything. I had just lifted a pile of his folders to my lap, when a sound at the door caught my attention.

I looked up.

"What are you doing?" he demanded, striding toward me.

I stood, frightened at his expression. The files slid to the floor.

"The deed to my land," I said, my voice little more than a whisper. "Where is it?"

A smile replaced the dark anger on his smooth face. "I can explain, darling," he said.

Yesterday's words about the mining companies and their devastating practices came back to me. I thought my heart might stop its beating for the fear that filled it. Did he want to help the poor children of the mining companies to relieve his guilt? I scarce could consider such betrayal. "You didn't," I said. "You wouldn't."

"Let me explain." He came toward me, raking back his flaxen hair with his fingers, looking down at me with warm eyes of undecided blue. "I'll tell you everything."

Fourteen

Zeb stepped to my side, still smiling. "I think you'll agree that the deed was too important to leave so carelessly unattended."

"Tell me you haven't done anything with my land," I said.

He laughed lightly, shaking his head. "Surely you don't suspect—?"

"*My* land," I repeated. "The land Poppy left to me." I knew the law. A woman didn't have the right to own property. Legally, it belonged to her husband to do with as he chose, with or without his wife's blessing.

"You had no right to take it." I spoke softly. "Where is it?"

He smiled, his face wide with wisdom. "It's here—where it belongs." He walked across the room, pulled out the middle drawer of his desk, and reached in for a key. It glittered in his fingers as he crossed to the framed English hunting scene beside the window. He removed the painting and swung open the door to the steel safe box.

He flipped through several envelopes and papers, pulling out a yellowed document. "You should have brought it to me in the beginning." Turning, he handed the deed to me. "It was careless of you to keep it in your chest."

I scanned through the words I'd memorized, at once relieved. I looked up to meet his gaze, trying to read his expression. He touched my arm. "What if we'd had a fire?" He shook his head. "All your important papers belong in here." He nodded to the safe.

"You didn't place my bank deposit paper with the deed."

"You don't need a deposit slip to withdraw your funds," he said evenly. "That paper is proof of your grandfather's deposit, of course. But to receive your funds—should you ever decide to—all you need to do is go to the bank in Dover Town."

I gazed at him steadily. "Is it possible for anyone else to withdraw my money? Anyone who might choose to…without my consent?"

He moved closer, studying my face. "Surely you don't think I would do such a thing." His expression was guileless, open, frank.

I felt foolish for my suspicions. Why did I always suspect the worst of my husband? Where was my trust? I tried to sort out my feelings. "I don't know what I think, Zeb," I said quietly. "Perhaps I'm simply bothered that you went through my private papers." I drew in a deep breath. "You should have mentioned what you'd done and why."

He slipped his arm around my shoulders affectionately as we walked back to the wall safe. "I'm sorry for the misunderstanding, Fairwyn." He took the deed from my hand and placed it among the other papers. "You're making too much of this." He closed the safe and locked it with a loud click. Instead of placing the key back in the desk drawer, he dropped it into his vest pocket. "But as I said before, you really shouldn't have been so careless."

"I am not one of your students," I said evenly. "I am not the naive young woman you brought here four years ago." I walked to the safe, stared at it a moment, then turned back to him. "I suspect that the day I said I wanted to return to Blackberry Mountain, you set about seeing to it that I couldn't leave you. You thought you could keep me here if I had no home to return to."

He took a few steps closer to me. "Is that really how you see me?" He frowned. "Capable of such a heartless act, I mean?"

My heart was pounding hard. I didn't answer.

"Does my love, my concern for you, mean nothing?" He sighed. "I was watching out for your best interests. That's all."

His voice was anything but harsh, and within a tick of the mantel clock I was ashamed of my accusations. With a sigh, I gestured lamely. "I'm sorry, Zeb. I don't know what's gotten into me lately."

He reached for me then and gathered me into his arms. His voice was husky when he spoke. "Poor, poor Fairwyn," he said, his arms circled around my waist. "My precious darling, the confusion that must be within you."

June 7, 1887

Dear Micheil,

Welsie True, my beloved friend, has written of you often, telling how you spend time with her and care for her in her times of frail health. I am greatly troubled because it has been so long since her last letter.

It would ease my mind considerably if you might write and tell me how my friend is faring. Welsie speaks kindly of you and has told me of your journey from Ireland and your troubles. I understand how your heart must ache for home.

A longing for home is something I understand. Heartaches, too, though of a different sort than yours.

Welsie tells me you were once a priest, and though you long ago turned away from that calling, you are still a man of God. Perhaps you can tell me how you pray for God's mercy. I have lost my way, and also my courage, and cannot seem to find either one.

Please write soon about my beloved Welsie.

Until then, I remain,

Fairwyn March Deforest

Jeannie rode up the winding driveway on a spirited black mare. When my friend saw me, she waved and smiled, then headed to the pasture just beyond our barn to let her horse graze. It was a ritual born of her comfort as our friend and of being a frequent visitor to our home. Minutes later, she strode up the walkway, looking beautiful and trim in her riding habit.

As always when we were together, I tried to set aside my apprehension about her feelings for Zeb and his for her. She hugged me, then grinned. "You're looking glorious today, Fairwyn."

I glanced down at my plain attire, then back to Jeannie. "I've been working on the 'soiree of all soirees,' as Zeb calls it. I wasn't expecting visitors." I touched my mussed hair.

She laughed, seeming not to notice. "That husband of yours. When he gets a bee in his bonnet, there's no getting it out. He intends to make this an event to remember. He's working everyone too hard."

"Thank you for your help, Jeannie. I don't know what I'd do without all your ideas, your help with menu and guestlist."

"It's nothing. I'd do anything for the two friends I love best in this world." She brushed back a strand of hair that had fallen across her forehead. "But I didn't ride out to talk of soirees or plans. I came to see if you'd join me in a ride. You need a break."

I was delighted. Jeannie was the sister I had always wanted: loving, accepting, merry. I was sorry that I couldn't completely believe in her loyalty to me. Oh, how I wanted us to be true friends of the heart.

"Let me change first."

She grabbed my hand. "You're perfect just as you are. This is impromptu. Let's just throw caution and proprieties to the wind." Laughing, she tore off her hat and shook her hair loose from its knot at her neck. "There, that's better."

Minutes later, we were galloping across the fields, Jeannie on the black, me on one of Zeb's prized Arabians. I hoped he wouldn't mind. We laughed like girls and called out to each other as we rode, racing for a bit, then letting the horses slow to a walk. Finally, we stopped at the edge of Strawberry Creek to let the horses drink.

The June sun beat down on my shoulders, and I drew in a deep breath with my eyes closed.

"See, I knew you needed this," Jeannie laughed when I looked up.

I grinned at her and slid from the saddle, landing lightly beside the Arabian. Jeannie swung off the black and led the way to a sandstone boulder. We sat down facing the creek. A pale thicket of rhododendron covered the slope on the far bank. A gathering of finches flittered through the branches of an elm, hopping and singing.

I could breathe again. "Thanks, Jeannie. You're right. I needed this."

"Let's talk books," she said. "I just finished Henry James's *Portrait of a Lady*."

"All three volumes?"

She raised a brow as if there could be no doubt.

I tossed back my head, delighting in the warmth of the sun on my face, and smiled. It had been several weeks since we had last discussed a book, *Pride and Prejudice* by Jane Austen. "I finished the second James volume last week. Tell me, what did you think of the story as a whole?"

"It's a masterpiece," she said. "I don't see how James will ever top the work." She stared at the creek for a moment, then turned to me again, her expression earnest. "Isabel Archer is a victim of her own provincialism. It's clear throughout."

"I've not finished the third volume, but I can see what's coming when she gets to Europe. She has such promise, yet..." A twinge of my heart stopped me.

"Yet what?" Jeannie pressed.

"Our American myth of freedom and equality is cut through with a kind of blindness. Maybe even pride. Isabel's promise can't be fulfilled. She's still a victim of her class."

She studied me for a moment. "You're talking about Fairwyn March, aren't you?"

"No," I said too quickly, "I'm speaking only of Isabel Archer."

"It seems that you're the only one who can't accept who you are," she said softly. "Everyone else here in Oak Hill thinks you're one of us—even Zeb's mother and father." She studied the rippling creek. "You just said that Isabel is trapped by blindness and pride—"

"You're still thinking I mean myself."

She shrugged, her expression expectant and kind. "Do you?"

"Pride in me?" I thought about it. "Perhaps."

"Blindness?" she said thoughtfully.

"Likely." I nodded. "Both in good measure...with me, just as with Isabel."

"I thought of you too as I read."

"That's why you came to see me today?"

She was staring up at the sky now, the cottony string of high clouds that dimmed the sun for a moment. "Partly, I suppose. It's been too long. That's the real reason."

"You said others in Oak Hill accept me…" The thought brightened my spirits.

She glanced my direction with a smile. "That's one of the reasons Zeb thought a party of this kind would be good for you—and for the town. He wants you to feel accepted for who you are."

"He told you that?"

"Yes."

I didn't want to ask when they'd spoken of it, but my imagination took wing. Was it during those evenings Zeb stayed late at the college, or those weekends he went riding, only to disappear for hours? I pictured them meeting, Zeb's smile of delight as he beheld Jeannie. Her sweet smile and contagious laughter as she reached out to take his hands.

Jeannie, head tilted, was watching me curiously. "He wants you to sing, for he thinks your music has been missing from your heart for much too long. He thinks it might alleviate your dark spells."

Such intimate things about his wife for a man to discuss with another woman. I was troubled with an emotion I couldn't identify. "We should be getting back," I said.

She glanced up at the sun and shrugged. "Yes, you're right."

Without speaking we mounted our horses, letting them walk as we headed from the creek to the open field. She looked across at me. "I'll stop by tomorrow to help with the invitations."

I nodded but kept my eyes straight ahead, still trying to sort out my feelings. She touched my arm. "Fairwyn, have I spoken out of turn?"

Meeting her clear-eyed gaze, I saw that I needed to put her mind at ease. "No, not at all. I-I enjoyed our book discussion."

"I fear I said too much about Zeb, about those things we discussed."

"He once said that you're his dearest friend. With such a relationship, how can I be troubled by your conversation about me and my problems?"

She halted her horse. "I did hurt you. I knew it! Oh, Fairwyn, please forgive me. I didn't mean anything by my bumbling words." Her fingers twisted in distress. "I wished only to reassure you."

I shrugged. "Zeb must talk to someone. Goodness knows he doesn't talk to me." I flicked the reins and headed the Arabian across the field, Jeannie's mare trotting behind me.

During the following weeks Jeannie, Zeb, and I spent hours planning the details for our grand gathering. Zeb arranged for a barbecue pit to be dug between the vegetable garden and the wood. An iron grate was fashioned in town, and two men hauled it out on a wagon and dropped it into place three weeks before the party. Zeb also sent for a dozen redwood tables from the north country of California, said to withstand the moisture in our climate even if left outdoors year-round. When they arrived by train and I beheld their vermilion beauty, I worried about the money Zeb was spending on this affair, but he assured me it was for a good cause.

I bought bolts of red-and-white gingham cloths from Grand's Mercantile to fit the new tables. Jeannie and I each took a bolt to sew into table covers. When we'd finished, we sat together at the large dining table and wrote out the invitations, Zeb smiling as he watched from one end of the room.

Next we set about planning the details for the menu, Jeannie spouting ideas, Zeb interjecting his, and me writing it all down. In my spare time, I pulled fat worms from tomato stems, weeded between the rows of corn, and broke up dirt clods around the potato hills, worrying that not all the abundance I had planted in the spring would be ready on time. I sang as I worked, old songs I remembered from my childhood, many near forgotten until my lips began to move and I discovered the words still deep in my heart.

> *Whistle, daughter, whistle, and you shall have a cow—*
> *Lolly too dum, too dum! Too lolly day!*
> *Whistle, daughter, whistle, and you shall have a cow—*
> *I cannot whistle, mother, because I don't know how.*
> *Lolly too dum, too dum! Lolly too dum day.*

Grinning as I worked, I went on to the next verse.

> *Whistle, daughter, whistle, and you shall have a sheep—*
> *I cannot whistle, mother, and I'm just about to weep.*

And the next…

> *Whistle, daughter, whistle, and you shall have a man—*

And I began to whistle happily.

A shadow fell across the row I was weeding, and I looked up to see Zeb smiling down at me. I stood and brushed off my hands.

"The invitations went out today," he said. "All two hundred."

I drew in a quick breath. "There's no turning back."

"There never was."

I glanced down at a large, cloth-wrapped bundle he was carrying in one arm. He followed my gaze, and met my eyes with a smile. "For you."

"Why, Zeb," I said, feeling my cheeks flush with pleasure. "What on earth?"

He held out the parcel and placed it in my hands, smiling into my eyes. "Something I should have done a long time ago."

We walked slowly toward the wooden garden chairs. I sat in one, and Zeb settled across from me in the other, his face eager. Fingers trembling, I untied the ribbon and let it fall loose in my lap. Slowly, I unwound the velvet cloth, noticing its dark, seductive softness in my hands.

When it was undone, I gasped in surprise. A new dulcimer gleamed in the slant of the late afternoon sunlight.

"Zeb," I breathed, turning it, examining the workmanship. It wasn't Poppy's handiwork, but it was exquisite nonetheless. I strummed a few notes, tightened the tuning pegs, and wondered if Poppy's hand-carved tuning pegs would fit.

I met my husband's eyes and wanted to believe in his love, that this gift was a symbol of his acceptance of me, my ways, my music, my heart. Jeannie's words came back to me about how Zeb understood my music, my longings. I wanted to believe her.

I pushed aside my recent suspicions. Maybe now Zeb and I could begin again. Singing for Zeb's friends, the families of Oak Hill, his colleagues from Providence, would at last set me free to be myself. Oh, how I wanted to believe that such a miracle could happen!

" 'Tis a treasure," I said. "Truly."

He grinned. "Sing 'Dabbling in the Dew.' "

I smiled with him. "One of the first songs I ever played for you. You remembered."

"I don't forget anything."

I strummed a few chords, tightened the pegs again, and let my fingers dance over the frets and the fingerboard. The soft zings and taps of the strings transported my heart to the carefree days of my childhood. I closed my eyes, letting the melody wash away the years.

I sang the first two stanzas, and began the last:

Oh, fine clothes and dainties and carriages so rare
Bring gray to the cheek and silver to the hair.
What's a ring on the finger if there's rings around the eye?
For it's dabbling in the dew makes the milkmaid fair.

"I've given you fine clothes and carriages," Zeb said when I'd strummed the final note. "But there's no gray in your hair or rings around your eyes."

I touched the damp tendrils at my forehead self-consciously. My yellow hair had faded. The last time I studied myself in the looking glass, my eyes showed a new darkness beneath them. I held no illusions about any beauty I might still hold. I didn't answer Zeb. Instead I looked down and continued strumming.

"It has a mellow tone," I said finally. "The wood is cherry. I've never seen one made of cherry." I rubbed my fingers across its smooth side. The color reminded me of blood.

"Sing something else," he said.

And I did, then another. And another. The songs of my childhood. The songs that linked me to the mountain, to my heritage across the sea. Long into the ashen dusk I sang. Zeb finally left me.

But I remained under the spangled skies, singing as if tomorrow might never come.

July 1, 1887

Dear Micheil,

I opened your letter with trembling fingers, worried about what you might say about Welsie's health. I am relieved to know she is regaining her strength after a bout of consumption. You say her constitution is fragile, but that her spirit is unusually strong. I knew this about my friend, and how joyful I am that someone else recognizes the same in her.

I am puzzled by your words about prayer. I thought you might help me learn to pray for God's mercy. But you said to find myself a clergyman here in Oak Hill, someone to counsel me here. I cannot do that. I thought you might know my soul yearnings and fears, because of your closeness to Welsie True. Though, as I consider it now, she—being the friend she is—has likely kept my personal heartaches in confidence.

I am but a simple and plain mountain woman. Any beauty I once had has faded. I have an education, and though it has filled my mind with glorious ideas and knowledge beyond imagination, my heart remains empty. I once sinned by not following what I knew was God's best for me. As a result I am filled with remorse, for myself and for the one I sinned against—my husband.

Lest this sound too obscure, let me explain. I married, thinking myself in love. Only later did I discover that it was the *idea* of love that captured my heart, not love itself. I want to ask my husband's forgiveness, but I can't admit to him that I married him without true love.

So that is why I asked you about God's mercy. In my head I know that God's forgiveness is there—if I shall but ask. But in my heart, I can't believe he has given it. How can he love and forgive one such as me?

I have given up asking, for I fear my Lord tires of my pounding on heaven's door. Oh that I could believe that his mercy is mine! That his forgiveness would wipe clean the slate of my heart! All that remains is the knowledge that long ago I did wrong and that my present darkness is punishment. If only I knew how to accept God's grace for one such as me, my darkness might be gone.

Thank you for writing of Welsie True. Give her my love, and tell her I will write to her again soon.

Until then I remain
Your grateful,
Fairwyn March Deforest

An hour before dawn on the day of our soiree, I woke feeling ill. I sat gingerly on the edge of the bedstead. I held my stomach and doubled over as the room spun. Quickly, I leaned back on the bed, stretching out on my back and breathing deep and slow until the strange queasiness disappeared.

Out on the back lawn, Zeb was barking orders to the men he'd hired to set up the tables and chairs. I heard the rattle of a farm wagon heading up the driveway as another crew arrived to set up the dais. I lay still, listening to their voices, then finally swung my feet over the side of the bed, sat still for a moment, then stood shakily.

It was the third morning of the strange malady, and a slow growing realization made me smile. Surely not! I touched my stomach and smiled again, deciding to keep my secret to myself until I could be sure.

Later, as I worked by Zeb's side overseeing the placement of the tables and laying out the cloths, I was back to my normal robust health. I cut a profusion of roses, peonies, sunflowers, and petunias from my garden and tucked them into the small watering pots at the center of each table. But with every step I took, every blossom I snapped, the secret tucked in my heart made me sing.

All was in place by the time the sun rose, but the air was heavy and damp. By noon a bank of clouds rose in the south, and the wind was already beginning to lift the edges of the cloths. By midday the sky turned gray, and thunder rumbled in the distance. I could see by the rigid line of Zeb's shoulders that his displeasure was great.

At noon Jeannie rode up our long drive in her buggy. I'd never seen her look fairer, with her long dark hair piled in a loose knot on her head, her blouse with its leg-of-mutton sleeves and high collar that accentuated her slender neck.

She gave me a hug. "I found another book at Providence library that you simply must read," she said.

Suddenly at my side, Zeb chuckled. "Do you two talk about anything but books?"

Jeannie smiled up at him, raising her perfect brow. "There's nothing more interesting, Zeb. I'm just glad you married someone who loves reading as much as I do." She looked back to me and winked. "Fairwyn's the only woman in town I can talk to."

Her words created a glow that spread from deep inside me to cover my face. "We do speak the same language," I said with a grin.

"And I'm feeling left out." Zeb's words were directed to Jeannie, not me. Her gaze caught his and seemed unable to let go.

The glow in my heart disappeared. "I must be seeing to things in the kitchen," I said and turned without another word to head to the rear of the main house. I wasn't needed. The cooks we'd hired for the occasion had already laid out the slabs of meat for grilling, hams for roasting. Pots of black-eyed peas bubbled on the stove, and the scents of honeyed ham and molasses beans wafted from the oven.

I hurried upstairs to my bedroom. With a sigh, I sat on the edge of my four-poster bed, staring at the looking glass across the room. I compared my sallow complexion and dark-circled eyes to Jeannie's perfect heart-shaped face, her peaches-and-cream skin, her lively eyes.

I took a moment to calm my fears, pushing the silly thoughts from my head. Surely my suspicions were imagined. I considered the tenderness Zeb had shown me of late, the gift of the dulcimer.

Standing, I smoothed my skirts, brushed my fingers through my hair, and left the room. As I descended the stairs and headed to the library to fetch my dulcimer, I scolded myself again. It was unhealthy to always suspect the worst. Why, Jeannie herself had told me that Zeb wanted me to play and sing for his colleagues this day—so they would see the talent in me that made him proud. He wanted them to know me, to appreciate my mountain ancestry, my folklore, my music, my voice. The thought made me smile.

I passed the window that looked out over the lawns where the tables were set. A sense of pride filled me. Yes, I was becoming the suitable wife Zeb's parents had wanted for him and he had wanted for himself. If they could put aside their fears about me, surely I could put aside my fears about everyone around me.

I strode down the hallway with renewed confidence. This day would make all the difference for Zeb and me. All the difference in the world.

I paused at the library door, on the way to fetch my dulcimer from within. I decided that for once in my life—given Zeb's new attentions toward me—I would tell him of my longings to start over. This very night, once our party was an evident success and we had worked together to make sure of his promotion to dean, we would sit together here, in our favorite room, and talk over the wonder of what we'd accomplished...together.

I smiled at the thought and turned the crystal knob. Zeb would at last understand my heart, I decided, because I would tell him everything in its depths. Even my secret that I might be with child. I imagined the look on his face.

I pushed open the door, then hesitated, hearing low voices.

"Precious Jeannie," Zeb said, his voice husky and low, "please don't push me away again. I can't bear it..." His voice broke off.

Jeannie answered in a voice so faint I couldn't make out the words. I only knew it was filled with heartache and passion. I started to back toward the doorway, but curiosity drew me closer. I might as well have been a moth drawn to a bright ember. Silently, I walked deeper into the room.

My husband and my friend stood near the window, backlit by the waning light of the cloud-filled sky. Zeb gathered her close to his heart, bent over her upturned face, and covered her mouth with his. Their kiss seemed to last for an eternity.

Then pulling back slightly, Zeb breathed, "It's always been you. Only you."

Fifteen

I stepped backward, groping for the library door, unable to make out more than blurred images because of my tears. It didn't matter if Zeb and Jeannie had turned to watch me flee, though I suspected they had not. They had been too lost in each other.

I stumbled through the house, pushed open the back door, then raced past the garden toward the clusters of early arrivals who were talking among themselves in lighthearted voices punctuated with laughter. I lifted my chin and pasted on a smile, just as any good Southern woman would do. Our guests were waiting. I couldn't leave them standing there without a word of welcome, no matter what my husband was doing inside the house.

"Greetings, one and all," I said. "My husband will be out to join us in a moment. For now, please help yourself to lemonade and cider. We've got both in abundance." I gestured lightly toward the table at the rear of the house.

At the outer edge of the cluster of the guests nearest me, I saw Zeb's father and mother exchange a worried look. I moved toward them, gave them both reassuring smiles, then kissed the air beside Charlotte's cheek.

"Zeb will be with us in a minute," I promised.

Zebulon glanced toward the back door. "I thought I saw him go inside with Jeannie several minutes ago—"

"Ah yes. 'Tis true," I said, with my smile still spread wide. "You did indeed." Without another word, I turned to greet Jeannie's mother and father, the president of Providence.

"Thank you for coming," I murmured. "Please help yourself to some lemonade." I looked up at the threatening sky, feeling the close, heavy air settling around us. "It's certainly the day for a cool drink."

Quickly I moved to each knot of visitors, his faculty colleagues, our friends from town, giving them a personal word of welcome, a bright smile, and then moving on. Zeb would be proud. I was an utterly charming hostess. Then the yard was full, and still more carriages were halted in a line before the house, moving slowly forward to let out their passengers.

With a jangle and creak of wheels, the last carriage had just headed around the curve to park with the others behind the barn when I raised my eyes to the stone stairs at the back of the house. Zeb and Jeannie stood together on the porch.

They met my gaze with surprising calm. When I stared hard at them, they exchanged a glance. A heartbeat later, they strode down the walkway to where the crowd milled about. Zeb took his place near me, easing quickly into words of welcome and polite chuckles with his friends.

I moved beside him as if in a fog, hearing my light conversation as if someone else were speaking the words. Ever the gentleman, Zeb guided me with a hand at the small of my back as if nothing had changed between us. Jeannie kept her distance; not once did I catch her eyes on either Zeb or me.

When we had finished our greeting, Zeb finally spoke to me. "Are you ready to sing?"

For a moment I stared, uncomprehending. "Sing?"

Zeb frowned. "You've forgotten?" He stepped closer so others wouldn't hear. "This is a benefit for the children of your mountains. You're planning to sing folk songs from your childhood."

"Oh…yes. That." I swallowed hard, remembering I had gone to the library to fetch my dulcimer and had left without it. It seemed hours ago, though only a half-hour had passed, if that. "I'll need my instrument. It's in the library."

"I'll get it." Before he turned away from me, a flicker of apprehension crossed his face, a look of puzzlement, of unease.

I didn't move my unblinking gaze from his. "The library," I repeated.

Grim-faced, he hurried away from me, took the porch steps two at a time, and slammed through the back door. Around me, the guests chatted and laughed. No one had noticed our exchange. Not even Jeannie, who had kept as far away as possible from me since her exit from the house with my husband.

Zeb returned a moment later and, without another word to me, bounded up the steps to the dais. He was now the gracious host, smiling broadly, calling for the attention of our guests. Then he turned to gaze at my upturned face.

"Darling," he said, inclining his head my direction. "Please, come join me. This is your party too. In fact, in many ways it's more yours than mine." I stepped up the stairs to stand beside him as he continued. "As many of you know, my wife is originally from the Great Smokies. I found her there—a jewel among the uncut gems of that glorious mountain culture.

"She had already taught herself to read—and gone far beyond the book learning of most women, even in our cultured region. She understood very quickly the import of my work connecting Elizabethan English to the language of the Appalachian people.

Her help in my project—and the ultimate publication of my first book—was without equal."

Zeb gave me a quick bow, reached for my hand, and kissed my fingertips. "Thank you, my darling." Our guests clapped and shouted their approval.

Zeb grinned and went on. "A project that has become dear to my heart, and to that of my wife, is the plight of the children and families of Appalachia now that the mining companies have lured many of the men from their land. The first published reports, only months ago—about the ravaging of the land, the mass evacuation of the men and resulting ripping apart of the caregiver from his family—have prompted us to do something about it. Something that will bring assistance to these people.

"This picnic is our first step. Let's not talk about this assistance in dollars and cents terms quite yet." He chuckled. "We'll hit your pocketbooks later. For right now, we want to celebrate my wife's heritage.

"Though she's been part of my life, and many of you have either met her at Providence or talked with her in town, you've probably never heard her sing."

He turned to me and smiled, handing me the dulcimer. "And she sings like an angel," he said softly. "For her music is her soul."

My eyes turned moist as I held the dulcimer close. My husband's trade was that of words, a study of their history, their country of origin. I didn't realize until this moment how desperately I longed for his words to contain a truth I could hold on to. Now I suspected that they never had.

So, accompanied by thunder rolling across the Piedmont and the air heavy with the coming rain, I opened my mouth and sang to my husband. The tune wasn't toe-tapping fast. No, I slowed the tempo, turning it into a ballad, full of sorrow and heartbreak.

> *There was a little ship and she sailed on the sea*
> *And the name of the ship was the Merry Golden Tree,*
> *And she sailed on the lonely, lonesome water,*
> *And she sailed on the lonesome sea...*

I continued through the verses, lifting my voice above the hush of the crowd with their faces tilted toward me, above the distant thunder. Then I reached the last verse. Halfway through, Zeb turned away from me as if unable to bear my pain-filled eyes.

> *She turned upon her back and down sank she;*
> *Fare ye well! Fare ye well to the Merry Golden Tree!*
> *For I'm sinking in the lonely lonesome water,*
> *For I'm sinking in the lonesome sea.*

When I was through, I handed the dulcimer back to Zeb, tears streaming down my face. There was not a sound among our guests. With my head held high, I walked from the dais, stepped to the grassy ground, and didn't turn to look until I reached the house. I hurried inside and up the stairs, then locked myself in my bedroom.

From my window I heard Zeb apologize to our guests, saying I was indisposed. The party went on without me, but by sundown the rain had started. The dinner was ruined as folks ran for their carriages. By the time the carriages had been driven from behind the barn, the red mud on our road was ankle deep.

Later, much later, I heard the drone of voices—Zeb's, Charlotte's, and Zebulon's. I could not make out their words, only their worried tones.

I was still awake when Zeb tapped on the door at midnight. I rose from my bed, turned the brass key in the lock, and stood back so he could enter the dark room. Now and then a flash of light brightened the walls, illuminating his face. It was kind, which surprised me. As thunder rolled in the distance I shivered.

"You're distraught," he said gently.

I let out a sigh. That was mild compared to what I was feeling.

"We need to face your illness. This darkness that attacks you without warning. You've been ill for a long, long time. I just didn't see it clearly until tonight."

I frowned at him in the dark, trying to figure his meaning. "You said as much tonight before our guests. You called me indisposed."

"You remember what Dr. Crawford said."

How could I forget? I let out a mirthless laugh. "Perhaps my darkness has reason," I challenged.

"What do you mean?" His voice was wary.

"I saw you tonight…you and Jeannie, in the library. I heard… what you said to her." My voice was low, my words clipped. I refused to cry in front of him, but the sting of unshed tears filled my throat.

Zeb didn't speak, didn't defend himself, as I thought he might. Nor did he try to reassure me that it had all been a mistake. A momentary lapse. Maybe something about a blunder in the heat of passion, something he would always regret. But the moment passed, and he said nothing.

I walked to the window, pulled back the drape, and peered

into the rainy midnight sky. A jagged streak split the sky, followed by a clap of thunder that shook the room. I bowed my face into my hands, and remained utterly still. Zeb moved closer and circled me with one arm.

"How can you suggest sending me to the hospital when it's you who's caused my darkness?"

"Me?" he said with a soft laugh. "Darling, it's you who's driven me away. Perhaps I've needed someone who doesn't dwell only on herself and her own problems."

I spun, tearing his arm away from my shoulders, and pushed against his chest with both my hands. "How dare you blame me for your indiscretion!"

He didn't answer.

"You're not taking me anywhere," I muttered. "You have no right."

"I have every right."

"I'm not ill. I see that now. It's you, not me."

A downpour of rain pounded the roof above us; until it passed, neither of us spoke. Another jagged lightning bolt did a macabre dance across the sky, followed by a low rumbling clap of thunder that kept building in intensity until it caused the windows to rattle. All the while I pondered the fact that he was set on blaming me, looking for a cause that spoke of my instability, not his guilt.

When the rain had died enough for us to hear, Zeb spoke again. "You haven't met my needs," he said at last. "Been the help-meet I needed. I should have listened to those who warned me…" His voice trailed off, lost in the ping and patter of rain on the eaves.

Something inside me died. The wasted years, a future without love or hope. "But you came for me," I said. "If it hadn't been for you I would never have left home."

"I thought you loved me," he said, his voice cold and hollow in the dark of the room. "Perhaps my love died when I found out yours never existed." I heard him step to the door. Seconds later it clicked closed behind him.

Still dressed, I curled on the top of my bedclothes, willing the sweet depths of sleep to overtake me. I lay still, lulled by the waves of rainfall crossing the roof. Trees near the house creaked and groaned in the wind, and the rain slashed hard against my window.

It was then I heard a sound from the corner of the room.

Do not be afraid, child. For in the night my song will be with you.

"Who is it?" I whispered, clutching my bedclothes to my bosom, wondering if it was truly a voice I heard…or my imagination. Perhaps I was dreaming.

I am the One who never leaves you, who never forsakes you.

"You are the same One who was there that day. That time beneath the chestnut tree?"

I am with you always, even unto the ends of the earth, beloved. Even till then.

His voice, so familiar, so strong and sweet, filled me. "I'm afraid," I whispered. "In the depths of my spirit I tremble."

Do not fear the dark, my daughter. I am here.

"Are you my da?" I choked back the long-dormant sorrow that seeped into my heart. There was no answer.

Then I jumped as a clap of thunder rattled the room and roused me from my sleep. I sat up, staring into the corner. "Are you there?" I whispered. "Are you still with me?"

I heard no answer, but peace, as comforting and soft as a blanket, settled over me. I lay back down and stared at the ceiling. I pondered it awhile and had nearly drifted off to sleep when a new thought came to me.

I must leave! I must put as much distance between my husband and me as possible. He and Jeannie could have each other. I didn't care. I shouldn't have married Zeb in the first place. I would leave and start over again. Let my husband start over…with Jeannie.

The peace of moments earlier disappeared, and I was at once filled with both self-pity and self-righteousness. I would fill my heart with music and fill my heart with the glory of my mountains. I didn't need Zeb. I didn't need all he had given me.

I am here, beloved. Give me your heart, your life, your darkness.

I swung my feet over the side of the bed just as downstairs the grandfather clock struck four. Time was short. Zeb would rise by five, heading to the barn to feed his horses. An ashen light was already tingeing the rain-laden skies.

Do not run away.

Pulling a valise from my wardrobe, I quickly stuffed enough clothes to get back to Sycamore Creek. I washed at my basin, changed into fresh traveling clothes, threw a cape over my shoulders, and started for the door. Then I remembered the tuning keys and dulcimer drawings and turned back to retrieve them from Poppy's wooden chest in my bureau drawer.

Long ago I had designed a small leather pouch with a long neck ribbon to hold the keys close to my heart. I pulled out the pouch, folded the drawings and bank receipt, and looped the ribbon around my neck, tying it securely. The pouch fell securely into place beneath my chemise. I refastened my shirtwaist, tucked it into my skirt, and slipped into the hallway and down the stairs. I tiptoed to the library, my cape over my arm, valise on the other. I was careful of every board that creaked or groaned beneath my weight.

Almost afraid to breathe, I opened the middle drawer in Zeb's desk and rummaged for the key. A moment later, I touched its cool metal and pulled it out. I hurried across the room to the painting, lifted it from the wall, and leaned it against the desk.

I fumbled with the key, dropping it in my hurry, then finally finding the keyhole. I turned it once the wrong direction, then turned the opposite way until it clicked. The safe door swung open.

First I counted enough bills to buy a train ticket to Dover Town from the small box at the back of the drawer. Then I searched quickly through the stack of papers for Poppy's deed. Frowning, I lifted them all out and placed them on Zeb's desk and lighted a lamp.

The sky was turning paler by the minute, and my heart pounded with fear of Zeb's discovery. Holding my breath, I sorted through the papers. Once. Twice. Then again to be sure I had not missed the deed.

It was not there. I looked again, then sat back in dismay. Zeb's final betrayal twisted my stomach nearly in two. I sat for a moment, my head in my hands, breathing slowly to calm the anger that burned deep inside. How dare he take my inheritance! He deserved to wake and find me gone.

Do not run away, beloved. Trust me with your heart…your all…

My heart still thudding with anger, I rose and stacked the papers in the safe, closed it, and replaced the framed painting of the English hunt.

I had opened the desk drawer to replace the key when a familiar-looking envelope caught my eye. Puzzled, I pulled it out and held it beneath the lamplight. It was from Welsie True, addressed to me in her distinctive script, postmarked just two weeks ago. Its seal was broken, and the folded letter inside was rumpled as if hurriedly read and stuffed haphazardly into the envelope.

Time was passing too swiftly for me to stop and read it now, so I placed the letter in my valise to read later. I closed the drawer and extinguished the light, then silently retraced my steps to the library door and headed through the dining room to the back porch.

Without hesitation I ran through the pelting rain to the barn, saddled one of the Arabians, my fingers moving quickly as I strapped the valise on behind. Next I found the broken dulcimer —just where I'd left it—wrapped in Poppy's worn counterpane. I secured it above the valise. I swung my leg over the saddle, arranged my rain cape over horse and baggage, and nudged the mare through the barn door, swinging it closed behind us.

I stopped in the shadows of the wood for one last look at the house. After a moment, I turned the Arabian, and we headed for the train station.

Sixteen

I walked the mare into the shelter of the stables near the train station, then led her to the small covered corral. I hurriedly wrote a note to the keeper and instructed him to return the horse to my husband. I left the paper visible beneath the edge of the saddle.

Dodging puddles of thick red mud, I headed through the rain to the station. The stationmaster opened his window as I stamped the water and mud from my feet.

"Why, Miz Deforest, you're up and about early this morning," he said amiably. The stationmaster, Tupper Wardell, had once been a clerk at the mercantile and knew me from my visits to buy seeds for my garden.

"Good morning, Tup." I gave him a wide smile, hoping to mask my nervousness. "I'm needing to head to Dover Town today. When's the next train leaving?" I knew it likely wasn't soon because the station was empty.

"Dover Town, eh?" He raised a bushy red brow, looking interested. "You heading back home for a visit?"

I laughed. "No, nothing like that. Just have business to attend to there." I smiled, trying to keep my eyes from the round clock on the wall behind him.

"Well now," he said, frowning at the schedule, "I'd say you have about two hours till the Dover Town train comes in."

I glanced nervously toward the door and the muddy street

beyond. Any minute I expected Zeb to burst in, ready to force me into the sanitarium.

Tup still watched me. "Did you want to buy a ticket?"

"Yes, please." I pulled out the bill and handed it to him.

"Is that round trip?"

I met his eyes, then looked down at the money on the counter. "No," I said. "One way."

He nodded, then turned to retrieve my ticket from a maze of cubbyholes behind him. A moment later he handed it to me. "The trains are running late this morning, Miz Deforest. Heard by telegraph that the rain's washed out some of the tracks. There's been detours along the way. May be more on the way to Dover Town."

I shivered, remembering my fears of high trestles and deep gorges.

"That must do," I said, my voice coming out in a squeak. I resisted another urge to glance toward the door. "I'll wait." Once I was on the train I didn't care how long it might take to reach my destination.

"All right then. You're set for the nine o'clock." He tipped his head toward the empty waiting room. "You can sit over there, if you want." He looked sympathetic. "You look plumb wore out. I brought hot coffee if you'd like some."

I nodded. He hurried to the back of the small room and came back with a blue-speckled mug. "I'm sorry I haven't any fresh cream."

I gratefully wrapped my cold fingers around the cup, then headed to the corner farthest from the door. I sat down, facing the window overlooking the tracks. The morning was dismal, even in the light of day.

I shuddered again, keeping my trembling, icy fingers wrapped tight around the warm mug. My eyelids were heavy, my lack of sleep catching up with me quickly. I fought to stay watchful, keeping my eyes on the track, listening for the clatter and clank of pistons and wheels and the roar of the steam engine coming into the station.

There was nothing. I strolled back and forth until the station filled, then took my seat again, facing away from the other passengers, my back to the door. One hour dragged by, then two. Nine o'clock passed. Then nine-thirty.

I remembered the letter, reached down to unsnap the valise, and pulled out the envelope. I pictured Zeb opening it and wondered if he planned to give it to me after he had mended the seal. How many other letters had he read through the years? The thought fanned the flame of anger already in my heart.

I unfolded Welsie's letter and began to read.

San Juan, California
June 20, 1887

Beloved Fairwyn,

You must come to me quickly, child. Please hurry.

Though Micheil laughs and tries to assure me that I look better every day, that my strength is returning, I suspect he is wrong and that my days are not long. I have something important to tell you. Something I should have divulged many years ago. It's only because of a promise I made to your grandfather that I've kept these precious truths to myself.

With your grandfather gone and with my own life

ebbing, it's time at last to tell you everything. But, beloved Fairwyn, I want to see your face as I tell your life's story. I've kept my distance far too long, child, and it is at last time to tell you why.

I am sending train fare. A journey across the nation does complicate matters, especially if your husband does not agree to the trip. I will understand if you cannot come to me.

Through the years I have rejoiced in every detail of your life, even from this distance. Your letters have always brought me the deepest comfort and joy—almost as if you were sitting here talking to me in person. Through the words you've written—and even what I've read between the lines—I know you almost as well as I know myself.

I know you're going through times of questioning— and believe me, beloved, these questions will increase. Remember that God is full of love and forgiveness, mercy and grace. His gifts are freely given. His arms are open wide as he stands waiting for you. He cares about every heartache, doubt, and fear. He loves you, Fairwyn, as if you were the only one in the world to love.

Should you come to me, Micheil will show you the way to my home. It's easier for me to tell you how to find the mission—a landmark you can't mistake—and Micheil, who spends as many hours there as he can, than to tell you the directions up the winding lane leading to me. Should Micheil be out at Saddleback Ranch (a distance away) when you arrive, you can ask others in town to show you to my little cottage by the sea.

I pray that I will see you face to face soon. Until
then, I remain

The one who loves you dearly,

Welsie True

I read the letter again and then searched the envelope for train fare.
Obviously Zeb had removed it. It didn't take an advanced degree to
figure out that he had kept the letter so I wouldn't go to my beloved
Welsie True. I pushed aside the nagging thought that my conclu-
sion didn't make sense: Because of his love for Jeannie, getting me
out of the way should have been uppermost in his mind.

I stood, fighting to contain my distress, and paced the floor. I
would go to Welsie True. Now. As quickly as I could get there.

More impatient than ever to be on my way, I glanced at the
clock again. 9:52.

At 9:59 I heard the faint whistle of the train in the distance.
With a sigh of relief, I stood a few minutes later as the train slowed
and screeched to a halt before the platform with a final blast of
steam.

Minutes later, the conductor shouted "All aboard," and I hurried from the station through the pouring rain to the first car I
reached. I settled into my seat on the side of the car facing the station. I had a clear view of the platform and anyone who might
walk its length. Almost afraid to breathe, I kept my unblinking
stare hard on the doorway.

So far no one else ventured into the rain from within the station; only a man and two women stood at the center of the platform with heads covered, waving to those they were sending off.

My heart raced as old fears rose in my throat. I swallowed my looming dread of high bridges and rail switchbacks that snaked on mountain cliffs. My stomach was a mass of jitters and nausea, seething anger toward Zeb, and fresh worry about Welsie. I bit my bottom lip and tried to remain calm, tried to dismiss the pouring rain and thoughts of washed-out rails. Instead, I focused on my unfaithful husband and my justification for leaving.

I glanced down at the letter, still clutched in my white-knuckled hand. If I hadn't had proof before of my husband's lack of love, I did now.

The conductor called again, and within minutes the heavy doors slammed closed on each car, one by one.

That was when I saw Zeb.

Looking frantic, he raced up and down the platform, shouting at the conductor to open a door. He ran toward the locomotive as the train slowly began to move from the station.

My car passed him, and he looked up. He moved with the train, shouting something to me and waving his arms. Finally, the train moved faster than he could follow. The curve of the track soon blocked both the platform and Zeb from view.

I turned in my seat to once again face forward. The engine gained speed, and rain pelted my window, drips flying backward. I trembled, an unnatural fear playing at the back of my mind. I looked across at my seat partner, a red-haired girl, who was watching the rain and nibbling on the tip of her long plait.

"I'm Fairwyn March," I said with a smile when she turned. I hoped reassuring her would calm my own twisting stomach.

"Tansy MacFie." She gave the window another nervous glance, looking as worried as I felt. "I'm pleased to make your acquaintance." Then she frowned. "I hear tell there might be some bridges washed out."

"The stationmaster said as much. He also said it may take us longer because of detours."

She swallowed hard and nibbled at her braid again. "I almost didn't get on this train."

"These iron beasts can go anywhere they want without trouble." I sounded braver than I felt. Behind me the rain sliced against the window.

Tansy leaned forward. "I'm going to Saint Louis. My brother's there. I'm taking this train to Dover Town, then transferring to another to Knoxville, where I connect again to one agoin' to Saint Louis." She sighed. "Where you goin'?"

With her flame red hair hanging in two long plaits and a face full of freckles, Tansy MacFie didn't look more than fifteen. "That's a long ways to travel alone," I said.

"My brother's all I have in the world. He'll be right pleased to see me." She smiled. "But you didn't tell me where you're headed."

I glanced at the letter, crumpled in my hand. "California," I said.

She let out a sigh of appreciation. "That's a long ways too."

"It is. And I've only just decided."

Her eyes widened. "That a fact?"

"It is."

"Where 'bouts in California?"

"A place called San Juan. It's near one of the old missions built by the Spanish."

The train lurched, and Tansy grabbed hold of my hand. I continued talking, mostly to keep her mind—and mine—off the heavy rains still sluicing off our window. "That's where swallows return every spring. Come rain or come shine, on the nineteenth day of March. My friend who lives there says it's quite a sight.

They soar to the heavens as if flying among the angels themselves. She says 'tis a sight to behold. It's as if God's Spirit himself was right there among them."

The train swayed suddenly, then jolted as if it had hit some loose track. Tansy wore a look of terror and clutched my hand yet tighter.

Talking about family seemed to help keep her mind off her fear, so I asked about her brother.

Her voice took on a prideful tone. She smiled. "He went west for gold, thinking maybe the Gold Rush wasn't truly over. Read too many of them dime novels, seems to me. Everybody knew the gold was long gone. He panned for a while. Didn't find a single nugget, so he came back to Saint Louis and started working the railroad, training to be a conductor. Last I heard he's running locomotives out of Saint Louis or thereabouts."

She watched the passing rain-blurred landscape for a moment, then turned again to me. "He doesn't know I'm acomin'. Stephan left for California three years ago—right after our momma and daddy died all of a sudden in a buggy accident. I've been with my aunt till now."

She fell silent again. The train rattled over a trestle, and she bit at her thumbnail. "I know Stephan must surely miss me even though he's got his other responsibilities and all. We was allus close, being it was just the two of us." She looked nervously toward the window again.

"We'll be in Dover Town before you know it," I said, trying to ease her fears. "Maybe we can ride together to Saint Louis."

"Where are you from?"

I thought of Poppy's cabin, the meadow beyond, and the lavender hills. "I'm coming from Oak Hill where I've been living for a few years. But before that I was from Sycamore Creek." I laughed lightly, wondering how to describe the place. "I lived just beyond a meadow on the knob of a mountain. We called it Blackberry Mountain, though I don't think you could find it written on a map." I pictured returning there after my visit with Welsie True. The thought lightened my heart considerably.

She leaned closer. "I've heard tell of Blackberry Mountain. 'Tis not far from where Stephan and me lived with our momma and daddy before the buggy wreck." She seemed to be puzzling something, then looked up at me. "You hear tell of Possum Creek near Laurel Fork?"

"I have—just a stone's throw from Sycamore Creek. Can't be more than a day's journey afoot."

She grinned, leaning back in her seat, more relaxed. "We're neighbors practically. Someday maybe I'll come over to see you if'n you go back." Then she frowned. "You got a schoolhouse in Blackberry Mountain?"

"No, not yet."

"How about Sycamore Creek?"

I shook my head, smiling at her persistence.

" 'Tis a pity," she said. "Possum Creek's got a schoolmarm. Name's Missus Page. Can you fancy that? I learned to read and write and cipher up till my eighth year." She smiled. "That's what I want to be someday. A schoolmarm."

"That's a fitting profession," I said.

We rode along in silence for an hour or more. The rain hadn't let up, and we were starting through the low rolling hills outside Dover Town. The train swayed again, first to the right as we rounded a curve, then to the left as it snaked the opposite direction.

"We're coming up on Granite Falls," Tansy said, her voice

sounding small and scared. "Not more than ten minutes I reckon. The bridge is high off the river."

I reached for her hand again and found it cold and trembling. "Would you like for me to sing?" It might help relieve some of my own jitters.

She nodded. "Yes. I'm fearful of that bridge something fierce."

So was I. "I'll sing us across."

"What kind of singing?"

I smiled at her. "Singin' from the mountains." I released her hand and leaned back in my seat. Then, keeping my voice low, I sang a lullaby, one Granny had sung to me every night as far back as I could remember.

Her face widened with wonder as she listened. And when I stopped, she clapped her hands. "Sing it again," she said. "It's one I remember my own momma singing."

The skies were dark and thunderous as we started across the trestle bridge. Tansy reached for my hand again, clutching it tight. I'd just started to sing again when I felt the first shudder of the train.

Time slowed so that it seemed not to pass at all. Timbers ripped, groaning as if human. Then an eerie silence filled our car. We hung in midair for an eternity. Beside me Tansy whimpered.

The passenger car shuddered, and I buried my head in my hands, too panic-stricken to move.

Then I heard a still small voice, the same as the One who'd come to me in the night.

I am with you, beloved.

I wanted to get up from my seat to go to him, but the steep angle of the train prevented movement.

You are not alone.

It was a voice so sweet it was almost unbearable, so filled with love it washed over me completely.

I reached out my hands. "Da?" I cried. "Da, is it you?"

"Who is it?" Tansy whispered, very near me. "Who are you talking to?"

"It's One who comes when I'm afraid."

"I'm afraid," she said.

"He is here."

"I hear a sound," she said. "Like music, the music of water and light rushing together. It covers me."

The train creaked and shuddered again, still hanging suspended above the river. Tansy reached for me. "I'm not afraid now," she breathed, gripping my hands with both of hers. "Would you sing again?"

Behind me a baby whimpered. A man prayed, calling out for God to send his angels. A woman cried, "Today in paradise... today!"

I opened my mouth and sang again. All fell silent, listening to my song. When a loud rumble of thunder sounded in the distance, a soft weeping accompanied my singing.

Timber splintered, and beams groaned under the weight of the train. We hovered on the brink between life and death for an instant. Then we plunged downward.

Utter darkness enveloped me. Utter silence. Then I heard the blast of rushing water entering the passenger car through broken windows.

I sank into blessed nothingness.

Seventeen

Before I opened my eyes I felt the wet sand beneath me, tasted its grit, smelled the soil and rocks the river carried in its swell. I looked around, confused, before realizing where I lay. Rain poured down, sheeting off me, and I peered through the veil of it seeing nothing but gray.

At first I could hear only the pouring rain and the rush of the river to my right. I tried to move then, surprised at the pain. I had no memory of what had brought me here or of anything before this moment.

Upstream I heard a shout, then another. Followed by a moan. I frowned, trying to remember why it was important to move. To get to those I heard crying for help.

Then it came to me. The train. The splintering timbers. The screams. The plunge into darkness. I put my head on my arm and closed my eyes, trying to think what to do next. Rain poured over my head, and I moved my face to the side of the puddle that had formed beneath it.

Later, much later, I woke again. In the distance I heard the shouts of rescuers. The men called out each time they discovered a body or found another of the injured. They yelled to each other up and down the river as they moved, trying to reach those still trapped underwater.

The rain had stopped, and the cries of the injured carried on the wind from upstream. I tried to sit but realized I was too weak. Then rolling to one side, I inched my way toward the brush at the riverbank.

My right arm was swollen and useless with pain. Holding it close with my left hand, I tried to stand, but I could not. Trembling, I tried again and staggered to my feet. Hobbling slowly, I made my way to the cover of the willows. I sat, lightheaded. I needed help. I needed to be seen so the rescuers would come for me. Judging by the sounds of voices upstream, I figured I'd been swept about a hundred yards from the bridge. Likely the search was focused on where the train had plunged into the water—just beneath the bridge.

I stood again. If I could just walk a few more yards, I would be heard when I called for help. My knees felt like water, and I collapsed on the wet sand once more. I curled, holding my face in my hand. It had begun raining again, and I inched back into the shelter of the willows. Exhausted, I fell on my left side, holding my right arm tight.

I woke again sometime in the night to the racket of crickets and frogsong. A round moon had risen, and a light summer's breeze carried across the still-rushing river. Standing with more strength this time, I realized how thirsty I was. The river still carried the heavy scent of mud and debris, so I moved deeper into the willows onshore until I found a shallow pool of rainwater on a broad rock. I cupped my left hand and scooped the sweet water into my mouth.

I tried to remember how far the train was from Dover Town when it derailed, but my memory was foggy. I wondered if I had the strength to walk any; I needed to get word to Zeb that I was alive.

My jaw dropped at the thought.

Would Zeb believe me dead? Had he learned of the accident? I stood and limped to the river's edge. The moon reflected on the rushing surface, dancing like a million fireflies across the chopping waters.

What if I let him believe it?

I argued with myself. I couldn't do that. It was wrong to deceive another person in such a tragic way. I thought of those who died in the wreck. What their families would give to have them back. But Zeb...would he care?

I couldn't help but think he would be relieved. I would be out of the way, I thought bitterly. He could marry Jeannie, the love of his life. Hobbling toward the bridge, I pondered the question, turning it over and over.

Slowly moving up the riverbank, I considered every detail. Zeb had spotted me on the train. Tupper would verify my ticket purchase to Dover Town—the fact that I was on the wrecked train.

When all the bodies were accounted for and all the injured rescued, I would be missing. I shuddered thinking about the twisted metal at the bottom of the river. They might never find all those who died when the train plunged into the waters. Zeb and all the others would think I had gone to my death under that water.

Quick tears filled my eyes as I thought about the girl sitting next to me—Tansy MacFie. I prayed she was one of those rescued.

I reached the bridge and walked among the broken timbers, then raised my eyes. The dark twisted trestle, with its gaping hole where the track should have been, looked like a gallows glistening in the moonlight.

Death might bring me a new beginning. My heart trembled with both fear and hope.

Of course, I must still get to California first. Time must pass before I could go back to Blackberry Mountain. I had to make certain Zeb was satisfied that I had died in the river.

Could I indeed try something so daring? My mind spun with the possibilities. Finally, dizzy with fatigue and pain, I lay down between two trestles on the smooth, damp sand. Sleep came quickly, deep and dark.

The next morning a group of men arrived driving four empty wagons. I shrank back into the cover of brush. All four had solemn slopes to their shoulders as they began their search. After a half-hour or so, a younger man said he thought he might try a dive to examine the contents of the cars at the bottom.

"Can't do it till the water dies down," a graying man called back. He seemed to be their leader. "The river'll take whoever goes down right now. I say let the dead rest if they're down there. Let 'em rest in peace."

The other two agreed, but the younger man looked disappointed. They looked around, picking up muddy bundles, valises, and clothing. The graying man found a doll, and for a moment none of them spoke. They just stared at the china face without speaking, each seeming lost in sorrowful thoughts. Not much later, they gathered up some of the articles they'd found, loaded them into the backs of the wagons, and drove off.

I walked out to the beach where the men had been standing. *My broken dulcimer, wrapped in Poppy's counterpane...* I stared into the murky depths of the river. It too was lost. Almost of its own accord, my hand fluttered to the soggy pouch still hanging from my neck. With trembling fingers I pulled the pouch loose and opened it. The tuning keys were tangled in the shreds of soggy paper. I unfolded one wet lump first and my spirits plunged. Poppy's note from the bank was blank. Only faint smudges of ink remained.

I fell to the ground as new weariness overtook me and unfolded the second soggy paper. It was fragile, and split into pieces. Then I smiled. Poppy's stubby pencil marks had survived the river. If I arranged the pieces just right, his drawings showed me how to make a dulcimer.

I hobbled back to where I'd found the granite pool of rainwater the night before. I brushed aside the willows and walked toward the large flat stone and bent to scoop water with my left hand.

As I did, from the corner of my eye I spotted a small faded bit of color—the hue of Poppy's counterpane—hidden under a pile of twigs and twisted metal. I knelt beside the ragged, damp cloth, recognizing it as Poppy's counterpane. I moved a forked branch, threw it to one side, and brushed off a layer of wet leaves. Then I gathered the old quilt close to my face, remembering Poppy.

Even before I unwound the tangled wad, I knew my dulcimer was lost. There was not a splinter of it caught in the quilt. I shook it out and gave it a hard look. If I was to start my life over again, I decided, it wouldn't be with a wet and tattered quilt being dragged along behind like a lassie with her cherished baby blanket.

For the first time since the wreck, I smiled. Then I laughed, a new freedom filling my soul. Feeling at once stronger of body and spirit, I headed up the bank and away from the wreckage.

I hobbled, limped, rested, then hobbled and limped again. All the while I paid little mind to my injuries, so busy was I seeing the world afresh, thinking about being alive. The sun was out now, and the colors of the river and the sky, the touch of the breeze on my face—all took on new meaning.

As I walked I pondered what I would leave behind should I decide to remain dead. It truly was not a hard decision since I had already begun my journey away from Zeb and Oak Hill.

But to allow people to grieve for me, knowing I had deceived them? This was a new thought, a new turn of my heart. Unbidden, Poppy's words came to me, words from long ago when I asked him to bless my marriage to Zeb.

"There's a new brittle cover to yer heart," he'd said. "Like frost on the edge of a pond. Ye know what is right…and surely ye're going to do what ye will."

I knew what I wanted this minute, and frost on the edge of my heart or not, I aimed to see it through. I wanted to remain dead to Zeb and everyone else in Oak Hill. To never be found. To begin life afresh.

Poppy always told me, "Ye canna run from yer troubles, Fairy lass."

For certain, I was planning to do just that. I decided to ignore the memory of his words. Poppy hadn't known what sorrows might befall me.

I walked on, the sun beating hard in my face. Dead I was. And dead I would remain.

Eighteen

I walked all day, keeping off the road, eating blackberries when I found them. Along the way I found a field of new corn and picked four ears, one to eat and three to take with me.

Sometimes I lost myself in the tangle of vines and undergrowth, and new scratches joined the still-swollen cut on my leg. The shade of the woods kept me cool as I crept along, and I found three springs of fresh water to quench my near unbearable thirst.

A cloud of mosquitoes kept me company, hovering around my face. Soon welts as big as the centers of black-eyed Susans grew on my arms and neck.

I could see my Smokies now, rising up pale lavender and blue against the sky. By sunset they had darkened to shadows, and soon bright stars spangled the indigo skies behind. They called to me in a voice so strong I could almost hear it.

The following day I would reach Dover Town. At least that was my hope. I spent the night in a cornfield, shivering in the damp soil, more from the fright of my experience than from the cold. I ate more corn in the morning, then was sick in the row of corn beside me.

I knelt to the ground then, clutching my stomach as a dull aching pain bent me double. I thought of my suspicions about being with child, and promptly dismissed them. It couldn't be. Not now.

I started walked again, slowly and unsteadily, keeping to the side of the road lest I be seen. My glorious mountains were my guide, and I followed them west. By midday, I walked to an outcropping at the top of a gentle rise and saw Dover Town lying serene in the distance.

When darkness fell, the glow of lights in the windows of the houses told me I was almost there. Needing a place to sleep, and soon, I puzzled my choices, dressed as I was in ragged, dirty clothes. How could I walk into town—especially to convince the banker that I was Fairwyn March—unless I could find clean clothes and a bath?

Tired and hungry again, I sat heavily on a stump near a clear stream, and let my face fall into my hands. The water rolled and bubbled along its bed, and I stared at it, knowing what I needed to do.

I'd read about the travelers who'd headed west on wagon trains. They had little more than I did now. I looked down at my skirt, then examined my shirtwaist, my smile widening. Before I lost my nerve, I quickly removed everything but my chemise, waded deep into the stream and scrubbed my shirtwaist and skirt with sand. Then I ducked under and rinsed my hair in the dark liquid depths.

I was refreshed when I rose from the water, and I quickly hung my garments on a maple branch, praying it wouldn't rain. Exhausted, I fell on a grassy patch of the riverbank and slept until dawn.

The next morning, the sun shone bright on my little patch of land. My clothes had dried, and I pressed hard to smooth their wrinkles with my hands. After realizing the attempt was futile, I quickly stepped into my skirt and fastened the multitude of buttons at the back of my shirtwaist. I brushed my hair with my fingers and let it cascade to my shoulders.

An hour later, I entered the First Savings and Trust of Dover Town. Trembling, I stepped to the teller's window.

A bald man with a green visor looked up and nodded amiably. "How can I help you?"

"My granddaddy opened a savings here years back. He did it as a gift to me. Last I knew there was ninety-one dollars and thirty-six cents."

"Your name?"

"Fairwyn March."

A flicker of something akin to recognition lit his eyes. "And the date of deposit?"

"I don't have the date. When my granddaddy—Angus March—died, he left his savings to me."

"You have the transaction paper?"

I pulled out the blank, still-damp paper and handed it to him. "I have it, as you can see, though it met with an unfortunate accident."

He frowned, fingered the paper with distaste, and handed it back to me. "You have proof of who you are?"

I shook my head. "No. Not with me."

He smiled. "Then you'll have to get it and come back. Then we can see about your money."

Fatigue and hunger were making me lightheaded. "Please, sir," I whispered, leaning against the counter. "I can't get it, not now. It's a long distance away, you see. Too far to go back."

"I'm sorry. These are our rules."

I hung my head, puzzling what I might do.

Then behind me a woman's voice spoke. "This here's Fairwyn March, Nab Quarrie. Don't ye know a March by jes' lookin'? Why, they family jes' about owns these hills. Scattered all over 'em, they are."

Before I could turn, the teller smiled at the woman behind me. "She's the spittin' of her grandpappy, the lassie is."

I turned then, to see Selah Jones waving a cane toward Nab Quarrie. Standing beside her was her grinning friend Lettie Jameson. Selah was so withered and wiry it was a wonder she still could stand upright.

For a moment I didn't speak, just stared at the two women, my mouth gaping.

"Well, Fairy lass, ain't ye gonna say hello?" Selah said, hobbling closer and peering into my face. "See there, Lettie," she said with a frown, "I told ye it was our Fairwyn March. Didn't I tell ye so? Purty as ever, she is. Purty as ever. Jes' look at that yeller hair."

I stared at Selah, wanting to gather the tiny woman into my arms, though I knew she'd have no part of it. Her embraces were few and far between. The last I remembered was the day I found out Poppy died. "Oh, Selah," I said quietly, "just the sight of ye blesses my heart."

She grinned up at me with her nearly toothless smile. "I missed ye, lass."

Before I could answer, the teller cleared his throat. "I guess we've established that you're who you say you are."

I turned to give him a triumphant smile, only to see his worried frown.

"There's another problem," he said, looking down at his ledger. "I see in my records that your husband, a Mr. Zebulon Deforest the Third, came here a year or so ago. According to law, you know, your property—real and otherwise—belongs to him. He changed the name on your account to both your names—Mr. and Mrs. Zebulon Deforest the Third."

I stepped closer to the counter and gripped it hard. "D-did he take the money?" I asked, my voice barely above a whisper.

"No, no. He didn't."

I let out a small sigh of relief. "I must have my money," I said, my voice low. "You must give it to me. My name is on the account, both as Fairwyn March and Mrs. Zebulon Deforest the Third."

By now, Selah was standing on one side of me, Lettie on the other. "I can vouch fer the lass," Selah said.

"Amen," said Lettie. They moved in close as if to keep me from falling.

The teller nodded finally, then smiled at the two women. "I know of no better souls around than these two women. If they vouch for you, then the money is yours."

Selah looked proud.

"It's made interest," Nab Quarrie said as he counted out the bills. "Some of it's been here for more than a decade."

I gasped when I saw the stack. "Do you have something I can carry it in? A valise...anything?"

He laughed. "With this you can buy a whole haberdashery." But he tucked the money into a thick envelope-folder and tied it with twine.

I started to turn to leave, then hesitated. "The bridge that washed out—"

"Oh yes, a tragedy." He shook his head. "A terrible tragedy."

"Is there a list posted of the dead? Somewhere here in town?"

"I'm sorry, but there's nothing official yet. I hear they're still searching for bodies."

"One more thing..."

He nodded.

"Is there another way to take a train out of town?"

"Oh yes. There are tracks leading north, south, and west—just can't go east because of the bridge."

Selah Jones and Lettie Jameson did their banking, and I waited to walk with them to the hitching post where they'd left their mules. We left the bank and made our way down the street.

"Since last year the road goes near all the way to Blackberry Mountain," Lettie said. "Still have to go the rest by mule though." She shrugged. " 'Bout the onliest good thing the mine company's done fer us."

"Are ye comin' home agin now? Back to Blackberry Mountain?" Lettie said. "Is that why ye're here?"

Selah's eyes were bright. "I've missed ye somethin' fierce, Fairy lass."

"I was coming back, but my friend Welsie True has written that she needs me."

Selah looked stricken. "That so, child?"

"I only received the letter yesterday."

"So ye're heading to Californy?" Selah said softly. "To see yer Welsie True at long last."

I nodded. "On the first train west."

"Welsie True…" she began, her eyes bright with tears. "So she's sent for ye."

"She wants to tell me my family history. Says she wants to see me face to face when I hear it."

"That would be her way," Selah said. She stopped in front of two swaybacked mules. She studied my face as if memorizing it. "You tell Welsie True fer me that I think on her. More'n she knows, I do."

"I'll tell her."

"You tell her for me, there's not a day goes by what I don't pray for her." She swallowed hard. "And love her. You tell her for me."

I tilted my head, surprised. "You never said you knew her well. Only that you knew her."

"She's blood kin," Selah said. "My own true sister I love." Before I could answer, she climbed onto her mule. Looking down at me, she added. "God's got ye in his hands, lass. Don't ever be forgettin' it."

The slant of the sun hit my face, and I shaded my eyes, still looking up at her. She smiled then and tipped her hat. "Don't forget to tell Welsie True." Then, side by side, the two mules ambled slowly down the street, Lettie and Selah with their heads held high.

After I bought a ticket for Saint Louis, I walked to McKenna's store and replaced my lost belongings. Then, I again visited the First Savings and Trust. Nab Quarrie stood behind the teller window, his visor low over his eyes. With a deep breath, I approached him again.

He recognized me and smiled. No other customers were in the bank.

"It is important," I began without preamble, "that Mr. Deforest not discover I have been here. Should he come back, that is."

He cocked his head as if puzzling my words.

I drew in a deep breath, willing courage to flow through my bones. "Selah Jones vouched for me once. She would again. Regarding this request, I mean."

He frowned. "What if your husband comes to collect the money? What am I supposed to tell him?"

What I'd asked of him was illegal, which shamed me. I let my gaze drift away from his eyes, feeling the threat of welling tears. "Tell him whatever you like," I said with a sigh and turned to walk away, my sorrows and worries weighing heavy. "I'm sorry I asked such a thing of you."

"Oh, balderdash!" The shout came from behind the counter just as I reached the door.

I turned to look back. Nab Quarrie had knocked over an inkwell. The dark liquid was spreading quickly across the ledger. He stood, glaring at the mess, hands on hips. "Sometimes I can be so clumsy!"

He grabbed a blotter and began to dab at the large book, shaking his head slowly. "Well, I declare," he said. "I can see all the day's transactions but one."

I smiled at him. " 'Tis a crying shame."

Nineteen

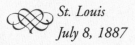

St. Louis
July 8, 1887

Dearest Welsie,

I am hurrying to you as quickly as I can. I am sitting in
the train station in Saint Louis, waiting to board the next
train heading west. I will be in California in a matter of
days. This letter may not reach you before I do, but in
the event it does, I wanted you to know I'm coming.

The family history you want to tell me is a secondary
concern in my heart next to your health, and to my seeing you for the first time. I've many times wondered what
our relationship is beyond friendship. I know there is a
connection, and I suspect that we are kin, but beyond
that I won't guess. I'll wait patiently for you to tell me
when we meet at last.

I also won't speak yet of how I've come to be traveling
west—it wasn't what you'd planned or offered for me. It's a
long story, an emotional and not entirely happy one. It
also needs to be told when we're sitting face to face.

Quite by accident I met Selah Jones in Dover Town.
As we were parting she sent her love to you. She also said

that you are blood kin, sisters. How my imagination goes wild with that word—the idea that she might also be related to me, for I love her dearly. But then, my imagination is getting ahead of the story you have to tell me.

You have been a friend like no other, Welsie True, full of love and acceptance, from the time I held your first letter in my hand till now. Hold on to life, beloved friend, for I am hurrying to you.

With affection, both family and friendship, I remain Your,

Fairwyn March

Outside Santa Fe, New Mexico
July 14, 1886

My beloved Welsie,

Again I am unable to sleep. My car is crowded and noisy even at midnight, with children fussing and crying and their mothers whispering comfort. In front, four men play cards, hooting and hollering and swearing and smoking, and beside me an old man snores. We are passing through the Rocky Mountains, and the train sways this way and that. So forgive my splotches of ink and shaky writing.

By the light of a small gas lamp near my seat, I will begin another letter to you, beseeching you again to live with the hope of my coming.

I have so much to ask you, so much to tell. I especially want to speak of forgiveness and mercy, for your words through the years have been steeped in wisdom.

Welsie, I have done things recently that cause nightmares to plague me. I have wandered down a path that at the time seemed reasonable enough, even justified, and now I am filled with doubt and remorse. I have told you that I feared I made a mistake in marrying Zeb, and now I have left him under circumstances that cause my heart to ache with the knowledge that I will always remain unforgiven, by God, by Zeb, by myself.

No matter how hard I try, it seems, I fall short of my intentions. When I try to make things better (which truly isn't often), I fall on my face in shame and error.

Welsie, how I long to sit at your feet and learn from you. I pray that day will be soon.

It saddens me to put down my pen, but I must. The car is rattling through tunnels and around curves, making it difficult to form even a single word.

With love, I remain

Your devoted,

Fairwyn March

The train rounded a long curve as it passed through Cajon Pass. We had just crossed the most barren land I had ever seen—hot, arid, filled with salt flats and dark rock formations. It could have been the moon for its lack of resemblance to anything I had ever seen on earth.

The car was as hot as an oven now, and little children whimpered to their mothers and daddies about being thirsty and hot. Three women near me looked miserable in their gussied-up dresses, and two men, sitting in the row behind, had removed their jackets long before we crossed the desert. The air in the car was fetid from sweat, and I kept my scented handkerchief to my nose to block the smells.

Even so, I could not help leaning forward in anticipation, peering through the open window as we descended into a long, golden brown valley. *California!*

The train wound around a switchback, then another, through a formation of red-brown boulders and at last headed down onto the valley floor. The sun now was in its downward arch, visible in front of the train, turning the tracks silver. We headed west, toward the ocean, and my heart caught in my throat imagining it.

A dozen times in the next hours I checked for my belongings, patting my small satchel to make certain it was still beside me. The whistle blew as we headed through several small villages, but the train did not stop. Soon I saw the dusty town of Los Angeles straight ahead.

Everyone in the car fell silent, even the children, staring through the windows as the train rattled and clanked along the tracks and the whistle blew up front. A layer of lavender haze hung above the ground, and a small orange ball of a sun was slipping quickly behind the squat buildings.

"So this is California," I sighed, mostly to myself.

The woman seated next to me laughed. It was a contagious sound, and I looked up to be greeted by a merry, round face. "In all its dusty glory." Her husband, a balding man sitting on the other side of the bench, chuckled with her.

I was surprised I was overheard and turned with a smile. I'd seen the couple board in Santa Fe, but until our last water stop they'd been seated at the rear of the car.

"This your first trip here?" the woman asked pleasantly.

"It is."

Her husband leaned forward with a friendly smile. "Where are you from?"

"Oak Hill, North Carolina," I said without hesitation.

Their smiles brightened at the same instant I realized my error. "Ah yes," the man said. "I know it well. Used to know someone at the college there—what is it again?"

"Providence," I whispered, a feeling of dread fear coming over me. "Providence College." I was twisting my wedding ring on my third finger, and looking down, quickly covered it with my opposite hand.

"We're Eliza and Alexander Roget," the woman said, sticking out her hand. "But you can call my husband Doc. Everyone does."

"Nice to meet you both," I said quietly.

"Oh me, what was the fellow's name?" Alexander Roget frowned. "Met him in Washington a couple of years ago." He turned to his wife. "You remember, don't you, El? Heavyset man, graying at the temples? He sat in on the council to study female diseases."

"He teaches at Providence?" I ventured, searching my memory for one of the professors who might fit the description.

The train was slowing now as the station came into view.

"What was his name?" Alexander Roget paid no mind to the approaching station, so fixed was he on the name he had forgotten.

Eliza rolled her eyes at her husband while smiling at me. "Once Doc gets something in his craw, he can't give it up. He never forgets a face, but sometimes names can elude him." She hesitated. "By the way, dear, you didn't give us yours. Your name, that is."

"Fairwyn," I said, "Fairwyn March De—" I halted just in time. Eliza did not notice, for at the same moment I spoke, the train screeched to a halt in a blast of steam. "Fairwyn March," I repeated more confidently when she could hear me again.

"Pleased to make your acquaintance," Eliza said, pumping my hand again. "Such an unusual name."

Doc chuckled as he shook my hand. "Fairwyn March. Now that's one I promise I will not forget. One of the loveliest I've ever heard." His smile was genuine.

People were milling in the aisles now, gathering their valises, travel boxes, and small trunks. The car was a mass of laughter, chatter, and confusion. I placed my hat above my knot of hair, pinned it into place, and picked up my two valises.

I had just started down the aisle to the door, when Doc called out above the hubbub. "Fairwyn March! I just remembered the name!" He wove in and out of the people between us, finally reaching me.

The look on his face was triumphant. "Gerald Hamilton! Do you know him?"

Now Eliza was standing by him, loaded down with valises and satchels. "And his lovely wife is Letitia. Very dignified, lovely woman, wasn't she, dear?" She glanced up at her husband, who was nodding vigorously.

The conductor called for the passengers to disembark. I stared into their faces as the ramifications settled in. Gerald Hamilton was a faculty colleague of Zeb's. We had seen the Hamiltons socially a few times. They had attended our wedding. One word to Gerald from Doc or his wife—should they meet again—would be passed along to Zeb. My deception would be discovered.

"Are you all right, dear?" Doc stepped closer, looking worried. "You look flushed."

"Just feeling lightheaded," I said, leaning against the back of a nearby horsehair bench. "That's all."

"It's been a long journey," Eliza said, touching my arm as if to steady me.

I laughed weakly. "Longer than you know."

"Let us help you to your connecting train." Doc took my two valises and led the way down the aisle to the door. "Where did you say you're going?"

More information for them to pass along. I blinked, and cleared my throat. No easy lie came to me. "San Juan," I said shakily.

"A lovely destination," Doc said. "You must visit the mission. Though it's in great need of restoration, it's in one of the fairest settings of the entire chain."

Within minutes they had helped me find the right track. They placed the valises beside me, and Doc pulled out his pocket watch. "You have a few minutes."

"Thank you for your help." I hesitated. "You don't need to wait."

Doc and Eliza said their good-byes and walked a few steps down the platform. Then Doc touched Eliza's arm, and they halted, only to turn again and wave.

I waved back, but worry flooded my heart. One word written to Gerald Hamilton about me would crush my plans, for it surely would be repeated to Zeb. I stared after them, long after they disappeared into the twilight mists.

"Aye, but to be sure," came floating into my heart in Poppy's rich mountain tenor, "yer sins will find ye out."

A train's mournful whistle sounded in the distance, and I

turned to watch the roaring approach of the steam engine. But instead of elation at the sight of the train that would take me to a place I'd dreamed about for years, I felt only a catch in my heart.

Here I was worried about telling a small untruth to Doc and Eliza when my whole life from the moment I decided to remain dead was one big lie. I swallowed hard and picked up the valises as the train halted in a cloud of steam.

The three-passenger-car train was the last of the day to San Diego. I was one of only a dozen or so passengers in my car. Wearily, I sat down upon my horsehair bench seat and leaned back, my knuckles white where I clutched the satchel handle. My valises were close beside me, one on either side.

Darkness was complete, but I stared through the window, wondering what lay beyond. The unseen ocean, stretching into the horizon, likely would be close enough to touch. The gulls roosted on roofs and in the sycamore trees. They would rise into the sky at dawn, calling and crying, just as Welsie True had told me. I would run barefoot through the sand, arms outspread, rejoicing in the wonder of my new world, my new freedom.

Then why did my heart not leap with joy?

I leaned my head back against the seat and closed my eyes, feeling a familiar ache creep into my heart. An ache for something I could not identify. A call to something I did not know.

Puzzled, I sat up and stared again into the darkness. It was as dense as my own future. I shuddered and turned away. What if the peace I sought could not be found? Here or anywhere? The train whistle moaned in the night, joining with the clatter of pistons, the rhythm of the wheels.

The warmth of my small packet of dulcimer tuning keys drew my hand to my bodice. I drew it to the outside of my clothes and clutched the warm leather in my palm, feeling the small lumps of keys inside. I was surprised at the comfort they brought.

I would see Welsie True at last, and she would help me find my way through this maze of deception and darkness. Tomorrow, I would begin to set things right. I lifted my chin and stared again into the black night.

Yes, tomorrow I would start my life all over again. The past would be forgotten. I would sing as never before, and my heart would spill over with love and music and joy.

I wondered why I didn't believe it could happen. Ever.

Twenty

I spent the night in a small, tile-roofed Spanish inn across from the small train station. At dawn the scent of salt air filled my nostrils even before I opened my eyes, just as the lonely cries of seagulls filled my heart. I hurried into my clothes and headed downstairs, through the parlor to the dusty street.

It had been dark when I arrived the night before, but now I could see that the squat adobe inn sat squarely atop a small cliff near the sea. A lacy froth of bougainvillea covered half the roof and cascaded to the ground below. Two seagulls marched jauntily along the rooftop peak; another perched on one foot, looking out toward the ocean.

As soon as I rounded the picket fence that framed the inn, I climbed along a path past an outcropping of sandstone. The cool ocean breeze touched my cheeks, lifted my hair, and stung my eyes. In the distance, waves hit the sand with a rhythmic rushing roar, and I climbed farther up the small cliff to have a look.

A gasp escaped my lips as I took in my first view of the ocean. I felt like laughing and crying at the same time. A sense of wonder fell over me, wrapped round me, filled me, as nothing before had ever done. I almost forgot my heartache.

My gaze fell to the horizon, and I scarce could imagine the distance to that place where the sky met the sea, blending together so completely it seemed it must surely be where eternity began.

My cheeks were wet with tears, but they dried nearly as fast as they flowed because of the soft sea air that touched them. I wanted to fall to my knees but felt shy about doing so.

"O God," I whispered, "are you truly in this place?"

Suddenly my mind was filled with possibilities I'd never before reckoned on. That there were whole worlds God had created, that he was not just the God my Poppy had spoken of, or the preacher in Oak Hill had droned on about in a monotone voice. He was something bigger that all that. I stood astounded, unable to take it in.

The seagulls soared, floating above me like nothing I'd ever seen before. They cried and called and swooped. I laughed and danced in a circle, holding out my arms in the purest joy I had felt in years. Then, removing my shoes and lifting my skirts above my ankles, I headed along a path leading from the cliffs to the sand below.

I wanted to shout with joy, but instead I stopped dead still, grinning as wide as I could remember, letting the lacy waves lick my toes. I hiked up my skirts and waded deeper, to my ankles, then to my knees, feeling the sway of the water lift me upward. Giggling, I felt the sand disappear from beneath my feet when the tide ebbed.

Little crablike creatures skittered across the wet sand, diving and digging, and all around me seashells of every color dotted the beach.

I stared at the ocean, the gulls, and the pelicans, under the sky looking more like heaven than I could ever have imagined. I ran and played and skipped along the beach, twirling through the shallows. Words and music seemed to come out of my heart without bidding. I opened my mouth and sang songs long forgotten as I danced into the waves and out again.

My joy turned into a quieter kind of peace then, and I settled onto a dry patch of sand, letting the sun beat strong on my head and shoulders. How long I sat, I could not say. For the moments seemed to settle so deep into my soul that time seemed not to exist at all.

Finally, my rumbling stomach brought me from my reverie. The day ahead would be long and perhaps not entirely pleasant. Reluctantly, I headed back up the cliffs to the boardinghouse for breakfast. Once I reached the top, I turned to look once more at the ocean. At that moment the low mellow tones of a bell echoed across the valley and mixed with the rush of the waves.

Shading my eyes against the sun, I took in some low, rolling hills in the distance. A bell tower rose above what appeared to be a long white wall with taller buildings above it. Clustered around what surely must be the mission were several smaller buildings— houses, I supposed. Light from the rising sun slanted against it all, causing the small village, the mission, to stand out against the darker trees behind.

I wondered if Micheil might be there this moment, pulling the rope in the bell tower. If I hurried I might catch him before he left for Welsie's ranch, the one she called Saddleback.

An hour later, I hired a carriage to take me to the mission. I grabbed hold of the upholstered bench seat as the cabby drove across the small valley, the wheels creaking, the vehicle jerking and bouncing as it hit ruts and bumps in the dirt road. On the right side of the carriage rose velvet-brown hills dotted with live oaks. To my left stretched the ocean, sparkling like a million jewels in the sunlight.

When I stepped out in front of the mission, I was immediately disappointed. What had appeared pure white and gleaming from a distance was little more than a long pile of cracked and crumbling adobes. Perhaps they had been whitewashed at one time, but now they were stained with age and in sad need of repair.

I headed to a small grape arbor just beyond the front gate and placed my two valises on a stone bench near an olive tree. Still clutching the smaller satchel, I headed tentatively into a tangle of overgrown plants and rosebushes that had turned to rosehips and barren sucker stalks. Farther out, nearly to the corner of the crumbling wall, a covered well stood beneath another olive tree.

A shallow, stagnant pond lay just behind the overgrown, dead garden. I skirted it and headed to what appeared to be the front of the sanctuary. It rose domelike above the rubble around it, a crooked wooden cross on its topmost point. The place had no doors, so I walked inside.

It took a few minutes for my eyes to become accustomed to the dim light. I sneezed three times and looked up to see the beams of dust dancing in bars of sunlight through the gaping holes in the dome roof.

Welsie True had told me of the mission's disrepair, its tragic history of earthquakes and storms. Still, I was not prepared for the sorry state of the place. Even the original tower bell lay on its side where it had fallen in the 1812 earthquake. Dozens were killed the morning it fell. I turned away, unable to bear the images that the broken, once-majestic bell brought to mind.

I turned to walk back to the tangled gardens, but then I heard footsteps approaching from the altar at the front of the church. I stepped into the shadows as a man passed me, his head down, his shoulders bent as if under a burden even greater than my own. He was slight of build, and even in the dim light his eyes seemed to hold great sorrow, his face lined with care.

My heart went out to him as he stepped into the glare of sunlight. He stopped, looking puzzled, glanced back into the sanctuary where I hid, then moved on.

He wore Western pants, frayed from hard labor, and a flannel shirt with rolled-up sleeves. A heavy silver cross, suspended from a chain around his neck, rested against his chest. He moved quietly, perhaps out of habit from years of wearing robes. I knew the man had to be Micheil.

I stepped cautiously into the sunlight and shaded my eyes, surprised I did not see him striding through the dead gardens or around the stagnant pond. Puzzled, I stood utterly still, trying to figure where he had gone. From the branches of a live oak tree above me, a mockingbird sang. Another fluttered along the branch above the first, calling out. A hummingbird buzzed near my cheeks, then stopped to take nectar from a nearly spent hollyhock stalk.

" 'Tis a lovely day," said a deep voice behind me. "Would you care for water, lass?"

Startled, I whirled. Standing near the covered well was the man in the flannel shirt. He held out a gourd with water spilling over the sides. It seemed like a long time ago since anyone had called me lass. Though I knew it was a manner of speech for this Irishman—and meant neither married or unmarried, young or old—still it caused my eyes to dampen.

I walked toward the well, cautiously, slowly, until I stood before him. "Tell me it is better than the water in the pond," I said, taking the ladle-gourd from him.

A smile crossed his haggard face, and he nodded. "This is the purest you will ever drink. Straight from a fresh spring hidden beneath the ground."

I drank and it was indeed sweet.

"You are a stranger here." It was not a question.

I nodded. "Yes."

He studied me, looking deep into my eyes as if to see my soul.

"I am Fairwyn March," I said finally.

"I thought as much," he said, his voice kind.

I tilted my head, puzzling. "Then you must be Micheil."

"I am indeed." He turned the crank at the side of the well, letting the wooden bucket drop once more into the water. When he had pulled it up again, I gave him the gourd and he filled it. I drank again, thirsty in this dry climate.

"Welsie True wrote that I needed to hurry to her," I said. "She said you would take me to her cottage."

"Aye, lass. I know she was expecting you any day." His brogue was thick and rolled from his tongue like cream. The sound of it reminded me somehow of the one who had filled my dreams when I was trembling with fear. Though there was no sense of rushing, musical waters or of streams of light. Only gentleness.

Micheil leaned against the base of the stone well, hooking one booted ankle across the other. "Welsie True knew everything about you, from your yellow hair to the near count of freckles on your nose. She knew that some called you Fairy lass, and she especially knew of your musical heart. She knew you well, and she loved you with utter joy."

I frowned, leaning forward. "You said 'knew,' like she might be gone." My words were barely a whisper.

He nodded to the stone bench beneath the grape arbor where

I had left my valises. "Let's sit for a while in the shade. I have much to tell you."

I trailed after him across the small courtyard to the place where I had entered. I settled onto one end of the short bench; he sat down at the other. For a moment he did not speak; he stared at his feet, his shoulders hunched and still.

"When Welsie wrote to you last, she was very ill," he said, looking up again. I realized I was wringing my hands and made an effort to quiet them. "She had been suffering for a long time."

"She spoke of her ailments," I said, knowing with dread fear what he was about to tell me. Tears blurred my vision. "I knew her time might be short."

"She desperately wanted to see you, but she also knew she hadn't much time. That's why she wrote to you at last. She also knew your life was troubled, and she understood you might soon need a sanctuary." He was silent for a moment and then added, "She died only a week ago." The grief in his face was raw, and I thought he might weep.

For a moment I couldn't speak. I stared across the courtyard, away from Micheil's sorrowful gaze, out to where the church lay in ruins. "Why did she not send for me sooner? Through the years, I begged her. Before I married Zeb, I wanted to come to her." I met his eyes again. "She thought I might need a sanctuary—then why didn't she offer it?"

"After your marriage, she thought you could better work out your problems with your husband if you remained with him. It wasn't her desire to separate you."

Thoughts of Zeb and our troubles brought on a wave of dizziness and nausea. Swallowing hard against the ache, I continued in a whisper. "She always wanted the best for me, God's best...but

I've never been able to fathom all she told me about his love and his forgiveness. I had hoped…" My voice trailed off. How could I selfishly think of what I needed from Welsie when I'd only begun to grieve over missing her presence, even from a distance, in my life? "Mostly I just wanted to see her." I met his gaze. "In the end she was my one true friend." Neither of us spoke for a moment. "I just wanted to meet her at last. Now I feel robbed of…so much. Robbed of *her*." My reasons still seemed selfish, which added shame to my grief.

Micheil looked worried. "Are you not feeling well, lass?"

I smiled at the name, so familiar from my childhood. Fairy lass, I'd been then, to Poppy and to Selah. Hearing it from Micheil brought me comfort somehow. "I'm weak from my journey," I said. "And hearing your news about Welsie…it's more than I can bear right now." Tears pricked the backs of my lids.

"She understood your circumstances," he said. "She made me promise to tell you all she'd planned to." The kindness in his expression was mixed with something I could not read. "She told me every detail so I that could tell you in her place."

"Can you tell me now?"

" 'Tis a lengthy tale," he said. "Are you certain you're feeling well enough to sit through it?"

A new wave of nausea swept over me. I brought my hand to my mouth, mortified I might be sick in front of him. I closed my eyes, breathing deeply.

"Lass, your face is the shade of the clouds in the heavens." His voice held alarm. "You must rest."

I nodded, my hand still covering my mouth.

"Have you eaten yet this morning?"

The thought of food brought a fresh pang of sickness. I closed my eyes and shook my head violently. "No food," I murmured from behind my hand. "Please, do not speak of food."

He was standing now, looking more alarmed than ever. "What can I do to help...should you lie yourself prone...or have some soup? Oh my, there I go again, talkin' of food. Oh, lass, tell me..." He looked helpless, but I was in no condition to see the humor in how he was wringing his hands.

I lifted myself heavily to stand near the bench, swaying a bit as I tried to regain my composure. I reached for it to steady myself. "The journey...Welsie's death..." I started to cry. "It's all just too much to bear."

"Let me take you back to your inn. I'll see you indoors and find someone to watch over you."

Biting my lip, I nodded. "Yes, please." I swallowed hard, struggling to keep my breakfast down, then managed to give him directions.

He left me at the bench and hurried off across the courtyard. After no more than ten minutes, he was back with a carriage hitched to a team of swaybacked grays. He settled me inside and drove me down to the small Spanish inn. There, he held me upright as he spoke to Mrs. Blum, the innkeeper. Then, one on either side, they helped me up the stairs to my room. I fell exhausted onto the bed, vaguely aware of Micheil's leaving and Mrs. Blum's bustling around the bedroom, closing the window shutters and covering me with a counterpane.

I woke to the sound of mission bells a few hours later. Feeling immensely better, I rose to open the shutters and peer out at the ocean, gulping in huge breaths of air. My room, on the third floor, was large and full of light. It had a single small iron bedstead near a window that overlooked the ocean, an oak rocking chair, and a writing table.

Still filled with weariness, I did no more than take supper with the other boarders and walk along the beach at sunset. I gathered shells and examined tide pools. I tried not to think of Welsie's death, but it was impossible. Until now, I hadn't realized the anchor her love had been for me.

Sorrow washed over me as the sun slipped into the pearl-gray waters of the ocean and darkness fell. Long ago Poppy said I needed to listen for God's song in the night, but right now in my soul's dark musing, I could find no music at all.

I had counted on Welsie True to help me find my way through the darkness, and now she was gone.

I did little more than sleep and eat for three days. Even the ocean lost its pull. Mrs. Blum told me that Micheil had stopped by twice a day to check on me, but arrived while I was sleeping.

On the fourth day, I felt stronger. I walked along the beach, studying my disappearing footsteps in the wet sand. The waves washed them away as if I'd never trod upon this beach, just as I had washed away the footprints of my life in Oak Hill. I thought of Zeb and wondered if he grieved for me. And what about Jeannie, the woman I thought was my friend?

Even those musings seemed minor compared to my own grieving over Welsie. It was time to find out what she'd meant to tell me. I touched my stomach and felt the barely perceptible swell of my growing baby, whose existence I could no longer deny. For this child, for our futures, I felt compelled to find out all Welsie True had planned to tell me about herself, about our family.

At dusk I pulled on my cape and walked to the livery next to the train station. I didn't expect Micheil to be at the mission this late, but I would leave a letter for him. I would return in the morning at ten. I couldn't wait any longer. I wanted to hear everything that Welsie had told Micheil.

As I settled into a hired buggy and flicked the reins, the mission bells rang in the distance, their tones low and mellow, echoing across the valley. It seemed they were calling me.

I rested one hand on my stomach, wondering again at the child's life growing inside me, and turned the horse onto the mission road.

Twenty-One

The last tone of the bells seemed to echo in my heart as I stepped through the entrance to San Juan Mission. The sun had long ago set, and a lacy mist off the ocean drifted among the olive and eucalyptus trees. The air was chilly, and I shivered as I passed the overgrown gardens. I glanced around the front courtyard then walked toward the arches at the north of the large complex. In the center was a fountain made of dark clay, with a small empty pool around it. Both were dry, and as I moved closer I could see they both were cracked and chipped with age.

I sat on the short wall that circled the pool and glanced at what must have been a plaza, with square rooms that might have once housed a smithy, a carpenter's shop, a candle factory, and a kitchen. Perhaps rooms for traveling monks walking from one mission to the next. I strolled to one of the long buildings and peeked through a window. An aged wooden bed was inside, and a table and chair, all appearing to be at least a century old.

I walked along the covered walkway outside the little rooms, peering inside each one. Darkness was now falling, and, because of the gathering mists, I strained to see across the courtyard past the fountain. I had almost rounded the entire square when I came upon the last in the row of cells. I inched along the wall until I reached the window. I peered in, surprised at what I could see in the dim light.

The room was swept clean, empty, except for a small corner table with a candlestick atop it, a large chair appearing to have been fashioned from tree branches, and, at the farthest wall, an ancient and scarred worktable hewn from a single massive tree. Tools hung neatly in a row above it.

They were familiar, so familiar. My heart quickened as I stepped inside and drew closer. I reached for the matches on the table beside the candlestick and lit the candle. I looked around in wonder. This square room was so like Poppy's woodworking shed out back of our cabin that it nearly took away my breath.

I pulled a small chisel from its hook and checked its sharpness. Someone had recently worked it on a stone. It was as sharp as Poppy's. Next I pulled down the first of three saws in various sizes. From one to the next I moved, the possibilities of using each filling my head. I pictured Poppy's big hands as he held the tools, carving and scooping and fashioning. I could almost see him bent over his work, his forehead smooth with pleasure in his work.

I reached for the pouch that hung at my neck, opened the drawstring, and pulled out his dulcimer drawings. Gently smoothing the torn pieces, I laid them on the worktable and moved them about until they were in the proper order. The figures were crudely fashioned, and some were so faint they were barely legible.

But there they were, sketches for the soundboard, the tail block, stock, frets, and fingerboard, even tiny drawings of the soundboard holes. Poppy's own designs: small meadow flowers and swallowtail butterflies.

All I needed was wood, blocks of hardwood, to make a dulcimer. Poppy mostly used sassafras, maple, and walnut, and I knew such trees might not grow in California. And they needed to be seasoned, not just hewn from a fresh limb or trunk. Poppy's instruments had an earthy sound, woody and fuzzy, instead of the bright twang of some. I wanted my instrument's tone to sound mellow and true like his.

Still puzzling over where I might find such wood, I refolded Poppy's drawings, extinguished the candle flame, and headed to the doorway. I glanced back at the carpenter's shop with pleasure once again before stepping outside and making my way back to the gate.

Darkness had fallen now, and the chilly mists hung low and dense. I shivered again, walked quickly across the compound. I had gone but a short distance, through the arches to the tangle of gardens by the stagnant pond, when I heard the murmuring of voices, or more accurately, one voice coming from the dilapidated sanctuary. I recognized the soft Irish brogue as Micheil's and made my way through the deep darkness to the entrance of the church and stepped inside.

I didn't want to disturb him, but only wanted to let him know I would meet him here, or wherever he might suggest, tomorrow morning.

Candles flickered on the dusty altar, casting macabre dancing shadows on the adobe walls. I still could not see anyone, but the voice was clearer now. I followed it down the center aisle. I had taken but a few steps when I realized I was listening to a prayer.

Embarrassed that I had intruded, I turned to leave. I held my breath when I heard him utter the word mercy. I hesitated, wanting to retreat now, but fearing my footsteps would be heard. So I remained still.

"Father God," Micheil said, his voice low, "I have prayed for it so oft I do not know if you are hearing or simply turning your back on me, your servant."

I halted midstep, statuelike, knowing I should leave but unwilling to move my feet.

"I have worked for you from the time I was a lad," he went on. "Done for others, served at your altar, performed the sacraments. Yet in all, Father, I have failed to know your mercy...forgiveness."

A great silence followed. I drew in my breath and held it, knowing surely even the sound of my breathing could be heard in this place.

"Who goes there?" the voice demanded. "Who is it?"

" 'Tis Fairwyn March, sir," I said.

There was a creaking of the altar rail, then a figure, almost ghostlike in the dim candlelight, rose at the front of the church. Micheil turned his head to look down the aisle, staring hard. His piercing gaze bored into me, even though he was several yards away.

"What are you doing here?" he said, his voice sounding weary. His countenance looked even wearier as he slowly moved toward me.

"I'm sorry I intruded," I said. "It wasn't my intent. I-I just wanted to find you, to—"

He held up his hand to quiet me, and his expression softened. " 'Tis not a meddling, Fairwyn. Not at all." His eyes were dark and troubled. "But you heard my supplication?"

I nodded, unable to lie about such a thing. "You seek the same from God as I am searching for." I hesitated. "Yet you were once a priest," I said.

"And you think I should know all the answers then?"

"No, of course not. Welsie told me about your exile, that your own troubles have been many."

He smiled, his face gentle. "It seems our Welsie True told us each about the other. About our struggles, our hearts' desires, our searching for God to reach down and lift us out of our present troubles."

I tilted my head, amazed at his words. "You search for God? Welsie didn't tell me anything except about your exile. And about your leaving the priesthood. She never said why."

"She didn't break confidences."

"Except in my case. She's told you everything about my family."

"There's a difference, lass. She told me about your family and hers. She has told me almost nothing else."

I waited for him to go on, to perhaps tell me how he came to this place. But he fell silent as we walked to the rear of the sanctuary. "You are looking well rested," he said.

When we stopped at the doorway, I said, "Could you tell me your story…why you plead for God's mercy?" Under ordinary circumstances, I knew the question would seem to presume on a relationship we didn't have, and I didn't expect him to do as I asked.

But he seemed to realize my question didn't come from idle curiosity. He searched my eyes. " 'Tis not an easy story for me to tell or for the hearer to hear."

I thought of my own sins, my need for mercy. I needed to know if there was hope for one like me. Perhaps his story might help me believe there was.

"What about your story, Fairwyn March?" he said gently. "Wouldn't it be more fitting for me to tell all Welsie wants you to know?"

"Perhaps I fear what she's asked you to tell."

He raised a brow and, surprisingly, guessed my thoughts. "Do you fear you cannot forgive her for not telling you sooner?"

My cheeks warmed, and I let my gaze drift away from his piercing look. "Everything comes back to that, it seems," I mused, without answering. "Forgiveness and mercy."

"And do you then, lass, have the ability to forgive easily?"

I pushed aside his question about Welsie and thought instead about Zeb and Jeannie. "Not easily," I said. "Sometimes not at all."

We stepped outside. The mist swirled around us, and in the distance drips fell from the tile roof. "When we find it hard to forgive others, or ourselves, 'tis difficult to believe in a God who so lavishly forgives us."

"You understand that about God, yet I just heard you begging for his mercy." I walked a few feet away from him, staring at the ghostlike trees and shivered.

His voice was barely audible when he spoke. "I am in greater need of God's forgiveness than anyone I know."

I turned, pulling my cloak tighter against the chill.

He was looking off in the distance. "It was during the famine. People were dying. Men took to the streets armed with pitchforks and scythes, going after those who had more than they did. I tried to calm them, but their families were dying. There was nothing I could do.

"One young man went mad with desperation in the dark of morning. His wee baby was starving to death, and he was desperate to get milk. Stole into the barn of an Englishman to get milk—not steal the cow—but merely to milk the old creature. I was trailing along after him, my robes flapping in the wind, trying to talk some sense into him. 'Ask the Englishman,' I said. 'Tell him your wee babe is starving. Appeal to his human nature.' But the young man wouldn't listen.

"Just as I feared would happen, the Englishman woke to the

sounds of us clattering around in his barn. He came after us with a gun, ready to pick off first one then the other, thinking of course that I was in the plot to steal his cow. The young da flew into a rage and lunged with his pitchfork, thinking to spear the man in two.

"The gun discharged, first in the air, then the Englishman took better aim. He pointed the gun straight at the young da's chest. Before I knew what I was up to, I grabbed the pitchfork from the boy, thinking merely to wrestle it away. In the confusion, the Englishman shot the boy, knocking him down wounded in the knee. He stepped closer and took aim again, this time straight at the young da's head."

When Micheil stopped speaking, his chest rose and fell with emotion, and the lines in his face seemed deeper. I thought he might weep, but after a time he continued. "The fork was still in my hands, and before the man could get off a shot, I flew at him, hoping to keep him from firing again."

His voice dropped to a whisper. "The gun went off and killed the boy sure as I'm standing here. And when I lunged, I speared the man through. I was the cause for both men dying that day... I slipped away in the gray drizzle of dawn, praying someone might come forward as a witness. No one did.

"The following day I confessed all to my bishop, and he ordered me to turn myself in to the British authorities.

"I was fearful that other lads in my village might take to arms in my defense, the troubles between the English and Irish would increase. More would be killed." He fell silent. "They were already starving. I didn't want to add to their troubles."

"So you came to California?"

"My bishop had planned to suggest to the English that I be exiled as punishment. He planned to suggest this abandoned mission.

"When I decided to run, I decided it would be to this place of self-exile." He heaved one long, troubled sigh. "I never lost my passion for my calling, though to this day, I still doubt my worthiness."

For several minutes, we stood without speaking, each lost in thought.

"I ceased being a priest the day I took another's life," Micheil said. "How could I kill God's child and call myself a man of God? I started praying for mercy, while doing every good work I could think of to earn his favor again."

"That's why you cared for Welsie True?"

"No, lass. That was done out of utter love. Even after I told her I was a murderer, she hired me to run Saddleback Ranch. She gave me the home I'd longed for all my life. My call to serve God, even before I became a priest, was out of a servant's heart. I found that I still had a desire to serve him by helping those less fortunate than I.

"Welsie True wasn't the only one God brought into my life." He looked back to the front of the church where the candles still flickered. "Perhaps I care for others in hopes that God will grant me mercy and rest at last.

"I asked for a sign, thinking if God understood, he would tell me. He would absolve me of my great sin. Had the young man lived, I would have thought that sign enough, but when I lunged with the pitchfork, the gun went off. I killed two men, not one." He fell silent for a moment. "Now, lass, when I look at my callused knees, I realize I'm still begging for mercy because I don't know what else to do."

Letting a silence stretch, we walked through the tangle of overgrown gardens. Tiny droplets from the mist had formed on my hair and cloak. "It came to me when I saw the carpenter's shop," I said, "that I need to make a dulcimer as sure as I need healing for my own soul." We stopped near the mosquito-clouded pond. The heavy air caused a stench to rise from the water, and I tried to wave away both the smell and the mosquitoes with one hand.

"You found our wood shop then?" he said. In the dim light I thought I saw a smile at the corner of his mouth.

"I did." I watched him, wondering how honest I could be with him. "As you're talking just now, it occurred to me that you're building something new here at the mission—more than just a new life for yourself. Welsie told me of the school you've begun for the Indian children, the food you give to those without homes and families, the restoration of the mission grounds." I paused, wondering how I could see God's work in his life—and be so blind to it in my own. "Though born of grief and sorrow and tragedy, you're building something good. Something good in your soul to diminish the bad."

"Just as your dulcimer will diminish the bad in yours?"

I drew in a quick breath. He didn't know my sins, but he had guessed my reasoning. "Yes," I said.

"It was Welsie's idea, you know," he said, "to turn a monk's cell into a woodworking room. She asked me to find the tools and wood just after she wrote to you to come. The only thing lacking is a solid block of the finest seasoned hardwood. And that we've taken care of as well…but I'll tell you later more about how and where."

"Seasoned hardwood?" I laughed. "She told you even that."

"She said sassafras is the best, especially if it's grown near Blackberry Mountain."

I sobered. "She was from the Great Smokies, wasn't she?"

"Aye, that she was, lass. And if you can stand to hear my Irish brogue get through another long tale, I promise I'll tell you Welsie's tomorrow." His expression was gentle. "I've gone on too long with my own, and I fear for another bout of ill health from you if I continue on tonight."

As eager as I was to hear it, I realized my fatigue had again taken its toll. I nodded in agreement. "Tomorrow morning then?"

"Good then. I'll come to the inn, and we'll talk again."

"I would like that." I hesitated. "Perhaps a stroll along the beach?" I thought of all the wondrous descriptions of the ocean in Welsie's letters and imagined that she would smile if she knew where we walked to speak of her.

He accompanied me to the buggy, and, with one hand, helped me step to the driver's seat. I seated myself, smoothed my skirts, and looked down at his upturned face.

"My husband accuses me of thinking of no one but myself. Tonight…listening to your story…" I frowned, trying to explain it even to myself. "I realized that others struggle to understand their faith, their hearts in relation to God, just as I do. My own pain lessened somehow. I don't feel quite so alone."

"That wasn't the reaction I was expecting, lass. I imagined you running the other way when you found out I killed two men."

"It was wrong to press you to tell me your secrets. And if it hadn't been for Welsie as the bridge between us, I think I wouldn't have asked." I fell quiet, looking at the calm in his lined face, the gentleness in his eyes that had drawn me from the first. "You gave me a gift tonight, Micheil. By telling me, I mean. A gift that has brought a small measure of quiet to my troubled soul."

" 'Tis the first time anyone has thanked me in such a way for my gift o' gab," he said. He laughed then, a rolling, rumbling sound, surprisingly strong for such a slight man. He stepped back from the buggy as I lifted the reins.

"I'll see you in the morning then," I said with a smile and a nod. I chirked to the horse to start.

We had gone only a yard or two when he called after me. "About your dulcimer..." he said. "Will you be staying long enough to finish it?"

I slowed the horse. "As soon as I get that block of hardwood, I'll start work."

"You plan to remain here then?" he said, now walking alongside the buggy. "Long enough to make a dulcimer?"

My smiled faded. How could I tell him I couldn't think beyond tomorrow to consider the day after, next week, let alone next year? That I didn't know where to go or what to do?

Now it wasn't just me I had to care about. Now it was *us*, my baby and me. A little one who would need me, depend on me. I stared at Micheil as my tomorrows, my fears, settled heavy on my shoulders as surely as the mists did on the road.

He wore a puzzled look as I attempted a lighthearted wave good-bye, and then turned the horse down the mission road, leaving Micheil standing beside the road beneath an ancient oak, watching me.

"I cannot think beyond tomorrow, my friend," I called back to him. "Until then..."

Twenty-Two

Micheil arrived the following morning as the sun rose high in a cloudless sky. I had just started down the wooden stairs leading to the wet sand when he called out to me.

" 'Tis a lovely day for a walk on the beach," he said.

I turned and waited for him to join me. A light breeze lifted his hair from his forehead. He caught my hand, helping me step from the bottom stair onto the sand, then he released it when we sat down to remove our shoes.

The wet sand was cold to my toes and threatened to disappear beneath my feet as the water ran around them. I grinned with delight, breathing in the scent of the salt air, the sounds of the gulls and pelicans.

"I've planned a surprise for you today," he said after we'd walked a stretch of the beach. "A place you'll be taken with, lass."

A place? I stopped with a frown. The thought of travel caused my delicate stomach to lurch a bit. "Is it far?"

"Just a ways up the beach—over there, toward the cliffs." He gestured north. "We'll need to take my wagon." I questioned him with a look. "I've brought it from Saddleback. 'Tis time to pick up a shipment of supplies."

I laughed, looking up at him in wonder. It seemed the man moved smoothly from mission caretaker to ranch overseer without so much as a ripple of trouble. "I'd like to see Saddleback. Welsie told me all about it, the cattle, the wide open spaces."

"That will be our second trip—if you're up to it, lass. First I'll take you by the cottage. That was to be my surprise." He grinned. "She wanted you to see it before anything else."

The thought pleased me. "She did?"

He led me to a formation of stout sandstone outcroppings and brushed off a flat, smooth rock. I sat down, and he sat beside me, both of us facing the breaking waves.

"Everything of Welsie's is yours," he said, staring out at the surf. Above us a flock of gulls cartwheeled and cried, accompanied by the sounds of lapping waves.

I frowned and turned to him in disbelief. "She never said as much."

"When she took sick, she made out a new will, leaving everything to you."

"But it's her—her friendship and love—I want. Not her ocean cottage or her beloved Saddleback or anything else." My voice dropped to a whisper as the weight of my loss pressed down on my heart. "I really don't want anything else."

"Are you certain, lass, that it's your grief that's causing such words?" When I didn't answer, he went on. "Welsie thought you might be angry she never answered your deepest questions."

I focused on the waves while fresh grief flowed through me. Grief over all I had missed because of secrets kept, grief over her premature death. "I loved her, and there's nothing to forgive. I just feel, well, cheated."

"You'll understand when you hear her story, lass." He was watching me intently. "And if there is any resentment toward her in your heart, you must let it go. Not for Welsie's sake. But for your own." When I didn't speak, he went on. "Without giving up such feelings you can't grieve properly." His voice dropped, and it was almost tender when he spoke again. "Whether it's because of physical death or that of a broken relationship."

I shook my head, tears still blurring my vision. But with his reminder, it was the broken relationship with Zeb I thought about, not Welsie's death.

"She told me a great deal about you, especially your connection to her. You have not grieved properly since I told you she died."

"I can't," I said, but my voice broke, and I began to cry.

Micheil moved closer and awkwardly wrapped a thin arm around my shoulders. I wept into his soft flannel shirt. I cried until I couldn't cry any more. For Welsie, for Poppy, for Zeb. For lost friendships and loves. For mistakes and sorrow. Finally, I pulled back, almost embarrassed that I had cried so in this man's arms.

"I'm sorry," I murmured and wiped at my tears with my fingers. I looked away until I could stop hiccuping and breathe again. He handed me his handkerchief, and I buried my face in it. "I want to go to her cottage now," I said finally. "I would like to see where she lived."

" 'Tis nearer than you might expect."

I walked slightly ahead of him as we ascended the stairs leading to the road. He led me around the inn to the farm wagon parked in front. A white mare nickered a soft greeting. Micheil stopped briefly to rub the velvet between her eyes and murmur a gentle word, before helping me into the wagon. I climbed up onto the bench seat. Micheil took his place beside me, chirked to the horse, and flicked the reins.

We headed down a narrow dirt road by the ocean. After a few

minutes he turned the mare to the north along a wider road. Several buckboards and carriages passed us as we drove to a plateau atop a steep cliff. Rounding a corner, we passed through a grove of live oaks and eucalyptus trees and halted in front of a small cottage.

Still seated in the wagon, I looked up and down the dusty road in wonder. Flanking it were rows of adobe houses, their red roofs bright, their whitewashed walls gleaming in the sun. I hadn't ever lived within view of neighbors, certainly not on Blackberry Mountain, not even in Oak Hill. Yet here, mothers tended little ones in prams or in arms, neighbors chatted across picket fences, and children seemed to spill from the yards into the streets with their hoops and sticks, their laughter carrying on the ocean breeze.

In wonder I turned again to Welsie's cottage, set slightly apart from the others, on the hillside facing the ocean. The foliage around the small house was lush and bright, a bougainvillea covering one end of the roof, cascading across the shingled covering of a nearby well, and pepper and willow tree branches woven together above the other side of the house. A wild froth of blossoms flanked the brick walkway leading to the front door.

"They're mine," I whispered, mostly to myself. "Exactly the same." A few of the neighborhood children had walked to the road where Micheil had tied the mare. They stood silent, watchful, as Micheil and I stepped through the gate.

Micheil looked at me with a puzzled expression as he helped me from the wagon.

"My garden in Oak Hill," I said, still frowning. "Welsie planted everything I told her was in my garden, the same order and patterns." It was true, but with her illness, her gardening had obviously ceased. The whole array was tangled and wild; milkweed and dandelions and dead grasses sprouted between the growth of cultured plants and flowers.

I ambled slowly along the pathway. "It's all here," I said. "Though it's hard to make them out among the overgrowth and weeds, she planted clumps of daisies here, rows of irises there. Pink and white tea roses. Even cascades of rosemary flowing down from tall, round urns along the path." I turned and smiled at him.

"She thought you the cleverest lass on earth." His smile was full of sorrow. "A grandmother's pride, to be sure."

I stopped dead still, wondering if I'd heard him right.

He watched me, knowing, understanding. "Welsie True was your grandmother."

"My grandmother…"

"Aye, lass. One of the many things she wanted to tell you in person."

I reached for the edge of a nearby urn to steady myself, letting the words sink in. *My grandmother.*

I turned my back to him then, wanting to lose myself in thought. I walked through the roses, examining each, from bud to full bloom. Micheil stood waiting in the shade of a pepper tree, as if knowing that my time of understanding Welsie True and who she was to me was a solitary walk into the depths of my heart. I was grateful for his silence. For several minutes I took in everything about the garden, picturing my grandmother on her knees working there, weeding and watering. Tamping the tender roots of pansies and daisies and bleeding heart ferns.

I turned to him after a few minutes of reverie. "What did she look like…my grandmother?"

"Ah, she had the fiery spirit of a flame-haired lass, though hers had long ago faded. There was something about her face that seems so like yours."

I tilted my head away from him at that, surprised at my pleasure. "In what way?"

"A turn of your round cheek, maybe. Or perhaps it's your eyes—both the color of the heavens on a sunny day. Her hair was snow white, but she told me when she was a lass her da said it was as crimson as a winter sunset."

I smiled with pleasure at the thought.

He nodded. "And curly as spring tendrils on a grapevine."

My grin widened. "Tendrils?"

"Just like yours. She said when she was a lass her nose freckled from her love of the sun—something her momma warned her against. Where most young women wore poke bonnets and such to shade their faces, she preferred to be bareheaded." He glanced toward the ocean. "One reason living in California came to mean everything to her. She took great pleasure in being right here, didn't want anything to hide the sunlight."

"Can we go inside?" I looked toward the cottage, wondering what lay on the other side, wondering what other mysteries about Welsie True would finally be revealed.

"Aye, lass." He walked up the brick walk to the paneled white Dutch door, unlocked it, and then stood aside so I could enter.

I stepped across the threshold and squinted against the bright light that poured through the windows lining the opposite wall. The ocean sparkled in the distance. A latticework gazebo stood squat and friendly to one side. I stepped close to the windows and listened to the faint crashing of the waves below.

A faint scent of violets seemed to hover near, or maybe it was the fragrance from the flower garden outside. I recognized the room, with its upholstered sofa and faded wedding-ring quilt that lay folded across the back, the scatter of crocheted pillows, the straight-backed rocker and petit point footstool. Not because I had seen it—or anything like it—before. I knew it because I knew my grandmother's heart.

I had known it all along, I realized. I knew her heart because it was so like mine.

Then I noticed the oval-framed painting on the wall. It was of a child, a little boy, maybe three or four years old. He had a squared-off haircut and was sitting on a wooden stool, one foot folded underneath him, the other hanging down, not quite touching the floor.

A solemn child, he seemed to be staring into my eyes.

"Your father," Micheil said, slightly behind me.

I touched the rounded glass that covered the canvas, a sorrow of loss mixed with joy of discovery boring into my soul. "What was his name?"

"Daniel."

"Daniel," I breathed and traced my fingers on the glass over his tiny hands. "Daniel True."

"Aye, lass. 'Tis your da."

"Tell me everything," I whispered, still looking into my father's little-boy eyes. "Tell me what happened."

Micheil took my elbow and led me gently back through the door and into the garden. He guided me to a small wooden table and two chairs under the shade of the pepper tree. "What I have to tell you will take awhile, and 'tis not always an easy tale to hear. For it will surely break your heart."

I sat opposite him and nodded for him to begin.

" 'Twas a spring day in fifty-five when they met," he said, "the young Daniel True and his bride-to-be, Fairwyn Enid March. They were no more than children, at least that is how it seemed to your Poppy and Granny Nana and to Welsie True." He paused, looking deep into my eyes, almost as if measuring how ready I was to hear the story.

"Go on," I said.

" 'Tis a tale of tragedy," he said, and, looking off across the valley where the mission lay, he began to tell me the story.

Twenty-Three

"Your grandmother told me her story many different times, now and again seeming to relive the events. Sometimes, lass, she wept as she spoke, other times she had to stop altogether only to continue another day. Toward the end, she made me retell what she'd said, making certain I had it right."

"Tell me everything," I said. "Every detail."

He settled back, a faraway look in his eyes saying he was somehow connected to the story he was about to tell. "Well, it seems the Trues and the Marches had long been friends in the Old Country," Micheil said. "They even sailed from Wales on the same ship, first settling in Virginia for a time, then moving on across the Appalachian Mountains into the hills and hollows around Sycamore Creek and Blackberry Mountain."

"The first March to come here was my great-great-grandfather," I said, remembering the tales Poppy had told when I was a child.

"It was the next generation that had a feud over land. Your granddaddy's father—"

"Anwar," I filled in.

"Yes, Anwar March, broke with the Trues after a fight with a man named Fagan True. Each swore to kill the other if they set foot on the other's land. Anwar had quite a temper, just as Fagan did. Welsie said they were enough alike to be brothers. Cain and Abel, she said."

"The only True I ever heard of was Welsie, and that was her married name."

"That's because Anwar found a way to run all the Trues off their land long before even your grandfather was born."

"How'd he do that?"

"There was a fight one night after both Anwar and Fagan were liquored up. Fagan was horsing around—or so it was said—with a rifle, threatening, but meaning no real harm. The gun went off and killed Anwar's young brother. As you can imagine, it nearly broke the hearts of Anwar and his family.

"They swore they'd run every True man, woman, and child off Blackberry Mountain and out of Sycamore Creek altogether. They got themselves up a posse one night and burnt seven cabins, going from one to the other. Those poor families had nothing to do with Fagan's drunken killing, but they all suffered. The women talked the men out of fighting back, and one by one the families left your valley for other parts. Scattered around the mountains, Welsie True told me. Her family ended up in Sugar Creek, about a hundred miles from where you lived."

"Poppy never said a word about any of this."

"He wouldn't. But according to Welsie, the bitterness ran deep on both sides."

"How did her son meet my momma if the families were so bitter against each other?"

"It was just after the Gold Rush here in California that Welsie and her son decided to head west. Her husband, John, your grand-father, had just died, and adventurer that she was, she wanted to leave the bitterness and closed surroundings of the mountains.

"So she and Daniel packed up their belongings in a wagon and headed out. Sycamore Creek was on the way, and she wanted to see her sister Selah for the last time."

I frowned, leaning forward. "How was it that Selah ended up marrying into our neck of the woods?"

Micheil laughed. "I've never met her, but apparently she's not one to be told what she can or cannot do."

"I know her well. Everything you say is right. And she didn't marry a March."

"That's what Welsie said. So her sins were not as grievous as your father and mother's."

My smile faded. "They did the unthinkable."

"Welsie and Daniel stopped for a visit with Selah. The first night they arrived your momma, Fairwyn Enid, came up the hill to bring Selah some preserves she had just helped put up." He paused as if gathering his thoughts. "She was beautiful, her cheeks the hue of peaches, Welsie said, her skin the hue of Devonshire cream. And her spirit held just as much beauty. She was filled with love for God, for others, for all mankind. A passionate kind of love. She had never heard of the feud with the Trues, and even if she had, she would have paid it no mind. She was a fiery one, according to Welsie.

"And of course, young Daniel took one look and fell in love. Deeply in love. And she with him. By the time Welsie was ready to move on—and time was growing short for making the trip by fall—Daniel no longer wanted to leave.

"He asked Fairwyn Enid to marry him, and she said yes. When she asked your grandfather, however, the answer was a resounding no.

"The young couple was not to be dissuaded. They went ahead and planned for their future. Daniel had no interest in the California gold fields. He was called to preach, he said. And together the two of them planned to head west together—with or without their families' blessings—and find themselves a little church. Or build one if they couldn't find one ready-made. They would raise their family and love others with great passion.

"Welsie said the two of them seemed made for each other. They had three favorite Bible scriptures they went by: the first, love the Lord your God with all your heart, mind, and spirit; the second, love others as you love yourself."

Micheil stopped, his eyes damp as if treasuring something special Welsie had told him.

"And the third?" I prompted.

"They figured out that another scripture from Zephaniah 3:17 put together with the first two made all the sense in the world for how a child of God should live his life. 'The LORD thy God in the midst of thee is mighty; he will save, he will rejoice over thee with joy; he will rest in his love, he will joy over thee with singing.' "

He leaned closer, earnestly. "This young couple thought that if God required them to love others as he did, that meant loving others with great joy, even singing over them with love.

"Welsie wept each time she talked about this young couple. They said there would be no hellfire and damnation in their preaching. They felt called to love others into God's kingdom."

I found my own eyes damp as I thought about my momma and da, the sorrow at what had happened to them in the end. I wondered how God could have allowed such tragedy to strike. I almost did not want to ask what happened next.

"They decided that your grandfather's bitterness shouldn't be allowed to keep them apart. They prayed about their direction, what path they should take. Together they spoke again to Fairwyn Enid's father and mother, trying to reason with them.

"Your Poppy said she could leave but she was no longer any daughter of his."

I drew in my breath, surprised. "So she did go with him."

"Aye. They rode out—Welsie True, her boy, Daniel, and your momma, Fairwyn Enid March. They made it only as far as the wagontrain camp on the western side of the mountains—maybe a week's ride from Sycamore Creek. The first night they arrived they asked the reverend who was traveling with the train to marry them. The whole encampment witnessed their vows, and a party commenced." He laughed. "I wish you could have heard Welsie tell of it. There was music and laughter and dancing to beat the band. People they had never seen before helped them celebrate.

"Of course, with the wagon train readying for the grand journey, everyone was in high spirits anyway.

"They camped at that spot for a week or ten days, Welsie recollected. They had just pulled out when a wild posse from the mountains overtook the train and stopped it.

I caught my hand to my mouth. "Poppy?"

"Aye, 'twas him indeed, with every shirttail cousin named March he could gather. He demanded your momma come home with him."

"Did she agree?" I was still trying to figure out the lone grave on Blackberry Mountain.

"Oh no. Welsie said your momma ran out to her da, crying and carrying on, pleading with him to let her go. Your Poppy saw his chance. While she was standing there, looking up and crying and praying, he had one of the ruffians with him grab her and haul her onto his horse.

"At that, young Daniel roared from their wagon with a rifle in his hand. He pointed it at your Poppy's chest and demanded he let

Fairwyn Enid go. Of course, your momma now was scared and crying harder than ever. Both sides—the wagon company and the posse—were getting nervous.

"Daniel wasn't going to take no for an answer. He raised his rifle as if to shoot, all the while demanding that Fairwyn Enid be set upon the ground at once. One of the others in the posse got reckless, took aim, and fired. The ball killed your da on the spot. Later it was found that there was no ammunition in Daniel's rifle at all. He was a peace lovin' man. But even so he wasn't about to let your momma be taken from him. He'd hoped the bluff would be sufficient.

"Your Momma screamed, but the posse was in a hurry to get out of there before the wagon captain commanded his men to fire. So she never got to say good-bye to her new husband."

I was crying now, a sorrow too deep to comprehend overtaking me. "But Poppy never said anything about all this. I never knew."

"Welsie wasn't surprised. When Selah wrote that Fairwyn Enid had died bearing her granddaughter, Welsie was so troubled she couldn't sleep for weeks. She didn't want you to grow up in the midst of the bitterness of those mountains. She wrote that she wanted to raise you as her own, thinking maybe because of the True blood running through your veins, your Poppy might agree.

"But he had decided to erase all memory of your father. Pretend he didn't exist. He wanted to raise you to be dependent on him."

"He loved me," I said, though my voice sounded small and uncertain. "I know he did. And after Granny Nana died, he tried to be both mother and father. He taught me his music..." My voice trailed off. I tried to make sense of the man I knew compared to the man in this tale.

I was startled when Micheil reached across the table and put his hand over mine. "Aye, lass. He did love you. You must believe that." He fell silent for a moment, and around us were only the sounds of the bees working Welsie True's spent roses.

After a time he spoke again. "Welsie True wrote to her sister Selah who had remained on good terms with your Poppy. She asked Selah to intervene. Your granddaddy agreed to letter writing. That was all. He wanted you to have an education, and because there were no schoolhouses near Blackberry Mountain, he finally gave his consent." He paused. "There was one condition."

I already knew. "Welsie True couldn't reveal what happened."

Micheil nodded his head slowly. "Or her relationship to you. She gave her word."

"What about after Poppy died?"

"She knew of your love for him. You wrote of him constantly, how he taught you music, the love and respect he gave you." He patted my hand, then withdrew his. "Can you see why she did not want to destroy the relationship, lass?"

I swallowed hard and looked away from Micheil, letting my gaze drift to my grandmother's garden. "I understand."

"It was only after she understood your desperate circumstances with Zebulon Deforest that she began having second thoughts. By then, she was aware that you would think she had deserted, betrayed you—"

"Yes, there were times…" I nodded slowly. "So many disappointments when she didn't acknowledge my questions. That's especially hard for a child. It seemed no one understood my need to know about my mother and father. Now I must wonder why she didn't insist to Poppy—or perhaps enlist Selah's help—to convince him I needed to know the truth."

"Welsie True had flaws," Micheil said gently. "She made mistakes, just like the rest of us. In the end, when she realized she was dying, she knew she'd done wrong by you."

"I loved her even so," I said.

He gave me a kind smile. "Aye. She knew that about you. She knew your heart."

Twenty-Four

I rose the next morning at dawn, stopped by the inn kitchen for a hurried breakfast of egg toast and milk, then found a winding path up the hillside at the north of the inn. I hoped it would lead to the plateau and my grandmother's cottage. It clung to the edge of the cliff, which was covered with yellow-and-pink ice plant on the ocean side and a row of slender eucalyptus trees on the other. I walked slowly to keep myself from tiring, knowing that fatigue led to the lightheaded dizziness and sick stomach I'd experienced lately.

My spirits lifted as I let myself through the gate. I circled the house to find a small shed filled with pots, spades, and rakes. On a potting table a pair of work gloves lay beside a copper watering can. I smiled to see the tools spread out, likely just as my grandmother had left them.

With my tools beside me, I knelt in Grandmother Welsie's garden, slipped on the gardening gloves, and set about pulling weeds. The soil was drier than I expected, since moist loamy Tennessee and damp, red clay North Carolina soils were all I knew. I brushed off my hands and stood to work the hoe.

The sun was rising now and beat down on my shoulders and head. I lifted my face to it and closed my eyes, aware only of birdsong, sea air, and the warm sun. Here, in a place so very different from Sycamore Creek or Oak Hill, I could pretend my old life did not exist. Then I laughed, though without mirth. If this were true—this pretending my old life was over—then why did it wait like an enemy at the dark edges of my mind?

I stopped and knelt again to pull some brush I had just loosened with the hoe and considered how the simple act of gardening seemed to also weed heartaches and ill thoughts from my mind. I had been too long riding trains, walking sand dunes, and wading in the waves. It was time to get to work.

I reached for a stubborn milkweed and gave it a hard yank, smiling as it gave way, roots and all.

"'Tis a happy thought you must be having," said a voice behind me.

I looked up to see Micheil standing at the garden gate. The early morning sun slanted into his face, erasing the shadows beneath his eyes. He looked younger, the weary lines in his face less pronounced.

I stood and brushed off my hands. He took in the small pile of weeds beside me and smiled. "You've wasted no time taking over where Welsie True left off."

"It was the first thought in my head this morning. I knew how it would please my…my grandmother to have her garden put in order."

He laughed, that deep rumbling sound that caused me to smile again. He scanned the bed I was working in and rolled up his sleeves. "Could you use some help then, lass?"

"Aye," I said, and he laughed.

I knelt beside him, and for several minutes we worked in silence. Only an occasional burst of birdsong broke into the quiet of the morning. That and the soft sounds of metal slicing into the soil.

"Damp ground might make our task easier," he said while

tugging a stubborn, thick-stemmed milkweed. The stalk broke, oozing thick white milk into his hands. "Aye, 'tis water we need." He rose and went to the water well, almost hidden behind the thick cascade of bougainvillea hanging from the side of the cottage roof. I followed with the watering can.

He drew water with the well's oak bucket, washed his hands with a portion, then poured the rest into the watering can. I carried it to the garden and sprinkled the contents across the ground. We fetched and watered until the flower bed was moist.

For an hour we weeded and dug and transplanted clumps of flowers from one bed to another. And without thought, I'd begun to hum, then sing...

Go tell Aunt Rhody, go tell Aunt Rhody,
Go tell Aunt Rhody, the old gray goose is dead...

Micheil glanced over at me with a grin. " 'Tis the loveliest voice I've heard since leaving Ireland." Then he held up a hand and shook his head. "I correct myself. 'Tis lovelier even than that. You, dear Fairwyn March, put even the finest of my homeland's voices to shame."

My grin widened. " 'Tis a fact?"

" 'Tis," he said, walking closer. "Please, keep singing."

The one that she's been a savin'
To make a feather bed...

He threw back his head and laughed out loud, a sound that seemed to roll through the garden, bringing life and light in its wake. It was contagious, and I laughed with him.

"How about you?" I gave him a teasing look. "If Ireland has such fine voices, surely you're one of them."

"Aye, my lass," he said while watching me with merry eyes, "you have no idea what you've just asked. Askin' an Irishman to sing is like askin' him to breathe. 'Tis my nature."

I knew his meaning. "Teach me your songs, and we'll sing together while we work."

In less than a heartbeat he began to sing in a heavy brogue,

By Killarney's lakes and fells,
Emerald Isles and winding bays,

I stopped working, rocked back on my heels, and watched as he pulled out a patch of dried grass, singing all the while. He seemed unaware of anything but his music. I understood that about him.

He grinned at me suddenly, eyebrows lifted. "Join me now, will you?"

He started the same verse again, and I hummed along. By the time he got to "Angels fold their wings and rest," I was carrying on word for word.

His booming voice took wing again on the second verse, and I fell quiet, letting him sing alone. His expression softened when he reached the final words.

Beauty's home, Killarney,
Ever fair Killarney.

"Killarney is your home?" I asked when he was finished.

"How did you know?" he said with a sad laugh.

"Your voice caught a wee bit when you got to 'beauty's home.' "

"Aye." He yanked on another milkweed, sat back on his haunches, and shaded his eyes as he looked across at me. "Micheil Grady Gilvarry from Killarney."

I had never thought to ask Welsie for Micheil's family name. "Gilvarry," I mused. "Micheil Gilvarry."

"And Fairwyn March," he mused. " 'Tis not your mountains I think of when I hear it, but the mists and lights across the hills and valleys of Wales."

I smiled then. "Fairlight is its meaning. Taken from a village in Wales."

"I have heard of it."

I pulled out a handful of dried grass beneath a woody-stemmed rosebush. He started singing about Killarney again, and I joined him, picking up the words as I could.

The sun was high when Micheil finally stood, grinned down at me, and reached for my hand to help me up. With an exaggerated groan I stood and leaned against the hoe handle, rubbing my side. My backed ached, but I felt better than I had in weeks.

"Welsie True loved this garden," Micheil said. I followed his gaze, noticing the play of light on the adobe walls beneath the wide spread of the pepper tree. The wall shadows danced in its breeze.

"It's almost as if she's here." I laughed. "The joy of her spirit, I think, spills across this place. Its color, the birdsong, the sound of the surf in the distance." I drew in a deep breath, closing my eyes, imagining her here, just as I had a dozen times during the morning. "Where is she buried?" It hadn't occurred to me to ask until now. "I would like to visit her grave."

"She is buried behind a small chapel near the mission grounds." He studied my face. "I'll take you there. Now, if you'd like."

"Thank you, but not today." I tired too easily it seemed these days, and after the morning's work, I knew I must rest. "I noticed some chairs in the back. Out near the gazebo. I would like to sit there for a spell, watch the ocean, rest a bit."

He nodded, carefully studying my face. "And how about some tea while you're resting?" I must have looked puzzled, because he laughed lightly and added, "You sit, lass. I know where my friend kept her tea. I'll brew you a hot cup of Irish tea. It will fix whatever ails you."

"Nothing ails me," I said too quickly, and then I blushed. "Absolutely nothing."

"I only meant if you were tired, lass, 'twould give you a pick-me-up. That's all."

As I made myself cozy in the shade beneath the gazebo, I heard Micheil whistling as he worked in my grandmother's kitchen. Pots and pans banged, the handle on the water pump squeaked, and the damper on the woodstove clanged as he lit a fire. I couldn't stop smiling at the trouble he was going to just to fix me a cup of tea.

A half-hour later he emerged, looking stricken.

"Whatever is the matter?" I imagined the kitchen was on fire.

"I made you a lovely spot of tea, lass. But any good Irishman knows tea must have cream. There's not a cow within a half-mile."

I reached for the mug of dark steaming liquid. "Did you find sugar...or honey?"

"Oh yes. Plenty."

"Then that's all I require. Truly, that's how I like it best."

"I'll be happy to search for a cow...or even a goat," he said, sitting down beside me. "For certain I'll be bringing you some from Saddleback tomorrow."

I took a sip. "Truly the best tea I've ever had," I said, meaning it. I couldn't remember when someone had offered me such a self-less gift of caring. Quick tears stung my eyes, and I looked out to the surf so that he wouldn't notice.

"Thank you for your friendship," I said after a few minutes. "I have need of a friend."

"Aye, lass. I understand better than you think."

I wanted to tell him the truth about me. I needed to tell him. Perhaps I just needed to tell anyone at all. He took a sip of tea from his own cup, and I stared at his careworn profile for a moment, wondering if I dared to tell him what I'd done. He must have felt my intense gaze, for he turned, looking puzzled.

"I am considered dead," I blurted. I waited for his expression to turn to alarm. But the alarm didn't come. "I am living a lie," I added, still watching him intently. I might have just told him the day was lovely, for all the reaction I got. "I let everyone at home believe I was killed in a train wreck."

His face was a portrait of strength. Still he didn't speak.

"I ran away from my troubles," I said. When he didn't answer, I stumbled on. "I found my husband with—" My eyes filled, and I looked away, unable to finish. I drew in a breath and closed my eyes to regain my composure. "With a friend," I finally managed.

Micheil frowned, a glow of anger slowly replacing the compassion. "He did such a thing to you."

"We had problems. But I thought…oh, I don't know what I thought, maybe that we might grow to love each other again." Fresh tears welled. I swiped at them, but they spilled down my cheeks. "I'm not even certain that's what I wanted."

Micheil handed me his handkerchief. My spilled tears were becoming a pattern. I blew my nose. "Maybe it was my fault. My dark spells, my unhappiness. Maybe I drove him away." I shrugged. "I don't know. And now I don't care."

His voice was kind. "He once loved you, lass?"

I bit my lip and looked down at my shoes. "He swore he always did…has," I finally whispered. "He swears it even now."

"Fairwyn?"

I looked up.

" 'Tis feelings of guilt that rack you so?"

"Maybe I shouldn't have run off, but I'm glad I did. Maybe I shouldn't have let everyone believe me dead, but I'm glad I did that, too. I wouldn't change any of it even if I could. No feelings of guilt," I insisted, my cheeks warming with the lie.

"Tell me what happened." He leaned back into the corner of the bench, his arms folded across his chest, his legs stretched out, one ankle hooked over the other. He seemed to have all the time in the world to listen.

"There was a terrible storm the day I left. The train to Dover Town derailed over a bridge. Many died. Others were swept downstream and listed as missing. By now, presumed dead."

"You're still considered one of them?" He watched me with that same look of understanding I'd seen earlier.

I leaned forward, my voice dropping. "My husband once took me to an asylum." I paused, trying to stop my tears. "It was right after my grandfather died, and a darkness had settled into my heart. I feared my husband didn't love me, and I knew I didn't love him. I…was afraid he would put me away." I halted, realizing I was telling too much of my heartache. "All of this…all the ugliness, I'd planned to tell Wel—my grandmother. To seek her help, her counsel."

"You said you need a friend," he said gently. "I'm here. You can tell me." His expression urged me to go on.

"My greatest fear is facing my own darkness. And if I entered *that* place inside where the darkness lives, it might hold me prisoner forever."

"Oh, lass, how sorry I am for your deep sorrow," he said, leaning forward. I thought he might touch my hand, but he did not. "For the pain you've endured."

"I can't ever go home again. If I am found out, my husband will have me committed."

He studied the sea, took a sip of tea, and kept his eyes on the horizon. For a moment I thought he hadn't heard me, and I started to speak again. "I can't—"

"You must," he said, turning to me again. "You must go back and face him," he said.

"I cannot." To make my point clearer, I added, "Any more than you can return to Ireland."

He gave me a sharp look, then smiled. "For some time now I've known I will return someday."

"You will face murder charges. Imprisonment...or death."

"Aye. Just as you will face the possibility of life in an asylum."

"Then neither of us can go," I said decisively. I stood and brushed off my hands. "That's all there is to it. The cost is too great."

He stood with me. "The cost might be greater if we don't get rid of our demons."

"It can't be."

" 'Tis, lass. For I know about the darkness that plagues you in the night."

I thought I might not breathe. "You know?"

" 'Tis the truth that will set us both free."

"Mine began long before I left Zeb, long before I lied about dying in the river."

He looked thoughtful. "You said you don't love your husband. Is that the source of the darkness?"

"I thought I loved him," I argued. "When he asked to marry me, I was the happiest woman on this earth. But through the years…I came to see that maybe what I felt for him wasn't love at all."

"Yours is a greater betrayal than his then?"

"He's told me as much."

"Love ebbs and flows, lass. Sometimes it's a great passion. Other times it's calm, like a lake on a sunny day. Don't be judging yourself too harshly or even figuring you can't go home again."

I stared at him. "I cannot," I said, my voice little more than a breath. "I will not."

There was no condemnation in his face, only deep caring borne on the wings of understanding and new friendship. "How about you, Micheil," I said. "When did your darkness start?"

"The day I left the priesthood," he said. He stood with a weary smile. "Would you care for more tea, lass?"

"Please," I said. I watched him return to the house, noticing again the sad slope of his shoulders.

Twenty-Five

Micheil drove me to the inn to collect my things, and I moved into the cottage as the late afternoon shadows stretched across the landscape. The sun hung like a brilliant ball over the ocean, now and then dipping beneath a bank of summer clouds and turning them orange and red and pink, the choppy waves reflecting the same hues.

After Micheil left, I strolled around to the gazebo where we'd earlier taken our tea. A cool wind whipped from the ocean as I stepped closer to the weathered picket fence that bordered my grandmother's land and protected walkers from the sheer drop on the other side.

I pictured Grandmother Welsie sitting in the gazebo, writing paper in her lap, pen in her hand, as she wrote to me. I thought of her longing to know me, her only granddaughter, her only connection with the son she adored. I walked to the heavy weathered chair and settled into it, looking out at the same view she must have gazed upon hundreds of times through the years.

How I longed to know her. Again I bowed my head, letting sorrow flow through me like the waves below. I thought of the sorrow she'd carried through the years, her son's loss, and her need to keep me a continent away.

Yet Welsie True had never once written of her bitterness or loss. How easily she could have nursed deep anger toward Poppy for bringing about the events that killed her son, for keeping me, her only granddaughter, at a distance.

My fingertips moved to my stomach and rested there, thinking of Welsie separated from the ones she loved.

I sat forward in alarm then, my hands still lightly touching my stomach. I was keeping Zeb from knowing his child and my child from knowing its father. As surely as Poppy kept the secrets of my parentage from me—so was I about to keep them from this precious life I carried.

Zeb would never know about the baby he'd desperately wanted for four years. I almost softened toward him, then I pictured him kissing Jeannie, and my heart turned again to stone.

He didn't deserve to know. But the child...*our* child? Didn't she, or he, deserve the truth? I bit my lip and refused to think about it any longer.

That night I woke with a start, my heart pounding. The familiar black fear had returned. I sat up in bed—in my grandmother's bed—and looked around, squinting into the dim light. Everything was as it had been when I had lain down to sleep: Grandmother Welsie's spool-backed chair in the corner, the mirrored dressing table near the window, the lace curtains hanging without motion to the floor.

Holding the counterpane to my chest, I shivered, feeling desperately alone. Only the ticking pendulum of the kitchen clock carried through the house toward me.

I swallowed hard. "You come to me in times of trouble and darkness," I said out loud. "Where are you now?

"Where were you," I said, my voice stronger, "when my da and my momma died? Why didn't you protect them? I wanted to know them all these years, yet they were taken from me. I wanted to know Welsie True...and now she is gone too."

I stared up at the ceiling, blinking as tears rolled from my lids to my earlobes and pooled on my pillow. "Who is left?" The thought terrified me. Zeb's face came unbidden to my mind.

"No!" I growled into the silence. "My husband is not the one. I will not go to him." I clutched my stomach. " 'Tis just my child and me now. *My* child. Not his. He doesn't deserve to know."

I turned on my side and curled into a ball. The clock ticked from down the hallway, and the waves beat a soft rhythm in the distance.

"You've been with me in my troubles…" I breathed. "Are you here now? Have you always been with me?" A sense of warmth settled into my spirit, and I didn't feel so alone. I drifted to the place between waking and sleeping, feeling loved. Unaccountably loved.

I am with you, beloved, even to the ends of the earth.

I sat up in bed and looked around, rubbing my eyes. The kitchen clock struck three. I had slept, or was I still asleep? "You are with me then? You are here?"

I am with you.

"I need you," I breathed. "But I'm afraid…"

Of turning from your darkness to the light, beloved, to my light?

"Can you take it away?" My voice was little more than a whisper. "My darkness, I mean?"

I can do all things, if you but ask.

Still on my bed, I bent forward, crying. "Then do it, I beg you. Take this darkness from me."

When the still, small voice spoke again in the depths of my heart, I wept in disappointment.

I already have, beloved. My son's sacrifice conquered death.

"Then why can I not know it?" I argued. "Why do I still feel imprisoned in it?"

He forgave those who nailed him to the cross. Can you do less?

"But I've been so wronged," I wept. "I should not have to forgive until Zeb begs it of me."

He forgave without being asked.

"You cannot know my pain."

I know your going out, your coming in. The very hairs on your head are numbered. You think I do not know you?

"But my heartache is deep, the deception by my husband, my friend…"

My son was betrayed by his friends.

I fell silent, ashamed.

I am the light of the world, beloved. In me there is no darkness at all.

I buried my face in my hands. "I can't do it," I cried. "I don't have the strength."

Lean on me, child, and learn of me. Try me, and know that I will give you the strength you need.

"What must I do?"

Forgive, as I have forgiven you.

"No."

I will help you.

"I cannot."

I tossed and twisted in my covers until the clock struck five. When I rose, the words in my heart seemed to have come in a dream. I pondered their meaning, knowing that somewhere in them was truth. Important truth.

Forgive, as I have forgiven you.

I stoked the stove and set water to boil for coffee.

Forgive, as I have forgiven you.

Then I stepped from the back door to the pathway leading across the small picketed enclosure. A blanket of fog had settled during the night, deep and thick around me, obscuring the sea even in the gray dawn. As I stood listening to the surf crashing below, the small, quiet voice in my heart came back.

Forgive, as I have forgiven you.

I thought about Zeb. How could I possibly forgive or return to him? I couldn't. I also knew I had no choice.

"God, help me," I whispered, staring into the ashen mist. "Help me."

The mists were burning off from the midmorning sun when I headed down the hillside for a walk into town. I was trailed by a passel of neighborhood children, wide-eyed and giggling into their hands.

Finally I stopped and turned to greet them. The youngest grinned up at me, her black eyes merry. *"Buenos días, señora,"* she said, exchanging a triumphant look with a little boy who might have been her brother. The other children looked duly impressed, likely because she was the first one to engage me in conversation.

"Bue-nos dí-as," I said slowly.

My pronunciation obviously wasn't what they expected, for the lot of them burst into laughter. They chattered away in Spanish. I shrugged and shook my head. "I don't understand," I said.

Finally, the child I thought was the little girl's brother stepped forward. "We want to know if you live here now." He pointed to the cottage. "Señora True was our friend. We miss her."

"I miss her too," I said gently. "She was my grandmother."

He translated my words to the other children. The little girl stepped toward me and tugged at my hand. Her face very serious, she said several words in Spanish, and I looked to her brother to explain.

"Señora Welsie made us little cakes. My sister wants to know if you will too."

I laughed then, bent lower to look into the little girl's eyes, and said, "What is your name?"

Her brother translated. "Rosa."

"And yours?" I looked up at him.

"Fernando, but I am known more by Nando."

All the other children moved closer, almost encircling me. One by one, they told me their names: Juan, Carlos, Nita, and Jaime.

"I will make you some little cakes," I said, "if you will help me."

Nando translated, and the others chattered excitedly, smiling up at me and nodding.

"Su casa?" Rosa asked.

"Sí," I said, glad I remembered at least that much. *"Sí."* I smiled. "First you must show me the way to some shops so I can buy some flour and sugar and eggs."

Nando grabbed my hand, pulling me forward, and called to the others to follow, explaining my request in Spanish.

"Wait, wait!" I said, laughing. "You must first ask your mommas. Please, run back and get their permission. I'll wait here."

There seemed to be no translation needed. The group trotted as one up the incline and soon disappeared from sight. It took only a short time for them to reappear at the top of the hill, this time with their mothers in tow.

I waved, signaling it was all right for the children to accompany me, and the women waved back. Minutes later, Rosa took one hand, Nita the other. Nando marched in front of me, the other boys trailed behind.

We soon arrived in the heart of San Juan, across the mission wall. The children led me first to a *panderia* for flour and leavening, to an open-air grocer to buy oranges and avocados, which they called alligator pears and insisted I try, then to a small ranch near the train tracks that sold eggs and milk and smoked pork.

As I trudged back up the hill to the cottage, my usual weariness seemed to almost disappear. The chatter and laughter of the children lightened my heart, and the sight of them gathered in my kitchen a half-hour later, aprons tied around their waists, some on stools or boxes, others perched on a worktable, made me forget everything but the joy of the moment.

I found my grandmother's recipe for little sweet cakes in a small tin box in her cupboard, and set about breaking eggs and instructing Rosa and Nando how to stir them, Nita to sift the measure of flour, and Jaime to set the wood in the stove.

As we worked, I began to sing "The Old Gray Goose Is Dead." Nando translated and gales of laughter resulted. The children tried hard to form the English words, then Nando attempted to teach me the Spanish words for the song. Finally we settled on a mix of both. By the time we put the small cakes on an iron sheet and slid it into the oven, we'd forged a friendship.

I looked around the kitchen, taking in the spilled flour on the floor, the smudges of the same on nearly every little brown face, the merry chatter. As the aroma of the baking cakes filled the room, their eyes widened and their voices hushed in anticipation.

They gathered round the stove as I clutched a heavy pad and pulled the iron sheet from the oven. Atop it the cakes were lopsided and lumpy, but the children didn't seem to care. They licked their lips and made small humming sounds.

"Outdoors," I said, gesturing to the grass this side of the

gazebo. "We'll eat them out back." No translation was needed. They scurried outdoors while I scooped the cakes from the flat pan and piled them onto a platter. Nando held open the back door, and I stepped through.

The children made a grab for the cakes, and above their chatter I heard a rumbling chuckle. I turned to see Micheil heading around the house. "Looks like I'm just in time," he announced.

"Hola, amigos," he said to the children, and greeted them each by name. To my surprise, he settled cross-legged onto the grass beside them, happily munching on a small cake of his own.

I sat down in the weathered chair by the gazebo and watched the scene before me. The small picket-framed yard seemed ready to burst with sunlight and laughter. Soon three of the children's mothers entered the gate on the opposite side of the cottage. They greeted Micheil like an old friend, and, after introducing me, he spoke with them in Spanish, carefully translating for me.

The women soon gathered their children to take them home, thanked me for baking the cakes, then disappeared into nearby houses. It seemed strangely quiet when they had left.

"I've never had neighbors," I said to Micheil with a half-smile. "These seem to come with the cottage."

He laughed. "You reminded me of Welsie when I saw you standing here with the children. She fed these little ones every chance she got, told them stories, sang them songs."

I tilted my chin downward, a warm pleasure sweeping over me with his words. "They loved it when I sang 'The Old Gray Goose,' but I didn't try any others. I thought I might confuse them by using too much English."

"Welsie taught the children many words. They understand

more than you know," he said. "Just start your singing and see what happens." His voice softened. "And, lass, I think they might be held spellbound by your dulcimer playing."

"Ah, but first I must make one," I countered, smiling.

"I came to see if you might want to ride to Saddleback Ranch with me. I've saved a chunk of wood for you there that just might strike your fancy."

"The seasoned hardwood you told me about?"

"The same, lass. Welsie picked out the best block months ago, knowing that in the end she would invite you to come to California. And hoping, of course, hoping with all her heart that you would come."

He stood and took the platter from me to carry into the cottage. Then ordering me to sit at the small round table beside the stove, he donned an apron and cleaned up the mess the children and I had made. He whistled as he swept the plank floor, and, after pumping water into the dishpan, wiped up the spilled cake batter on the stove.

"There now," he said, untying the apron and scanning the kitchen for spots missed. " 'Tis better than new."

I grinned at him. "Is there anything you can't do, my friend?"

His own smiled faded. "Only what I want to do more than anything in this lifetime, lass."

To return to the priesthood, I knew he would say if I asked, but I nodded slightly in understanding and said nothing.

"We'll need to be on our way now," he said. " 'Tis a ways out to the Saddleback, and we'll want to be getting back before dark." I started for the door, and he gently reached for my arm. "Perhaps you'll be needing a wrap, lass. I wouldn't want you to take a chill now."

His concern touched me, and I nodded. "Aye, kind sir," I said with a grin.

He laughed then. "I'll be makin' an Irishwoman of ye yet, lassie."

I climbed into the wagon and sat on the driver's seat. He circled the vehicle and settled beside me. At a flick of the reins the mare pulled away from the cottage. Within minutes we wound into the hills to the east of San Juan and onto a rutted road that stretched across a grassy valley. The horse clopped along, and the wagon jostled from side to side as the wheels headed through the ruts.

We'd gone only a few miles when Micheil slowed the mare and pulled over to let another rider pass coming the opposite direction. He pointed to a barren plateau up ahead.

"Welsie's cattle range is on the plateau, her ranch down the hillside on another steppe just below."

I gazed up at the wide sky in wonder. "My grandmother liked open spaces."

He laughed and popped the reins above the mare's back. "She always said it was a breath of fresh air just to be out of the hollows of home. It seemed she couldn't get enough of views that let her see forever—from her cottage, from the place I'm taking you."

"The shadows of the hollows sometimes block the sun most of the day."

"That's what she said. She loved the West because the views stretch to heaven itself. She couldn't seem to get enough of the sunlight and warmth she found here."

He turned the horse onto a path leading up a slope on the north side of the plateau. The mare whinnied and flicked an ear back as we headed up a steeper incline. Small clods of dirt rolled behind us. I grabbed hold of the bench as the wagon rattled along, seeming to rock and sway enough to topple.

"Ah," Micheil breathed audibly, as if the air were purer this far above the ocean. He rounded the easternmost switchback and climbed onto flat land. "This is Saddleback Ranch." He halted the horse and turned to me with a grin. "Fairwyn March's spread."

"My ranch," I mused with a frown. I'd almost forgotten that my grandmother had left it to me. I let my gaze travel across the windswept, golden grasslands. It held a beauty all its own. Clumps of cactus were scattered among the boulders and live oaks. And in the distance the ocean stretched beneath a hazy blue sky. I could see why Welsie True loved this place.

"Where are the cattle?" I said, looking up at him. "I thought this was a cattle ranch."

He laughed. " 'Tis, Fairwyn. 'Tis. And I'll explain their mysterious disappearance a wee bit later." Then he caught my hand and pulled me along as both of us ran like the wind to the far end of the plateau.

"Stop, stop!" I finally called, bending over, breathless.

He let go of my hand and, heaving great breaths of his own, fell on his knees and stared straight up at the sky.

I looked down at him, laughing again. "Why, Micheil Grady Gilvarry, I believe I might have outrun you after all! You're panting harder than I am."

He sat up. "Ah, but 'tis a long time since anyone called me that." He smiled. "Welsie True was the last."

"I thought maybe so," I said and turned to look out toward the open sea. "She loved this place," I said. "I bet you can see to eternity from up here."

"Aye, lass, that you can." He stood beside me now. "I'll show you," he said. And we walked slowly toward the far end of the plateau.

From there we could see Welsie's ranch tucked into a grove of fruit trees and eucalyptus and black pines. Farther out spread a thousand head of cattle, their soft lowing carrying on the wind. Beyond the little village of San Juan, an even wider expanse of the ocean could be seen. It sparkled blue-gray until it melted into the horizon. Even Santa Catalina Island rose up from the ocean, its mountain formation looking like the back of a great gray whale.

"How did she manage to buy this?" I asked.

"She came to California with a small nest egg. She started buying land, an acre at a time, mostly land no one else wanted. She started out with a small herd of cattle, some sickly scrawny things someone had ordered by train from Texas and never claimed. She got them for a song at an auction, then set about nursing them to health. Turned out to be a prize herd. She sold off part of it for a tidy profit a few years later. That's how she bought the cottage in town."

He turned to me. "Everything she did was for you. She hoped to leave you enough to never want again. She wanted you to make your own choices without worry of poverty or need."

"I can stay here then," I said softly, imagining it.

"Aye, that was her intention—if you chose to."

I turned to him. "Yet you're saying I must return to Zeb."

He didn't speak for a moment. "It makes the choices harder."

"This is where you live. It is your home."

" 'Tis."

"And should I…" I tried to formulate my thoughts. "If I decided not to stay…" I drew in a deep breath and started again. "If I did determine I needed to go back to Zeb—I'm not saying I am, only that should I feel I must…"

He raised a brow, his head tilted. "Lass, what is it you're trying to say?"

"If I did, and if I gave you this ranch—for I think my grand-mother loved you as much as she did me and would be pleased—if I gave it to you…"

He held up a hand. "Then it would truly make my choices even harder."

"Because of Ireland."

"The same."

"I have no need for a cattle ranch," I said, my voice soft. "Should I stay, the cottage is perfect for me."

"What about for your child, Fairwyn?"

I spun then, moving my hands to my stomach. I tilted my head and started to protest. But when I saw the compassion in his face, I stepped back and held my tongue.

"My dear ma bore seven after bearing me," he said. "I well remember the signs."

My cheeks warmed. "You guessed then?"

His smile was gentle. "I knew then."

I walked away from him. "That's why you've been telling me I must return to Zeb."

"Partly." He walked closer to stand beside me. "For the child, but also for you."

"I don't think I have the strength in me," I said, still looking out to the sea, the glint of sunlight playing on the distant waves.

" 'Tis our Lord who strengthens us."

I turned to him. "Are you just repeating those platitudes you learned in"—I grappled for the right word—"seminary…Catholic university…wherever it is you learn to be a priest?" He grinned, but I went on. "You remind me of those things I know to be true about God"—I tapped my forehead—"but have never taken root in my heart." I searched his face. "But you, Micheil Grady Gilvarry,

I suspect you, too, have learned these truths about God up here." I touched my head again. "But neither have they taken root in your heart." I resisted the urge to point to his chest—the very place where his silver cross lay.

I caught my breath, wondering if he might be angry at my honesty. Instead, he threw back his head and let out a booming, rumbling laugh. "Aye, lassie mine. You are speakin' the truth more like your grandmomma every day I know you."

I was dumbfounded. "I am?" I managed.

"Has it occurred to you that our heavenly Father, knowing you and knowing me, knowing our need for friendship and honesty, planned this time for our coming together? From the beginning of time, perhaps he planned it."

Quick tears stung my eyes.

"He knows our heartaches and sorrows and search for truth. Our search for answers to heartbreaking questions." He paused, nodding slowly, as if speaking only as the thoughts came to him. "Perhaps—and truly, we cannot know the thinking of God—but perhaps, just perhaps, he's brought us together to help us both on our journeys."

"Father Micheil," I said. "I do believe you're right about your calling."

His eyes filled. "If only I could believe it."

"You must. With his strength, you must." I gazed into his eyes solemnly.

He led me back to the wagon and helped me in, and we drove toward the adobe ranch house. With great pride, he told me about the workings of the ranch as we crossed the range, the numbers of ranch hands and the size of the herd, as we drove over the rounded hills and scrubby flatland. His eyes shone with delight as he told me how he'd worked with Welsie to turn the ranch into a working enterprise, profitable from hides, tallow, and beef. He explained that though he was overseer, his trusted foreman was in charge of the everyday workings.

We parked the wagon from time to time and strolled across the property as Micheil told me about leftover herds of Texas long-horn, the newer species from Brazil, the vaqueros that rode with them. We stopped at the top of a bluff and looked down on the sweep of brown, short grass. Not a steer or calf could be seen.

"The mystery you mentioned earlier. There's not a cow in sight."

Laughing, he pointed toward a double-humped rise in the dis-tance. "Saddleback Mountain, the namesake of your ranch," he said, "The vaqueros take the herds up there to higher ground where feed is more plentiful. Helps the depleted range restore its growth. Helps the cattle fatten for market. It's our pattern every summer."

He turned back to me. "That's why I can spend time at the mission this time of year," he said. He raised a brow. "And garden-ing with you at Welsie True's."

"And when the herds are back?"

He followed my gaze to the adobe ranch house and beyond. "Ah, lass. 'Tis always a dilemma. This is my home, where I live, where I spend most of my days during branding or when we're slaughtering, readying for shipment.

"We move the cattle by train to the Midwest, though I don't travel with the ranch hands. My foreman goes to market with the herd, settles on the price—with my approval, of course.

"But as for me, my time in town is over for a season. I'm needed here."

Before we climbed back into the wagon, he disappeared into the barn at the rear of the ranch house. Minutes later he returned and held out a block of oak, seasoned and ready for the working.

His eyes were warm as he laid the piece in my arms. " 'Tis time to rebuild what was destroyed," he said.

Micheil halted the wagon in front of the cottage, then walked around the vehicle to help me to the ground. The wind blew off the ocean, rattling the shutters and sending rose petals skittering across the garden. The wind tangled his graying hair, and I gazed into his worn and lined face, knowing that someday our journeys would turn and I would be left with only his image in my memory. Something pressed against my heart at such a loss.

He inclined his head almost as if understanding my thoughts, then turned back to the wagon. He had just hoisted himself to the seat when Nando called to me from across the road. I waved hello as he hurried toward me.

"Señora, señora," he cried breathlessly. "Someone was here to see you. Asking for you, saying your name many times as he banged on your door."

My heart began pumping too hard, which made it difficult to breathe. "Did he leave his name?" I exchanged a worried glance with Micheil, who was hurrying toward me.

"No, señora," Nando said. "We were afraid for you, so told him nothing."

Micheil stood very near me now, and I breathed a bit easier. "Did he say he would return?" I asked the boy.

"No, señora. *Mi mamá* told him the woman who lived there was dead. Died many days ago. I don't think the man will return."

He hesitated. "*Mi mamá* said she didn't care for the look in the man's eyes. He did not seem to be *su amigo*."

I grabbed hold of the picket gate to steady myself. *Could it have been Zeb…or his agent? Someone who'd come to take me home?*

"Are you all right, señora?"

The wind whipped frantically around us, bending limbs on the pepper tree and tearing leaves from the rosebushes. My skirts snapped and billowed. I swayed, feeling I might be sick. "I am all right, Nando. Truly."

Micheil caught my hand. The solid warmth of his fingers wrapped tightly around mine renewed my strength as we walked to the cottage door. Nando trailed along behind.

"*Gracias, amigo,*" I said. "And tell your mama *gracias* for me."

The boy trotted off, and I met Micheil's worried gaze again. "I think I could use some tea," I said shakily.

He smiled and helped me through the door, letting me lean against him. With his arm tenderly supporting me, I settled into a big upholstered chair near the window.

His lilting Irish brogue filled the kitchen, spilling into the room where I rested, mixing with the banging of the kettle, the squeak of the pump, the thud of wood dropping into the stove, the slam of the damper.

My eyes closed, and soon I drew in the scent of steeping tea. But it wasn't just the tea that lifted my spirits. It was this man who sang and clattered and prepared this soothing drink for me.

It was this man who walked toward me with a tray set with cup and saucer, a pitcher of cream, a dish of lumped sugar, and a vase with a scrawny-stemmed rosebud tucked inside.

It was this man, my friend, who set the tray before me and smiled into my eyes with tender compassion.

Twenty-Six

The kitchen clock struck midnight, and I woke with a start, my heart pounding hard beneath my ribs. In my nightmare, I had been locked in a cell, pounding at the door to be let out. Dr. Crawford peered in at me, frowning but not hearing. Cries of the other patients rose to a deafening roar. I covered my ears with my hands.

Zeb peered through the window to my cell, shaking his head as he saw me, knitting his brow in worry. Dr. Crawford appeared beside him. They spoke, though I couldn't hear their words, even after I dropped my hands from my ears. Only the din of the patients' anguished cries filled the air.

"Please," I cried to Zeb, "please, listen to me. I am well. I am whole! Please let me out! Please, don't do this to me."

It had been a dream. Only a dream. But my heart thudded harder as I relived it. Zeb's agent—or Zeb himself—had followed me to California. I had to leave. I couldn't stay here another day, wondering when he might return.

I rose in the darkness and lit a lamp, carrying it with me to the kitchen, where I fanned the still orange coals in the stove and put on the kettle for tea. *I must be rational,* I told myself, *about where to go and when to leave.* It had to be someplace safe for me and my child, but it also had to be a place where I could disappear without a trace. Someplace where Zeb would never think to look.

I didn't want to think about leaving California. Already, the place had become home. Just as it had captured my grandmother's heart, so it had mine, and more so every day. I thought of the children who played up and down the road, their mothers who were already looking out for me. And Micheil. He had brought me a sense of reasoned thinking, the realization that I wasn't alone in my sorrow and quest for healing. How could I leave him?

How could I leave this place? Leave my new friends?

I set out the teapot, filled it with leaves, and then sat at the table, resting my chin in my hands, to await the whistling kettle.

The lamp flickered in the center of the table, casting a warm glow across the adobe walls and the bright colored gingham curtains, the oak pendulum clock on its shelf next to the window, and the cheery iron stove with its ornate steel designs.

The place brought such comfort. I could picture my grandmother sitting at this table, her mind awhirl with decisions about the ranch, or helping Micheil oversee the latest building project at the mission, the children's needs at his school, or thinking about food for his work with the poor. Maybe she sat here and thought about her granddaughter on the other side of the continent. I wondered if she had pictured me sitting in this very spot.

The thought made me smile. The kettle whistled and sputtered, and I set the tea leaves to steep.

I felt at home here, and perhaps someday I would return. But I felt I must run. And keep running until I felt safe.

A few minutes later I poured my tea, thinking of Micheil as I poured the cream and added the sugar. I took one of my grandmother's woolen shawls from a hook by the back door, wrapped it snugly around my shoulders, then stepped outside with my mug.

Rather than hiding behind the usual ocean mists, the moon rode bright above the ocean. I walked to the gazebo and settled into the wood-slatted chair, facing the surf. Below me, the waves crashed in rhythmic comfort. I closed my eyes, breathing in the salt-air scent, wondering again how I could say good-bye to this place.

Dusty Los Angeles might be a place where I could flee, though it likely was too close for comfort. I considered San Francisco, a bigger city, where I might have an easier time of disappearing. Perhaps a Western town along the railroad route.

I thought how I might support myself. With my education I could teach if I had to, but the profession had never appealed to me. I was a storyteller and musician. I smiled as a thought took root. Perhaps I might sing and play my dulcimer for hire. I stood and walked to the picket fence and looked down at the ocean with its shining band of silver ripples under the moon. Then as I thought about the places I might sing and play, saloons and dance halls came to mind, and I let out a sigh of disappointment. My thoughts of singing for hire vanished. Above all, I wanted a wholesome and safe place to raise my child.

I turned back to the house. The lamp still glowed in the kitchen, casting a dim light throughout. The whole scene, from Grandmother Welsie's upholstered furniture to her family portraits and her frilly gingham curtains—all of it beckoned to me.

This was where I wanted to be. No place I'd ever been filled my soul the way my little cottage did. But I had no choice; I had to leave.

I finished a last sip of lukewarm tea and tossed the tea leaves into the soil by the gazebo. I squared my shoulders and walked into the house.

By daybreak my valise was packed, the house was scrubbed, and I was ready to close up. I locked the Dutch door and headed down the brick walk, through the newly manicured garden, before the neighborhood children came out to play. It felt unfinished somehow, leaving without saying good-bye, but perhaps it was better this way.

The day was clear and bright, the morning sun warm on my shoulders as I trekked into town. I'd walked only a half-mile when the milk wagon drew along the road. The milkman raised his hand in a solemn wave and nodded as he passed. His swaybacked horse clopped along, head down, the echoing sound dying away in the morning air.

By the time I reached the bottom of the hill, the town was waking. Shopkeepers, some on hands and knees scrubbing their doorsteps and walkways, raised their heads in pleasant greeting. They called out to each other, some in Spanish, others in English, as they worked. Farm wagons rattled along the dusty cobbles, bringing in loads of brightly colored autumn squashes, a rainbow of gourds and fat pumpkins. I resisted the urge to stop and talk with the farmers about their produce. Forgetting my determination to leave, I grinned in spite of myself, picturing the cattle back from their fattening in the Saddleback Mountains, the ribbon of sea in the distance, my fields of squashes and pumpkins shimmering like gold beneath the California sun.

I would teach my child to ride, and we would gallop together across the range. If my baby was a girl, I would raise her to be strong and independent, have a mind of her own and follow her heart. She would glory in the wide-open spaces; she would never feel suffocated or forced into bad choices. If this infant was a boy, he would grow strong and tall in the fresh sea air and beating sun. He would ride like the wind, take part in the roping and branding, the high-country cattle drives.

Behind me the mission bells tolled, interrupting my thoughts, as I stared at the pumpkins in the back of the farm truck. I turned away, clutching my valise and letting go of my dream.

Resolutely I marched to the mission gate and let myself in. The grounds were quiet and peaceful. My heartache eased as I surveyed the outer courtyard.

When I'd first arrived, I'd seen only the decay and disrepair. Now it seemed endearing somehow, a place that held Micheil's heart. I was still standing by the well outside the sanctuary when he emerged from the bell tower, just as I knew he would.

He brightened when he saw me. "Lass," he said, glancing down at the valise then back to my face, "tell me what's happened."

"I want to stay," I said. "But I can't."

"The man who asked after you?"

"Yes. I've tried not to be troubled about the visit…" I shook my head. "After all, he may never come back."

"Your neighbors sent him packing."

"It's still too dangerous. I thought with the distance between Zeb and me…a whole continent…I thought I'd be safe. But in the night I decided I haven't a choice. I must leave."

He took my hand and guided me toward the dappled shade of the grape arbor, where I sat wearily on the wooden bench beneath the cascading leaves. Sitting down beside me, he let out a heavy sigh and leaned forward, elbows on knees, and studied me.

"Where will you go?"

I looked at him steadily, willing myself to be stronger of mind and spirit than I felt at this moment. "I'll go by train to San Francisco. It's a busy city, hundreds of people arriving from around the world every day. It would be easy to get lost in such a place."

"Lost," he said. "Aye."

"I have it in mind that you could send me some of the proceeds from the ranch, enough for me to live on."

He nodded slowly. " 'Tis yours, to be sure."

"Yes," I said decisively. "That's exactly what I'll do. I have plenty of money to get started—from the nest egg my grandfather left me, you see."

" 'Tis so," he agreed.

"But I'll need more once this runs out."

"Aye." He stood. "You'll have to let me know how to reach you once you're settled."

I stood with him. "I thought I might take the hardwood, the tools…"

"You'll be looking for something to occupy your time."

I swallowed hard, thinking of the loneliness that would be mine once I left this place. "I'll go collect my things then."

"Aye, lass. You must."

I turned to leave, but he didn't follow me. I felt his gaze, and when I reached the archway to the center courtyard, I turned again to where he was standing by the grape arbor. "I was counting on your wisdom just now," I called to him. "I thought you might have some words of guidance, or, at the very least, comfort."

"You want me to agree with you, lass? Is that what you're expecting?"

"I thought you might disagree," I said as he drew nearer. "Maybe I wanted you to tell me not to go."

"Ah, lass. I will not do that. This is your decision to make, and you've told me your plan. You look weary and pale as if you've been up all night thinking it through, planning your journey." He was standing before me now.

"I have."

His clear eyes met mine, and his voice was gentle when he spoke. " 'Tis not my decision to make. You alone know the great dangers you might face should Zeb find you. You know firsthand the reality of his threats."

"You've said I need to talk with him, no matter the cost."

"Only when the time is right."

I leaned against the adobe arch, still searching Micheil's face. It struck me that when I left Poppy's to marry Zeb, I sought the same kind of approval. I begged for Poppy to give me a blessing to send me on my way. Was this what I needed from Micheil—a blessing to send me off? A blessing that made me think all would be well, even if this was the wrong decision? A dull ache of recognition lay heavy in my heart. It was an easy way to remove myself from the responsibility of choosing my own way.

My voice dropped. "I only know that it's too soon. You may be right, and yes, maybe, terrified as I am, maybe I'll need to confront him—"

"Confront?" he said gently.

"Ask his forgiveness," I said. "And tell him…about our child."

"Only God can tell you when the time is right," he said. "No one else."

I let my gaze drift to the tall pepper tree beyond his shoulder. "I only know I am afraid to stay."

"Does your fear mean it's time to go then?" There was a soft smile at the corner of his mouth. "Is that what your decision is based upon?"

Again I remembered leaving Blackberry Mountain, my fear of remaining a spinster, my fear of letting the opportunity for an education pass me by. "Yes," I whispered with a sigh. "Fear has caused it in the past. Dread fear."

Micheil didn't comment for a long moment, but reached out and took both my hands in his. "It takes courage, lass, to admit such a thing."

"If I stay—and I'm not saying I will—how can I be safe?" As if with a mind of its own, my hand settled lightly on my stomach.

"Only our heavenly Father can protect us, lass. And we cannot know his purposes, his timing, what he may call us to do as a sacrifice. Being his child isn't always safe. Our physical bodies will pass away, but the core of who we are—our souls—can never be taken out of his palm."

I frowned then, remembering Ireland. "And you? You fear returning home because of the certainty of death."

" 'Tis a certainty in human terms," he said. Then he raised a brow and grinned, breaking our somber tones. "And you've just guessed why I know the subject so well. You might say that I am intimately acquainted with the feeling of dread fear." He chuckled. Then, looking heavenward, he thickened his brogue. "Aye, lass, even your questions cause thinkin' about me own dilemma when it comes to God's grace."

"Grace?"

"Aye, his grace." His voice dropped. "That place between where our short arms reach out to him and his powerful hands stretch toward us. That place where we fall so short of our own expectations. Fall short of what we imagine God's to be." Tears glistened in his eyes. "And then if we keep reaching toward him, we see the bridge of his love crossing that space between. No matter what we've done, no matter how far short of his glory we've fallen—he's still reaching out. His big hands are open wide to catch us, to draw us nearer to his heart." He paused, wiping his eyes. "That's grace, child. That's grace."

My own eyes had filled. "Shouldn't this grace remove our fears then?"

He nodded slowly. "Aye, lass. It should. But we're human. We make mistakes. We run when we should stay. We're cowards when we should be strong. We say things we shouldn't. We act in ways unbecoming for God's children.

"But our Father doesn't give us just one chance to make it right." He wiped his eyes again. "He keeps giving us chance after chance after chance."

I thought of my headstrong ways, the hurts I'd caused others, the mistakes I'd made. "I don't know if I can reach far enough."

"That's the glory of it," he said. "You don't have to, lass. 'Tis God who does the reaching. You just need to hold out your arms and stand still."

Neither of us spoke for a moment. I tried to imagine such love, such grace. But the concept was almost too big, too deep, too wondrous, to take in. "I need to get my wood," I said finally. "And the tools."

He nodded with a sad smile. "I'll miss you, Fairwyn."

"And I, you," I said, then stepped through the archway to the courtyard. I didn't turn to look, but I felt his gaze following me to the monk's cell.

I stepped inside moments later and stopped to let my eyes adjust to the dim light inside. There on the workbench was the heavy block of wood from the ranch. I stepped toward it and rubbed my hand over its rough surface. It seemed to beg for sanding, and I couldn't resist just one quick swipe across the surface.

I set down the valise and reached for a sheet of sandpaper. I lightly smoothed it across the wood. Once. Twice. Pressing harder, glorying in the scent of the sawdust, I sanded a smaller area more intensely. I felt the surface with my left hand, letting my fingertips rub the wood. I pictured the rough-hewn piece finished and polished, shaped into the instrument I longed to play.

I lit the lamp and bent over Poppy's instructions. The soundboard would be my first cut, using one of the saws above the bench, following the grain. I peered at the black oak, scrutinizing the grain, touching it, turning it. The length was perfect, exactly thirty-three inches.

Poppy's instructions showed I was to draw a shape, hourglass, long oval, or something made entirely of my own fancy. His dulcimers were always hourglass shaped, though with varying designs, small and large. He had roughly sketched one of his most familiar for me to follow. But I was struck by the idea of designing a shape that would be uniquely mine.

Picking up a fat stick of carpenter's chalk, I drew a double swirl along one side of the oak, then I rubbed it away. I tried again, this time keeping the curve gentler. It was better, but still not right.

Bending lower, I pored over Poppy's designs, and then I looked back to my sketch. I hadn't allowed enough width at the base of the instrument for the sound holes. Poppy's drawings showed that each must be slightly less than two inches in diameter.

I couldn't help the smile of satisfaction that played at the corner of my mouth as I redrew the shape. I tilted the wood toward the lamplight, knowing the design was perfect.

Without hesitation, I reached for the smallest saw, checked the strength and sharpness of the blade, and then began to make my first cut. Holding my breath, I pushed and pulled on the saw's handle, holding to the chalk line. The wood was rock hard, and my right hand ached after just a few minutes, but gradually the cut appeared, taking the exact shape I'd drawn.

I stood back, grinning, to shake the cramp from my hand and to admire my work.

"Did you know, lass?" said a voice behind me. "Did you know that our Lord rejoices over us with singing?"

I turned as he crossed the distance between us and peered down at the block of wood. "You'll recall that passage in Zephaniah that was a special favorite of Fairwyn Enid and her Daniel True: 'The LORD thy God in the midst of thee is mighty; he will save, he will rejoice over thee with joy; he will rest in his love, he will joy over thee with singing.' "

Bending over the workbench, he ran his fingers over the wood, nodding slowly. He looked up at me and smiled, straightening. "I've heard your voice, lass. 'Tis a thing of joyous beauty." His voice dropped as if in awe. "Can you imagine that our God sings over us with the same joy—only a thousand times more glorious and filled with love?

"Softer than a mother's lullaby," he went on. "More powerful than the wind, more glorious than a rushing waterfall, more gladsome than birdsong in spring.

"He's given you a gift, Fairwyn March. One that reflects his joy in you." Micheil glanced down at the wood, and then back to my face. "One that reflects his life in you."

"I am staying," I said, making my decision in that moment. "I cannot leave yet. It's not time."

"You will know," Micheil said. "Just as I will, lass."

Minutes later, I heard him whistling an Irish jig as he crossed the courtyard. I turned back to my workbench and picked up the saw again.

As I moved the blade back and forth in rhythm, I started to hum a lullaby, then to sing as I worked.

If all the world were a sheet of paper,
And the sea an ink of blue,
And all the trees on the hills were eagle quills,
It couldn't write all my love to you.

A flutter like butterfly wings tickled the inside of my abdomen. Frowning, I stopped my work with the saw. Still humming I stepped back from the bench, my hands resting where I'd felt my baby move.

It couldn't write all my love to you, my little one, I whispered in awe. I pictured the tiny legs and arms, the fingers and toes. My breath caught at the reality of the child within me. A baby! A baby! A thousand questions came to mind. What color were her eyes, her hair? Would it be curly or straight? What would I name her? Or him? Would she giggle or sing or both? What would her voice…his voice…sound like?

Again came the delicate flutter. Beside myself with joy, I hurried from the workshop into the sunlight and lifted my face to the heavens.

"My child and I are here," I said out loud. I pictured God's hands stretching out to us, crossing the place where I fell so short of deserving his love. That bridge Micheil said was God's grace. "I'm not moving from this spot," I promised God. "No matter what happens, I'll not leave until it is time.

"I'm scared, Father. I still harbor fears that will not let me go. I still fear for the future, the uncertainties, my own tendencies to make bad decisions.

"All I know is that I cannot do this alone…cannot raise this child alone." I stopped to draw in a deep breath. "I cannot do it.

"Hold us in your big palm, my child and me. Hold us close."

Twenty-Seven

The weeks passed quickly, fading from a warm autumn as we headed into my first crisp, sunny California winter. The cattle had returned from the high country, and now Micheil spent longer hours at the Saddleback. Several times I rode in the buggy with him to the ranch, but because I couldn't risk riding horseback, I waited on the veranda for him to complete his rounds with the foreman.

But I didn't wait patiently. Most often I paced the wide porch, itching to saddle up one of the horses grazing nearby and thunder across the fields, glorying in the wind, the sun, the sea air. As my abdomen began to show a slight swell, though, even the buggy ride on a bumpy, rutted road seemed dangerous. I decided to remain in town.

By mid-December I had finished shaping and smoothing the dulcimer's soundboard and had begun work on the delicate fingerboard, sanding the wood until my fingers almost bled. Compelled to work faster and now feeling less tired, I worked as many hours during the day as I could, sometimes from dawn to dusk, other times just in the mornings, or even by candlelight late at night. Often, I stopped to walk around the deserted mission, stretching my back and rubbing away the ache from my hours bent over the workbench.

One Tuesday in early winter I walked to the outer courtyard, surprised to find Micheil shoveling out the stagnant pond.

" 'Tis a fine mornin' to be doin' such work, my friend," I teased with a heavy Irish brogue. "Though methinks the fragrance is not one of the finest I've found in California."

He straightened and shot me a grin. " 'Tis almost winter, and the rainwater will fill it, make it smell as fresh as an Irish meadow in spring."

I stepped closer. "By summer won't it be stagnant again?"

"Maybe in years before. But not this one." He leaned against his shovel handle and pointed to the dry creek bed that wound by the well and disappeared under the outer adobe wall that circled the mission. "I've fashioned a method of digging a channel from San Juan Creek, which will bring fresh water to the pond. I'll dig another channel on the other side to empty the pond and water the gardens."

He looked proud. I followed his gaze to the sorry tangle of old growth and weeds, then looked back to him. "It looks like back-breaking work." My tone softened. "I'm sorry I can't help."

He held up his hands in protest. "Don't be considering such a thing, lass. I know how you are when you spot a garden to weed. Can't leave it alone." He shook his head. "If not of yourself, be thinkin' of your wee one, if ever such a mood should strike you."

"I promise," I said, meaning it. The baby turned, and I felt a ripple of life scoot across my belly. "I do indeed."

He bent over his digging, and I walked back to the shade of the pepper tree to watch him shovel the hard dry soil from the furrow.

I came back days later when he poured the first bucketful of water from the well into the trench. Micheil's face lit up like the morning sun as he watched the water rush through the ditch to the tangle of dormant plants. Later that same day, we traveled through town in the farm wagon, gathering native cactuses, succulents, and even a small orange tree.

During the gray days before Christmas, I rode in the carriage with Micheil as he visited the families in his unofficial parish. I sat with him by the bedside of the aged, watching—sometimes with tears falling—as Micheil spoke words of comfort and healing. I baked breads and small sweet cakes with the children of the neighborhood, the *barrio,* wrapped the sweet delicacies with paper and bright bits of ribbon, and delivered them to families nearby.

San Juan became my village, my home, and the longer I was there the harder it was to think about leaving. Strangely, my fears of Zeb and what he might do to me lessened as time went on. But as my friendships grew with the women in my *barrio,* the more I knew I belonged in this place, surrounded by noise and clamor and laughter and song.

Antonia, the mother of Nando and Rosa; Elena, the mother of Carlos, Jaime, and Juan; and Carmelita, the mother of Nita, brought me warm sopaipillas and tortillas, often staying for tea and a visit. Each time they came, I picked up more Spanish words, and they tried hard to remember the English my grandmother had taught them. Hand motions and facial expressions filled in where words failed.

Carmelita, a pretty, vivacious woman, confided in me—in a combination of Spanish, English, and belly patting—that she was expecting her second baby. "In the spring," she said, her round face aglow.

I hugged her, patted my own rounded abdomen, and told her a baby would soon be cradled in my arms too. "In the spring," I repeated, first in English, then in Spanish. "The same as you."

Carmelita frowned, looking doubtful, and I hurried to explain. "*Mi esposo*—my husband—is away. In North Carolina, where I come from."

"You will go then," she asked, looking worried. "You will leave before the spring?"

I sighed, and let my gaze travel to the sea. "Someday," I said. "*Sí*. Someday."

Carmelita touched my hand as if reading the sorrow in my eyes. From that moment when our hearts seemed to connect, I sought her out. We strolled together into town, little Nita skipping between us, holding hands with both of us. We sat in the gazebo, talking over sopaipillas and Irish tea. I kept Nita during afternoons when I saw Carmelita was especially tired. She promised to return the favor once I returned to California with my husband and child.

I didn't have the heart to tell her I had no plans to return.

The children became my little shadows, following me to the mission almost every morning like I was the Pied Piper, pestering me with questions, playing in the mission courtyard, singing along as I worked.

Without instruction, Nando learned to sand scraps of wood with a surprisingly delicate touch. I soon realized that all the other children—Rosa, Carlos, Juan, Nita, and Jaime—wanted to help me with the dulcimer.

"All right, come with me," I finally said on a rare sunny January day. I gathered them into a circle just outside my door. They sat wide-eyed, and I handed each of them a spacer or a bridge.

They turned the small pieces over, examining each angle, faces bright with wonder and anticipation as I then placed into each pair of hands a small sanding block.

"Follow Nando's example," I said solemnly, beckoning him to step closer and demonstrate how to sand the wood, following the grain. "These are important pieces, for this is a special musical instrument. I want it to be just right."

Nando translated my words, his chest sticking out with pride, as he showed the younger children how to hold the sanding block.

Soon all were happily working, Nando in the middle, instructing them through each step. I stopped to examine Nita's spacer. Looking worried, she handed me the small piece of wood.

"Beautiful," I murmured in praise.

She beamed as I handed it back to her.

I examined each one. Though they held the wood awkwardly, the children were trying hard to follow instructions, and the results showed. With a grin I retrieved a basket full of more spacers and bridges and set it down by Nando. "After each is finished, you can give out another," I told him.

The children looked at each other, then at me, their pride showing in their dark eyes.

"Señora," Juan said with an arched brow and mischievous smile, "I like this almost as much as making sweet cakes in your kitchen."

Immediately the others started arguing which activity was the most fun. Laughing, I rolled my eyes heavenward and shrugged. "No reason we can't do both—but only one project at a time," I said.

I stepped back to the wood shop doorway and leaned against the thick adobe jamb, looking out on the scene before me, the circle of children, laughing and talking and sanding.

A squawk of ducks flapped by in a V formation. Sailing through the buttermilk sky, they flapped and talked and carried on, still flying, still heading to their destination. I sighed, feeling my heart in flight with them.

Still grinning, I glanced toward the archway leading to the outer courtyard, beyond the pepper tree, to the sparkling fresh waters of the pond.

Micheil looked up as if aware of my scrutiny. He waved and then loped toward the circle of children, his smile spread. "I see you've enlisted the help of experts," he said in Spanish.

The children looked up from their sanding and laughed.

He turned to me and walked closer. "Your progress should move faster now with all this help."

"She promises to teach us to play," Jaime volunteered. "Isn't that right, señora?"

"*Sí,*" I said to the boy, and then I looked back to Micheil. "They're the age I was when Poppy taught me. I remember his big hands making my instrument, showing me how to hold it, finger it, and strum it. I remember the joy of holding the dulcimer, knowing it was mine, strumming it and feeling the vibration of music touch my soul."

"May I see the dulcimer?"

I laughed. "I don't know if we can call it that yet. I'm nearly ready for the clamping. Just waiting for the spacers to be sanded. But you're welcome to examine the work in progress."

I hadn't shown him the entire design of the soundboard, the curve of the thin strips of wood that would hold it together once glued and clamped. With a smile, I stepped back and nodded for him to enter the shop.

He let out a sigh of appreciation as he headed to the workbench. "It may not be whole, but already 'tis a work of art," he murmured. "Is it just me, or does this piece of wood almost speak to you?"

I threw back my head and laughed. " 'Tis a bit o' Irish blarney I'm ahearin' for certain."

He laughed with me and then sobered. " 'Tis a glorious thing you're making, Fairwyn March. To be sure, a thing of beauty."

Micheil started for the door, then turned to look back. He

grinned then strode toward the children. He squatted on his haunches to talk with them in Spanish, their exchange punctuated with laughter. A moment later, he crossed the plaza, and a wave of tenderness washed over me.

Unwilling to think of the sadness of that coming day when I—when perhaps both of us—would leave, I studied the block of wood. Before clamping and gluing the two soundboards to the curved sides, I must cut the sound holes. I bent over the workbench in concentration, considering the overall shape. As with most of the mountain dulcimer makers, Poppy's sound holes were distinct and known throughout the county. He had cut everything from hummingbirds to hearts to moons and stars on either side of the fingerboard, but always with a flair that was entirely his own.

Outside, the low tones of the mission bells rang throughout the mission grounds. I pictured Micheil pulling the ropes and wondered who would ring them once he left for Ireland.

I stared again at the front soundboard, the one that would be atop the instrument. By the time the last bell echoed from the tower, I'd picked up the carpenter's chalk and begun drawing. I drew the shape of a mission bell to the left of the fretboard, then fashioned the image of two flying swallows on the opposite side.

Smiling, I admired my handiwork and began to make the cut. I bent over the workbench, carving and sanding a fraction of an inch at a time.

A small giggle from the doorway made me turn to see Nita standing hand in hand with her mother.

"Mommy's brought us lunch," she announced.

Carmelita smiled. "For all the children," she said in Spanish. She held a large basket in her hand.

Rosa and Nando crowded through the doorway to see, the others shouting and bouncing behind.

"Now, now," I said with a laugh. "We'll eat by the new pond. Pick up your tools and bring the spacers and blocks to me." Nando called out my instructions in Spanish, and the children skipped back to their circle to do as I asked. A few minutes later we marched across the courtyard to the pond and winter-dead gardens where Micheil was hoeing weeds.

I sat heavily onto a large flat granite stone, and the children nestled around me. Carmelita handed out the fresh-baked bread, spread with the strange green fruit of the alligator pear, and peeled orange sections. Micheil dusted off his hands and joined us, sitting between Juan and Carlos. He spoke to them rapidly in Spanish, with an eyebrow arched at Nando, who translated those words I couldn't understand.

Nando said with a grin, "Señor Micheil wants us to sing. All of us together."

Above us a flutter of sparrows hopped through the pepper tree leaves. Three lit on some dried brush beside the pond. The others hopped to higher branches, blending into the lacy leaves that rustled in the breeze.

"I'll start," Micheil said as he popped an orange slice into his mouth. He smiled and winked at me. "But only if you children join me."

I held up a hand. "And only if the children sing one of their folk songs for us." I laughed. "And please, don't try to sneak in 'The Old Gray Goose.'" I moved my gaze to Carmelita. "I'd love to hear a song of your heritage."

Micheil cleared his throat dramatically, causing Nita to giggle. Then he lifted his voice in song, singing at the top of his lungs.

As I roved out thro' Galway city
At the hour of twelve at the night,
Who should I see but a handsome damsel,
Combing her hair by candlelight.
"Lassie, I have come a courtin'
Your kind favors for to win;
And if you'll but smile upon me,
Next Sunday I'll call again."

"Sing with me now," Micheil said to the children. "Come on and let me hear ye belt it out!"

Raddy a the too dum, too dum too dum
Raddy a the too dum doo dum day.

The children imitated his brogue, which caused Carmelita and me to explode with laughter. We threw back our heads and joined them.

Raddy a the too dum, too dum too dum
Raddy a the too dum doo dum day.

Micheil started on the second verse, exaggerating his brogue even more and drawing out the words dramatically.

What would I do when I go walking,
Walking out in the morning dew?

What would I do when I go walking,
Walking with a lad like you?

"All right, my lassie," he said to Rosa and Nita. "This is the part ye're supposed to sing. Can ye join me, ye think?"

I whispered to the little girls, "I'll help you."

Micheil started the verse again, and a giggling Rosa and Nita sang along in their Spanish-Irish brogues. I filled in when they didn't know the words. When we'd finished, he started another verse, this time asking the boys to join him.

Did you ever see a copper kettle
Mended with an ould tin can?
Did you ever see a handsome damsel,
Married off to an ugly man?

Laughing together—the children, Carmelita, Micheil, and me—we all sang the chorus at the top of our lungs.

Raddy a the too dum, too dum too dum
Raddy a the too dum doo dum day.

The afternoon stayed sunny and bright as we traded songs of our heritage. The children sang in Spanish, teaching Micheil and me the words and music, Carmelita told folk tales from Mexico and Spain.

As a wind kicked up and a flurry of dry leaves skittered across the courtyard, I told the tale of the old people who invited the Lord to supper. The children listened solemnly, with Nando explaining the words they didn't know as I spoke.

When I reached the end, not a sound was heard except my voice.

"They kept the fire going and kept Jesus' supper ready. And finally they looked out and saw him coming. They went to meet him at the gate and said, 'We waited so long! We were afraid you'd never come.'

"The Lord took their hands and said, 'I've already been here twice.' "

Soon after, Carmelita left with the children to see them home, and I stayed to finish smoothing the edges of the carved sound holes. Micheil walked with me to the wood shop, hesitating as I turned to step inside.

"I don't remember ever feeling so much joy in my soul," he said, surprising me. "When you told your story just now…" I followed his gaze to the high dome and bell tower across the courtyard, the gulls that circled, the high puffed clouds skittering across the sky beyond. He seemed to be struggling to find the words to finish his thought.

"It seems he visits us when we least expect it," I ventured.

He smiled then. "Aye. I was thinking the same. That we see our Lord in the faces of children, hear his voice in their laughter—"

"Hear him rejoicing over us all with singing, when they lift their voices in song."

"And in your face," he said quietly, studying me, "I see his love shining in your eyes, lass. I do."

Without another word, he turned and strode across the courtyard, leaving me standing there, watching him, and knowing I saw the same in him.

Through the years, I'd wondered why God wasn't with me in my darkness and sorrow. The scales of anger, bitterness, and self-pity had blinded me. Now I knew he'd been there all along. He had visited me, but I hadn't known it was he.

I returned to the workbench and examined the sound holes, trailing my fingertips around the bell and swallows. I would finish smoothing the cuts today; tomorrow I would ready the pieces for fitting together.

Now that the California winter was about to begin, the three months of drenching Micheil said to expect, the glue would take longer to set, the varnish longer to dry. But come spring, likely March, just before my child would be born, the dulcimer would be ready to play.

I stood back, resting my hand on my abdomen, considering the instrument. It would be done in time to play lullabies to my child. I pictured the place I would play, and the image of Zeb's and my home in Oak Hill filled my mind.

The image was dark, frightening, and I caught my breath. I tried to replace it with the warmth and sunlight of the cottage, the music of the surf and calling gulls, the scent of the sea air. I pictured myself rocking my baby in the chair beneath the gazebo, but Oak Hill would not leave my mind.

I bit my lip, feeling the old dark fears slipping into my heart. How could I return to my old life, even if Zeb forgave me—and I forgave him—and we started over?

I stared at the dulcimer pieces, scattered across the workbench, knowing as a certainty that when the instrument was finished, it would be time to leave.

Time to return to Oak Hill and Zeb.

I again bent over the soundboard. "God, help me," I whispered. "I don't think I can do what you require of me." I smoothed the edge of the mission bell, lightly drawing a small cut of sandpaper across the edges of the opening. "I cannot."

Twenty-Eight

That night my fears returned. I tossed and twisted in my blankets and counterpane, willing sleep to come. The clock in the kitchen ticked endlessly on, and the distant surf pounded the shore. Finally, I fell into a troubled sleep. Dreams filled my mind, from sitting at Selah's table for elderberry tea to hunting ginseng for Poppy.

My old fears pounded my heart as the asylum rose dark and forbidding in my mind. I was running from the place, looking back over my shoulder at its towering brick sides and startling white dome. On and on I ran, my legs leaden, my feet sinking into the soil beneath me.

Monstrous shadows pursued me, faces hidden, bodies taller than the four-story pillars at the front of the asylum.

Panting, I tried harder to run, only to sink into the ground as if in quicksand. Just as I thought I might sink entirely to the bottom of the pit, I found myself in San Juan and hurried up a path that led from the ocean cliffs to the mission.

I moved with agility now, almost seeming to float above the path. The mission loomed tall and white against the gray skies.

I found myself at the gate, aware that the monstrous shadows still followed at a distance.

I stepped through and called out to Micheil, to anyone who might still be working there. But the courtyard was deserted. Only the hollow echo of my voice came back to me.

I ran through the dead gardens, skirted the pond, now stagnant again, and looked into the dark sanctuary.

"Micheil?" I called, walking slowly down the center aisle. "Are you still here?"

In its utter silence, the place loomed dark and frightening, its painted statues seeming to mock me. My heart pounding, I hurried outside again, only to be met by another blast of wind.

"Micheil?" I called again. "Micheil?"

Perhaps he was in the plaza. I gathered my courage as a greater darkness descended—from the skies and within me. Almost sobbing now, I ran through the arches. "Micheil!"

I stopped by the fountain, breathing hard, my heart thudding against my ribs. Zeb would come for me. I knew it. The terror of his confrontation, his carting me off to some asylum brought terror and images of wolves pursuing my soul. Dark-shadowed, with bared teeth, snarling, growling…the images crept closer once more.

I ran to the carpenter's shop, but it was empty. Not even my dulcimer remained. Frantically I tried to find it.

It was symbolic of myself, and without it I would disappear.

Leaning against the adobe wall, I tried to catch my breath, to still my heart, my breathing. The harder I tried, the more breath squeezed from my lungs.

"Lord, help me!" I cried. "Please, help me!"

At once a figure stood before me, his face so alight with love I couldn't bear to gaze into it for longer than a heartbeat.

I am with you, beloved.

I recognized it at once, with its sound of rushing winds and bubbling waters, with its music of a thousand dulcimers and harps and lutes.

I have been with you all along.

"I'm just beginning to understand." I swallowed hard, feeling my fears dissipate in his presence. "Sometimes my fears are too great for me to believe it."

I felt the warmth of love move nearer as he reached for my hand. His big hand tightened, solid and warm, around mine.

He led me through a graveyard I hadn't noticed before. A place of death. I shivered and clasped his hand yet tighter. I knew if I let go, the fears would come again.

We stepped into a meadow filled with bluets and buttercups. I smiled in recognition. A young woman sang and danced in the center of the meadow, her arms outstretched. She looked happy, carefree, young. So young. Her hair was the color of sunlight, her eyes the hue of the mountain skies overhead.

" 'Tis me," I whispered.

A shadow fell over the meadow in the shape of a man. Before I saw him coming up the trace, I knew it was Zeb. He walked over to the young woman, taking long, confident strides. He caught the woman's hands in his and whirled her around the meadow.

My heart caught when I saw the desire in his eyes, the desire for all that the young woman might bring him. The power he held over her at that moment. He was offering the one thing she couldn't refuse, an opening of her closed world.

Then I trembled as I saw the fire in the young woman's eyes, when I saw how desperate she was to achieve her longings.

Just when I thought I couldn't bear to watch the two faces any longer, I noticed a third figure in the meadow. I knew at once he had been there all along, only I hadn't noticed. His face was filled with sorrow, for he knew what lay ahead.

He stood next to her, beseeching her without words to follow him. He offered her hope and the light and love and comfort of his presence, but the young woman looked through him into Zeb's eyes.

I dropped my hand from the One who now stood beside me and covered my face with my hands. "I can no longer look," I whispered. "The sorrow is too great."

And when I looked again, we were in Oak Hill. Charlotte and Zebulon were standing near a window in the second story of their house, Zeb beside them. His parents wore looks of scorn, Zeb's expression was a mix of exasperation, determination, and confusion. Below the house in the garden, the young woman sat with a dulcimer in her lap.

Her face was a portrait of sorrow and shame. Her fears rose like a stench, forming thoughts I could see.

I am unworthy.

I am unlovable.

I am undesirable.

I am lonely.

I am afraid.

I started to look away, unable to bear the memory.

Then again, I saw the young woman was not alone. Someone stood beside her, a look of compassion on his face, as if he could feel every harsh word being spoken. He reached for the woman's hand, but she was too filled with the horror of what she had heard to notice.

Her face crumpled into a mask of failure and sorrow, yes even self-pity, and she turned away from the One who loved her, the One who wanted to share her heavy burden, who knew her innermost thoughts.

When she looked up again, her face had taken on a new look, one of defiance, brittleness, pigheadedness, and spite.

"I used my husband," I whispered. "I used him to get what I wanted. Escape from spinsterhood. Knowledge of the world. An education. I thought I loved him, but"—I looked down, ashamed—"in the end I used him for all these things."

I turned to the One beside me. "You were with me all along."

The love in his face was my answer.

"It would have been easier to bear if I'd known," I said. "If I had only known."

Next I saw the home Zeb and I built together outside Oak Hill. Its sweeping green hills, weeping willows, even my lush gardens. Zeb's prized Arabians prancing in the white-fenced corral.

Memories flooded my mind. Every harsh word Zeb had spoken to me, every criticism, every look that said I disappointed him, they all poured in, filling me with darkness.

They rolled around in my mind like storm clouds, mixing with the failures and spitefulness I knew now had grown like a cancer in my own heart. I shuddered and hung my head in shame, the memories too much to bear.

Beloved, he said with his voice of rushing rivers and gentle wind, *I felt your every heartache. I loved you even when you didn't love yourself.*

"He betrayed me," I whimpered, my voice small.

He didn't speak about Zeb's sins, and I knew his life was not mine to know, his betrayals were between his God and him.

Tears trailed down my cheeks. "I cannot bear it. I don't want to see any more."

His presence was nearer now, and I felt the light of his love flood into me until the darkness was no more. *Look again, beloved,* he said. *Look now.*

And I did. I saw the fluttering of the red-and-white-checked tablecloths in the breeze, Zeb's colleagues, our acquaintances from town, and the storm clouds building in the distance. Heat flooded my face, and I caught my hand to my mouth. "Oh no," I murmured. "I cannot. The pain is too great." The dark would surely come now, a shadow too dense, too great to find my way out.

I had seen them that day, locked in an embrace. Zeb and Jeannie.

I started to weep, knowing that when I saw the young woman standing with her husband upon the dais and heard the love song she sang to him, my heart would break once more.

For now I knew, looking deep into my heart, that I had loved Zeb after all. My fears of rejection, of not fitting in, my fear of failing him in this new life, had kept me from giving my heart to him.

When I saw him in Jeannie's arms, my pain had come from that place within.

If I hadn't loved him, he would not have had the power to hurt me so by his betrayal with another woman, by his suggestion of locking me away.

"She looks so young," I said. "And scared."

His voice was filled with compassion and understanding. *You were still a child, beloved.*

I couldn't hear the words the young woman spoke, or even those she sang when Zeb joined her on the platform. But I saw the sorrow on Zeb's face, his knowledge of his own betrayal.

Spread before the young couple was the beautiful house they had built together, the sweeping acreage and fine Arabian horses, but now, as I watched, they crumbled into broken dreams, broken lives, broken spirits.

I wept for us both.

Then I noticed the One standing between the young woman

and Zeb. He too was weeping, wanting to gather the young couple into his arms, wanting to heal our wounds.

"You were there," I whispered, my voice hoarse.

I will never leave you, he said. *Nor will I forsake you.*

The scene he'd shown me was fading. At once I was again walking with him through the graveyard, feeling a light mist on my face, and hearing the pepper tree leaves stirring in the breeze. My hand still in his, I turned to look back at the dark place we were leaving, the cold headstones, the shadows.

In me there is no darkness, he said in that voice that rushed like the wind. *No shadow, no turning.*

I woke with a start and sat up in bed, amazed to find myself in my bedroom at the cottage. It was almost dawn. Disturbed by the images in my dream, I rose and made my way to the kitchen.

I sat at my table and stared out toward the sea. Dark clouds billowed over the ocean. The first storm of winter seemed headed for shore. Roof tiles rattled in the wind, some breaking off and clattering to the ground. In the distance, I heard the clip-clop of horses' hooves on the cobbled streets as the milkmen made their deliveries.

The rain slanted toward the cliffs, the cottage, in sheets, turning what should have been daylight into a gray and wet gloom. I didn't go to the mission to work on the dulcimer. Instead I stayed inside by the fire, baking little cakes to deliver to the *barrio* children once the storm died down and thinking about my return to Zeb.

There was no darkness of spirit in me this day to match the gloom outside. Instead I found myself humming Spanish, Irish, and Appalachian folk songs while I baked, delighting in the scent of cinnamon and sugar, the sounds of the crackling fire.

And all the while, *I will return to Oak Hill come spring* played like a song's refrain through my mind.

Surprisingly, the prospect was not fearful. With God's strength, I would do as I must. I smiled, glad in my new courage. *I will return to Oak Hill come spring.*

While I waited for the last tray of cakes to finish baking, I walked to the window and pulled back the curtain to stare into the rain. As soon as the winter rains stopped, as soon as the dulcimer was finished, I would go.

Less than three months to finish my instrument. Less than three months to say my good-byes.

It rained for three days. Finally, on the fourth day, the sun broke through and the *barrio* children raced from their houses to play in the puddles, singing and shouting and laughing. The neighborhood once again came to life.

Rosa sped across the muddy road to hug me when I stepped out my front door. Antonia, her mother, waved from their adobe down the road, and Carmelita called a thank-you for the cakes I'd brought her during the breaks in the rainstorm.

When the rains had kept me indoors, in silent reverie, thoughts of my good-byes hadn't seemed as difficult as they did now, with the children's faces before me, their little arms hugging me tight, their mothers' friendly smiles and greetings.

That evening, an hour before sundown, I spotted Micheil trudging up the muddy road, his hat brim turned downward, the lines in his face looking wearier than usual. An unexpected wave of affection filled my heart. He saw me watching from the small front porch and called out.

Wanting to weed the garden while the soil was rain-moist, over my long smock I had pulled on an oversize man's flannel shirt I'd found in my grandmother's closet.

Micheil grinned when he saw me, and I struck a pose like a manikin. We both laughed.

"I've just put together a stew," I said. "Would you like to join me for supper?"

"Lass, you're spoiling this Irish lad for certain."

"There's a catch." I caught his hand and pulled him around the side of the house. I pointed to the ocean below. The tide was out, and a wide stretch of sand lay beneath us. "How would you like to cook our dinner down there?"

His brow shot up again. "On the beach?"

I grinned. "It's seems dry enough. The sun's been out all day. We'll have to cart it down there. If you'll dig the hole for the Dutch oven, I'll find some dry sticks."

"That may not be possible."

"We'll take a bundle from the stove bin."

I caught his hand again and pulled him along. We gathered blankets and towels and a shovel. Going to the kitchen, I gently placed the small Dutch oven in a basket. Inside were pieces of beef, carrots, onions, beets, and rosemary. Then I dropped in two blue-speckled plates and cups and cutlery for us both. Next I pulled a Mason jar full of fresh-squeezed orange juice from the icebox and tucked it along one side of the basket.

"Don't forget matches," Micheil said, watching me.

"Oh, and tea." I grabbed a small tin and dropped it into one of the blue-speckled cups. "It will be cold after the sun goes down. We'll need to hold the cups to keep our hands warm."

We found a sheltered spot in the center of a rock formation

and spread some old quilts. While he dug the hole for the cooking fire, I sat and watched him.

He was in silhouette, with the setting sun behind him streaking the sky with orange and lavender. He pushed the shovel blade into the ground and then leaned against the handle. He looked out toward the sea, and I wondered if his thoughts were of Ireland, halfway around the world.

He turned to me then, his expression one that I knew would haunt me forever. I could see beyond the shadows of twilight to his own fears of the future, his unwillingness to say good-bye.

I went to him and gently wound one arm around his waist. He laid his cheek on top of my head, and I thought he might be weeping. We stayed like that as the glow from the sun faded to dark purple.

"I need to make some decisions about my grandmother's ranch, the cottage." I spoke calmly, surprised at the peace in my heart. The waves swished across the sand, and a cool breeze came up where we sat facing the ocean. I shivered and tightened Welsie's shawl around my shoulders. "I don't think I'll be back once I leave."

I met Micheil's eyes, and he gave me an encouraging nod. " 'Tis as it should be, lass."

I was grateful for his encouragement. "I will miss your singing," I said, the corner of my mouth turning upward.

He laughed. " 'Tis one of my best assets."

"I was about to ask your advice about my grandmother's properties."

"Your properties," he reminded me gently.

"After I leave, I want you to have them."

He considered me for a few moments. The ocean swelled,

rushing to the shore, then ebbed again. Above us, gulls circled and cried, some gliding almost without movement on the winds. The baby scooted something that felt like an elbow across my belly, and I smiled to myself, resting my hand over the place.

"I'll be leaving, lass, though how soon I can't say," Micheil said. "All I know is that I can't promise you that I can oversee your property."

I leaned forward. "I don't mean as an overseer, Micheil. I mean for you to take them as your own. I want to give the whole thing to you. You can use the proceeds for Ireland's fight against the English. Or for feeding the poor there…or here. Maybe use part of the ranch as a school—"

He raised his hand to stop me. "I know your thinking, but no, lass. Welsie True left her lands to you, her own granddaughter. It isn't fitting for me to take them." I'd known what his answer would be before I'd made my offer.

When I didn't speak, he went on. "As I told you before, the temptation would be nearly too great for me not to leave for Ireland." He smiled, the sorrow clear in his eyes. " 'Tis hard enough already. But letting the ranch, this cottage, burrow deeper into my heart…well now, it might just be impossible for me."

I had no right to wish for his change of mind, but I had to admit I'd hoped the gift might turn him from his course. I tried to push from my mind the trial he would face, his walk to the gallows. I shuddered and turned away.

"Lass," he said softly. "your generosity moves me. More than you can know, it does. I will promise you this. I will stay on for a while, through the spring roundup, the calving, and the branding. My foreman is a man to be trusted. Perhaps you can hire him to run things. We'll make arrangements with a banker here in town to oversee the financial arrangements. Together, they can see to it that the ranch runs smoothly. They'll send you a full accounting and a draft of the profits each month."

I nodded bleakly. "Yes, I'll need to see the accounting, but we'll let the profits accumulate for my child. Someday perhaps she—"

"Or he," he added with a laugh.

"Perhaps *she*," I corrected with a grin, "will come here to claim her inheritance."

"Are you so certain she's a she, not a he?" he teased.

I patted my abdomen, looking down thoughtfully. "Sometimes I wonder if it's both," I said. "Such a tumble of arms and legs…" My cheeks warmed, speaking of such a delicate matter in front of a man.

"Twins?" He almost shouted the words, then threw back his head and laughed. "Glory! Now wouldn't that be a joy!" He leaned forward, holding my gaze intently. "I want you to remember, Fairwyn March, that when you deliver these wee ones—"

"We don't know there's more than one!" I protested.

He arched a brow and continued "When you deliver, lass, I want you to know that I'll be singing over you, over your wee ones, with joy! I'll be raising my voice to join the angels in heaven rejoicing, just as our heavenly Father rejoices over us."

We talked on into the night, staring out at the starlit sky and listening to the rush of the breakers. When the full moon broke over the eastern horizon, shining its beams across the rippling ocean, Micheil began to sing, smoothly at first, then with a broken, husky resonance.

The pale moon was rising above the green mountain;
The sun was declining beneath the blue sea

When I strayed with my love to the pure crystal fountain
That stands in the beautiful vale of Tralee.
She was lovely and fair as the rose of the summer
Yet 'twas not her beauty alone that won me
Oh, no! 'twas the truth in her eye ever dawning
That made me love Mary, the Rose of Tralee.

He stopped suddenly and was still, staring out at the ocean. Neither of us spoke. Perhaps he was afraid, as I was, to fully consider the meaning of his last words.

The waves broke and laced toward shore. My eyes stung as I held back the tears that waited to spill.

"When we've parted, I will carry you in my heart," he said, still looking out to sea. A small wave rushed toward the beach, its foam shining in the starlight. Seagulls cried in the distance.

"Aye," Micheil said after a few minutes. "That I can promise you, lass. 'Twill be until the end of time."

Twenty-Nine

After that night, I felt a new urgency to complete my dulcimer. Every morning at dawn I walked to the mission, sometimes with an umbrella in the rain, sometimes in the fair predawn light that promised a crystal, blue-skied day as only a winter in California could. On such days the seagulls flapped and soared above me as I fairly floated along the mission road, just as I once did along the traces at home, and the sparrows and finches and mockingbirds sang from the olive trees and sycamores that lined my path.

As the weeks passed, the drape of my smock ceased to conceal the swell of the baby, and my walking seemed to bring her special delight. She bumped and jumped almost playfully and turned over in rhythm with my stride. I prayed for her safekeeping, and mine, during my early morning strolls, wondering if my newfound happiness and peace had anything to do with her vigorous activity.

By mid-February I could no longer see my toes. Carmelita's mother, a midwife in our *barrio,* examined me and, with a beaming smile, announced what I already knew to be true: My child was robust and healthy.

One morning in early March I had just finished applying the first coat of varnish when I moved outside my workroom to stretch my back and enjoy a moment of the sun's warmth on my face and shoulders.

"Señora! Señora!"

From across the arches beneath the pepper tree Nando raced toward me. Rosa, Nita, and Carlos, following along behind, began shouting before they made it halfway across the courtyard, their faces glowing with some bit of news. When they reached me, all four tried to talk at once, bouncing and shouting above each other.

I laughed, holding up a hand to quiet them. "One at a time, please."

"Señor Micheil has asked us to sing," Nando said, his eyes wide with importance. "At the festival! All of us—Rosa, Nita, Carlos, Juan, and Jaime."

"And you, señora," Nita said, taking my hand and craning to look me in the face.

"And Señor Micheil," Carlos added. "Do not forget him. He says we will sing of our heritage. All of us, just like we did that day—"

"The day Nita's mommy brought us lunch," Rosa filled in.

"*Sí!* Yes, that was the day." Nando grinned up at me as if looking for approval.

"And when is this festival?" I hoped it was before the end of the month. I couldn't risk traveling any closer to my baby's arrival.

"March nineteenth," Nando said.

"Ah, yes," I said, tilting my head at the memory that filled my mind. How could I have forgotten the festival my grandmother wrote me about each year? "Saint Joseph's Day," I said, "the day the swallows return to the mission."

"*Sí! Sí!*" the children shouted, again bouncing and talking with excitement.

"Señor Micheil," Carlos shouted, vying for my attention, "he says he'll sing that night too, and also say a few words—"

"Of en-cour-age-ment," Nando added, struggling with the

unfamiliar word. "Because Señor Micheil says that the winds of change are soon to blow, and he wants to prepare us." He hesitated and scratched his head, frowning. "What does that mean?"

I smiled and ruffled his hair. "God has planned good things for us all," I said quietly. "But sometimes it means things will be different." I couldn't bring myself to tell them that I would be leaving in just a few weeks. That the cottage would be empty and dark. That no one would be there to oversee their cake baking, to listen to their happy chatter, to answer their troubled questions or settle their minor squabbles.

How could I tell them?

I couldn't. Not yet.

They ran off to play, and I turned back to the dulcimer. The days were warmer now, and I expected the first coating of varnish to dry overnight. I stepped closer to the workbench to examine the thin veneer I had just applied.

The dulcimer was nearly complete. I rubbed my fingers over the fingerboard, the only part of the dulcimer that wasn't sticky with fresh varnish. My fingers moved along the spacers, tapping out soft rhythms from long ago as if they were connected to my heart, not my arm.

I jumped when Micheil spoke behind me. " 'Tis almost done."

I turned and gave him a mock glare. "I'll have to start all over if I drop it."

My words were spoken in jest, but his expression was serious when he spoke. "Something tells me your time is nearing."

I smiled at the irony. "For my leaving, yes. Also for"—I looked down at my bulging stomach—"for, ah, well…"

"The coming little one," he grinned, helping me in my embarrassment.

He moved to my worktable and bent to examine the sound-board. "You'll be taking part of our mission home with you." He studied the sound holes, moving his gaze from the mission bell cutout to the swallows. "When will you go then?"

"I've only just now decided—after Nando told me about the festival. I'll leave the day after." I leaned against the workbench, my folded hands resting on the shelf made by the baby. "I can't miss the children's singing." The image of the candlestick sent to me by my grandmother came back to me. It had brought me so much comfort during my dark days with Zeb, with its glow of candle-light illuminating the relief of swallows. "Or the return of the swallows," I said with a sigh. "My grandmother wrote of its wonder."

He chuckled then. "Did she also tell you that it's more legend than reality? That sometimes they don't return on time."

I laughed. "She did, but I choose to believe the legend." I straightened, rubbed my back, and then moved through the door to the plaza, conscious that I now waddled rather awkwardly.

"Have you told Nando…and the others?" Micheil asked as we moved to the squat adobe bench in the center of the courtyard.

I sat heavily and smiled my thanks. "I will soon," I said, "though it will be difficult to tell them why. Perhaps harder on me than them."

"I know you'll be missing them when you leave, lass. They've become your wee shadows." He settled on the end of the bench, turning halfway toward me, resting one ankle on the opposite knee.

I sighed and closed my eyes, holding my face to the warmth of the sun. "I can't promise them I'll return. I hope to, of course. But it may be long after they're grown and gone." I shook my head. "How can you explain that to a child?"

"They'll have memories of the love you've given them," he said.

I opened my eyes to study his face, seized by the sudden flow of my own memories, the children's voices, their laughter and song. The way Nita had of kissing my cheek whenever she saw me or Nando's pride in helping with the dulcimer. The way they constantly peppered me with questions, from why robins' eggs are blue to why the tide flows in and out.

And Micheil? What would I do with my memories of him? I smiled at him gently. He, too, had shown me love and acceptance when I thought I was the least of God's children to deserve it.

My memories of Micheil would be tucked in my heart forever.

"The children tell me you're planning to speak at the festival," I said, forcing my thoughts away from the heart-wrenching loss I would soon face. "Will you tell them you're leaving?"

"Aye," he said softly, looking past me to the fluttering leaves of the pepper tree. "This is one of the few times the *barrio* families gather in one place. Though my departure won't be for a few more months, I want to ask some of the families to continue my work here."

"To take over your school?"

He nodded. "That will be the most difficult." He turned back to me. "The anguish of the Indians goes back a century or more. The hostilities between the local groups are just under the surface." He shook his head. "The sad thing is, lass, that each group has a rich heritage. I just wish they'd look at their riches and let the old wounds heal."

"By bringing them together—to help the less fortunate—you've hoped to help them overcome their differences, their hostilities?"

He let out a long sigh. "Takes more than just one, lass. Takes all of us working together."

I studied the profile of his face, those expressions of concern and compassion that had become so dear. "You've begun a good work, Micheil. Surely God will see that those seeds you've planted will grow."

"Aye, lass. But in his time, in his time." He turned with a sad smile. "I'm the most impatient of his children. I know in my heart that what our heavenly Father desires will come to pass. It's just that my heart's desire is to remain here to see it happen before my very eyes." He smiled sadly. "Desire and duty are at war within me too often."

"What you've done here won't be forgotten, any more than what you've done for me will be forgotten."

"Ah, my child, as I told you months ago, I believe this great big God of ours planned for our meeting at this exact time and place in our spiritual journeys. I will remember how I've seen him reflected in your spirit. How that recent joy that seems to glow from your sweet face has renewed my own courage."

I blinked in surprise. "I can't imagine that my spirit would cause anyone to be inspired," I said quietly. I remembered my dark days, my lonely musings, my unhappy spirit, from years gone by. These memories pressed down on my heart like a weight, so different than those I would take with me from this place.

"That's where you are wrong, lass. You may have considered yourself unworthy of inspiration, but 'tis an error in your thinking." He clasped my hand between his and held it gently. "You are worthy, Fairwyn March. Your heart belongs to the One who sings over you with gladness.

"And that, lass, is the glow of love and joy that you can't hide." His smile was radiant, as if he looked into the future and saw something that I did not. "That is the true music of your soul." He glanced toward the doorway of the wood shop and nodded slowly.

" 'Tis a fact that our Lord has gifted you with a voice like an angel, with the beauty of your dulcimer songs. But lass, 'tis the music of his love that brings it forth."

He released my hand and stood, looking down at me, as I nodded, understanding the truth of his words.

"And you, Micheil Grady Gilvarry," I said softly, " 'tis the music of *your* spirit that will stay with me forever. I'll be hearing that music long after I leave this place."

He rolled his eyes heavenward, a grin melting into the radiance on his face. When he again met my gaze, his eyes twinkled merrily. "As long as it's me soul's music you're ahearin', lass," he said, "and not the froglike croakin' of me voice."

With a chuckle, he gave me another nod and turned to walk back across the courtyard, whistling as he went. He almost seemed to bounce as he walked, a new lightness having taken over his step. I wouldn't have been surprised to see him dance a quick jig or click his heels in the air.

He seemed to sense that I was watching him and turned to wave. "Keep singing, lass," he called to me. "Don't you ever let your music die." With another wave he stepped through the archway and was gone.

The Cottage at San Juan
Early morning, March 19, 1888

My dearest Grandmother Welsie True,

I am whole at last, I am! How I wish you were here so I could gather you into my arms and tell you how it happened.

I have found mercy in the arms of One who was with me, loving me all along and bringing me to where he wanted me to be so that he could show me himself.

I know myself too well to fancy that I will never be afraid again. For as you know, I am predisposed to worrisome thoughts. But now I know there is One with me who walks by my side, One who will carry me when I'm in need of carrying.

Tomorrow I will lock up your little cottage. I hope someday to return, bringing Zeb and our coming child. If Zeb doesn't take to the idea, then I will bring our little one myself, to check on things, visit my new friends in the neighborhood, and introduce your great-grandchild to the waiting inheritance.

I write to you this morning as I sit in your gazebo, looking out at the slant of sunlight on the ocean. It's reflecting on the rippling waves, looking like a million shards of glass have been scattered across the blue waters.

It reminds me of my heart, Welsie True. Long ago it held all my hopes and dreams. It seemed almost translucent, guileless, I suppose. I thought my heart would remain filled with warmth and joy. But I went my own way, headstrong and determined. My heart turned brittle with hurts, disappointment, and self-pity. When it shattered into a million little pieces, I thought it would never be whole again.

Now, as I sit here watching the light play like rainbow prisms on the rippling waves, I'm thinking about that heart of glass. Oh yes, it was broken, and I can't place blame on Zeb for shattering it. Too much of the responsibility was mine.

All I know is that has God created jewels from the broken pieces. Micheil once quoted these words from the prophet Isaiah: "O thou afflicted, tossed with tempest, and not comforted, behold I will lay thy stones with fair colors, and lay thy foundations with sapphires. And I will make thy windows of agates, and thy gates of crystal, and all thy borders of precious stones."

My heavenly Father has done this for me! He's taken my brokenness and built me up with precious stones. Through you—and this little cottage—he brought me home. Truly home.

I look to the horizon, Welsie True, that hazy place between the edge of the sea and the sky. I like to think of you as still alive, waiting at the far end of my letters' journey, listening and loving me, just as you always did.

How grateful I am for how you loved me all these years. You have given me a legacy like no other.

I remain

Your loving granddaughter,

Fairwyn True Deforest

I folded the letter, tucked it into an envelope, and sealed it with a stick of wax. I placed it inside my grandmother's Bible and placed it in the oak secretary by the window.

A few minutes later, Nita tapped on my door. She gave me a hug and then took my hand and led me down the walkway to the family wagon. I held my finished dulcimer in my opposite arm like a baby. Carmelita and Fernando waved gaily, and Fernando jumped down to help me step to the bench seat. He held the instrument as I sat heavily next to Carmelita, and then handed it back to me. I cradled it against me to protect it against the jostling of the wagon.

My friend grinned, glancing at my round abdomen. I chuckled at hers. Nando's ears turned red as he chirked to the swaybacked horse. Nita clambered into the back, full of questions about the swallows coming back to the mission.

By the time we reached the mission, families had already begun to gather. The sounds of Spanish guitars carried toward us as we let ourselves through the entrance gate.

The day had dawned clear and crisp, and now that the sun was higher, the sky had turned a purple blue. I sat down on the stone bench beneath the grape arbor as Carmelita and Nando walked into the center plaza, the children skipping along beside them.

I wanted to drink in every detail, from Micheil's irrigation trenches to the pond where pollywogs and mosquito fish now flourished. The nearby garden remained a tangle of cactus, milk-weed, and dandelions, and my fingers itched to pull a few weeds. Glancing down at my stomach, I couldn't help chuckling at the image. If I bent over to pull a single weed, I would likely topple into the tangled brush and never get out.

For days the mission families had been at work preparing the foods, chopping and baking, and cooking pots full of sauces. The air was filled with the fragrance of simmering chilis and baking tor-tillas. I leaned back and closed my eyes. It seemed everything within the line of my vision, every scent wafting toward me, every trill of birdsong and distant strum of the Spanish guitar—all of it filled my senses.

A flutter of wings reminded me of the swallows, and I looked to the pepper tree near the arches. But the flapping had come from a mockingbird, up to its usual antics, flying in dancelike loops, landing and singing, then starting over again. I smiled to myself, wondering if the swallows would indeed return today.

More families were entering the courtyard now. Many stopped to crane their necks heavenward. Each time I followed their gaze. The sun was high, the sky still a bright blue, but there was no sign of a single swallow.

The Spanish music that floated from the plaza was irresistible. I tapped my foot, wanting to dance, and then laughed again at the silliness of such a notion. Soon I rose and, holding the dulcimer, headed through the arches. I stopped in surprise.

The place was a blaze of color and music and laughter. Already, more than a hundred people had gathered. I grinned at Micheil as he passed by dressed like a vaquero for the occasion, leading a small group on a tour of the monks' quarters. As the group moved off to listen to the guitar music, he headed toward me.

He glanced at the dulcimer in my arms, and smiled. "I saw it on your workbench yesterday, finished and glorious. Then it disappeared." He raised a brow. "Been worrying meself sick all night because of it, lass."

I strummed my fingers across the fretboard. "Surely you knew I would take it home to practice a bit."

"Truly, lass, I did indeed." He reached across to run his fingers lightly over the strings. "But I can also tell you this. I missed seeing the spread of your tools and the scattered pieces of wood." He glanced across the courtyard to the workshop. "Looks too bare for words."

Before either of us could speak, we were interrupted by Rosa, dark braids gleaming in the sun, as she flew across the bricks. "*Los pájaros!* The birds! I see them," she shouted in Spanish. "I see them. They're here at last!" The other children raced behind her, reaching for my hands and Micheil's.

Nita led me to the outer courtyard. Already a crowd had gathered. They craned skyward.

"See!" Nita shouted. "Up there! Look!" In her excitement she chattered happily in Spanish.

I grinned, following her gaze. Then I saw them myself. A flock, perhaps three dozen or more, circled above the mission. They gleamed in the sun, almost silver—just as Welsie True had said—swooping and dipping gracefully through the sky. Their tails were spread like fans, their soft voices carried in the wind.

My heart almost stopped with the wonder of the moment, the little girl's hand in mine, the vision of utter freedom and peace and joy.

The birds still circled, and I wondered if the crowds might frighten them away. Almost as one, the groups of families and children hushed. Still the birds glided and circled. Then more fluttered closer and joined in. One by one, they dipped and fluttered to the roof of the sanctuary, some perching in the arches on either side, some in the pepper tree nearby.

Just when I thought the sight of it all couldn't be prettier, still more arrived, their voices lifted in a chorus of rolling *churrrs* with small squeaks and clicks as if they were talking to each other. They circled several times and then fluttered to a roosting spot.

"Listen to their voices," Nita whispered, still hanging on to my hand. "Can you hear them?"

"I can," I whispered back and squeezed her hand.

When it seemed that surely all the flocks had arrived, still more fluttered to a landing. Now people spoke in normal tones, and the festival spirit arose once more. The swallows seemed to take it in stride, and simply gazed down at the group with calm expressions.

The sun was starting on its downward arch when the folks started back to the main plaza. The children ran off to play, their voices joining the chorus of squeals, laughter, conversation, and guitar strums. If I listened carefully, I could hear the low, peaceful tones of the swallows above us.

At dusk, Fernando and Micheil lit torches around the plaza. The scents of *posole,* tamales, and tortillas again filled the air, and families broke into small groups to eat, some on blankets, others standing, still others sitting on the edge of the pond or near the front gardens.

During a lull, Micheil walked to the platform where the guitar players had been playing and looked out over the crowd.

" 'Tis a night of celebration," he said. "We celebrate the gathering of the swallows, we also celebrate the gathering of family and friends, all those we love. And we celebrate the care of our heavenly Father who brought us all together in this place."

A hush fell over the crowd. In the front row, my young friends sat cross-legged in front of their parents.

"We are blessed," he said, "with abundance from God's storehouse." He nodded toward the tamales and roasting beef. "What better day than this could we have?" With a smile, he gestured toward the roosting swallows. "Good food, great joy—singing, dancing, and music. And the swallows actually returned on time."

Fernando whistled a cheer, followed by clapping from the others. The swallows fluttered, some taking wing, only to quickly return to their nesting places.

"Memories such as these can bring us comfort later on." Micheil's eyes sought mine.

"Aye," I mouthed with a soft smile. "Aye."

Micheil looked back to the families, his gaze resting on the group of children from the *barrio*. "Sometimes change comes. It's not always welcome, but it must come nonetheless." He looked back to me. "One of us is leaving tomorrow. Great change is coming to her life—"

"It is Señora Fairwyn," Nando said with importance. "She already told me. I was the first to know."

"Huh-uh," Rosa said. "I was the first."

"No! I was!" Carlos stood to emphasize his point.

A small peppery argument followed. I grinned, knowing enough Spanish now to understand. "I told you all at once," I reminded them, raising a brow.

"I was there," Carmelita said. She met my eyes with a sad nod. "Señora Fairwyn told us all, children. Over cakes and tea. But it does not matter who heard it first. We all will miss her."

Antonia and Elena, sitting nearby, had already given me their well wishes, but they stood and came over to me to say good-bye. Antonia, reaching across my stomach to hug me, whispered, *"Vaya con Dios."* Elena held me close for a moment. Then she pulled back and grinned, patting my belly just as the baby wiggled and turned.

After a few minutes, Micheil cleared his throat and the crowd quieted, though they still were hovering close by me.

"When people leave," he said to the children, "though you don't see them, you carry them in your heart. You remember everything about them. You will remember Señora Fairwyn's dulcimer making…"

Still holding my hand Nita looked up at me, and nodded her head. *"Yo lo recuerdo,"* she mouthed in Spanish. "I will remember."

"And baking little cakes in her kitchen…"

Nando licked his lips and rubbed his stomach, exaggerating dramatically for his friends, until a frown from his mother made him stop. His expression grew serious. "Señora," he whispered, "I will miss you."

I squeezed his hand, and turned back to Micheil.

"More change is coming," he said. "Later on, I will be leaving as well." He smiled broadly. "Going back to my home in Ireland, I am, but it won't be for yet a season or two."

The torches flickered and glowed, casting light on the faces of the men and women around him. I saw their expressions turn from dismay to sadness, and then to alarm.

He held up a hand to stop their questions. "I'm telling you tonight," he said, "because I need your help in the days to come." He paused. "God has given us each other. We're not alone in our journey, no matter our heritage, no matter who we are, rich or poor, from big families or small. He asks each of us to take the hand of another, to help them keep from stumbling, to feed them, to clothe them, to teach them.

"We can't always succeed," he said. "God doesn't ask us to. He only asks us to try to help those who need us.

"Here is a story that explains it better than I can:

"Then shall the King say unto them on his right hand, Come, ye blessed of my Father…for I was hungered, and ye gave me meat: I was thirsty, and ye gave me drink: I was a stranger, and ye took me in: Naked, and ye clothed me: I was sick, and ye visited me.

"Then the people asked him, Lord, when saw we thee hungered, and fed thee? or thirsty, and gave thee drink? When saw we thee a stranger, and took thee in? or naked, and clothed thee?

"And the King answered, Verily I say unto you, Inasmuch as

ye have done it unto one of the least of these my brethren, ye have done it unto me."

Micheil went on, making his plea for others to help feed the hungry and visit the sick in San Juan and on the reservation. But I stared at him, my mind still on the King's words, understanding at last. Micheil did not serve others as penance to gain favor with his Lord as he once suspected of himself. No, he served with a heart of ministry so great he might have been serving Christ himself.

I was stunned and blindly reached behind my skirts to find a chair. I grabbed hold and fell into it, still staring. This man, with a heart so pure, a love so deep...how could he possibly think of returning to Ireland and certain death?

"Lord," I breathed, "this world needs Micheil Grady Gilvarry, his heart and soul!" I pictured his trial...the gallows...and buried my face in my hands. "Don't take him from us."

For a moment, there wasn't a sound in the courtyard except the soft burrs of the swallows. I lifted my face to see Micheil standing with his arms outstretched as he pronounced a blessing on the gathering. His beloved voice, with its thick brogue, carried on the wind, mixing with the rustle of pepper leaves and coo of the flocks above us.

His weary, lined face was filled with deep conviction, his voice with great courage. I shivered and prayed again for his safekeeping.

Later, after the vaqueros and señoritas had performed their dance, the children shouted that it was their turn to sing. They scrambled onto the platform, first singing in their native tongue to the music of the Spanish guitars. When they finished, Rosa hopped from the riser, took my hand, and led me to my place just below them.

A few days earlier I'd taught them "The Bird Song" in honor of the swallows. It had quickly replaced "The Old Gray Goose" as their favorite. I hummed a note so they would begin in the same key and then lifted my hand.

They watched my fingers just as I'd taught them, and when I brought my hand downward, they began to sing, shyly at first, then gaining speed and gusto. Nando wiggled his way to the center of the front row. He opened his mouth wide and sang at the top of his lungs, drowning out the others.

Hi! says the blackbird, sitting on a chair,
Once I courted a lady fair;
She proved fickle and turned her back,
And ever since then I'm dressed in black.

Giggling, the children went on to sing verses about the blue jay, the leather-winged bat, the woodpecker on the fence, and the little mourning dove, each verse striking them as sillier and merrier than the last.

Nita stepped forward and opened her eyes wide, her thumbs and fingers forming round circles like spectacles atop her nose. The others hummed while she sang the next verse alone.

Hi! says the owl with eyes so big,
If I had a hen I'd feed like a pig;
But here I sit on a frozen stake,
Which causes my poor heart to ache.

The audience laughed and clapped. The children finished the final verse together, first pointing to the roosting swallows, then

standing tall with hands on hips and waggling their elbows like
wings.

Hi! says the swallow, sitting in a barn,
Courting, I think, is no harm.
I pick my wings and sit up straight...

When the song was over the children bowed and marched
from the platform.

"Now you, señora," Nando said heading straight toward me.
"It is your turn. You promised."

Micheil carried a chair to the platform and placed it in the center. Then, taking my hand, he helped me step onto the small riser
and be seated. The children settled on the ground below me, their
parents, brothers, and sisters slightly behind. A hush fell as I began
to strum.

The tone was perfect, mellow and sweet. I shivered with
delight, unable to stop smiling. It was finished, it was! As whole and
beautiful as I'd imagined it would be. I let my fingers dance over the
strings, closing my eyes and listening to the tone I'd missed.

The dulcimer Zeb had given me, the music it played, seemed
shallow and empty compared to the rich tones floating from this
instrument. I glanced up at Micheil, who was heading from the
platform to sit with the children. His expression said that his
delight in the sound was nearly as great at mine.

I strummed up and down the fingerboard, playing the first
chords of "Greensleeves" and watching the faces of the little children kneeling in front of me. The song, dating back to sixteenth-
century England, was familiar to Micheil. He smiled and nodded
in time with the music.

I purposely didn't sing out loud, but instead, lost myself in the haunting beauty of the melody, letting the lyrics play only in my mind. *Greensleeves was all my joy… Greensleeves was my delight… Greensleeves was my heart of gold…* Still strumming, I glanced down at the children, who had draped themselves over Micheil. Rosa rested her cheek on one shoulder; Juan hung on the other. Nita sat in his lap. Carlos played with the vaquero hat, lifting it and dropping it back onto Micheil's head in perfect rhythm with the music. Jaime leaned against one arm.

The sight of Micheil surrounded by the children made my throat tighten, and I swallowed the sting. Cradling the dulcimer, I slowed the tempo, still strumming softly, almost as in a lullaby.

Though he didn't sing the words out loud, Micheil's lips formed the words of the final chorus, his expression solemn as he kept his gaze on mine.

Greensleeves, now farewell! Adieu!
God I pray to prosper thee…

I boarded the first train east the following morning.

Thirty

The train pulled into the station in Oak Hill at 11:13 A.M. the following Thursday.

From the corner of my eye I saw the stationmaster give me a curious glance as I walked past his counter, my face slightly averted. In my present state, I didn't think I would be recognized. But I needed to be careful. I didn't want the word spread that I was back. Not yet. I would find out soon enough if Oak Hill thought me dead or if Zeb had tracked me to California and let it be known that I had deserted him. When I ran into the first old acquaintance, the resulting expression would answer the question: A look of horror would tell me they thought me a haunt. Disdain would tell me Zeb had indeed discovered I was alive.

I hired a carriage at the stables across from the train station, and soon I was heading down the dusty road to town. I directed the driver to take me to a rundown boardinghouse on the outskirts, a place where Zeb and his colleagues would have no connection.

My valise in one hand, I paid the driver with the other and waved him off before turning to assess the front of the graying, two-story town house. It certainly wasn't of the same distinction as the imposing Deforest home on Bank Street, or Jeannie's family estate a few blocks over.

I stepped to the front door and knocked. A small woman with

white hair and a face like a dried-apple doll opened the door a few minutes later.

"I need a room for the night…" I hesitated. "Possibly longer."

She frowned, looking me up and down and finally settling her gaze on my round abdomen. "What's your business in Oak Hill?"

Her question stopped me. I hadn't expected it. Worse, I didn't know how to answer. "Family here," I finally mumbled, knowing she likely would wonder why I wasn't staying with them.

"Estranged family," I added with a small smile.

She patted my arm. "Never mind an old woman's questions, dear. Come in, come in." She stood back to let me enter the house. "My name's Geneva Zacharias." Her cheeks wrinkled into a smile. "You can call me Eva. All my boarders do."

"My name is Fairwyn," I said. "Fairwyn March."

Eva's forehead furrowed in thought. "Fairwyn…now that's an unusual name. Heard tell of someone else in this town with that same name. Now isn't that something?"

I swallowed hard and nodded. "Yes, it is."

"She was married to that Deforest professor out at Providence College." She peered into my eyes. "You heard of the college?"

"Yes ma'am. I have."

She chuckled. "Well, that Fairwyn, the other Fairwyn, has a reputation just about as far and wide." She turned to lead me up the stairs.

"What have you heard, about that other Fairwyn, I mean?"

Eva moved slowly upward, taking two small steps on each stair, hanging onto the banister as she went. "Well now, I'm not at all certain what I've heard is the gospel truth—but I think she's one of those what died in that there train wreck last year." She shook her head. "Sad, sad time it was. So many lost here in town. Over in Dover Town, I heard tell, they lost more'n we did."

Eva stopped at the top of the stairs, pinching her little knot of white hair at her neck to make sure the hairpins were still in place, then moved slowly on down the dark hallway. I followed, breathing heavily as I climbed the stairs.

Eva waited for me at the door to the first bedroom on the right. I looked in and sighed when I saw the iron bedstead. The train ride across the country had taken its toll on me, and I was weary.

The bed graced one end of the perfectly square room. It was covered by a faded log-cabin quilt and flanked by two small scarred tables. An ancient wardrobe stood opposite the bed. And between the two, a worn curtain draped across the room's single window.

Eva fussed around the room, opening the wardrobe doors, pointing out the basin and towels, and chattering on about the necessary that was outdoors behind the peach tree.

She tottered to the open door, then hesitated and turned, looking worried. "Child, you look close to your time."

I nodded. "I am."

"You plan to have your child here? See a local doctor?"

My cheeks warmed as I realized how unprepared I was. My focus had been on getting to Oak Hill before my labor pains began, not on what would happen once I arrived. "I-I hadn't really thought about it."

Her face softened somewhat. "You need to think about it. I've had experience with such things. You look like you could have your baby any day."

I felt the room begin to spin and reached for the iron footboard of the bed to steady myself. "I am tired. It's been a long, long journey."

When she left I dropped to the edge of the bed and sat for a long while, thinking about Zeb, wondering how I should first contact him. I rose and walked to the window and lifted the heavy sash to let the spring breezes sweep in.

A tightening rippled across my stomach. I caught my breath until it passed.

I had to see him. Now. It couldn't wait, even till morning as I had planned. Feeling faint, I crossed the room to the basin, poured water in my hands and splashed it on my face. Then straightening the skirts of my voluminous smock, I headed slowly for the door.

Shortly later, I walked slowly along the road to the heart of Oak Hill to the livery at the corner of Central and West Bank Street. The proprietor was asleep, sitting on a bale of hay. I touched his arm, and he jumped, looking sheepish.

"I need a buggy for the afternoon. And a driver."

"Yes ma'am. Got just the thing." He stumbled to the corral and led out a high-stepping black mare. "I'll give you the fanciest one we got. But I ain't got no driver. You'll have to do the honors yourself."

My arms and legs ached from days of sitting on the bench in the coach car and trying to stretch out in the small sleeper at night. The thought of managing a horse, even flicking the reins, brought the smart of tears.

"I don't need fancy," I said. "Just gentle. Manageable."

Minutes later he had hitched up a quieter horse and helped me into the carriage. Gritting my teeth in determination, I forgot my discomfort and snapped the reins over the back of the old piebald mare, heading her to the south of town. The more I tried to guide her, the more rapid the flicking of one ear. I headed her onto the familiar road leading to our property, winding through the spring-green hills and across the wildflower-strewn fields.

The spring scents raised my spirits; and instead of past failures, I focused on our new start. I pushed the thought of the asylum from my mind as I flicked the reins over the piebald. She lifted her head and shook her mane with a low sputtering whinny, one ear flicking backward.

"All right, girl," I said with a laugh, "have it your way." I let her set the pace, and surprisingly she ambled along with ease.

The closer I got to our acreage, the harder my heart beat against my ribs, to the point of causing a dull ache. I slowed the mare, and she let me know her displeasure with another flick of her ears.

I reined the piebald to the side of the road and let two carriages pass me. I flicked the reins again and headed the mare toward the house. When I was a half-mile away, I stopped, surprised to see the place looking deserted. The fenced pasture where Zeb kept the Arabian horses was empty, the grass overgrown. My gardens near the back porch entrance were a tangle of wild growth.

I halted the piebald near the barn and eased myself to the ground. Still puzzled by the deserted look of the house, I walked closer. The curtains were drawn tight, the winter storm windows still in place. I stepped to the front door and knocked.

Perhaps Zeb was ill. Even so, he would have hired servants to keep up the place, tidy the yard, care for the horses, open the windows. I looked around the high, grassy lawns, frowning that he would let such a thing go. It wasn't like Zeb at all.

I knocked again, but no footsteps sounded from inside. Perhaps he had gone on a trip, an extended European tour. He had always talked of the two of us visiting England one day.

Still searching for answers, I skirted the house, through the gardens, to the back door. A small notice had been posted in the window, facing out. Curious, I stepped closer and bent to read it.

Grand Estate Auction
April 7, 1888, 10:30 A.M. to 5:00 P.M.
Owners Deceased

Owners deceased? I frowned and reread the notice. Zeb must have sold our home after he thought I died. That was the only logical explanation. The new owners had died, thus the notice.

Resting my hand on my stomach, I read the notice again, and then turned away, still puzzling over Zeb's being gone, over the notice that left too many unanswered questions.

I climbed into the carriage and turned the mare toward the road. As she trotted alongside the house, a sadness settled deep inside me. I craned to look back as we passed, trying to conjure up happy memories, but they didn't come. Instead, my heartaches and fears lined up in legion, waiting to march against the new-found joy in my heart.

I chirked to the mare, and once we were on the main road, she moseyed along at her own clip-clopping speed. The wheels creaked as we hit a rut. I braced myself, glad the mare was moving no faster.

We reached the outskirts of town and I reined the horse to the side of the road. I didn't have the courage to do what was next. I didn't! I turned to look back at the house, now lying deep in the shadows of the setting sun.

"I can't do it," I muttered to myself, picturing Zebulon II and Charlotte when they saw me. "I can't."

I watched the shadows deepen, the red sunset fade to amber and gold, then to a deep lavender gray.

The mare flicked her ears impatiently. I sighed and reined her back onto the road. As dusk fell, we reached into town. I turned the piebald onto Bank Street, flicking the reins to urge her forward.

Soon the Deforest mansion rose before me in the ashen light. Biting my lip nervously, I chirked to the mare once again and turned her onto the curved road leading to the wide porch.

A light glowed in the parlor window. Jeannie stood by it, facing Charlotte and Zebulon, who were just entering the room.

I stepped from the buggy and walked to the front of the house. I climbed the stairs, grasping the handrail for support. Inside, I heard the low voices of Zeb's father and mother, and Jeannie's higher, musical tone.

I lifted my hand to the brass doorknocker and hesitated. I didn't want to frighten them. I also had to admit I didn't want to face their hostility when they found out, if they didn't know already, that I had chosen to deceive Zeb.

The full impact of my deception swept over me, and I almost fell to my knees in despair. The baby kicked and rolled, and I touched the rippling spot, taking some comfort in the movement beneath my hands.

Finally I tapped the knocker, once, twice…then again. The sound cut through the frog chorus from the side garden and the cricket song from across the wide lawn.

The conversation inside quieted, and after a moment I heard footsteps coming toward me. A moment later, the door opened.

Zebulon Deforest II stood before me, a puzzled look on his face. He obviously didn't recognize me.

I bit my lip and stared at him, thinking of all the words I'd practiced saying to Zeb when we met. Never once had I considered I might first see his father and mother instead. I didn't know what to say.

"Yes?" he said, peering into the dimly lit porch. "Can I help you?"

"It's Fairwyn," I finally whispered. "I've come home."

His eyes bored in on me, and he didn't make a sound. Behind us the crickets screeched. "Is Zeb with you?"

I cocked my head, thinking I hadn't heard him correctly. "Zeb?"

"Who is it, dear?" Charlotte called from the parlor. "Do we have guests?"

His gaze was still fixed on me, unblinking, unbelieving. "Fairwyn," he said softly, shaking his head. Then his gaze moved from my eyes to my toes, and he looked back, stunned. "A baby?" he breathed, incredulous.

"Zebulon?" Charlotte called again. "Is everything all right?" I heard her footsteps approaching and braced myself. She took her place beside her husband and stared blankly into my face.

"It's Fairwyn," Zebulon murmured.

"It can't be—" She halted, and took a step closer. "Fairwyn?" Her voice was little more than a whisper. "Fairwyn?" She frowned, looking me over. "Whatever…? How can this…?" Finally she gave up trying to comprehend the impossible and reached for my hands.

When she had drawn me inside, she asked the same strange question her husband had asked. "Is Zeb with you?" Without waiting for my answer, she drew me into an embrace. "Please tell me he is," she said. Her shoulders trembled, and it seemed as if she was weeping softly.

I drew back, confused. "No," I said as gently as I could. "No, he isn't."

Jeannie stood in the parlor doorway, her face pale, her expression troubled, as she watched the reunion.

I had last seen her on the day I found her in Zeb's arms.

Her eyes filled. "We thought you were dead." She stepped toward me and took my hands.

I fought the urge to withdraw mine. "We thought"—her tears were spilling now—"that you died." She shook her head slowly. "The stationmaster said you were on the train."

How could I tell them what I'd done? I looked from Jeannie's face into Charlotte's tragic, white face, then to Zebulon's lined haggard face. Their grief was still raw. Was it all for me?

I remembered the notice on the house: *Owners deceased,* and stepped backward with a gasp. "Zeb...?" I uttered a small cry and covered my lips with my fingertips. "Tell me, please. What's happened to Zeb?"

Charlotte and Zebulon exchanged a puzzled look, and Charlotte started to cry again.

"Zeb died on the train, Fairwyn." She met my gaze, her own unwavering. "He knew you were running away, and he'd gone to bring you back home."

I felt the room begin to spin. "No," I cried. "Please. Tell me it's not true." I reached for a chair to break my fall, but it was too late. I heard it clatter against the wall as I sank into a velvet blackness.

Thirty-One

"Fairwyn, wake up." Jeannie's soft voice drifted like a haunt into the fog of my pain. "Please, wake up!"

I struggled to open my eyes, but the effort was too great, the pain in my abdomen so white-hot and terrifying I couldn't get away from its grip. I heard a moaning, a cry. It frightened me that someone might cry out so.

The cry came again, and this time I knew it was my own. I waited, my leaping, uneven heartbeat thundering in my ears, knowing another racking pain would soon overwhelm me. Already, I knew it had a rhythm, like Welsie's ocean, like my dulcimer playing.

I opened my mouth to speak to the shadowy face before me. *Jeannie?* But I couldn't get the word out. *Jeannie?* Another rushing wave of pain carried me on its crest. Higher. And higher. I heard my cry again—unearthly and frightening—and felt a cool, gentle hand take mine. I clutched it, squeezed it, holding on as if I would surely die if I let go. The pain reached its peak and held me there, silent and weeping, then lifted me and sent me whirling far, far away.

Now it was relentless. It ebbed, only to return higher than before, each time carrying me farther away. I was no longer fearful. Only weary. So weary.

I was drowning in pain. The thought didn't frighten me. I just wanted the pain to end.

"Fairwyn!" Someone's hands were on my cheeks. "Fairwyn, wake up! Now, this minute!" My head was moving side to side. Then someone lightly slapped my wrists.

"Fight, child, as you've never fought before!" A deeper voice moved into the foggy place where I floated. "Come back to us! Fight, child! Fight…"

Charlotte?

"I can't bear to lose you, too. Fight this, Fairwyn!" I heard weeping, a shadowy, sad sound, barely audible in the rushing roar of the pain. "Think of the baby…you must fight to save your baby!"

My baby?

The pain hung over me now, a white-hot cloud, pulsating, drawing me into its depths. I felt inches from death.

My baby?

I drifted back toward consciousness…Charlotte was wrong. It was too soon. My baby would die!

At the thought, the ache in my heart surpassed the physical pain. Another wave lifted me. I was carried again to that faraway place. This time I welcomed the drowning.

The death of another—that of my precious child—was on my hands. First Zeb. Now our child. Punishment for my mistakes.

I sank deeper into the formless, overwhelming pain and let myself go this time. I drifted farther away from the fuzzy voices…the shadowy sounds…until I thought I couldn't return.

There I stayed until I saw a man standing on the shore. He beckoned to me, but I turned away. I couldn't bear to look in his face.

"Father," I said. "Let me die, but don't take my baby."

Come to me, beloved.

Still I kept my face turned away. "I thought you had forgiven me, but now I know better. I thought the worst was over. But my sorrows have just begun."

Fear not, beloved, I have redeemed you.

"You cannot know the full extent of the evil within my heart. I caused my husband's death!"

I have called you by name. You are mine.

I drifted farther away from shore, sinking, unable to help myself, unwilling to fight any longer. "I want to know your mercy, but my sins are too great. Now, especially…" I thought of Zeb and began to weep. "I have failed miserably."

When you pass through the waters, I will be with you.

Even life's rivers, child, will not overflow you.

"I am not worthy…"

Reach out to me, beloved. I am here.

"I am sick. And weak. So very weak," I cried. "My arms can't reach that far."

Turn to me, child…

Micheil's words came back to me in a flood of images, tumbling together like a river of light and beauty.

Grace is that place between where our short arms reach out to him and his powerful hands stretch toward us. That place where we fall so short of our own expectations. Fall short of what we think are God's expectations.

If we keep reaching toward him, we see the bridge of his love crossing that space between. No matter what it is we've done, no matter how short we've fallen of his glory—he's still reaching out. His big hands are open wide to catch us, to draw us nearer to his heart. That's grace, lass. That's grace.

I turned to the One who stood waiting onshore. The kindness, the love, the light of his countenance quickened my spirit. I reached out my arms.

Just as Micheil had said, my arms were too short. For an instant, I despaired, thinking I surely was lost.

But glory of all glories, the waiting one reached out to me, his arms open wide. He lifted me across the wide gulf between us and brought me close to his heart.

He held me until I was no longer afraid.

"Fairwyn…" the fuzzy voice said again. "Fairwyn…"

I tried to move my lips. "Baby…"

"Did you hear?" someone next to me said. "She's trying to speak."

"Baby…" I fought to open my eyes, but didn't have the strength. I tried to touch my stomach, but felt only my fingers move.

Then a cool, soft hand cradled mine, moving it gently until it lay on my hard, bulging abdomen. "Your baby," Jeannie whispered. "Your baby is coming."

I heard footsteps approach, and Charlotte spoke next. "You've got to help us, child. You've got to fight. The baby is breech. The midwife will try once more to turn him. At the next pain, don't bear down. Can you hear me? You mustn't, Fairwyn."

My eyes still closed, I tried to nod. Someone held a cup to my lips, and I sipped.

The searing pain struck hard, and I gasped at the depth, the breadth, of it. *My baby, my baby…* I breathed, focusing on the life within. *My baby.*

The pain grew larger than before, but when I felt myself drifting to unconsciousness, I pulled myself back. Only my baby's face could keep me from that far place. I thought about his toes, and counted them in my mind…next his fingers and thumbs. I imagined his eyes, crystal blue like my Smoky Mountain skies…his hair, as yellow as a mountain daisy's.

"Breathe, Fairwyn," a strange voice said. The midwife, I knew. "Breathe, slowly now. And when I tell you, bear down. Do you understand?"

I breathed deeply and tried to nod. Seconds later, she said, "Now!"

Pain exploded, so huge and overwhelming, I was lost in its entirety. Just when I thought I couldn't bear it a moment longer, Jeannie cried out.

"It's a boy, Fairwyn! Your son!" Her voice was filled with awe.

A tiny cry filled the room. I forced my eyes open and stared unbelieving at the tiny bundle the midwife was handing Charlotte, who reached for him with an open blanket.

"Oh, the little sweetheart," Charlotte said bringing him closer. "Do you want me to clean him up first?"

Unable to speak, I shook my head. She was about to lay him in the crook of my arm when the midwife said, "You'd better hang on to that one, Miz Deforest. Fairwyn's going to be busy… We've got another one coming."

I bit my lip, my tears still flowing. I reached out a trembling hand to Charlotte. "Stay," I whispered, turning my head toward her to stare in amazement at my son.

"You've got one more push, Fairwyn," the midwife said. "This one should be easier—you'll know when."

The next wave of pain rose and fell, almost unnoticed, because my baby's face was all I could think about. I rose on the crest of it, this time unafraid, this time looking to the joy that I knew would follow.

"Here she is," the midwife said with a chuckle. "Tiny, like twins usually are, but healthy. Wiry and feisty."

A small mewing cry came next. I strained to see, but fell back on my pillow, exhausted. After the midwife finished with me, covered me with fresh linens and blankets, and carried the basins from the room, Charlotte and Jeannie carried the babies to me. Charlotte tucked my son beneath my left arm. I gazed down at him, his eyes closed in sleep, a silken crop of flaxen hair capping his head. Jeannie brought my daughter, gently helping me cradle the child beneath my right arm. It was too soon to know the hue of her fuzzy head, but in a certain light, it might just be red. Like Welsie True's when she was a girl.

I looked from one rosebud face to the other and back again, my heart flooding with joy.

Charlotte stepped closer. "Would it be all right for Zebulon to come in and see?"

"His grandchildren," I finished softly. "Yes. I want him to meet his namesake."

Her eyes watered. She turned and hurried to the door.

I closed my eyes, weary, sinking into my pillow. Jeannie, sitting by my bedside, said, "Do you want me to take them?"

"Not yet," I whispered.

Charlotte and Zebulon tiptoed in a few minutes later. I sensed them standing nearby and forced open my eyes. "Meet your granddaddy," I said to my sleeping son.

Zebulon moved closer, looking down at the child in wonder.

"His name is Zebulon Deforest IV."

The baby's grandfather smiled. "Thank you," he said softly, his eyes still on the baby's face. He looked across at my daughter. "And this young lady?"

I smiled down at the little girl. "This is Michela," I said. "Michela Fairwyn Deforest. Fairwyn is a tradition in my family."

"And Michela?" Charlotte asked. "Is that also a family name?"

I thought of Micheil and shook my head. "The name of a dear friend," I said.

The babies were taken from me, and I fell into a deep and peaceful sleep, waking only to feed them or to sip tea and soup. Charlotte and Jeannie took turns by my bedside. Many times during my convalescence I sensed that both women wanted to talk about what had happened on the train, what happened with Zeb.

I needed to ask forgiveness from them both. I was terrified of what they might say, so I waited until I felt stronger.

One April afternoon after the babies had been fed and were sleeping in their cradles, I sat in my room by the window in a wicker rocking chair. Below me, robins splashed in the fountain and sang in the gardens. The very spot where I'd overheard Zeb and his parents arguing about me.

They had disliked me, felt I was wrong for their son, back then. How would they feel when I told them the full extent of my deception? Would they blame me for his death?

Old fears rushed from the corners of my mind. What if they still thought me unfit to be the mother of their grandchildren? What if they tried to take my babies away?

I stood, my gaze on the fountain where so many heartaches had begun. "Father, I am so weak," I cried silently. "Help me."

When you pass through the waters, I will be with you.

"It would be so much easier to take my babies and run to my mountains."

Even life's rivers, child, will not overflow you.

I bowed my head and prayed for strength.

A light tap on the door interrupted my prayer. "Fairwyn?" Jeannie called from the other side. "I need to talk with you."

It was time. My heart pounding, I stood and moved to open the door.

Thirty-Two

I held the door open, and Jeannie entered my room. She glanced at me, looking worried, then she walked to the cherry wood cradles by my bed. Bending over Michela, she tucked the blanket around the baby's neck and shoulders. Next she tenderly touched Zebbie's cheek with the backs of her fingers.

"They're beautiful," she whispered. There was a soft anguish in her face when she straightened and turned back to me. "How do you keep from just looking at them and doing nothing else? "

"It isn't easy," I admitted. "Sometimes, when they're sleeping or when I'm feeding them, I just stare, completely lost in the awe of God's workmanship."

Her face was pale and solemn as she studied me. "I—we need to talk," she said.

"Please, sit down." I nodded to the damask upholstered window seat.

With a sigh, she crossed the room and settled onto it, nervously smoothing the folds of her long skirt.

I sat near her in the wicker rocking chair, my gaze intent on hers.

"I've talked to Charlotte," she began, "so she knows what I'm about to tell you."

I bit my lip, my heart pounding. "I can guess what you're about to ask," I blurted. "It's about the train wreck. Charlotte and Zebulon have sent you to find out what happened to me."

She looked startled, frowned, and shook her head. "Why, no. That wasn't why I came to you at all."

I rocked back gently in the chair and let out a pent-up breath. "I'm sorry," I said. "Please go on."

She let her gaze drift from my face to the window and the garden below. "I should have come to you for forgiveness long ago." She turned to me again. "I never wanted to hurt you, Fairwyn. I didn't. You must believe me."

I frowned as old jealousies and fears rose again into my heart.

She leaned forward, clasping her hands in her lap, so tightly her knuckles turned white. "I've been in love with Zeb since we were children. I never thought he might not love me in the same way I loved him. I assumed—especially since our families arranged for our betrothal—that life would be just exactly as I planned it. We would marry, live in a lovely home, have a houseful of children, and grow old together."

Her face was lined with pain. She looked down so that I couldn't see her eyes. "Then Zeb met you," she said quietly. "He followed the thread of his book to your mountains and fell in love with a young woman so beautiful and bright none other could compare."

Beautiful and bright? I stared at her, incredulous. I was an awkward, uneducated old maid when we met.

"When he came home, he could speak only of you." She was looking at me again, her eyes bright with unshed tears. "He spoke of everything in context of you…what you might think of his work, his handling of the material in the book, of the Appalachian heritage."

"He never told me. Never once did he seem to give my mind a second thought."

Her expression was almost angry when she continued. "You were so busy thinking you were somehow inferior to him that you didn't once notice how he really thought of you, Fairwyn. He was proud of you and your accomplishments. Proud of how you carried yourself, how you worked hard to fit into what he knew to be a difficult social setting."

Her eyes glistened and narrowed. "Did you see how he looked at you on your wedding day?"

"What do you mean?"

"The love in his eyes…" She shuddered and turned away. "It broke my heart." She fell quiet, and her voice was a whisper when she continued. "Yet even then I couldn't stop loving him."

"I know," I said quietly.

She turned to me again. "No, I don't think you do. I dreamed of you leaving him so that he would turn to me. I planted the thought of your…instability. Your emotional hysterics. I was the one who suggested he quietly put you away.

"That day he took you to the asylum?"

"Yes."

"He was supposed to leave you there—against your will." She was crying now. "Oh, Fairwyn, how could I have thought of such a thing?"

"It was you?"

She nodded, tears streaming down her face. "I hoped he would be mine. I daydreamed tragic scenes of how he would long for me, but remain true to his insane wife…finally unable to keep himself from me." She fluttered her lace handkerchief. "It's not worth telling." She quieted for a moment, then said, burying her face in her hands, "I'm just so ashamed."

"You don't need to tell me all this, Jeannie. Please, don't do it to yourself."

"No, there's more. And I must tell you. I can't live with myself if I don't."

With a sad sigh, I said, "Go on."

"I knew you would find us in the library that day."

I sat forward, intent on every word.

"I saw your dulcimer by the fireplace and called Zeb into the library to ask him a question." She paused, looking ashamed. "I wanted you to see us. I wanted you to behave exactly as you did. Or worse."

The scene came into my mind, every detail. I stared at her dumbfounded. "He looked perfectly willing to me," I said. "In fact, more than willing."

"I had practiced that scene…and others…for years. I knew your husband well. I knew his weaknesses, his strengths. I played on his weaknesses. I drew him into my arms, Fairwyn. It wasn't the other way around."

"I heard him say…" I knew the words perfectly so often they had played in my heart, stabbing it with sorrow each time. "He said it had always been you."

She smiled. "He'd always held a tenderness toward me. I was his childhood sweetheart. What he said meant nothing more than that." Her face softened. "He never stopped loving you, Fairwyn. You must believe me."

"Did he know that I saw you…saw you kissing?"

"I saw you come in the door, of course. I was waiting for you.

But Zeb didn't know until later. I didn't tell him until the following morning."

"The following morning?"

She nodded, remorse flooding her dark eyes. "Just as I expected, you ran away. I watched by my window, hoping to see you ride by. And there in the distance…in the rainy dawn…you did."

Fresh tears formed. She cleared her throat and stared at me. "I couldn't go through with it.

"You were giving up everything, your home, your life with Zeb. I thought of his love for you, and I dared to think that if I came to you, explained how it was, what I had done, maybe your love for him might be given a second chance.

"I ran to the family carriage and drove as fast as I could to Zeb's. I confessed everything. Before the words were out of my mouth, he rode like the wind to the train station. I prayed he would catch you in time, bring you back, let me explain to you my deception, my terrible deeds."

Michela fussed in her cradle, and I crossed the room to pick her up. When she was cradled in my arms, I sat again and rocked her gently.

Jeannie was openly weeping now. "But he never came back."

"He boarded the train."

"Yes," she whispered. "The brakeman said he grabbed the rail of the caboose as it moved past him. He was so distraught they feared for his safety if he tried to move to the next car. With the storm and all…" She didn't finish.

"They found his body?" For a heartbeat I prayed that maybe he'd lived…that maybe he had gone looking for me…not telling anyone he was alive.

Her gaze never leaving mine, Jeannie shook her head. "His body was found."

I swallowed hard, looking away from her beseeching eyes, concentrating on my nursing infant.

"Fairwyn," she whispered, coming toward me. Reaching my lap, she dropped to her knees, looking at me with so much anguish and fear and sorrow I thought I couldn't bear to look.

"Will you…can you…forgive me?" she whispered.

My heartache, my failed marriage, Zeb's life…so much of it attributed to Jeannie's deception. She had loved Zeb too much. Even now his flaws were covered by the haze of her love for him. My own doubts about myself—my fears of failure, my certainty that Zeb couldn't love someone like me—had played right into her hands. I stared at her now, wondering how different my life, Zeb's and my life together, might have been without her meddling.

Jeannie. My friend. I thought of the hours she had spent in our home, talking and laughing with me, reading and discussing books, speaking of our mutual passion for learning. Listening when I told her my fears and sorrows. My friend had betrayed me.

Forgive others as I forgive you, beloved.

Tears rolled down her cheeks, and she started to get up, certain that I couldn't do what she asked.

She was no different from me. She was human. Her choices hadn't been the right ones any more than mine had been. Yet at this moment, her courage shone bright. She didn't have to tell me any of this. I would never have known.

I reached out one hand, clasped hers as she stood, releasing it as she walked back to the window seat. "My own failures are great," I said. "It's hard to forgive without also asking your forgiveness."

"For your deception?" she asked.

I nodded. "You know then?"

"I suspected that you didn't die in the wreck. Your body wasn't found, which made me wonder. After what I did, I was determined to follow you, find you, and tell you everything." She fell quiet and turned to stare out at the fountain. "After…after Zeb was…killed, I knew I couldn't live with myself, if I didn't find you."

"You weren't surprised to see me." I lifted Michela to my left shoulder and patted her back as I rocked. Smiling at her tiny burp, I snuggled my head close to hers and continued rocking.

"I feigned surprise for the sake of Zebulon and Charlotte. But when you fell sick and I thought you might die too, I told them everything. Including the fact that I hired an agent to search for you in California. He found Welsie True's home, asked around the town of San Juan. It didn't take him long to find someone who described you, even giving your name."

Zebbie was fussing now in his cradle, and Jeannie stood to fetch him. She rocked him gently in her arms as she paced the room. "I just hadn't decided what to do with the information," she said. "I didn't know whether to travel there…or wait until you came home. All I knew was that to be rid of my own darkness, I had to find you. Beg you to forgive me."

"I forgive you," I said. "But Jeannie…" She turned, her head tilted affectionately toward the baby. "Have you forgiven yourself?"

She sat down on the window seat, now holding Zebbie against one shoulder and patting his back. He sucked one fist, making hungry, fussing sounds. I smiled and we traded babies. She went back to the window seat to change Michela's diaper, while I nursed my son. "I don't think I can," she said. "After all that I've done… the hurt I've caused others…"

I settled back in the rocker, the baby making little sucking sounds in the back of his throat. A wave of tenderness enveloped me. "Let me tell you about a bridge I heard of in California," I said.

She shot me a puzzled look, then finished pinning the diaper and picked up Michela. "A bridge?"

I laughed. "You wouldn't think such a thing would be life changing. But it was."

Jeannie sat down again with the baby, staring down at her sweet face with awe.

"You see, it has to do with God's mercy…his forgiveness."

"Tell me," she said. And I did.

Oak Hill
July 1, 1888

Dearest Micheil,

Your letters lift my heart! Half the time they're more filled with sea shanties than facts about the ranch or San Juan. I can almost hear ye singin' the words, with your deep Irish brogue. 'Tis almost like sitting with you, my friend, listening to your music and laughter and talk.

The days are passing quickly. Spring utterly disappeared in the midst of changing diapers, feeding the twins, changing the diapers again. And again. Rocking and singing. And changing diapers. Again.

You once said I might be carrying twins. At the time I thought it a wondrous idea indeed. A family, readymade, since I would not be having any more. But now, I worry I can't keep up with them. Already they're running me ragged, and they've not yet begun to walk!

Oh, but you should hear how they quiet down at night. When they fuss, I pull out the dulcimer and sing, sitting cross-legged in the center of my bed, strumming and humming. I always end with "Greensleeves," which seems to lull them to sleep better than any other. And while I sing, I remember that grand day the swallows returned to the mission.

I plan to stay on with Zebulon and Charlotte until the babies are strong enough to travel. I have become closer to Zeb's parents than I ever thought possible. They dote over the babies and me, spoiling us all with their love.

The twins are now round and rosy-cheeked. Oh, how I wish you could see them, Micheil. By the first of June they were smiling and cooing, and now they're laughing out loud. Their eyes follow me across the room, making me want to kick up my heels and dance. And they've just begun to reach up for me to hold them, their little arms waving like windmills. My heart turns cartwheels in rhythm with them, and I almost forget to breathe because of my joy!

I know by the end of summer you will head into the high country for the roundup. It will also be a sign that Ireland calls. You promised me you would stay for these "seasons," and I will forever be grateful.

My time here is coming to a close as well, dear friend. Next letter you write to me, please send to me in care of general delivery at Sycamore Creek. I will then give you a full report on my journey to Blackberry Mountain with the twins.

Until then, I remain
Your friend,
Fairwyn True Deforest

I settled onto the upholstered horsehair bench in the first car of the train, my dulcimer in a large valise to one side, my smaller case with my clothes on the other, two more piled atop holding baby clothes and extra diaper cloths. Facing me, on the opposite bench, were two small wicker baskets, sitting side by side, that Zebulon had made in Oak Hill. Each held a twin. Bright-eyed, they gurgled and cooed, hands moving like swallowtail butterflies in the spring.

I bent forward to the window, searching for Zebulon and Charlotte. They spotted me and waved. Charlotte was crying and blowing kisses. I smiled and blew one back.

Around me, the other passengers spoke of their journeys. Children scrambled to get closer to windows. Voices rose. Laughter and squeals, murmurs of mothers talking to their children, businessmen to each other about their fields.

Across from me a woman met my eyes and smiled, then lost herself in the book open on her lap. Beside her an old man adjusted his hat low on his forehead, leaned back and closed his eyes to rest. Ordinary people, ordinary sights and sounds, just like the journey I began a year ago when I boarded in the rainstorm.

Back then I didn't know the fragility of life…or know the light that shone on the far side of the darkness.

We pulled away from Oak Hill station, snaking through the center of town, past the red-soil earth and the acres of tall corn ready for harvest, past the rolling green hills and silver-hued river. The train gained speed, and soon the small town with its proud history lay far behind me.

Strange, I thought, how when I arrived from California I feared that truth would destroy me.

Instead it had set me free.

Michela started to fuss, and I reached for her hand. She

gripped my index finger tightly. *Just like God has hold of me,* I thought with a smile.

Dover Town
August 7, 1888

Dearest Micheil,

Because of the proximity of a post office, I decided to write to you tonight and post this letter in the morning before the twins and I head into the mountains. They are sound asleep here in our hotel room, though the saloon next door is raucous. A tinny piano plays, and from time to time a group of merrymakers spills into the street below our window. Yet Zebbie and Michela sleep on...

I bought a horse, a sturdy chestnut mare, and a pack mule to hold our clothes and other belongings. I can fasten the twins' baskets to my saddle, one on either side. They'll be close enough to touch if they fuss, and safer with me than on the mule. We will be a sight to behold once packed up. Because the mining companies have improved the trails, in some cases making new ones, I believe I can make the trek in one long day. I will begin before dawn and, Lord willing, arrive at Poppy's cabin by dark.

There's a promise of a full moon to light the way if the mists don't settle, which will ease the night journey. And I have brought a lantern, should we need it.

My friend, I can't help but wish California was my destination. It's all I can do to keep from boarding the train tomorrow morning and heading west.

But Selah is getting up in years. She's my great-aunt, Welsie True's sister, and I want to see after her for all her days. There's also the matter of the feud between the Marches and Trues, something I would like to straighten out. I can hear your laughter now at such grand ambition!

But California calls, with its windswept lands and great big sparkling ocean. My little cottage and the *barrio* around it, all of it remains in my heart, and will until the day I die.

Enough thoughts of melancholy from me. I meant to cheer you, my friend, as the time for Ireland nears. I've begun a new prayer, one I hope will not offend you. I am praying that by some wondrous intervention by God, you will be absolved of all charges, that you will be free to return to San Juan and the work you've begun there.

Forgive me, for I know why you return, but I pray for such a miracle each night before I go to sleep.

It is ten o'clock. The tinny piano plays on, and my little angels are not even stirring. I think I shall pull out my dulcimer and play a lively Irish jig to drown out the noise below.

You remain in my prayers tonight and always.

And I remain

Your friend,

Fairwyn True Deforest

Thirty-Three

With the babies wrapped snug and safe in their wicker carriers beside me, I yanked on the rope that tethered the mule behind the mare. We climbed quickly and soon found ourselves deep in the hardwood forest, making our way through the poplars, chestnuts, and maple trees. On either side of the trail grew red fern spread over miniature forests of mushrooms hidden beneath. The scents of decaying leaves and loamy soil filled my nostrils.

Gnats danced around my head. I shooed them away from the babies until the buzzing disappeared in the clearings. Upward, ever upward we climbed, sometimes crossing valleys sprinkled with farmhouses, other times riding for an hour or more with no sign of civilization.

I headed the chestnut mare to an outcropping of rock. I halted her and slid off the saddle, stretching my legs. Zebbie slept, but Michela chortled, chewing on her hand. I lifted her from the basket and cradled her in my arm to feed her. When I had finished, Zebbie was awake and ready. It took me nearly an hour to feed them both and change them, an hour I hadn't planned on.

I looked up at the sun, gauging my time. This time when I placed the babies in their baskets, I covered their faces lightly with flannel blankets, hoping they would fall asleep again. Zebbie did, but Michela howled and fussed so loud she made the mule's ears flick and the mare snort nervously. A half-hour later, she settled to a whimper, then slept soundly.

I reined the horse onto level ground, still keeping to the trail. My eyes drank in the beauty of the pink sea of rhododendrons on a slope in the distance. It was known by the hunters in Sycamore Creek that deer got caught in them, unable to move in one direction or another because of their thick foliage. An adult deer could starve to death right there in the middle of beauty and fragrance.

I shuddered and moved on down the trail.

Beyond the rhododendrons, the lavender mountains faded into the pale blue summer sky. I halted the horse at the final outlook above the valley where Sycamore Creek lay tucked up against the mountains bathed in sunlight, deceptively bright in the slant of the afternoon sun.

I thought back to the sad stories that Micheil had told me of my kinfolk. It struck me now that beauty covered our darkness, the feuds and fighting and death that had passed through the generations.

I nudged the horse with my heels and headed her back to the trail.

After three more stops to care for the babies, and once for me to eat a packed lunch and drink from a clear stream, we finally rode through Sycamore Creek. I stopped for supplies at the mercantile, holding the babies while I instructed wide-eyed Dearly Forbes, who was minding the shop, what to pack. Still grinning ear to ear, he strapped the provisions to the mule while I fastened the twins in their baskets.

"Glad ye're back, Fairwyn March!" he shouted after me as I pressed my heels into the horse's flanks. "Ye've sure got yerself some purty lap babies there."

I waved gaily and then turned in the saddle as we headed up the trace. The mule ambled on behind us.

The sun was hanging low as we started up the trace to Blackberry Creek, and dusk had settled in, misty and gray, before we arrived in the meadow. I halted the mare and drew in a deep breath.

There, on the far side of the meadow, at the edge of the thick canopy of forest, sat Poppy's cabin, squat and solid. A fresh tangle of kudzu grew up one side and cascaded from the roof on the other.

Grinning, I urged the horse to move faster across the grassy meadow. We drew to a halt in front of the cabin. The babies were sleeping, but I carefully removed the baskets, and set them one by one on the porch, followed by our supplies. Unburdened and unsaddled, mule and horse headed a short way into the meadow to feed.

Next I lit the lantern and held it up while I opened the door. The place smelled slightly musty and looked to have recently been cleared of dust. Everything was the same, Poppy's iron bedstead in one corner, mine kitty-cornered to his, two wooden chairs before the cold and empty fireplace.

The books Welsie True had sent me through the years lined the small bookshelf by the fireplace, and I ran my fingers lovingly over their spines, thinking how she had loved me all those years. I pulled down *Great Expectations* and tried to flip it open. A stench of mildew filled the room, and huge clumps of pages stuck together. Grimacing, I quickly placed it back on the shelf. Likely everything in Poppy's cabin would need replacing if we stayed, from furniture to dishes and eating utensils.

I set the lantern on the table and looked around, worried about mice or any other critters that might have taken over the cabin. Again, I noticed it looked surprisingly clean to have been shut up for so long.

I brought in the twins from the porch, placing their baskets on the table to serve as cradles. Weary beyond imagining, I settled onto a chair between them, dropping my head onto my folded arms.

Hours later I woke to the hoot owls calling. A big moon had risen over the meadow. I picked up my dulcimer and went out to the porch. My fingers moved almost of their own accord as I played. I started with songs taught me by my Granny Nana and Poppy, then moved on to some I'd written myself, and finally, just as dawn's gray light crept over the silhouettes of the trees, I strummed "Greensleeves."

Everything seemed so easy and pleasant as the sun rose above the meadow, causing the dew to sparkle and chase away the mists that shrouded the trees. I had a strong hankering for eggs, some of Selah Jones's perfect brown eggs, laid by her prized chickens. I stretched and headed back into the dark cabin.

That's when dismay settled into my heart. I gazed around the inside of the cabin. Cracks of light showed through the weathered boards. One of the windows was broken, and the floorboards cracked and moved beneath the pressure of my feet. When the babies learned to crawl, it couldn't be on that floor. I shuddered, thinking of the splinters, the spiders, and worse.

The babies were awake now, calling me with their coos and gurgles. As I hurried into the house, the full extent of the cleaning and fixing drew me nearly to despair.

I fed Zebbie first, sitting by the table while Michela fussed. Her fuss turned to a louder cry. Red-faced, she complained, waving her little fists in the air. I burped Zebbie, laid him in his basket, tucked the blanket around him, and picked up Michela.

I'd no sooner started to nurse when Zebbie let out a high-pitched screech, turning as red as Michela had a few minutes before. I weighed how I might feed both at once, then quickly dismissed the idea. There wasn't a chair big enough to support my arms while I held them. And the beds were too dusty to lie down.

Zebbie squalled on while I tried to relax and feed Michela. Around me the cabin seemed to get darker and close in on me.

What could I have been thinking to come back here? Tears formed in my eyes. How could I manage? Two babies and no help.

Michela sensed my mood and refused to eat. I propped her on my shoulder to burp her, but she cried louder.

When both babies stopped crying to gulp for a breath before howling again, a cackling sound at the door caused me to whirl.

Selah stood before me, grinning a toothless grin. "Dearly Forbes tol' me ye'd come back, Fairy lass, but I had to see it with my own eyes." She moved closer, almost yelling above the sound of the still-fussing babies. "So these are yer lap babies." She scooped up Zebbie. His eyes opened wide, and his mouth snapped closed in surprise.

She laughed into his eyes. "This here's yer auntie Selah," she said. "And who's this wee lass?" Juggling Zebbie in one arm, she tickled Michela under her chin with the opposite hand.

Michela stopped fussing in mid-cry and blinked at Selah.

"They're purtier than Dearly Forbes said. Purtier even than yer letters let on." Selah didn't read and write as capably as her sister Welsie, but she knew enough to read my letters from California and the one announcing the babies' birth. She had even written back to me with a wide, childlike scrawl.

Selah scooted a chair from beneath the table and sat with Zebbie in her lap, bouncing him and singing, while I leaned back in my chair to finish feeding Michela. The cabin was quiet again.

I looked across the table at Selah, to find her studying me. "Yer shorely not plannin' on stayin' here," she said.

"I came back to be with you. We're blood kin. This is where I belong, where I need to raise my children. I want them to know their mountain kin."

"To take keer o' me, I reckon." She cocked her head and stared at me hard-eyed. "That's why ye came back."

I feared I had offended her. "To be with you."

"I kin take keer o' meself, Fairy lass." She kept her gaze on me. "When was the last time you et?"

I swallowed hard. "Yesterday sometime."

She wagged her finger at me. "Aye, lass. I knew 'twas at least that or longer." She placed Zebbie back in his basket. "I brung ye some eggs. Also some coffee. I knew thar wasn't much here. Rats would've had it sure."

I smiled as she bustled around the house, gathering wood and lighting a fire, and brought in two pokes filled with supplies. From time to time she looked at me and frowned as if still upset I thought she needed taking care of. I couldn't get enough of her bird-bright eyes. The irony wasn't lost on me. I'd come to see after her, and she was rescuing me.

"I brung Verily with me," she said. "She's ready fer milkin'."

Sure enough, when I glanced through the front window, the scrawny milk cow looked back, eyeing me nervously. My stomach growled at the thought of pouring myself a glass of thick, creamy milk.

Within minutes Selah had set a place at the table, and presented me with a meal fit for a lumberjack: grits, eggs, berries, and corn-pone covered with honey from her bee gum. I ate every bite, delighting in her vigorous, pleased nods.

"Now," she said when I was drinking the last of the milk, "tell me everything."

I blotted my mouth with the large checkered lap towel she'd brought in one of the pokes. I couldn't put it off any longer. "I have some sad news."

" 'Bout my sister. 'Bout Welsie True," she said.

"Aye." I reached for her hand. " 'Tis about her." This was news I hadn't wanted to send in a letter. I had to tell her face to face.

For two hours we sat at the table, and I told her everything about my grandmother, about San Juan, the mission, the town, the *barrio* children. I told her about Micheil, Welsie's friend and mine. Several times she wept as she talked about her sister and the years they missed together.

"Are ye goin' back, lass?" she asked, her voice unusually gentle.

I looked away from her bright eyes. "I don't know." Thinking about the question, I stood and walked to the window. Selah was a connection to my past, just as Welsie True had been. I turned back to her, a wave of affection filling my heart.

"Tell me about your childhood," I said. "About you and my grandmother. There's so much I don't know about my family. I want to learn about your momma and da, about where you lived before moving here."

She patted my chair, looking pleased. "Sit yerself down again, Fairy lass. 'Tis a long story.

"Well, you see, long ago and faraway, came our people to these mountains…"

We bathed the babies, put them to bed, rocked them and fed

them, and put them down again while Selah talked. The sun was on its downward slope when she finished.

"Will it ever change?" I asked. "The hatred and feuding?"

"I hain't been back thar since I wed," she said. "Nigh onto fifty years back. I'd be shunned yet."

"Have you ever thought of going back?"

"Most are gone, I reckon. Left the mountains for the mines. Spread out all over God's creation, they are." She looked hard at me then, her little round eyes piercing. "You hain't thinking of goin' thar to try to patch things up among 'em, are ye? That's not why ye come back?"

I shook my head and laughed lightly. "I have to admit it's crossed my mind. But from what I know about the Marches and the Trues, it's going take more energy than a widow with baby twins can muster up to fix what ails those folks." I reached for her hand. "I only want to make things right about my momma and da. I came back to see you and to take care of them. That's all."

"How're ye fixin' to do that?"

"I'll start with the graveyard. I want to see to it that my da's grave is marked, and that my momma's proper married name is on hers."

Selah grinned. "I'll help ye, Fairy lass. I been carin' fer that graveyard long as I kin remember. 'Twill bring me pleasure to set things right for the Trues."

Later we sat by the cook fire while the babies slept. A bubbling stew scented the room. Selah's bright eyes met mine. "Ye canna stay here, lass. Ye know it, and I do. There's nothing here fer ye now."

"You are here."

Her voice softened. "I won't be forever, lass."

I leaned forward, a grin spreading across my face. "When we've finished with the graveyard…have it in order, the right stones made, my da's in its rightful place…"

Her eyes seemed to glow as if she knew what I was about to ask.

"Would you consider coming to California with me?" Outside the crickets sang and the tree frogs croaked. A hoot owl called from near the meadow.

"So ye kin take keer o' me?"

My grin widened. "How can you think such a thing after today? You were the one caring for me and my babies." My eyes turned moist. "I don't know what I would have done without you."

"That a fact." Her wizened face broke into a wreath of smiles. "That a fact."

" 'Tis." I couldn't stop smiling.

She sighed. "Well now, Lettie'll have to come up to see after Verily. Gather the eggs and pick the berries so's the birds don't git 'em all." She smiled at me. "Unless you think Verily might come with us."

"I don't see why not," I said. "I know of a ranch up in the mountains above the sea. It's called Saddleback, and it once belonged to Welsie. I think Verily might just think she's gone to heaven with all that nosing around in the tall California grass."

"Well then, it's settled," Selah said with a nod. "I'll go!"

Blackberry Mountain
September 25, 1888

Dearest Micheil,

I'm on my way to California! Selah, the twins, and I are leaving tomorrow for Dover Town. We'll be in San Juan by the first of October. Oh, how I hope this letter reaches you before you sail. I would love to see you once more before you leave…Please, please, tell me it is possible!

Dear friend, what a joy it will be for me to see you with Michela and Zebbie! And I can't wait for you to meet Selah. Something tells me she is so like Welsie True in spirit.

I await seeing you again—my dearest hope!—with joyful anticipation!

Until then, I faithfully remain

Your friend,

Fairwyn True Deforest

Thirty-Four

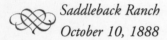
Dearest Micheil,

We arrived in San Juan just three days ago, Selah, the babies, and me. How saddened I was to discover you never received my letter telling of our return. I found it unopened here at the ranch.

You are surely still sailing and will be during the coming weeks. I pray for your traveling mercies, my dear friend. I also pray this letter will reach you. I am sending it in care of your parish church in Ireland, knowing it is there you will likely head first.

The train travel to California was wearying, much more difficult than my earlier crossing. You can imagine the troubles of caring for two babies in such a cramped space. The most joyous part of the trip was watching Selah's face with each new modern discovery. She is quite the seasoned traveler now and proud of it, hankering—she says—to be on the road again. I do believe she is ready to load us all into a ship and sail for Ireland!

That isn't to say she hasn't fallen in love with California.

She settled into her sister's cottage as if she'd lived there all her life. Already she's made friends with the *barrio* children, promising to continue the tradition of baking little cakes and singing with them.

The children and I are making ourselves comfortable here at the ranch. I've hired some young women from the *barrio* to help me with the everyday care so that I can find moments to myself to rest. Selah comes by often to help, but, feisty and headstrong as ever, she's made it clear she is used to living alone and likes it that way.

As for me, my friend, California reminds me of you at every turn, our long talks about God and his mercy, and the joy you brought to my spirit.

Please write to me soon and advise that you have arrived safely in Ireland.

Until then I remain
Your devoted friend,
Fairwyn True Deforest

Saddleback Ranch
December 4, 1888

Dearest Micheil,

Your letter arrived yesterday! I have read it at least a dozen times already! I laughed and cried at the same time when I read your account of going before the magistrate with your crimes. To think you had a witness on your behalf all along and that all was forgiven before your arrival! And joy of all joys, you are coming home to California!

You said you have some business to take care of before sailing. I send this letter in hopes it reaches you before you leave. Though, on second thought, I would rather you miss the letter and sail into Los Angeles harbor sooner!

Lest you worry about being displaced by this widow woman and her two infants, I will set your mind to rest. The ranch lands are large enough to split in two. Half will be yours—to build a school or quarters for those without family or home.

It is yours, Micheil Grady Gilvarry! And I cannot wait to see you riding across it like the wind.

I remain

Faithfully yours,

Fairwyn True Deforest

Saddleback Ranch
February 22, 1889

Dearest Micheil,

Such a long time has passed since your last letter. My heart is sick with worry. You mentioned you had business to conclude before you sailed out of Dublin. Yet you did not say how long it might take. Perhaps I expected your sailing to be sooner than you meant.

I am praying that it was my mistake and nothing worrisome has overtaken you.

If you receive this before you sail, please know that all is well here. Michela, your sweet namesake, took her first step yesterday. Zebbie is content to crawl, though he now says more words than she does. "Ba" is his favorite. It means everything from "ball" to "muffin."

Selah has utterly captured the hearts of the children in the *barrio.* Nita and Rosa have become her little shadows; they knock on her door at dawn and would likely stay all day if she would allow it. She's bought a dozen laying hens, and Nando has made her a coop.

Oh, I think I've forgotten to tell you the new addition to the ranch. Selah insisted on bringing her milk cow, Verily, from Blackberry Mountain. Though she refuses to be corralled, the old girl has made herself at home. Like me, she prefers the wide-open spaces.

You remain in my heart and prayers, dear friend. I pray God's comfort is with you wherever you may be— on the high seas or still in Ireland.

Until we meet again, I remain
Your friend,
Fairwyn True Deforest

Saddleback Ranch
June 7, 1889

Dearest Welsie True,

It's been over a year since my last letter, and truly I thought I wouldn't need to write to you again. But something has happened, and I need to pour out my heart to you. I need to tell someone who understands a friendship more dear than the love of kin.

You see, Welsie True, in Dublin on Christmas Day last, there was an Irish uprising against the British rule. It was part of the Irish troubles, and I'm certain now it had something to do with the business that Micheil wrote he had to attend to.

After I wrote to the shipping company he sailed with last fall, they checked the manifest for his name and found it but wrote back that he never claimed his passage.

They also said I might be interested to know that in Dublin that very day, many had been killed, and many more arrested and sent to prison for the uprising. Several others went missing that day, they said, and were thought to be hiding out.

It's the not knowing that troubles my heart. If he were in an English prison, I might know how to pray. If he lost his life, then I would grieve for him, but also rejoice in his new life with his Father in heaven. It's the uncertainty that is hard to bear. And to think that I might never see him again causes a heartache like none I've ever known.

As I pen this letter, though, I can almost hear what Micheil would say, the same words he comforted me with when I grieved over your passing:

Aye, lass, 'tis God's light we need in dark times like these—in tragedy and in joy—for 'tis the One who walks with us who sustains us.

We need to remember, he said, *'tis God who brings others to meet us on our life journeys, to help, to love, and*

*to guide us. When he moves two wayfarers onto a different
path, both are richer for their meeting.*

Yes, riches beyond expression have been mine—in
you, Welsie True, my precious friend and grandmother.
And in Micheil Gilvarry.

I've seen the face of God in you both.

Forever, I will remain

Your loving granddaughter,

Fairwyn True Deforest

Saddleback Ranch, March 19, 1893

Of the four years the children and I had attended the festival of the
return of the swallows to the Mission San Juan, only twice had the
flocks arrived on the right day.

Today, as I rode with the twins across the golden poppy-
drenched ranchlands, I wondered if the swallows would indeed
delight us with their presence.

Within the hour it would be time to leave for the festival. Zebbie and Michela had recently learned to play their first Appalachian
folk songs on their dulcimers. They would join the other children
from the *barrio* to sing and dance in the glow of torchlight in the
balmy evening air. Nando, now twelve years old, had been practic-
ing his solo for weeks. And though Rosa and Nita sang better than
they played their dulcimers, their giggling enthusiasm made up for
their lack of fingering skills. Carlos had decided he wanted nothing
to do with music, but he loved to tell folk tales of Mexico and Spain
with brightly attired Juan and Jaime acting out his stories.

The informal music and instrument-building classes I'd begun
at the mission were a resounding success. Seven of the children had

finished their own dulcimers, and three more were nearly completed. We had recently begun a new project with the help of the children's fathers. All the children, including Zebbie and Michela, were learning to play Spanish guitar with the patient help of the *barrio* musicians. As usual, when they performed, the music would combine the best of their cultures.

During the festivals, I was so taken by the rich heritage of the folk songs that a year ago I began work on a book of American folklore and folk songs. Zeb's work had covered only the connection of the Irish, Scots, Welsh, and English in the Appalachians to the lands of their heritage. I plunged heart and soul into the riches of the Spanish and Indian songs and stories. I planned that, after this book was done, I would begin work on other heritages that already captured my imagination: the Germans, the Scandinavians, the French, the Africans, and beyond.

I rode on, leaving Zebbie and Michela lagging slightly behind, looking for Verily, who as usual had wandered away from the confines of the ranch.

The sun had burned off the mists from the ocean, leaving the sky filled with streaks of buttermilk clouds. A breeze brought the saltwater scent inland and swept it across the ranchlands.

I halted the bay mare and stared skyward with a smile as a few swallows dipped and wheeled in flight on their northward migration. Though I had no way of knowing if they would light at the mission, their soft burrs carried across the sky, filling my heart with their music.

Memories came with the sight of even these few, just as they did every year. Sometimes they brought regrets for choices that hurt and harmed others; sometimes they brought fresh grief for those I'd lost—Poppy, Zeb, Welsie True, and perhaps Micheil. But joy always filled my heart at last. Joy in the knowledge that no matter my mistakes, there was One who walked with me on my journey, loving me, accepting me just as I was, through it all.

As I gazed heavenward, the cry of a single young swallow caught my attention. Her scruffy look of pinfeathers and down told me she was likely on her first journey northward. Away from the flock, she flapped and wheeled, fluttering and working her wings hard against the wind. I wanted to call out to her and explain that if she would quit trying so hard to make her own way, if she would relax on the warm thermals, she would sail through the sky as if cradled in her Creator's hand.

"Soar, little bird, soar," I whispered, still following her awkward flight. Then I laughed to myself. Of course she would soar, but not until her wings were strong enough and the time was right, perhaps not even until later in the spring.

To everything there is a season, I thought, remembering the wisdom of Ecclesiastes, *and a time to every purpose under the heaven.... A time to weep, and a time to laugh; a time to mourn, and a time to dance.*

I wondered if the joy that filled me today would have been mine if I hadn't known sorrow, if my spirit would know light and freedom if it hadn't known the bondage of darkness and fear. The depth carved by despair in my soul had allowed me a greater capacity for happiness. Wasn't that also part of God's grace?

Hooves pounded behind me, and I turned to see Zebbie riding across the poppy fields, his cheeks pink, his flaxen hair gleaming in the slant of the morning light. Michela raced slightly behind on a bright palomino, trying her best to overtake him, her mass of red curls blowing in the wind, her face freckled from the sun.

Just before they reached me, Michela squealed and pointed to the sky, drawing her gelding to a hard stop. "Momma! Look! They're here! They've come back!"

Zebbie halted his horse and followed her gaze with awe. "They're going to the mission, they are!"

There, in white relief against the blue heavens, flew whole flocks of swallows, wheeling and dipping, and soaring as if to the sun. I wanted to skip through the buttercups and poppies that spread across the fields, dancing until I could fly heavenward on spirit-wings.

It struck me then that all I'd ever wanted was to fly…whether it was from Blackberry Mountain or Oak Hill or here, straight into the heavens with the swallows. And now I could. Oh, yes, I could. For it was my heart that took wing, rising into the heavens.

I watched the swallows until they disappeared over the flower-draped valley and into the eucalyptus groves and smattering of oaks beyond. A few minutes later, the mission bells rang out, echoing across the wide valley, telling San Juan of the swallows' return.

I closed my eyes, letting the joyful ringing join the music of my heart.

Dear Friends,

This has been quite a writer's journey for me as I traveled with our Fairwyn, step by step, page by page. As I wrote her story, I often discussed her life-choices, sorrows, and triumphs with other women; many told me, with tears in their eyes, that they understand Fairwyn, because they've "been there." They've taken wrong turns. They've wondered about God's forgiveness and grace.

Fairwyn's journey is for all of us who've "been there." Her circumstances may seem extreme in our day, but maybe, like Fairwyn, we've taken matters into our own hands because of our wants, fears, and impatience. (I can't help but think of Abraham and Sarah here.) *Heart of Glass* explores the "What if…?" questions we might all entertain. It also explores God's tender love, healing mercies, and utter sovereignty in our lives, no matter how we think we've messed up. No matter how undeserving we believe we are.

Sometimes events beyond our control shake our very foundations. Sometimes our own daily challenges with families and loved ones vastly change the Story we're living. But there is One who never changes. Nothing takes him by surprise. He is the same yesterday, today, and tomorrow.

For who is God, except the LORD?
And who is a rock, except our God?
It is God who arms me with strength,
And makes my way perfect,
He makes my feet like the feet of deer,
And sets me on my high places.
　　　　　—Psalm 18:31-33, NKJV

May God's peace be yours in abundance today and always,

Diane Noble

Diane Noble

Diane Noble is the award-winning author of eighteen books, including historical and contemporary fiction, novellas, and inspirational nonfiction books for women. In recent years she has twice been the recipient of the Silver Angel Award for Media Excellence. In the year 2000, Diane was a double finalist for both the prestigious RITA for Best Inspi-  rational Fiction and for the HOLT Gold Medallion honoring outstanding literary talent.

A popular writing teacher and speaker, Diane makes her home with her husband Tom in the mountains of Southern California. For more information about Diane's books or her women's retreat ministry, please visit her Web site at http://www.dianenoble.com. You can also write to her at either of the following addresses:

Diane Noble
P.O. Box 3017
Idyllwild, CA 92549
E-mail: diane@dianenoble.com